Ominous Odyssey

Ominous Odyssey

Herbert Klug

Adams Press

Ominous Odyssey

International Standard Book Number: 978-0-9827908-2-3
Library of Congress Catalog Number: 2011940525

This is a historical novel based on a true story that took place during World War II. Except for the surnames Klug and Werner, all non-historical surnames have been altered and therefore are fictitious.

Cover, interior design, and Post-War North Central Europe map on pages 276-277 by Tom Kepler

Printed in the United States of America

This book is printed on recycled-content paper.

This book is dedicated to my aunt and uncle, Ida and Emil Werner, who many years ago took in two waifs in need—and to my wife, Marcia, who put up with my self-imposed banishment in our rec room where, after wearing out my old computer and resolving the compatibility problems with the new machine, I finally was able to get this story transferred to paper. Last, but not least, a "thank you" to my editing team in alphabetical order: Corrine, Mary Sue, Peggy, and Vicki.

Chapter 1

Hertha Klug arrived at the pier with her three children at about 7:30 P.M. She was accompanied by her friend Ihde Johte, who had helped her with the children and would stay to see them off. Noting that the dock was crowded with passengers getting ready to board the huge liner and with friends and relatives on hand to wish them bon voyage, Hertha commented, "We'd better stand aside a bit and close to the pier entrance, otherwise Walther and Rudy will never find us in this crowd. Walther estimated that they would get here about an hour after we did."

Remembering her husband's comment, Ihde said, "Rudy wasn't quite as optimistic. He was thinking something like an hour and a half when we left for your place."

Hertha was an attractive woman—five foot two inches with dark hair (almost black) and dark brown eyes. Smartly dressed, she wore a white silk blouse under a gray jacket, embroidered with a red plaid pattern, and a black skirt. Nylon stockings and half-high black leather shoes completed her ensemble.

"Oh, Ihde, I am so happy," she exclaimed exuberantly. "I have been looking forward to this day for a long time." She looked at four-year-old Hannelore whom she was holding and the other two, twelve-year-old Rosemarie and Herbert who was eleven. She was pleased with what she saw. The girls wore dresses with a floral pattern on a white background, white ankle-length socks, and black patent leather shoes. Herbert was neatly dressed in sports shirt and short pants.

About fifteen minutes after their arrival, Hertha heard her name called out. She turned to see her brother Emil and his wife Ida walking toward them.

"Are the Klugs all ready to board?" he asked. And in the same breath, "Where are Walther and Rudy?"

It was Ihde who answered, "When we left they were getting ready to wrestle with the steamer trunk."

✚✚✚

Walther Klug gave a sigh of relief as he stretched and straightened his back. He and Rudy had finally managed to lower the steamer trunk from the fourth floor apartment down to the sidewalk where Rudy's car was parked. Rudy just grunted and said, "Break time!" He reached into his shirt pocket and pulled out two cigars.

"Have one?" he asked his friend.

"Sure, why not."

Rudy offered Walther a light and then lit his own stogie. Walther sat on the trunk, while Rudy leaned against the car. After a few puffs, Rudy said, "Well are you all set for your big trip?"

"C'mon Rudy, you know that this is not my idea. Hertha has been pushing this for years, and every year she pushes harder. She has been homesick ever since she got here. She thinks it's the same over there as it was when she was a young girl."

"Why not make it a round trip, an extended vacation?" Rudy asked.

Walther thought a while before replying, "Rudy, I couldn't come up with one-way fare for the five of us. If it weren't for the steep discounts arranged by Hertha's uncle who has some lofty position with the steamship line, we wouldn't be going." He hesitated, then added, "Besides, there are other considerations." He did not elucidate the other considerations.

Rudy decided not to press any further. "Well, we better get this thing loaded into the car trunk and be on our way. We're already behind schedule," Rudy commented.

✦ ✦ ✦

After they secured the trunk, they went back up to the now empty apartment, freshened up and exchanged the coveralls that Rudy had brought along for their street clothes. Rudy was first to finish.

"I'll see you downstairs," he said, as he left the apartment.

When Walther rejoined him, Rudy was again leaning against the car. Rudy looked at his friend with approval. With his five-foot eleven-inch frame, curly blond hair, sharp facial features, gray suit with buttoned-down white shirt collar and blue tie, Walther looked as if he had just stepped out of a magazine ad, Rudy mused. Well, almost.

"You look like a million bucks," Rudy said. Walther thought a moment, then retorted, "You know, there was a time back in the old country when I was worth a million. Of course, the exchange rate at the time was about 33,000 to 1 in favor of the dollar."

"You too, eh?" Rudy queried.

"Yep."

They both had a good laugh and then got into the car.

✦ ✦ ✦

Rudy made good time driving the car from Brooklyn to Manhattan. They were on 55th Street heading west toward the Hudson River. At Lexington Avenue they stopped for a red light with one car in front of them at the intersection. As the light turned green, the driver of the first car put his trust in the light without reservation and therefore probably never saw the northbound car barreling toward him and seconds later hitting him broadside.

"Wow! Did you see that?" Rudy exclaimed as he slammed on his own brakes.

After a moment of indecision, Rudy and Walther got out of the car to offer assistance. As they approached the wreckage, they could see that both drivers, the only occupants of either car, were injured and apparently unconscious.

"Don't move them," a voice called out. It came from the elderly gentleman who had emerged from the taxi that had pulled up behind the northbound car. "I'm a doctor," he added, as he surveyed the scene and assessed what he could do to help the injured.

"I asked my cabbie to call emergency—they'll be along soon." Pointing to a rapidly growing puddle under one of the cars, he said, "You guys may want to back off a bit—that car seems to have a ruptured gas tank."

The pungent smell of gasoline quickly verified the good doctor's assessment, and the distant sound of sirens signaled that police and ambulance were on their way. Rudy and Walther retreated back to the car and got back in.

"Looks like we'll be stuck for a while," Rudy said, "Can't go forward and can't back up. Cars are backed up behind us all the way to the other intersection and all those double-parked trucks sure don't help any."

It had been dusk when they left the apartment. Now darkness had fallen, and the flashing beacons of the arriving ambulance and police cars added an eerie touch to the scene. Walther opened the passenger side window completely as one of the police officers approached the car.

"Did you guys witness the accident?"

"Yes, officer, we were right behind him waiting for the light to change," Walther answered.

"OK, I'll be back in a little bit to get your version of what happened."

The officer's "in a little bit" turned out to be about forty-five minutes, since he first busied himself with finding pedestrian witnesses and obtaining statements from them. When the police officer returned, he first asked to see Rudy's license. After Rudy complied, the officer asked, "So, what happened?"

Rudy told him what he had seen, in particular that the driver ahead of them did have the green light. The officer recorded Rudy's statement and asked him to sign the report form. He then thanked Rudy for his cooperation and said, "The fire department is almost done purging the intersection of the gas spill. Once the wreckers clear the intersection, you'll be on your way. It will be another fifteen minutes to half an hour." With that he left and headed back to his patrol car.

When they finally continued across town toward the pier, Rudy did not say much since he sensed that Walther was preoccupied.

Walther was reflecting on the accident and asked himself: Was this an omen? Not the accident in itself but the delay incurred. Was fate suggesting that with sufficient delay the ship would depart without them? Nah, it was just an accident—they happen all the time.

✚ ✚ ✚

Bright pier lighting now illuminated the scene and accentuated the white superstructure of the ship against the black hull even more so than daylight did. Three of four gangplanks had been pulled in, leaving only one to complete the boarding process. The dock was quite empty now except for several small groups congregating close to the remaining gangplank—the retinue of already boarded passengers having either left or having been directed by security personnel to a section of the pier reserved for those who wished to stay until the ship departed.

Hertha Klug and her party were one of the groups remaining on the dock. Hertha looked at her watch and exclaimed, "It is 10:30," and "Where can they possibly be?" she asked of no one in particular. "Rosemarie, Herbert, how many times must I tell you? I don't want you running all over the pier. Now get back here!" she admonished them again.

The children could tell that she was somewhat anguished when she said Rosemarie instead of addressing the older girl with the familial Romi. They quickly rejoined the group.

"Can't we go on the ship now?" Romi asked.

"Child, as I have said before, we can't board until your father gets here."

Emil again tried to reassure her, "Perhaps they had a flat tire, or a failed radiator hose," he ventured, although he knew that Rudy was an auto mechanic by trade and neither of these occurrences would take him long to repair.

"You don't suppose they had an accident," Hertha asked him.

"No, I don't suppose that at all," he answered, adding, "Try to relax, Hertha. You're getting yourself all unraveled."

"When does the boarding have to be completed, Oscar?" Emil asked the man in the white ship steward jacket who had come down the gangplank and had joined the group.

His full name was Oscar Diebohl. He was a friend of the Johtes. Often, when the ship put into New York he would visit them in their home or reciprocate by inviting them on board while the ship was in the harbor. In one of his visits to the Johtes, he had also become acquainted with the Klugs.

"They like to have everyone on board by 11:00 P.M., although the gangplank won't be pulled in until a few minutes before departure," he answered.

How can I relax, Hertha asked herself, deeply embroiled in all kinds of scenarios. Surely he hasn't changed his mind at the last minute and was purposely trying to miss the departure time. *What* would they do? They had given up the apartment. They had sold or given away all the furnishings. *Where* would they go? No, he wouldn't do that, she told herself and erased those thoughts from her mind, albeit unconvincingly.

It was almost 10:45 when Hertha spied her husband and Rudy coming down the dock. "There they are!" she cried out as she rushed toward them and asked, "Where have you been?" while embracing Walther and then ushering him to the group with her arm locking his and tears welling in her eyes.

Rudy and Walther alternated in telling the group about the accident, in particular how the gas spill hampered the rescue procedure and the ambulance crew went in at great risk to extricate the injured before the fire department got there to purge the intersection, knowing that any spark would spell disaster. Oscar Diebohl politely broke up the reunion with, "Folks, I think it's time for you to board."

Hertha's eyes were welling tears again, as were other's as they said their goodbyes. Then the Klug family walked up the gangplank, followed by Oscar Diebohl and two porters carrying the Klug hand luggage.

✚✚✚

On deck they were accompanied by a steward who showed them to their cabin. After a perfunctory inspection—mainly to ensure that they had all their hand luggage—Hertha and Walther herded their brood back up to the ship's deck where they were lucky to find a spot on the dockside railing.

Emotions were contained by engaging in small talk with their entourage on the dock until departure time. Precisely at midnight, the cables connecting the ship to several tugboats gave up their slack, and the ship slipped away from the dock into the shipping lane of the river.

While the ship's pilot guided the liner out of New York Harbor, the Klug family caught one last post-midnight look of the brightly illuminated skyline on this 31 May morning—the skyscrapers taking on a majestic appearance, with the Empire State Building towering above all.

One hour later, the pilot debarked, and the liner headed into the open sea. The year was 1939. The ship's destination: Germany.

Chapter 2

Once the Manhattan skyline appeared to recede into the horizon, the children started to become restless, so Hertha decided to take them down to the cabin. Walther indicated that he would stay on deck a while longer.

While getting Hannelore ready for bed, Hertha's eyes glanced over the cabin and the adjoining bath. The cabin was equipped with a double bed, a two-tiered bunk bed—Herbert had already claimed the upper tier—and a crib that had been brought in for the little one. A table and two chairs completed the furnishings. The table was located on the outside wall under the porthole.

"Herbert, stop climbing up and down on that bed! That's not a..." Hertha was groping for the right word in English.

"Not a monkey bars?" Herbert interjected.

"That's right, not a monkey bars," she said, giving him a stern look. "I want you to put on your pj's and go to sleep. You, too, Romi." Once the children were bedded down, she decided to also retire.

She lay down with a sigh of relief. It had been a long day, and once again she had worried needlessly. Not that Walther's late arrival had not been a matter of concern, but she felt a little guilty that she had thought that he might deliberately try to put the kibosh on their departure. Well, now they were finally on their way.

She was just dozing off when she heard the low-pitched sound of the ship's horn. She had been startled by that sound before. Semi-consciously she remembered. It had been fifteen years earlier when she had been an unwilling passenger on another liner going in the opposite direction. In a state of drowsiness she relived the particulars. To do so, she had to go back another ten years. It was 1914. She and her mother had just bade farewell to Hertha's father, Emil Werner, who was leaving on another trip to America. He was employed by a German passenger line that ran the transatlantic route between Hamburg and New York. He was a musician, a member of the ship's orchestra.

The date of her father's departure in late July had ingrained itself in Hertha's memory because Germany, just one week later, became embroiled in what would become World War I.

Hertha recalled the great anxiety the family shared, not knowing the father's whereabouts until a letter from the shipping line advised them that the ship had docked in New York, but in view of the risks involved, the ship would not be returning to Germany in the near future. The letter went on to say that the crew would be returned to Germany via a neutral ship.

A week or so later, her father's letter arrived. It confirmed what the line's letter said but then went on to tell them that he had chosen another option. He had jumped ship!

Even in her semi-conscious state, Hertha couldn't suppress a smile when she remembered her mother's response as she read the letter, "Jumped ship? Has the man gone mad?"

Her mother read on: He reasoned that if he came home, he'd be out of a job—he figures there wouldn't be much of a call for musicians in a country at war and even if there were, he thinks he could provide for his family far better by staying in America. He goes on to say that he has easily blended in with the population of New York, but he has taken the precautionary measure of listing a fictitious company name and a post office box as his return address.

"This is a *fait accompli*!" Mrs. Werner shrieked, after she reread the letter aloud to her three children.

"What is a *fait accompli*?" ten-year-old Emil, Jr., asked.

"Never mind," Mrs. Werner responded, brusquely cutting him off. "Your father has decided to stay in America—there is a war going on and he has decided to stay in America—your father has a wife and three children, and he has decided to stay in America—your father thinks he may not find a job, so he decides to stay in America!" she lamented and broke into tears.

"He will be labeled a draft dodger," she exclaimed between sobs.

Nineteen-year-old Hedwig, Hertha's older sister by five years, tried to console her mother. "Mama, Father is approaching fifty. He is well past the draft age. He won't be labeled a draft dodger. But suppose he would have trouble finding work if he came back. What would you do? What would *we* do?" she asked, broadening the scope of the dilemma.

Mrs. Werner thought about her daughter's practical assessment of the situation. "I guess we will have to make the best of it and hope that your father knows what he is doing," she responded while wiping away her tears, her voice lacking conviction.

Hertha continued her surreal reminiscence. Father did know what he was doing! He supported them well during the war years—even after the United States entered the war and postal contact was interrupted—he managed to support them via a friend who was still plying the Atlantic on a neutral vessel.

Mother, although missing him dearly, thought he was an absolute genius when the dollars kept coming in during the devastating inflation years after the war. She would hurry to the bank and then scurry to the grocery store. The storekeeper would greet her with, "Hello, Mrs. Werner. You're not going to empty my shelves again, are you?"

But he did so good-naturedly. He knew she had helped a lot of her neighbors during those trying times. While concluding one of her shopping sprees early on during the inflation period, he might say, "You have fifteen hundred Marks in change coming."

She would wave him off with, "Forget the change, just give me two more loaves of bread."

A little later on, as the inflation spiraled, the conversation would go something like this, "You have a million and a half Marks in change coming."

She would wave him off with, "Forget the change, just give me two more loaves of bread."

Hertha recalled that although her mother could have used the income that Father was sending to really enrich herself and her children during the inflation years, she only used it to meet their immediate needs. To do otherwise, she felt, would not be right.

The events of 1924 were particularly ingrained in Hertha's memory. The *Reichsmark* was replaced by the *Rentenmark,* thus bringing the inflation cycle to an end. Father's letters indicated that he was ready to return home. He yearned to be back with his family.

Unfortunately Mother had other ideas. She was afraid that bad years still lay ahead and therefore urged him to stay put a little longer. As an inducement she offered to send Hertha to America. Hertha could keep house for him, and the experience of visiting a different country would broaden her horizon, was how mother put it.

Hertha was aghast when Mother proposed this idea. "I don't want to go there," she told her mother. "I don't even know the language," she added.

"Your father has been very good to us these past years, and perhaps it's time for us to reciprocate," Mother replied.

"Why not let Hedwig look after him? She and her husband Joseph have been in America for over three years now and apparently are doing well."

"But they don't live in New York City."

"Then why don't *you* go?"

"I can't go! Who would look after young Emil?"

Hertha relived all the anxieties as these memories emerged. She knew there was more to this than placating her father. She had been seeing a young man who, unfortunately, was engaged to someone else. Even more unfortunate, Mother knew that he was engaged to someone else. Hertha recalled the many arguments she and Mother had had, wherein Mother insisted that she break off the liaison.

"If you don't end this, you will no longer be welcome under my roof," Mother finally threatened.

Hertha acquiesced. What else could she do? She was totally dependent on Mother, she had no skills to make it on her own. The decision at first left her in a state of despair, and then a despondency set in that would not go away.

"As soon as I know of someone leaving for America, someone I can trust as a chaperone, I'm sending you off to your father," Mother finally said. "A new environment will stop this moping around day after day!"

Mother found her trusted someone in the fall of 1924. It was her boarder who one morning excitedly told her, "I'll be immigrating to America in about a month!"

Prior to this revelation, Hertha's attitude toward the boarder had been amicable—now she suddenly loathed him.

The low-pitched sound of the ship's horn interrupted Hertha's "reverie." In a state of utter confusion she fumbled for a light switch. Seeing her children peacefully asleep, she gave a sigh of relief. For a moment I thought I was back on that dreaded other ship, she said to herself as she put her head back into the pillows.

Chapter 3

Walther Klug stayed on deck long after most of the other passengers had retired to their cabins. Having walked up to the bow, he reached into his pocket for his pipe and tobacco pouch. His first attempts to light the pipe were for naught because of the strong wind blasting across this foremost part of the ship. Finally he squatted beyond the edge of the bulwark and got his pipe lit. Straightening up, he peered into the dark unknown into which the ship seemed to be heading. His imminent future also seemed like a dark unknown.

With the future so uncertain, Walther's thoughts dwelled in the past. He had left Germany years ago to catch up with his fiancee who had emigrated to America three months earlier. After arriving in New York, he traveled to Columbus, Ohio, for their reunion only to find that he had been jilted. Devastated, he decided to return to New York where he found a job as a laborer in a shipyard.

Several months later he decided to visit an acquaintance whom he had met briefly after his arrival from Germany. Walther was not real keen on meeting this fellow again, but the man's daughter piqued his interest. After Walther rang the doorbell a third time, his acquaintance responded. Looking at Walther quizzically for a moment but before Walther could reintroduce himself, he said, "Ah, yes, I remember you. You're

Walther. You're my wife's former boarder. Please come in." Walther responded, "I'll be glad to, Mr. Werner."

Six months later, he and Hertha Werner were married.

✚✚✚

Walther recalled the early years of their marriage. They were happy ones, but occasionally he would come home and sense that she had been crying.

"What is troubling you, honey?" he would ask.

"Oh, I guess I'm just a bit overwhelmed. A new country...a strange language...unless I find a German shopkeeper, I run into all kinds of problems just to do my shopping. On top of all that I suppose I'm just plain homesick," she would tell him.

Walther realized that the transition was much more difficult for her than it was for him. Up until that time she had never been outside of her native Hamburg; whereas he had been called up for service late in 1917 and then, after having been discharged, had left his parental home to accept a position in Hamburg. He further mused that while he had completed *Gymnasium* (high school) and had studied English for four years, she had never been exposed to a foreign language. Walther recalled that he didn't really perceive the depth of her feelings until that evening when Hertha suggested that they go back to Germany.

"Go back to Germany...are you out of your mind?"

"Well, why not? It wasn't *that* bad over there, was it?"

"It wasn't for you. You had your father supporting you from over here, while I remember getting paid twice a day just so I could run out and purchase something that might cost twice as much four hours later," Walther replied.

"But it's different now, they have a new currency," Hertha said.

"They may have a different currency, but unemployment is still widespread, and the way democracy is working out in Germany, it will be a long time before things get better. What about your father? He's staying with us now. What are you going to do—send him back to some boarding house?"

"Oh, he'll be all right. I suspect he'll be returning home in the near future."

"Are you sure that you're not still pining for your boyfriend over there?" Walther asked, trying to camouflage a real concern as a jest.

"Of course not, silly. I did marry you, didn't I?"

"You did. And you also knew that I look at America as a land of opportunity and that I was not planning to go back. When opportunity knocks, you don't let it go unheeded!"

"I was hoping I could change your mind."

"Honey, things will work out. It's all a little new to you right now. Give it some time. Try to be a little patient," Walther said, as he took her into his arms.

"I'll try," she said as she thought, but I'll also keep on hoping.

Walther remembered that her longings for the old country had subsided or at least had not been verbalized as often after the older children were born. He assumed that the children had given her a greater sense of purpose; also, all the mundane tasks of looking after two little ones naturally left less time for introspection. The downside was that while nurturing the little ones there was little time for socializing. They were homebound, spoke mostly German at home. As a consequence Hertha had little opportunity to expand her social horizon in the new country. On the rare occasions when they did go out, it would usually be with German-speaking friends.

Their circumstances had vastly improved after Walther left the shipyard and went to work for a large bakery concern in late 1927, the same year Emil Werner, Sr., returned to Germany. Within two years Walther had been promoted to manager of one of the company's retail outlets, which allowed them to rent the upper level of a two-family house in a nice section of Brooklyn. The future was looking bright for the Klug family, even well into the Depression years.

Inexplicably, in 1935, Walther lost his job. No reason was given other than that his services were no longer required. It was quite a while before he found work as a maintenance man in a private girls' school at about half his former pay scale. In the interim, most of their savings had been expended. Walther relived their having to give up the nice apartment and having to move into a fourth floor walk-up. While still in Brooklyn, they were now on the other side of the tracks. Their lifestyle changed drastically—approaching a hand to mouth existence.

Two years later they met Oscar Diebohl for the first time. The Johtes had invited Oscar to their place and also had invited the Klugs. After dinner they settled into the living room. The women, Hertha and Ihde, were each nursing a glass of wine while the men enjoyed a beer.

"So, how are things in the old country?" Rudy asked Oscar.

"Getting better all the time; unemployment will soon be a thing of the past," Oscar replied.

"But most of these jobs are in the armament field—isn't that true?" Walther asked.

"Oh, by no means. They are building the Autobahn; Hitler is pushing the Volkswagen," Oscar declared, adding, "no pun intended. He envisions every family in Germany having one. A lot of jobs were created to prepare for the Olympic games, which were held last year. If you recall the news coverage, you'll remember that the games were well received by all the participating nations."

"But those jobs, the ones involving the games, were of a temporary nature," Rudy implied.

"True enough," Oscar conceded. "Folks finishing those jobs will go on to other things. There are many other construction projects underway in Germany." Walther recalled the glowing terms with which Oscar Diebohl described the situation in Germany—not only during this get-together but also in subsequent ones. He also recalled how Hertha had perked up whenever Oscar had alluded to the improved conditions in Germany. To Walther it appeared that Oscar was rekindling a fire that he, Walther, had tried to extinguish.

One evening, in late 1938, Walther knew that his premonition was correct. Oscar had indeed rekindled the flame. Hertha again started talking about returning to Germany.

"Why do you want to return to Germany at this point in time?" he asked her.

"For one thing, according to Oscar, we could be doing as well in Germany, if not better, than we are here. This Depression just seems to be never-ending. Look at what happened to Hedwig and Joseph. They were working in domestic service for a banker in Peekskill, New York—she as a cook, he as a chauffeur—and for a while did well. As a matter of fact, they did very well. He was able to amass a small fortune, some 50,000 dollars, by buying stocks recommended by his boss. Then the crash occurred, and they were practically wiped out. Not only that, both eventually lost their jobs. What did they do? They went back to Germany two years ago! Do you remember what you once told me about opportunity knocking? Well, it's not knocking here!"

Walther had to concede that this was a point well taken, and he was somewhat ashamed that he had not always been mindful of how difficult it was for her to make ends meet. He was remorsefully reminded of the times when he had chided her for what was offered at the dinner table after he got home from work.

"What's this? Another casserole? Or is it the same one we had yesterday?" he would grouse.

The first time she said nothing. She was too busy quelling the tears.

"As soon as the household money improves, so will the cuisine," she said the second and last time he challenged her in this manner.

"I realize that we have seen some rough years, but I think there is more to it than just that," Walther said to her.

"There is! I miss the *Gemuetlichkeit* [relaxed atmosphere]," she replied.

Walther remembered that she had not wanted for anything while she lived in Germany with her father supporting them from America during the war years and the terrible years following. He realized that she had lived in a cocoon that shielded her and therefore kept her unaware of the privations that had befallen the old country. She had little concept that somehow someone always had to bring home the bacon and that a relaxed atmosphere sometimes had to yield to this primary objective.

Walther knew that she was as apolitical as he was. Their meager understanding of what had happened in Germany since 1933 was obtained by simply reading the newspapers—in their case a German language newspaper that they bought once a week—and by listening to Oscar Diebohl. But he felt that the political aspects might help change her mind.

"You think you'll still find that Gemuetlichkeit with this new fellow in charge?" Walther asked her.

"Walther, Germany has been a monocracy before. Prior to Hitler it was the Kaiser. It's…it's the same thing, only the title is different."

"But the Kaiser didn't make territorial demands nor did he utter anti-Semitic statements like this guy does."

"Hitler is a politician. Politicians say things to scare the opposition to get what they want. They are means to an end. In this case one of the means is so ludicrous, you know he can't be taken seriously."

"You don't think the situation could become explosive? Two months ago when he took over the Sudetenland, it seemed as if the world was approaching an abyss."

"You mean, will there be war? Why should there be? He is just reclaiming what is rightfully German, and the other countries appear to be in concurrence. Why else would they let him get away with it? He has said that after the Sudetenland he would have no further territorial demands."

"What else is bugging you?" he asked.

"Walther, fifteen years ago my mother practically kicked me out of the house. She uprooted me from my familiar surroundings and sent me half a world away! What she did was wrong! I want to, just one time, tell her how wrong she was in sending me away!"

"You can convey those thoughts in a letter."

"No. It has to be face to face."

"You're willing to stake your future on a...a grudge?"

She did not react to his inference; she just asked, "What future?"

Walther was astounded that she, who usually was so security-minded—whenever he brought up the subject of looking for a better paying job, she would tell him that she didn't think the time was right and that he'd better hold on to what he had, else he might find himself on the street again—would now be willing to gamble on an uncertain future.

Walther was also astounded at the depth of her resentment toward her mother. He didn't know to what extent that resentment, or her longing for the old country, or their financial plight contributed to Hertha's anguish. He guessed that it was mostly the latter. He did know that he couldn't change any of them. He also did know that he was tired of the badgering. He feared that if he sent Hertha and the children over on a visit, which he couldn't afford, she might not return. He did love her, and he loved his children. He did what he had to do.

He capitulated.

In April of 1939 they had obtained their passage. Hertha gleefully exclaimed, "Well, the die is cast!" Walther had no comment. He just thought that if things do blow up over there, you'll have to rearrange those words, because, in that case, some of the cast will die.

Walther made several attempts to relight his pipe but was forced to quit because he ran out of matches. He cast one last look into the darkness and then headed back to the cabin.

Chapter 4

The throttling of the ship's engines awoke Walther on the third morning out of New York. He glanced at his watch. It was 6 A.M. Curious to why the ship apparently was just drifting, he arose and quickly dressed preparatory to going up on deck. Herbert too had been awakened.

"Where are you going, Papa?" the boy asked. "Sh, you'll wake up your mother and the girls," Walther admonished in a whisper.

"Can I go with you?"

"Yes, but hurry up and be very quiet."

+ + +

As they joined several other onlookers on deck, they noticed another ship had stopped; it was on the port side of the liner, about one hundred yards away. The other ship, which appeared to be a freighter, was parallel to the liner with its bow facing in the opposite direction. A cable and what appeared to be a rope had been launched from the freighter to the liner.

"What are they going to do, Papa?" the boy asked.

"I don't know. It looks like they're either going to transport something from that ship over here or something from this ship over there."

Walther and Herbert watched the activity on the freighter. The cable connecting the two ships appeared to be controlled by a winch on the freighter's stern. Close to the winch several crewmen were attaching what appeared to be a stretcher to the cable via a pulley arrangement. The pulley arrangement was tied to the rope to the liner and also to a rope on the freighter side, thus affording control from either ship.

"What are they doing, Papa?" Herbert asked.

"It looks like they are going to transport someone to this ship on that stretcher."

"Why?"

"Well, someone probably has taken ill and needs more help than the people on the freighter can supply."

The crewmen on the freighter had indeed placed a man on the stretcher after carefully wrapping him in blankets.

Walther now could visualize what was about to happen. The crewmen on the freighter would carefully play out the rope until the stretcher reached the low point of the catenary formed by the cable connecting the two ships or, more precisely, until the stretcher reached the halfway point. Crewmen aboard the liner then would pull the stretcher in while the freighter people continued to pay out their rope. Herbert watched the activity with fascination.

"What happens if the cable breaks, Papa?"

"Don't even think about it," Walther answered.

Although the sea was calm, the two ships had drifted closer together by the time the stretcher was approaching the halfway point, causing the stretcher to be uncomfortably close to the waves below. The crewmen of the freighter stopped paying out the line and did not continue until the winch operator had reduced the slack in the cable. Once their human cargo was halfway across, they signaled the liner crew to start pulling from their end.

As the stretcher finally was pulled aboard the liner, the group of onlookers as well as the deckhands on the freighter broke out in applause.

"Well, did you learn anything from that?" Walther asked his son.

"Yeah. Don't get sick when you're on a boat!"

They continued to watch as the unoccupied stretcher was returned to the freighter by reversing the process, and the cable and rope were released from the liner.

As the ships got underway again, the crewmen of the liner and the group of onlookers exchanged farewell waves with the freighter crew. Herbert watched the freighter until it was almost out of sight. He had noticed the stars and stripes fluttering at its stern. When he looked to the back of his ship, he saw a different flag. It was a white circle on a red background. In the white circle was a symbol he had seen before. He had seen it on the tail of the German zeppelin as it flew over New York. It was a swa…swas…a swastika!

Chapter 5

Starting on the third day on board, all of the Klug family took their meals in the dining room. During the first two days Hertha and the two older children had been seasick, and one or more would not show up. Also, during those two days, one or more might leave the table in a hurry to avoid an embarrassing moment.

During some of their meals Oscar Diebohl would stop by to inquire about their well-being and to chat a while. Walther thought he looked rather dapper in his white shirt, black bow-tie, white steward's jacket, and black pants. His black oxfords were always polished to a bright shine. I can see why the world looks rosy to you, Walther thought as he observed the steward.

✦ ✦ ✦

The children had been enrolled in a shipboard day-care center. Romi and Herbert had been included per their mother's edict to keep an eye on little Hannelore. They thought it redundant to babysit at the babysitter's, so they would play hooky, feign seasickness, or try to slip away unnoticed. When Hertha questioned them about their devious behavior, Romi would tell her, "Mama, all the others are just little kids!"

Hertha relented and told them they would not have to stay but would have to deposit and pick up their little sister at the day-care at the prescribed times. Thus, the older two could enjoy the mild June weather on deck, playing shuffleboard or just sitting in a deck chair, given that one of the parents were available.

At the end of the sixth day the ship anchored in the harbor of Cherbourg, and passengers wishing to disembark were taken ashore via launch.

On the following day the liner docked in Cuxhaven, Germany, located at the mouth of the river Elbe. Since the draft of the loaded ship exceeded the river's depth further upstream, disembarkation was done here. Thereafter the ship would continue up the Elbe to Hamburg for refitting for the next voyage. The steamship line provided several special trains that would take the ship's passengers the some sixty miles to Hamburg, if they so desired.

✦ ✦ ✦

The Klug family was standing on one of the Cuxhaven station platforms as the special train slowly pulled in.

"Why does it have so many doors, Papa?" Herbert asked as the cars were slowly moving past.

"It's a commuter train. It's designed to handle many people very quickly. That's why each compartment has its own doors, one on each side," Walther explained.

"Why do some cars have a number 2 on them and others a number 3?" Herbert asked.

"They denote second and third class. In second class your tush sits on upholstery, in third class it sits on wood," Walther patiently replied.

"Oh."

Once the cars had stopped, Walther selected a compartment, and Hertha and the girls boarded. Walther and the boy busied themselves with the hand luggage, which Walther stowed in the overhead bins. Shortly after they were all seated, the train slowly pulled out of the station. Herbert observed to himself that Papa was right; number 3 cars did have wooden seats.

They were the only ones in the compartment, which normally could seat about ten people. This meant that they all enjoyed a window seat, Hertha and Walther opposite one another on one side of the compartment and the two older children on the other side. Little Hannelore had a view of the outside world from her seat on mother's lap.

Having been city dwellers for all of their young lives, the children were very much enthralled by the countryside as the train passed through the northwest German farmlands.

Romi had moved over to sit next to her mother and was pointing things out to her little sister. "Look at the cows," Romi exclaimed, and, "Look at the chickens—see, they only have two legs!" This was in reference to little Hannelore's chicken drawings in which she always drew them with four legs that always resulted in jeers from her siblings.

"Now don't be making fun of your little sister. The only chickens she's ever seen were in magazine pictures or pictures you drew," Hertha reminded her.

"Yeah, but none of them had four legs," Romi impishly remarked.

"Look at that funny looking truck, Papa. It only has three wheels," Herbert chimed in. Walther got up and moved over to the children's side of the compartment to look at the truck traveling along the road running parallel to the railroad track. It had the normal two rear wheels, but only one wheel mounted at the extreme front of the vehicle at the center of the engine compartment.

"Why do they build them like that, Papa?" Herbert asked.

"Probably to make them less expensive, son. But I don't know. I've never seen one like that either," Walther answered.

It wasn't long before the farm landscape gave way to the suburbs of Hamburg. The farms had been displaced by single-story dwellings and multi-storied apartment complexes. In the distance the skyline of Hamburg, yet indistinct, had come into view. As the train rumbled toward the city, Hertha started to point out the various landmarks, "That is the Michaelis *Kirche* [Michaelis church]. That one over there is the Nikolai *Kirche.* And that one with the green steeple is the Jakobi *Kirche.*"

Walther noticed the exuberance in her voice as she identified these landmarks and felt that she was truly savoring this, her homecoming.

The rumbling of the train became less muted once it was on the railway bridge crossing the Elbe River. To the left and to the right, the Klug family was exposed to the panorama of the harbor facilities with the many shipbuilding yards and the many piers where ships of all flags were either being loaded or unloaded.

About fifteen minutes later the train was easing into the Hamburg *Hauptbahnhof* (main station). Herbert noticed that they were entering an arched structure that spanned across what must have been about twenty tracks entering the station.

Once inside, he noticed that they were still in complete daylight. Looking up he could see the sky through the steel grids that connected to the main girders. At first he thought that the roof was unfinished, but a closer look told him that the grids had been closed by what must have been thousands of individual glass panes. No place to throw stones, he thought to himself.

After the train came to a squealing halt, they got off onto a crowded platform. "No sense trying to find your parents in this crowd," Walther commented to his wife. "Why don't you and the girls stay over there by that big clock, while Herbert and I put our hand luggage in a baggage locker. I'll come back later and pick it up."

The crowd had dispersed considerably once they returned, but there was no sign of Hertha's parents, Mr. and Mrs. Werner.

"Perhaps they are waiting for us outside," Walther said.

"Let's take a look."

As soon as they exited the railway station Hertha almost immediately exclaimed, "There they are!" She was pointing to an elderly couple standing about fifty feet from the entrance. Romi and Herbert, who were trailing a little behind their parents, looked in the direction she was pointing.

Mr. Werner was of average height. His ruddy complexion, combined with his white goatee, made him look rather distinguished. He was wearing a dark suit and a homburg hat. Mrs. Werner was attired in a dark blouse and a black skirt just short enough to reveal her laced black shoes that reached up past her ankles. She was a small woman whose salt and pepper hair was combed back into a bun. The severity of her coiffure and her piercing eyes gave her a somewhat harsh look.

Romi immediately noticed Grandmother Werner's shoes. She nudged her brother and whispered, "Look at the funny shoes she's wearing." Herbert shrugged his shoulders and gave her a quizzical look, which she returned. Then they burst out laughing.

Walther turned around and admonished, "Hey, you two, stop the clowning—you're about to meet your grandparents."

Hertha's reunion with her parents was subdued. Seeing her mother, she was reminded of the animosity she had felt toward her the last time they were together. She embraced her father and kissed him on the cheek. She then gave her mother a hug, but without a kiss. Walther broke the awkwardness of the moment. "It's a pleasure to meet you again." With a nod toward the little girl cradled in his arms he added, "This is our youngest, Hannelore."

He then introduced the older children to their grandparents. Herbert and Romi said *Guten Tag* (good day) in their best German, followed by a bow and a slight curtsy, respectively.

"We could call a taxi, but since it's such a lovely afternoon, why don't we just walk to our house," Mr. Werner suggested.

As they started out Walther addressed the older children, "I want you two to stay ahead of us, but within earshot, understood?" The children nodded in assent.

Staying within earshot allowed the children to hear the grown-ups' conversation, which now was all in German. "Do you understand everything they're talking about?" Herbert asked his older sister.

"Nope!"

"I don't either. We're lucky that it's almost summer vacation. When we have to go to school in the fall, we'll probably be the class dunces!"

Romi thought about this for a moment, then said, "Mama always told us that we should speak more German at home because it might come in handy some day."

"Yeah, but she didn't tell us that we'd *have* to talk German until recently. Are they talking high German or low German?"

"I don't know," Romi replied.

They were walking down Steindamm, a major thoroughfare. At each crossing they would check with their parents whether to keep going straight ahead or perhaps turn a corner.

"Look at the trolleys," Herbert commented. "They all have two or three cars, not like ours in Brooklyn, which have only one car.

"Did you notice that a lot of the boys are wearing brown shirts and short black corduroy pants? The older ones have a swastika armband on their left sleeve."

"I think they're like Cub Scouts and Boy Scouts in America," Romi suggested.

Herbert noticed that all the uniformed kids each carried a knife enclosed in a black sheath that was attached to their belt at the left hip. He thought those knives were pretty snazzy.

Shortly after the Steindamm merged into Luebecker Street, they turned left onto Muehlendamm. "See the second house from the corner ahead?" Hertha asked the children. "That's where Grandma lives. That's where I was born."

Chapter 6

The Werners had an apartment on the second floor. It was essentially a railroad flat. The entrance from the street led into a long hall that ran along an outer wall for almost the length of the house. Three rooms opened onto the inside wall of the hall, the largest of the three facing the street. Another large room, also facing the street, opened onto the entrance end of the hall. The other end of the hall narrowed to accommodate a bathroom, leaving a corridor that led to the kitchen. Beyond the kitchen was a partially enclosed balcony furnished with table and chairs.

After they entered the apartment, Mother Werner said, "I've prepared one of the front rooms for you. Not the one that opens onto the end of the hall—I have that one rented out to a boarder. Why don't you freshen up a bit while I make some coffee. I bought a cake at Nagel's bakery."

"Nagel's bakery?" Hertha asked, "Are they still around?"

"They're still around."

+++

Later that evening, while Walther was still chatting with his in-laws, Hertha was in the front room getting Hannelore ready for bed. Romi soon joined them. "Are we all going to sleep in this one room?" Romi asked.

"Your father and I and you two girls will be sleeping here. Your brother will sleep in the little room off the kitchen."

"Isn't it going to be a little crowded in here?"

"A little bit."

"How long will we be staying here?"

"Until we can find a suitable apartment of our own, hopefully no more than a couple of weeks."

Their conversation was interrupted when Herbert came running in from the hall. "Mama, they don't have a real toilet," he excitedly confided.

"What do you mean 'they don't have a real toilet'?"

"It's just like a bench with a hole in it."

"It flushes, doesn't it?"

"Yeah, if you pull the chain."

"So, what's your problem?"

"It's just so...so old-fashioned."

Hertha turned toward him and placing her hands on his shoulders, she said, "This is an old house. When it was built, modern toilet fixtures were just not available. OK?"

Hertha directed her attention back to Hannelore, thinking Herbert's misgivings had been resolved. But Herbert was still perplexed. "Where is the bathtub?" he asked.

"The bathtub? There is no bathtub." Hertha answered.

"How will I take a bath?"

Hertha turned her attention back to him. "To bathe or shower we will have to go to the bathhouse. It's right around the corner on Luebecker Street. You'll see, we'll go there tomorrow." After a pause she added, "Tell me, since when are you such a bathing enthusiast?" He just looked at her sheepishly.

"OK, I want you two to get ready for bed."

As Herbert trudged out she could hear him mumbling, "Gee whiz, what a bathroom—a holey bench and no tub!"

✚✚✚

During the first few weeks, the Klug family would take in the sights with Hertha acting as tour director. One day they took the streetcar all the way to its terminal point and visited Hagenbeck's *Tierpark* (Hagenbeck's Zoo). "It is even bigger than the Bronx Zoo! You do remember when we went to the Bronx Zoo, don't you?" she asked the older children. The children nodded in assent.

Another day they visited *Planten un Blomen* (Hamburg's horticultural park). "Wasn't that interesting?" Hertha asked the children as they left the park. This time, the children did not nod concurrence. Romi just shrugged her shoulders, while Herbert said, "I think we should have gone back to Hagenbeck."

Closer to home, they would take walks along the Alster River. The river flows north to south and fills a great depression near the city center, thus forming a huge lake on its way toward confluence with the Elbe. During the summer months, sailboats ply the lake and swans float on the water, or look for handouts supplied by city residents along the shoreline.

They also visited members of the extended family, and they became acquainted with friends of the Werners who would stop by to visit. Among these friends were Mr. and Mrs. Jockel.

✚✚✚

The Klugs and Werners were enjoying a lovely early June evening on the balcony, when the Jockels stopped by for the second time since the Klugs' arrival.

Mrs. Werner greeted them by saying, "We're all out on the balcony, and we're just getting ready for cake and coffee. Please join us."

Walther took them to be his age, perhaps a few years younger. He noticed, as he had during their first meeting, that Mr. Jockel was wearing a National Socialist Party pin on the lapel of his suit jacket.[1] He's either a government worker, or perhaps just a Party member, Walther thought to himself. Mrs. Jockel struck him as rather plain looking.

Her plainness was accentuated by, or perhaps even due to, the way she wore her blond hair. It was combed straight back and gathered in a bun, just like Grandmother Werner's hairdo. Her faintly lined face suggested that life had not always been easy for her.

"So how is Mr. Werner?" Mr. Jockel inquired.

"Oh, I'm fine."

"Still playing that clarinet?"

"Yes, I played in three performances with the Thalia Theatre orchestra last week. I do it on a part-time basis to stay in tune, so to speak."

"That's wonderful," Mr. Jockel commented.

Turning to the Klugs, Mr. Jockel queried, "How are the newcomers doing?"

"We're doing fine," Walther answered. "As a matter of fact, we will be hitting the road again in about a week. We'll be traveling to Kassel to see my parents and my brother and sisters."

"Well, then you have quite a trip ahead of you. How long will you be staying?" Mrs. Jockel asked.

"No longer than a week. By then, I'll have to be busy looking for a job during the day, while during the evening Hertha and I will be apartment hunting," Walther replied.

1 The word Party appearing alone and capitalized refers to the National Socialist Party for the remainder of this book.

Mr. Jockel inquired whether the Klugs had taken advantage of the fine weather with outdoor activities.

"Oh, yes," Hertha replied. "We love to take long walks along the Alster, and we have been to Hagenbeck's and to *Planten un Blomen*. The children loved the zoo, but they were less impressed with the botanical gardens."

"Not very exciting, eh?" Mr. Jockel asked the children.

Romi and Herbert both shook their heads.

"Well, I have something that may be of interest to all of you," Mr. Jockel announced. "The *Fuehrer*, Adolf Hitler, will be coming to Hamburg in a couple of days. He will be traveling from the airport by motorcade to the convention center, where he will give a speech. Would you be interested in catching a glimpse of the Fuehrer along the motorcade route?"

The Werners declined. Hertha asked, "When will this happen?"

"Two days from now, on Wednesday."

"Our steamer trunk is still in baggage-hold at the main station. On Wednesday we have to make arrangements to have it put into storage until we have found an apartment," Hertha said.

"Well, how about the children?" Mr. Jockel asked. "I could pick them up."

Romi shook her head.

"How about you, Herbert?" Mr. Jockel asked.

Herbert shrugged his shoulders, while looking at his mother.

"If you want to, you can go," she told him.

"OK."

"Does OK mean yes?" Mr. Jockel asked. Seeing Hertha nod her head, he said, "Then it's all settled, I'll pick you up on Wednesday morning at 10:00."

After visiting a while longer, the Jockels left.

✚✚✚

Mr. Jockel was punctual, when he picked Herbert up on Wednesday. They walked up the Steindamm toward the city center. As they approached the main artery the motorcade would be traversing, they could see that people were already lined up, apparently three or four deep, along the motorcade route.

They were still half a city block away when Mr.Jockel said, "I'm afraid we got here too late." After a moment of indecision, he said, "Maybe all is not lost. Maybe we can still see him—if he's standing up. Let's just wait here. Why don't you fetch that orange crate by the lamp post, and bring it over here. You won't be able to see anything at all, unless you stand on it to raise your eye level."

After about fifteen minutes, they could hear distant cheers. The cheers grew louder and louder as the motorcade approached nearer and nearer. When the cheers were at their loudest, Herbert saw a brown visored cap bobbing laterally just above the crowd. It reminded him of a duck moving along its predetermined path at a shooting gallery.

"That's him, that's the Fuehrer," Mr.Jockel cried out.

"I only see somebody's cap," Herbert ventured.

"Well, yes, but it's *his* cap! We just saw the Fuehrer drive past," Mr. Jockel exclaimed.

After the cheers had died away, Herbert asked, "How do you know it was the Fuehrer's cap?"

"Because this is his procession. No one else in that car would dare stand up, if the Fuehrer were still seated! It's a matter of protocol!"

Herbert didn't quite understand what this meant, so he responded with a simple, "Oh."

Upon their return to the Werner's apartment, Mr. Jockel left Herbert at the front door, indicating that he had some errands to run.

Hertha responded to the doorbell. "Your father and I are just getting ready to go to the main station. Want to come along?"

"Nah."

"Did you see the Fuehrer?"

"Nah, we only got to see his cap."

"Why did you only see his cap? Did the wind blow it off? Did he lay it down somewhere?"

"No! No! No! It was on his head! Because of the crowd, we could only see his cap, not the rest of him."

"How did you know it was his cap?"

"Because Mr. Jockel said he's the only one allowed to stand up in the car."

Hertha didn't quite know what to make of this, but she didn't press the issue.

Chapter 7

The Klug children spent considerable time in the little park located near the Werner's residence, where huge trees offered a canopy of foliage that provided relief from the early summer's heat. There was a sandbox for the tykes, while a playground attracted the older children. The playground offered swings, parallel bars, seesaws, and climbing poles.

The first few times the children ventured to the park, the older two sort of stuck together. They were somewhat inhibited to talk to the other children, because their German language capability was, at best, rudimentary. They had learned their German as preschoolers, for Hertha had spoken to them, almost exclusively, in German at home. They had learned English while they played with neighborhood children. By the time Hannelore was born, the older children were attending school, and by then they were speaking mostly English at home. As a consequence, Hertha's English improved considerably, but Hannelore was exposed to very little German, ever since she started to talk.

But little Hannelore was not the least bit inhibited. Playing in the sandbox, she would talk to the other little occupants in English. They would stare at her in astonishment, wondering what she was trying to tell them, and then would shy away.

Romi and Herbert were amused by their little sister's efforts. They also felt sorry that she could not communicate with her would-be friends.

One day, while they were again keeping an eye on their sister playing in the sandbox, two girls, one blond, the other brunette, approached Hannelore. The blond girl asked her, "*Wie heisst Du denn*? [What is your name?]"

Understanding that much German, she answered, "Hannelore."

The blond girl asked Romi, "Is she your little sister?"

Romi and Herbert both nodded.

The blond, who appeared to be Romi's age, then said, "She sure is a pretty little thing. Her hair is much lighter than either of yours, but she has the same dark brown eyes that you both have."

She then introduced herself. "My name is Annemarie." Pointing at the brunette, she said, "This is my friend Helga."

Romi completed the introductions. She said, "My name is Rosemarie, and this is my brother Herbert."

"You're new around here, aren't you?" Helga asked.

"Yes, we're staying with our grandparents who live just a block from here," Romi answered.

"Why are you living with your grandparents?" Annemarie asked.

"Because we just arrived from overseas a couple of weeks ago."

"Oh, then your whole family is staying with your grandparents?" Helga asked.

"Yes," Romi replied.

Cries, coming from the sandbox, prompted Herbert to check what the fuss was all about.

Returning her attention to Romi, Annemarie asked, "Where did you come from?"

"From America."

"All the way from America? Will you be staying in Hamburg?" Annemarie asked.

"We'll be staying somewhere in Hamburg. My parents will be looking for an apartment soon."

"I hope it will be nearby," Annemarie stated. "Then we could go to the same school, perhaps be in the same class, and you could tell me all about America."

"Annemarie, your mother is expecting us. I think we have to go now," Helga interrupted.

"You're right," Annemarie remarked. "Will you be coming back to the park tomorrow?" she asked Romi.

Romi nodded, "If the weather is nice."

"We'll see you then," Annemarie said, as they departed.

Having pacified Hannelore, Herbert returned from the sandbox. "Did your friends leave?"

"Yes." After some thought she added, "Aren't you surprised?"

"That they left?"

"No. That Hannelore broke the ice for us. But for her, those girls probably wouldn't have stopped to talk to us."

"If not today, they would have, sooner or later."

When they went back to the park the next day, Annemarie and Helga were already there. The two German girls were accompanied by two boys who appeared to be approximately the same age as the girls. When the Klug children approached the group, Helga cried out, "Here come the Americans!"

Annemarie introduced the boys, "This is Wilhelm, and that is Ernst," she said, pointing respectively to them.

Romi and Herbert nodded in acknowledgment.

"Are you taking Hannelore back to the sandbox?" Annemarie asked.

"Yeah," Romi said, "but first we're going to give her a ride on the seesaw."

With Hannelore in tow, Romi went over to the seesaws. Herbert and the German kids followed.

"You sit on one end," Romi suggested to Herbert, "and Hannelore and I will ride on the other end."

"How do you like living in Germany?" Helga asked.

"It's OK," Romi answered.

"Where did you live in America?" Wilhelm asked.

"In New York," Herbert replied.

"Did you see many Indians in New York?" Wilhelm asked.

Romi laughed. "The only Indians I ever saw were in the movies," she replied.

"But there still are a lot of Indians in America, aren't there?"

"Yes," Romi said.

"Well, where do they live?"

"Mostly out in the West. A lot of them live on reservations," Herbert commented.

"Reservations? What are reservations?" Wilhelm asked.

"They are like camps," Herbert explained.

"They live in camps? Why do they live in camps? Are they bad people?"

Herbert rolled his eyes and said, "No, they are not bad. After they lost their land, the government decided to take care of them by letting them live in camps."

"Oh."

"Did you live in one of those skyscrapers?" Annemarie asked.

"No. The skyscrapers are used for offices and stuff," Romi replied.

"Do the skyscrapers really reach up into the clouds?" Annemarie asked.

"They do, if the clouds are low enough," Herbert answered knowingly, although he really had no idea whether they did.

"Did your father have a car?" Ernst asked.

"No," Herbert answered.

"Oh, I thought everybody had a car in America."

"My father says that every family in Germany will soon have a car. It's called a Volkswagen," Wilhelm said.

"How does your father know that?" Herbert asked.

"My father says 'The Fuehrer said so.'"

"Oh."

Romi and Herbert made more new acquaintances as several children joined the group, and they continued to answer many more questions posed by the German kids. By the time they had to head back to the Werners' apartment, poor little Hannelore never got to play in the sandbox, but there were about ten hands waving goodbye as they left the park.

Late in the evening, prior to preparing for bed, the Klugs often would gather in the front room to spend some quiet time amongst themselves. On one of these occasions Hertha asked, "Well, how did it go in the park today? Did you make any new friends?"

"I didn't make any new friends today, but some guys I already met were back in the playground," Herbert answered. He continued, "You know, there still are a lot of kids we don't know yet, but they seem to know us. Every time someone mentions the Americans, everybody immediately looks our way. It's sort of like...like they're talking about us behind our backs."

"Oh, they aren't talking behind your back. They are just spreading the news: Hey, we have some American kids coming to the park!" Hertha said. "Imagine yourself back in New York and some German children moving into the house next door.

Wouldn't you find that exciting? Wouldn't you be telling all your friends about it?" Hertha asked him.

"I suppose so."

"Well, there you are. They are just talking of you. They certainly aren't talking about you 'behind your back,' as you put it."

Hertha turned to Rosemarie, "How about you, young lady? Did you have a good day in the park?"

"It was OK," Romi said, "but I have a question."

"What is the question?"

"Why do all the German girls wear black undies?"

"What have you been doing—comparing underwear?" Hertha asked.

"No, no! When they are climbing up the poles or are trying a routine on the horizontal bars, you can't help noticing what they are wearing, and they're all wearing black undies."

"Black underwear..." Hertha wondered. Then she broke out laughing.

"What's so funny?" Romi asked.

"Oh, honey," Hertha said, still chuckling, "they're wearing gym shorts! In German schools all the kids are required to take gym classes, even in elementary schools, and they wear white jerseys and black gym shorts for those classes. Those girls are wearing their gym shorts when they go out to the playground." Hertha frowned for a moment. "Have you been climbing around out there, Romi?"

"No."

"Well, don't, until we get *you* a pair of those shorts."

Chapter 8

Herbert liked this train a lot better than the one that took them from the ship to Hamburg. He was watching the countryside go by, while standing in the aisle that ran the length of the car. He stayed in front of the sliding door that led to the Klug's compartment, mindful of his father's admonition: Don't be wandering around in the aisle, but stay close enough where I can see you.

Herbert enjoyed his view from the train window. Because of the constantly changing panorama, his attention was drawn to horses and cattle grazing in the fields, to more of the little three-wheeled trucks that had piqued his interest on the train ride from Cuxhaven, and to the thatched sloping roofs of the farm houses.

When a waiter bearing a tray with sandwiches and drinks came down the aisle and stopped at the Klug compartment, Herbert decided it to be a good time to return to his seat. The waiter pulled up a collapsible table top located between the window seats Hertha and Walther were occupying. He locked it in place and set the tray on the table.

"Your father ordered some refreshments for us," Hertha said to her son. "Sit down a while, and eat something."

"What do you have to drink?" Herbert asked.

"Lemon or lime soda."

"Can't I have a Coca-Cola?"

"They don't have Coca-Cola."

Herbert sighed and said, "Nobody has Coca-Cola. When I asked Grandmother Werner for some, she didn't even know what I was talking about."

"Lemon or lime soda," Hertha reiterated.

"Aw, gee whiz, give me a lime," he crabbed. When he saw the expectant look on his father's face, he quickly amended his request to, "Give me a lime, please."

His mother handed him his drink with a beseeching look, saying, "Please, don't spill it—these seats don't clean up as easily as do the wooden ones."

"They sure are much softer than the ones on that other train." Herbert said.

"Just don't make a mess," Romi piped in.

Herbert didn't respond, other than sticking his tongue out at her.

"I knew before we entered the car that we wouldn't have wooden seats again," Herbert declared.

"And how did you know that?" his mother asked.

"I saw the big number two painted on the outside of the car."

"Aren't you the clever one."

"Papa, how long is the train ride from Hamburg to Kassel?" Herbert asked.

Romi intercepted the question, "About four hours."

"Papa, why do the farmhouses have those funny looking roofs?" he asked. "They look like they are made of straw."

"They are made of straw," Walther replied.

"Why?"

"The farmers always have a lot of straw after the grain harvest, and they found that they could put all that straw to good use, such as using it for roofing material."

"Doesn't it leak?" Romi asked.

"No. Because the roofs are sloped, the water runs right off."

Everyone but little Hannelore, who was busy pounding on the tabletop with a spoon, chuckled when Herbert mused, "All those straws but not one Coca-Cola..."

When the intercom announced that the train would soon be arriving at the Kassel main station, the Klugs prepared to disembark. Walther reminded the older children to stay close by and said, "Your Aunt Elfriede wrote that she would pick us up at the station, so we'll just stay on the station platform until she finds us."

Once off the train, they didn't have to wait long until they saw a young lady, perhaps in her late twenties who, after she had agilely made her way through the crowd, approached and said, "You're Walther, aren't you?"

"Yes, Elfriede, I'm Walther."

"It...it has been such a long time since I last saw you—almost twenty years. I couldn't be sure. Let me give you a big hug." She embraced him and kissed him on the cheek. Walther introduced Hertha and the children.

"My, what a lovely little girl you are," Elfriede said when she saw Hannelore. Hannelore gave her a big smile.

"Come," Elfriede said. "We'll get a taxi to take us to Father's house."

Arriving at the elder Klugs' apartment a little after dusk, they were greeted by Walther's parents and his brother Alfred. It was an emotional reunion. While Hertha and the children momentarily were relegated to being bystanders, Grandmother Klug cried, Alfred shook his brother's hand vigorously, and Grandfather Klug's stern demeanor changed into a brief smile as he embraced his son.

Herbert, looking at his father, thought he saw a tear or two trying to emerge. Elfriede said, "I'm so happy to see my big brother again."

When Walther introduced his family, Grandmother Klug cried some more, and Grandfather Klug smiled once more.

"Did you have any trouble finding them at the station?" Alfred asked Elfriede.

"Well, since the most recent photograph I have of Walther dates back to when he was married, I couldn't be sure what he would look like today. I did not look for Walther, I looked for two adults trying to keep three youngsters corralled. I only saw two such couples. The first man I asked said his name was not Walther, it was Heinrich. A lady who was standing nearby, probably his wife, gave me a dirty look."

Everyone laughed except Grandfather Klug.

"Did you, really?" Hertha asked.

"No. I'm only kidding. Walther was the only one I addressed."

"You must be hungry after your long trip," Grandmother Klug said. "I'll fix a light supper. Elfriede, will you give me a hand, please?"

✚✚✚

After they had eaten, Grandmother Klug assigned them their rooms. While the children were getting ready for bed, Romi asked her father, "Papa, was your father very strict?"

"Well, he was strict but not overly so. Why do you ask?"

"Oh, he just looks so stern all the time," she answered.

"That's just his way, honey. His tough demeanor is really trying to hide a kind heart."

✚✚✚

On the following day all of Walther's siblings were present when dinner was served in the elder Klug's dining room. Grandmother Klug had invited Walther's older sister Ella, her husband Fritz, their son Walther, and Walther's sister Elizabeth who, at nineteen, was the baby of the family.

After dinner, when the women had cleared the table and were busy in the kitchen, Herbert, who was leafing through some magazines, couldn't help overhearing his father's discussion with Grandfather Klug.

"What do you think of the political situation?" the elder Klug asked.

"It worries me," Walther replied. "Hitler said that he would have no further claims, after he annexed the Sudetenland. Now he wants access to Danzig via a corridor through Polish territory."

"He's willing to make some concessions," Grandfather Klug said.

"What kind of concessions would you accept if your neighbors in the apartment on your left wanted access to the apartment on your right—through your living room?" Walther asked his father.

"I get your point," Grandfather Klug replied.

"I think it is a completely unworkable proposition," Walther went on. "The Poles are dead set against this proposal, and if Hitler keeps pushing it, I'm afraid he might bring Germany to the brink of war."

"I totally agree with you," the elder Klug said. Leaning forward, he continued, "Walther, there is something I want you to remember. You are not in the U.S.A. now. Over here the powers that be recognize only two options. You are either for them, or you are against them. There is no between. Open dissent can have serious consequences, and mark my word, there are ears out there just listening for dissent."

Herbert's involuntary eavesdropping was interrupted when Aunt Ella's son approached him and said, "I brought my soccer ball with me. Want to go out in the yard and kick it around?"

Herbert sized him up. Young Walther was about his age, maybe a year younger. They were about the same height, but Herbert noted that he, Herbert, was the huskier of the two.

"OK," Herbert said.

"What's OK?" young Walther asked.

"It means yes," Herbert explained.

They went outside and kicked the ball around. Later in the afternoon, Herbert's father and Uncle Fritz joined them. Play didn't end until Ella called them in for supper. As they walked in, she commented, "Well, did you boys do a good job ruining your shoes?"

✚ ✚ ✚

That evening Herbert asked Romi whether she had noticed anything about their father's sisters' names.

"Yeah, they all start with the letter E," Romi said.

"I wonder why," Herbert mused.

"I know why," Romi said. "It's because Grandma and Grandpa Klug's first names are Emma and Ernest—both start with an E, right?"

"OK, smarty," Herbert said. "How come they didn't name the boys Eric and Eddie?"

"Eric and Eddie?" Romi asked incredulously.

Herbert shrugged his shoulders, and they both giggled just as their mother walked into the room.

"What's so funny?" she asked.

"We were just wondering why Grandma Klug didn't name her boys Eric and Eddie," Romi said.

Hertha took a moment to let that sink in. Then she said, "I'm sure I don't know, but I do know that it's getting close to your bedtime."

"Mama, is there going to be a war?" Herbert asked.

"What makes you think that there might be?"

"Grandfather Klug and Papa were talking and—"

"There won't be a war—do you hear me?—there will not be a war!" Hertha said brusquely.

✚✚✚

One morning after breakfast, Elfriede announced, "Today I will take you to *Wilhelmshoehe*, where you will see the castle that was the summer residence of Kaiser Wilhelm II. You will also see the statue of Hercules, which, like a perpetual sentinel, overlooks the city of Kassel from a nearby hilltop."

An hour later Elfriede, the elder Klugs, and Walther's family boarded a streetcar for the rather lengthy ride to the western outskirts of the city.

✚✚✚

After the trolley reached its terminal, the three generations of Klugs started their walk into the park. Since the elder Klugs would be setting the pace, the others let them lead the way. Walther, carrying Hannelore, and the two older children followed his parents, while Hertha and Elfriede brought up the rear.

"Papa, who was Kaiser Wilhelm?" Romi asked.

"He was the emperor of Germany," Walther said.

"Was that in olden times?"

"Well, he was the emperor when your mother and I were children. I wouldn't call that 'olden times.'"

Pointing toward the Hercules statue, which had become visible while they were still on the trolley, Herbert asked, "Who was Hercules? Was he an emperor, too?"

Walther laughed and said, "No, he wasn't an emperor. According to Roman legend, he became famous after he accomplished twelve different tasks given him by his king."

"What did he have to do?" Herbert asked.

"I don't remember all of the assignments, but I know that he had to capture a boar, slay a lion, and fight a nine-headed hydra," Walther said.

"What's a hydra?" Herbert asked.

"It is a nine-headed snake, and it posed a real problem for Hercules."

"What was the problem?" Herbert asked.

"Hey, any nine-headed snake is a problem in itself, but with this particular snake, every time you cut off one head, two new ones would grow!"

"Holy cow! What did he do?"

"Hercules hoped that the snake had an Achilles' heel. He had to find that heel."

"Snakes don't have feet, Papa."

"I don't mean Achilles' heel literally; I mean it figuratively, like a vulnerable spot."

"Did Hercules find the...the heel?" Herbert asked.

"He must have found it. His report to the king read: mission accomplished."

"But why does Kassel have a statue of this Roman guy?" Herbert asked.

"Because the city of Kassel originated as a Roman settlement way back in the tenth century," Walther said.

"Oh."

✦✦✦

Having arrived at the castle, the elder Klugs sought refuge on a park bench to rest a while. The Klug family viewed the imposing structure, and Elfriede, acting as tour guide, provided some historical details.

Their attention soon shifted to the Hercules statue, which appeared to be several times life-size. Starting at the castle level, stairways of several hundred steps on either side of the statue curved upward and met at the top of the hill in a horseshoe pattern. Inside the horseshoe pattern created by the steps leading upward on either side, a series of larger steps, obviously not intended for pedestrian traffic, led straight up to the statue. On the bottom, these steps terminated in a pond on the castle grounds.

"What are the big steps for?" Herbert asked his father.

"The hydra climbed up those steps when it emerged out of the pond to fight with Hercules," Romi interjected.

"Yeah, yeah," was Herbert's derisive comment.

Walther didn't respond to Herbert's question immediately but asked Elfriede when the water would be turned on.

"At 2:00, that would be in about five minutes," Elfriede said.

Turning to his son, Walther said, "If you can wait five minutes, your question will be answered."

At 2:00 sharp, water started pouring from the base of the statue, and flowed from the top of the hill down the center steps into the pond below. Each of the approximately three-foot-high steps in the water's path created a waterfall, or cascade. With sunlight reflecting off the water, the series of cascades, perhaps fifty of them, commencing at the top of the hill and ending at the pond below, was a stunning sight.

"Wow, that is neat," Herbert exclaimed.

"What do you think of it, Romi?" her father asked.

"I think it is beautiful."

It would have been a perfect day, except for two instances. On the return trip, the trolley was just coming to one of its many stops, when Herbert tugged on Hertha's sleeve and said, "Mama, I think I have to throw up." Hertha knew her son well enough to know that if he said I think I have to, he would. She got the boy off the trolley just in time; then, through the car window, she told Walther to go ahead with the girls but to wait at their intended stop until she and the boy arrived.

✦✦✦

The second instance followed right on the heels of the first one. As Hertha and the boy finally arrived at their intended stop, Romi came running toward them and said, "Hannelore forgot that she was toilet trained and wet herself while Papa was carrying her. Hannelore is all wet, and Papa's shirt is all damp." Hertha noted that not only his shirt but also his mood had been dampened, when he said, "Here Hertha, take your little girl."

✦✦✦

During the remainder of their stay, Walther's family took in the sights of Kassel's city center and went for long walks along the Fulda River, where Walther pointed out the spots where he used to swim as a boy.

Having taken leave of Alfred at the elder Klugs' apartment earlier, Walther's family said goodbye to the elder Klugs and Elfriede who had accompanied them to the train station.

"Do we go into a number two car again, Papa?" Herbert asked as the Hamburg-bound train pulled into the station. Walther nodded at his son.

After they had boarded, Walther lowered the window of the compartment to enable some last minute conversing with his parents and sister.

"Come and see us again," Elfriede shouted, as the train slowly pulled out of the station.

Chapter 9

During the train ride back to Hamburg, Hertha asked Walther, "Well, did you enjoy the trip and the reunion with your family?"

"Yes, I enjoyed both the trip and the reunion, but I would have enjoyed both of them a lot more if I now had a job to return to."

"Don't worry," Hertha said, "everything will work out just fine."

+ + +

Walther started his job hunt early in July, immediately after returning to Hamburg. A week went by without any results. A second week passed—still nothing.Hertha noticed his increasing irritability as he came home day after day without any good news to report.

At the start of the third week, he came home early one afternoon, and announced to Hertha, "I start work on Monday morning!"

"Oh Walther, that is wonderful! For whom will you be working?"

"I'll be working for an import/export company. I start out as assistant buyer. My new boss told me that if things work out, he will cross out the first word of that title."

"I'm so glad for you." She looked up at him and said, "What's the matter? You don't seem overly enthused."

"I'm pleased, of course, about finding a job, but..."

"But what?"

"There is so much talk going on about the Polish situation, and the papers don't seem to have anything else to report. I'm afraid Hitler will use force if his demands are not met."

"You men and your talk about war...you already have Herbert asking me whether there will be war."

"How is that?" Walther asked. "I haven't mentioned war to him."

"He overheard you and your father talking, when we were in Kassel."

"Oh."

Changing the subject, Hertha said, "Why don't you tell my parents your good news? They are out on the balcony."

✚ ✚ ✚

July turned into August. One day in mid-August Hertha told the older children that she was taking them to register for school.

"Where will we be going to school, Mama?" Herbert asked.

"You'll be going to the school on Wall Street. It's only two blocks away from here. I'm not sure yet where we have to register Rosemarie," Hertha said.

"Why can't we both go to the same school?" Romi asked.

"Because over here they don't have coeducational classes in elementary school or in high school, for that matter."

"Aw, gee whiz, we have to go to separate schools?" Herbert asked, in spite of what he had just heard.

"I won't be able to talk to anybody," Romi said.

"You talk to the kids in the park, don't you?" Hertha asked.

"Yeah, but they already know I speak funny German," Romi answered.

"I've been telling you two to be talking German to one another. Speaking English all the time won't make you proficient in German. Do it every day. You'll be surprised how quickly your German will improve," Hertha said.

"Yeah, but we don't have a zillion days till school starts," Herbert mumbled.

Hertha sighed and said, "Get yourselves ready. We want to leave in half an hour."

At work, Walther picked up snatches of conversations between his co-workers which indicated that the possibility of war was on most everybody's mind. He discerned that people, his age or older, appeared to be disinclined toward another conflict, although they did not say so outright. Walther felt that much of the younger crowd was less risk averse. They believed that since Hitler was merely trying to recoup what was taken from Germany after the World War, he was on the right track.

As the Polish issue reached crisis proportions toward the end of August, Walther listened to the radio broadcasts that alluded to the shuttling of diplomatic emissaries all across Europe intent on either defusing the situation or establishing a plan of action, in the event that all negotiations with Germany came to naught.

On 21 August, the non-aggression pact between Germany and the U.S.S.R. was announced.

On 25 August, Great Britain announced a formal alliance with Poland, and the world held its breath.

Chapter 10

The suspense was broken on 1 September, when Hitler decided that arms would resolve the Polish issue. A few hours after this decision, the radio broadcast that German troops were crossing the Polish border.

Late that evening, Hertha and Walther were taking a stroll along the Alster banks. It had become their way of getting away from the close confines of the Werner apartment which allowed for very little privacy.

Referring to the day's news, Hertha said, "Walther, I never thought that he would go this far and take the country to war. But for me, we would not be in this predicament. I want you to know how sorry I am. I fear for us, and I fear for our children."

Walther thought, I feared all along that this might happen, but, noting her anguish, he said, "Don't worry too much. If this war stays localized, it might be over before long."

"Oh, Walther, do you really believe it will be over soon?"

"Honey, all I'm saying is that there is some hope," Walther said while reminding himself that hope, at times, is not justified by the expectations.

+++

Two days later, on 3 September, Great Britain and France declared that they were in a state of war with Germany.

Once the conflict started, everyday life of the populace experienced some major innovations. Almost immediately, the air raid siren was introduced. Both radio and newspapers advised that a wailing sound would signify an alert, whereas a constant pitch would indicate all clear. Profuse testing of the air raid sirens in the all clear mode soon familiarized everyone with the sound.

One person in each house had to be designated to take on the responsibilities of an air raid warden. The air raid warden had to ensure that a bucket of sand was available on each floor of the house to contend with incendiary bombs and that the tenants would seek shelter, preferably in a cellar, in the event of an alert. Blackout procedures were instituted. Adherence to these procedures was another responsibility of the air raid warden.

Block wardens, assigned by the Party, would oversee the air raid wardens.

Food rationing was instituted toward the end of September. Each person received several cards each month. The cards, differing in color and measuring about five inches by seven inches, consisted of tearaway coupons such that increments of a month's allotment could be redeemed. The color code of the card identified the food group for which it was valid. Children under the age of five and workers engaged in heavy industry received more than the standard allotment. Hoarding of food was designated as a crime against the people, and violators of the law faced prison sentences.

Listening to enemy radio broadcasts was prohibited, and dissemination of foreign radio content was considered as abetting the enemy and was punishable by death.

✚ ✚ ✚

"This food rationing is a real pain in the neck," Grandmother Werner commented one evening at the dinner table. "Not only can't you get as much as you want, but the printing on those tearaways is so small that I have to get out my glasses every time I pull out a card. Even then, I sometimes have trouble reading the coupon."

"Why don't you take Herbert along when you go shopping? He has young eyes; he'll be able to tell you what the coupon is worth," Hertha suggested.

Herbert grimaced and said, "Why do I have to go shopping? Why can't Romi go?"

"Because she's already helping me a lot by babysitting Hannelore," Hertha said. She continued, "Don't be giving me that scowl, young man. It's not asking a lot for you to help out a little."

Herbert removed the scowl, but he could not conceal a remaining look of annoyance.

✚ ✚ ✚

While helping Grandmother Werner shop for about the third time in the past two weeks and fulfilling his mother's edict, as he put it, Herbert noted that the shopping consisted of a simple routine. They would go to the butcher, then to the dairy store around the corner, then to the grocer, and finally to the produce market. Back in Brooklyn, Herbert would have gone to a Bohack's and done all the shopping in one store, but here there was no Bohack's.

Since some customers entered the stores saying good morning, as Grandmother Werner did, while others entered uttering *Heil Hitler*, Herbert monitored the storekeeper's responses to the customers' greetings. Some storekeepers would always respond with good morning, while others would always acknowledge with *Heil Hitler*. Some storekeepers would always respond by matching the customer's greeting.

He felt that their shopping took much longer than it should. A trip that should have taken a half hour seemed to always turn into an excursion of an hour and a half. And Herbert knew why it took so long. Before they even reached the butcher, Grandmother Werner would run into Frau Koogelhofer, and they would chat. As they turned the corner to the dairy store, Grandmother Werner would see Frau Voss, and they would chat. On the way to the grocer, Grandmother Werner would stop to chat with Frau Klingenmacher, and there probably would be another rendezvous, either before or after entering the produce store, with another Frau.

Feeling that he could do the shopping much faster if he went by himself, Herbert proposed to Grandmother Werner that he should do so. He emphasized how much easier it would be for her, rather than dwelling on the time he would save.

"Well, if you think you can handle it alone, that would be a great help to me," she said.

"I 'm sure I can," he replied. "I'm already familiar with all the ration cards, and I can bring back a sales receipt."

"All right, we'll give it a try," Grandmother Werner consented.

"Grandmother, can I ask you a question?" Herbert asked.

"Sure."

"Why do some people say *Heil Hitler* when they enter the stores?"

"That is the Party salute," Grandmother Werner answered.

"Why don't you say *Heil Hitler*?"

"Because we are not Party members. Besides, if I want to wish someone a good morning, can I say *Heil Hitler*?"

He did not answer. He just gave her a puzzled look.

Herbert thought he had put himself in a win-win situation. He would have more time to spend with his newfound friends in the park, and he would enjoy the extra sandwich or sausage slice Grandmother Werner promised to slip him, every time he returned from shopping.

Chapter 11

During the month of September, the radio in the Werner residence announced many *Sondermeldungen* (special reports), which conveyed the progress of the German troops in the Polish campaign. By the end of the month, fighting had almost ceased. The Germans occupied the western half of Poland, and the U.S.S.R. took over the eastern half.

Grandfather Werner's hopes, that the swift resolution of the Polish campaign would bring the great powers back to the conference table, were shared by all in the Werner apartment.

+++

Hertha had made arrangements with the respective school officials to allow Herbert and Rosemarie to start school early in October, instead of the normal September starting date. She had done this to allow the children some additional time to become adjusted to their new environment.

Two weeks after the children had started school, they were coming home with all kinds of complaints.

"Mama, I'm having to learn to write all over again," Herbert said with a groan.

"Why is that?" his mother asked.

"Because they use some German lettering style. They don't use the lettering that we learned," he replied.

"You mean they don't use the Latin script, don't you?" his mother asked.

"Yeah, whatever."

"I have to learn that German lettering, too," Romi piped in with a moan. "Not only that, but we have to know all about umlaut," she continued, referring to the diacritical marks used in German writing that change the normal vowel pronunciation. "How can we know when to use an umlaut when we can't even recognize a lot of the words?" Romi asked.

"I talked with your teachers when I registered you for school, and I told them that your proficiency in the German language would be weak. They told me that they would be considerate of your predicament, but I don't want you to take advantage of their consideration. After school hours I will help you with the German script and the umlaut. I know it will be hard for you, at least in the beginning, but I want you to take a positive attitude, without a lot of groaning and moaning," Hertha said adding, after a pause, "You don't want me to have to address you two as groan and moan, do you?" Romi and Herbert both giggled and shook their heads.

A day later, Hertha returned to the Werner's apartment after one of her visits to the *Wohnungssamt* (housing authority). She found her mother alone in the kitchen. Walther was at work; Mr. Werner was performing with the orchestra at the Thalia Theatre; the older children were in school, and little Hannelore was napping in the Klugs' front room.

"Well, how did it go, Hertha?" Mother Werner asked.

"Same as last time and the time before, they don't have anything available yet. I'm beginning to wonder, why, with this huge bureaucracy the Party has generated, they can't find an apartment for us. Why does the Party have to be involved in the first place? Years ago all you had to do was to find a landlord who had rental space available. Now you have to stumble through a mountain of red tape!"

"The country is no longer what it was years ago. The Party has stuck its fingers into everything, because they have to control everything," Mother Werner said.

Hertha looked at her with a sigh and said, "It sure is different now. The woman that I had to see at the housing authority had the audacity to ask me why my husband was still an American citizen."

"What did you tell her?" Mother Werner asked.

"I told her that it was none of her business!"

"Oh, my," Mother Werner said, "next time you go there you might want to talk to another person."

Hertha sighed again, while Mother Werner got up to fetch the coffee pot. "Let's you and I have a cup of coffee," Mother Werner said, and "this is the first chance, since your return, that we've had to talk alone to one another, and there is something I want to talk to you about."

Hertha stirred her coffee and looked expectantly at her mother. "Well, what is it that you want to talk about?"

"Hertha, you have been very resentful toward me since your return. When we met you at the railroad station, you could hardly bring yourself to shake my hand."

"Mother, does that surprise you? Fifteen years ago, you sent me thousands of miles away. You sent me away to keep me from seeing a man whom I had already stopped seeing long before you made your decision," Hertha countered.

"Yes, you stopped seeing him, though not because of my admonishments, which apparently just went in one ear and out the other. You stopped seeing him because I told you that you would be leaving my house if you did not stop."

"But I had complied with your request, yet you still sent me away. Why?"

"Honey, do you remember your attitude, after you broke up with this fellow?" Mother Werner answered her own question, "You were morose and deeply despondent. I couldn't even talk to you."

"Mother, it was very unsettling for me. You could have sent me to your relatives in Hanover, which is what—a three-hour train ride away? You didn't have to opt for transatlantic banishment!"

"Hertha, at the time I was faced with a dual dilemma. I was worried about you to the extent that you might do yourself harm. I was also worried about what your father's long absence was doing to our marriage. I was worried that I might never see your father again."

"But it was you who suggested that he stay in America a while longer," Hertha commented.

"I know, I know," Mother Werner said, "I wanted him to come home, but I wasn't sure that the worst was over. That is why I suggested that he stay a little longer, at the same time worrying how his continued absence would affect us as a family. My decision was to solve both dilemmas by sending you to your father and to a new environment."

"A housekeeper's environment, Mother?" Hertha interrupted.

"No. An environment that hopefully would retain a sense of family for us," Mother Werner answered.

"Mother, why are you bringing this all up at this time?" Hertha asked.

"Because I understand your resentment. Because I've felt bad ever since. Sending my daughter away, as I did, was a harsh thing to do."

"Yes, it was, Mother." Hertha said. Then, after some hesitation she added, "Luckily, the good outweigh the bad experiences I had while I was gone."

"How is that?" Mother Werner asked.

"Well, your former boarder became my knight in shining armor," Hertha answered.

"You love Walther very much, don't you?"

"Yes, I do."

"No hard feelings then?" Mother Werner asked her daughter. Hertha pondered for a moment and then replied, "No hard feelings, Mother, but there will always be mixed feelings."

In the middle of November, the housing authority finally allocated an apartment for the Klug family. It was located on the Iffland Strasse, about half a mile westward from the Werner residence. The apartment was located on the first floor of a three-story structure. Entry to the apartment was into a small foyer. Upon entering the foyer, the rooms were located as follows: to the right, toward the back of the house, were the kitchen and a large bedroom; to the left, toward the street, were the living room and the master bedroom. Opposite the foyer entrance two doors led to the bathroom and a storage room, respectively.

Hertha and Walther worked hard to make the place livable. They bought new furnishings and accepted some castoffs made available by the Werners. Walther had the steamer trunk removed from storage, not only because he now had a place to put it, but also because the onset of cooler weather made access to his family's winter clothing imperative.

Hertha was determined to have her family in their new home in time for the Christmas holidays. Her diligence enabled the family to move into their new quarters one week before the holidays.

As they moved in, the first thing Herbert did was to inspect the bathroom. "Well, we still don't have a tub, but at least we now have a real toilet," he said to his mother.

Not responding to him, but addressing Walther, she said, "I get the feeling that your son may grow up to be a plumber."

Chapter 12

Early in 1940, the RAF started invading German airspace in the coastal areas of northwest Germany. Because of Hamburg's proximity to the coast, those incursions often caused the city's air raid alerts to be activated.

The RAF activity consisted of high altitude reconnaissance during the day and propaganda leaflet drops during the night. At times, sporadic antiaircraft fire could be heard in the distance, but no bombs were dropped.

The OKW (German Army High Command) reported the night flights as nuisance raids, if they were reported at all. Nevertheless, the streets had to be cleared and the populace had to seek shelter every time the sirens sounded an alert.

The shelter assigned to the inhabitants of the apartment building where the Klugs were living was a large storage room, which was located in the rear of the glazier store on the ground floor of the building. Benches and chairs had been aligned along the length walls of the storage room. Behind the benches and chairs, leaning against the walls, large sections of plate glass were being stored.

The first time the Klug family had to seek shelter in the storage room, an irate Walther asked the landlord, "You call this a shelter?"

The landlord merely shrugged and said, "This is the lowest floor in the building. The building doesn't have a basement."

"I'm referring to the glass, man. How can you call this a shelter with all this plate glass leaning against the walls?" Walther asked him.

"What would you have me do? The glazier needs the plate glass for his business. He has nowhere else to store it."

"But all this glass is as menacing as the bomb injuries that we are trying to avoid. If a bomb were to hit within fifty meters on either side of us, the concussion alone would cause shards of glass to fly like shrapnel around our heads," Walther said in an agitated tone.

The landlord shrugged again.

"Can't we seek shelter in another building?" Walther asked.

"The shelter system is based on each building having its own shelter. You must remain in your own building," the landlord answered.

"But I would feel safer standing in the street rather than being in here."

"The streets have to remain cleared during an alert," the landlord countered.

"Well, how about a public shelter? Can we go there?" Walther asked.

The landlord shook his head and said, "There are no public shelters, Herr Klug."

Walther looked at his family sitting on one of the benches and wondered why he had allowed himself to get into this kind of predicament.

✚✚✚

In early April of 1940, the OKW reported that German ground troops had occupied Denmark and that the German

Navy was landing troops at various points in Norway. One month later, the occupation of Norway would be all but complete.

Several weeks after the start of the western offensive against France on 10 May, the air raid alerts for Hamburg became more frequent and occurred mostly during the night, and the enemy planes were moving further inland.

As a consequence, the Klug family started to spend an increasing number of nighttime hours in their "glass reinforced" air raid shelter. During many of these alerts, some of which lasted more than two hours, no antiaircraft firing was heard. After this happened several times, Hertha asked Walther, "Why are they keeping us in the shelter, when apparently nothing is going on out there?"

"Honey, there may be aircraft in the vicinity but out of range of the guns. The authorities have no way of assessing the RAF's intent until after the fact, so the alert stays in effect."

In time, the antiaircraft guns were heard more frequently, and in time, the planes, instead of dropping propaganda leaflets, were dropping bombs.

The anxiety level of the cellar dwellers varied with the din created by the flak and the bombs and peaked with the discernible tremors of the near misses.

Outside of being awakened from a sound sleep and having to dress quickly, the older children at first did not mind the interruptions all that much. Any alert starting after 11:00 P.M. and lasting more than two and a half hours resulted in a two-hour school delay.

Herbert would track time in the shelter by watching the old wall-clock in the storage room. Whenever the clock reached the two and a half hour mark he would yell, "Hooray! We don't have to be in school before 10 A.M."

Romi was inclined to sympathize with her brother's outbursts, but, noting her mother's look of disapproval whenever he did this, she did not comment.

✦✦✦

Hertha was folding laundry. When she came to a pair of Herbert's dress shorts, she noticed that the side pockets had some ragged holes in them. "Herbert, where are you?" Hertha called out.

"In here," he answered from the children's bedroom.

"Come into the kitchen," Hertha said, "I need to talk to you." After he had entered, she said, "Look at the side pockets of these shorts. They are full of holes. What have you been putting into these pockets?" she asked.

Herbert stood there and shrugged his shoulders.

"What does that mean?" Hertha asked, mimicking his shoulder shrug. "Does it mean you don't know, or does it mean you really don't want to tell me? Let me see what's in the pockets of those shorts you are wearing now."

Herbert pulled a pocketknife out of his right pocket. He pulled a not too clean handkerchief out of his left pocket. He pulled a length of string out of his right pocket, and then he stopped.

Hertha looked at him expectantly and said, "Your pockets are still bulging, let's see what else is in there."

Herbert emptied both pockets on the kitchen table.

"What is all this junk?" his mother asked him.

"These are antiaircraft shrapnel," Herbert informed her.

"Well, I guessed as much," Hertha said "But why do you carry them around with you?"

"My friends and I collect them, and we trade them back and forth," he told her.

"Trade them? They all look alike to me," Hertha ventured.

"No, no, Mama," Herbert said. He picked a piece up and said, "This is ordinary shrapnel—see, it is rough all over." He picked up another piece and said, "This one is more valuable—see, one side of it is smooth. This one was part of the outside surface of the projectile."

He picked up a third piece and said, with some pride, "This one is even more valuable. It has a smooth side with some numbers and letters stamped on it."

"What do the numbers signify?" his mother asked.

"I don't know."

"Why do the numbers make that one more valuable?"

"Because I probably can get two plain smoothies for that one."

"Ah," Hertha said, as if she had been let in on a secret. "As long as your shrapnel hunt doesn't interfere with your homework, I guess it's OK. But you have to promise me two things: If you ever come across a whole projectile, a dud, one that didn't explode when it was supposed to, I don't want you to bring it home, and I don't want you to even go near it—understand? I also don't want you to carry these things around in your pant pockets anymore. Ask your father for two of his little tobacco tins to store that stuff. Our clothing allotment doesn't take shrapnel collecting into account. OK?"

"Yes, Mama."

"OK, you can go back to what you were doing."

Hertha watched him trudge off, and she suddenly realized how worried she was about her children. She worried about awaking them on so many nights and rushing them to the shelter; about dressing little Hannelore when the alarm sounded, only to find, after she had left her for a moment to pick up a few essentials to take along into the shelter—woe to whoever did not have a *Kennkarte* (identification card) on their person—that the little girl had removed her clothes and was again fast asleep in her underwear; and about how the older children would recoup the many school hours they were losing because of the many nightly alerts. Hertha was mainly concerned about Herbert's schooling, for she knew that he would have to be a breadwinner some day.

Chapter 13

When the German armies approached Dunkirk, Grandfather Werner again voiced hope that the war might be over soon. He opined that perhaps the remaining opposition, namely Great Britain, might not be prepared to fight an extended war. Walther did not share Grandfather Werner's view; he remembered the American intervention in the World War.

The school Herbert attended offered the last four years of the elementary grades and four years of *Oberbau* (high school). On a sunny morning, while Herbert was in the schoolyard during recess, one of the high school boys approached him and introduced himself.

"Hello, my name is Ewald Kroner."

"Hi, I'm Herbert Klug," Herbert responded, looking up since Ewald was about a head taller than he.

"You're the American kid who recently enrolled in this school, aren't you?"

"Yes, I started here last October," Herbert responded.

Ewald smiled and said, "I'm in my first year of high school and my first year of English."

Herbert was surprised that one of the high school boys would seek him out, particularly since he was only in the sixth elementary grade, but, from what Ewald had just said, his reason quickly became apparent.

"You want me to help you out with your English homework, don't you?" Herbert asked.

Ewald seemed somewhat embarrassed when he answered, "Well, yes, if you don't mind."

"I don't mind," Herbert said. "Let's take a look."

Herbert was able to answer Ewald's questions just in time before the bell signaled the end of recess.

"Thanks a lot," Ewald said, as they were on their way to their respective classes. "Maybe I can return the favor one of these days."

✦ ✦ ✦

Herbert and Ewald would get together quite often after their initial meeting. Herbert helped Ewald with his English assignments, and Ewald assisted Herbert with his German homework. Even though an occasional American slang term would perplex Ewald's English teacher, they became good friends.

While walking home from school together one afternoon, Ewald asked, "How do you like living in Germany?"

"It's OK," Herbert answered.

"Just OK?" Ewald asked.

"Well, when I was in America, I didn't have to spend a lot of nights in an air raid shelter," Herbert said. "It sure isn't a lot of fun."

"Do you think your family will be returning to the United States?"

Herbert shrugged and said, "I don't know." After a moment's pause, he asked Ewald, "Why did Germany have to go to war, anyway?"

"Well, to answer that, you have to go back to the end of the World War. The particulars get a little involved and it will take a while to explain them."

"Go ahead. I've got time," Herbert said.

"After the armistice in 1918, a treaty was signed in 1919, known as the Treaty of Versailles. The treaty forced the German delegation to admit to total responsibility for the war. Furthermore, the treaty resulted in large territorial concessions, such as the Rhineland, Sudetenland, Memel, and parts of Pomerania, and it demanded large reparations from the Germans and reduced the German Armed Services to skeleton size.

"Many people thought the treaty was too severe, including some non-Germans. Even your President Wilson said that if he were a German, he would not sign it, and your Senate did not ratify it."

"Well what happened?" Herbert asked.

"There were a sufficient number of signatories from the other nations to impose the treaty on the Germans.

"When the war ended, the Kaiser abdicated, and Germany became a democratic republic. Democracy did not work out in Germany; there were too many disparate parties. And the effects of the treaty soon caused economic chaos in Germany. Inflation, partly due to the reparation demands, reared its ugly head, and by the end of 1923 the value of the German mark had dropped from a post-war rate of about eight marks to the dollar to 60,000,000 to the dollar. Many people lost their life savings during those years, and many less fortunate, who were on a fixed income, starved to death or committed suicide. Can you imagine that?" Ewald asked his younger friend.

Herbert shook his head. As a matter of fact, much of what Ewald was telling him was over his head, but he let Ewald continue, since he had not yet answered Herbert's original question.

"In 1924 inflation was reined in by the issue of a new currency, and the next four years of everyday life approached a normal pattern. Misery returned in 1929 when the world-wide economic crash occurred and unemployment in Germany ballooned to three million.

"The Fuehrer at this time was busy building the National Socialist Workers' Party. In his many speeches he promised the German people that he would relieve them of the yoke of the Versailles Treaty if he were to become Germany's chancellor.

"By 1933, he had sufficient votes to be offered the chancellorship, and in the last six years he made good on these promises; he stopped the reparation payments, and he recouped all of the territories lost after the World War, except for Pomerania and the city of Danzig. The Versailles Treaty had ceded Pomerania to Poland, while the city of Danzig and the surrounding area was declared a free state under the auspices of the League of Nations.

"Since the population of Danzig was eighty-nine percent German, Hitler wanted the city returned to German jurisdiction; he also wanted overland rail and road access through Pomerania to effect a link not only between the German motherland and Danzig but also between the motherland and the German province East Prussia—both of which had become separated by granting Pomerania to the Poles. Polish refusal to meet these demands then led to the start of war."

"You mean the war started because the Poles wouldn't let Hitler have access to Danzig?" Herbert asked.

"Yeah, that's about it. The Fuehrer didn't even ask for the return of Pomerania, he just asked for access to Danzig and East Prussia through that region," Ewald answered and then asked, "Did I answer your question?"

"I think so," Herbert said and then queried, "Where did you learn all this?"

"In my history class," Ewald replied.

"Oh."

The boys had reached the street corner where their homeward paths diverged.

"See you around," Ewald said as he turned into a side street. After taking a few steps and suddenly remembering that the coming Friday would be the last day of the current school year, he turned and yelled, "I hope you have a nice summer vacation."

"You, too," Herbert acknowledged.

As Herbert continued toward home, he thought about what Ewald had told him. That treaty must have been really bad, if even the president of the United States said that he would not sign it—if he were a German.

He was impressed with what that Fuehrer guy had done in just six years, and Ewald had not even mentioned the past nine months when Hitler's armies had vanquished Poland and were about to do the same to France. Herbert surmised that this Fuehrer guy was not an ordinary local yokel.

During the night of 18 June, 1940, Hamburg suffered its most severe bombing since the war began. Bomb explosions, although not close by, were distinctly audible in the shelter of the apartment building on the Iffland Strasse.

Chapter 14

The Klugs stopped by to visit the Werners on a Sunday afternoon in early July. Both families were seated around the table on the Werners' balcony, ready to enjoy the cake that Mother Werner had bought at Nagel's bakery.

While Mother Werner was pouring coffee for the adults, she asked Hertha, "Do you remember Miele?"

"Yes, of course, I do. She was the orphan girl you and father took in when she was ten years old. I was only about three at the time. Her name was Emilia, but you nicknamed her Miele, because whenever you called her or Father, almost invariably both of them would respond. I remember that she married when she was still very young. Whatever happened to her?" Hertha asked.

"She has had her ups and downs, but she is doing quite well now," Mother Werner replied. "As you indicated, she married very young, and she soon had two children, a girl and a boy. Shortly after the birth of the second child, her husband became ill and passed away. A year later she married a fellow named Joseph Lienhof, and they had six children of their own. They are now living in the Sudetenland, where he owns a paper-processing factory."

"Did they move there since the annexation?" Walther asked.

"No, they've been there for quite a number of years," Mother Werner responded.

Grandfather Werner stopped puffing on his pipe long enough to ask his wife, "Didn't you say that she will be coming to Hamburg soon?"

"Yes," Mother Werner said. Looking at Hertha, she continued, "She comes to Hamburg about once a year and then drops by to visit us. I have invited her to have dinner with us next Sunday. Hertha, why don't you and your family join us for dinner so that you and she can become reacquainted," Mother Werner suggested.

"I'd like that very much," Hertha replied.

+++

When the Klugs arrived for dinner on the following Sunday, Emilia Lienhof was already there, seated on the balcony with Father Werner. Mother Werner made the introductions: first Hertha, then Walther, and then the children. Emilia was immediately taken by little Hannelore. Turning to Hertha, Emilia said, "What a lovely little girl you have here."

"Thank you, Miele," Hertha replied. "I hope you don't mind my calling you Miele."

"I wouldn't feel I was back in my old home, if you didn't call me Miele," Emilia said, and then asked, "How old is the little one now?"

"She just turned five," Hertha said.

"That's not much older than you were when your parents took me in, all those years ago," she said to Hertha. "Isn't that right, Mother Werner?"

"Hertha was about three years old when you came to us," Mother Werner replied as she came out of the kitchen carrying a stack of dinner plates.

"Here, let me give you a hand setting the table," Miele volunteered.

Hertha watched her go back into the kitchen with Mother Werner, and she thought that if she had run into Miele somewhere by chance, she never would have recognized her. The last time Hertha had seen her, Miele was a young, blond girl getting ready to be married. She had never been an exceptionally pretty girl, but her freckled face always radiated a certain serenity. Although now much of her blond hair had fallen claim to streaks of silver, her face still radiated that serenity. Her attire substantiated Mother Werner's comment that she was now doing well. Hertha was favorably impressed by Miele, who had apparently developed into a rather stately lady.

"Herbert, we will need two more chairs out here. Will you please fetch them out of the living room?" Mother Werner inquired.

"OK."

After dinner, Walther and Father Werner took the children for a walk, while the women busied themselves with the dishes. Once they were done, Mother Werner complained of a migraine headache and thought she would lie down for a while. Hertha and Miele went back out on the balcony and sat down to visit.

"I was very excited when your mother wrote to me and informed me that you were returning from America. I have been looking forward to seeing you again and meeting your family ever since. So how are you doing?" Miele asked.

"Well, we are settled now," Hertha said. "Walther is working; we have our own apartment, and the older children are in school."

"Do you still feel that your decision to return to the old country was the right one?" Miele asked.

"I was at peace with myself until shortly after we returned, but I became very ambivalent as soon as I realized that we had walked into a war. I believed Hitler when he said that he would not seek any further concessions after annexing the Sudetenland. Obviously he lied, and I was wrong in trusting—"

"Careful, Hertha," Miele interrupted. "You want to be very, very careful when you talk like that, Hertha. This is not the old Germany where you didn't have to look around in all directions before voicing an opinion. This government is very critical of anyone who dares to fall out of step. Anything that does not coincide with the Party line has become a transgression, and severe punishment is meted out where a transgression is perceived," Miele advised.

"I know, I know," Hertha said, raising her hands. "The Germany I once knew and the one I see now differ like night and day. In the new Germany, everyone must carry an identification card at all times; everyone must report to the police and provide a forwarding address whenever leaving town for more than two weeks; everyone must get the approval of the housing authority to move into an apartment. The Party seems to want to know your every move. Why did the people let this happen?" Hertha asked.

"The people did not elect Hitler into power," Miele answered. "Although he built up the National Socialist Party to where it received more votes than any one of the other parties, his Party never was able to garner a majority, which would have allowed him to govern without forming a coalition. After the many indecisive votes during 1932, the then German president, Hindenburg, finally offered Hitler the chancellorship. Hitler accepted, but only because it might provide the means to his goal of complete control.

"At the opening of the first *Reichstag* [legislative body] session of his chancellorship, Hitler requested a vote for an Enabling Act that would allow him to govern by decree. He beguiled the assembly into believing that he would maintain the sanctity of the presidency, the Reichstag, and the constitution. In the ensuing vote, all the parties succumbed to his demand except for the Social Democrats. But their no vote was insufficient to deny him the required two thirds margin for victory. After that first vote, Germany had become an authoritarian state!" Miele exclaimed.

"Couldn't the other parties reverse the trend in a subsequent election?" Hertha asked.

"They could not. Why? Because he disbanded them. Germany became a one party state." Miele answered.

"Uh,uh!" Hertha exclaimed. Then she asked," What made the other party leaders go along with that?"

"Some of them apparently made deals with Hitler, while the others were pressured to cave in."

"And the people—what did they do?" Hertha asked.

"After the devastating inflation following the war, the people were disillusioned. After the depression hit, the people had become desperate. Many accepted Hitler, merely because he promised to put bread on the table. With one-party rule and with the many Nazi storm troopers roaming the streets, there was little else they could do," Miele answered.

Hertha sat still for a while, pondering what Miele had told her. Then she said, "You are in a somewhat similar situation as we are, in that you were living in a foreign country up until about two years ago. In your case, you didn't return to Germany, but Germany returned to you—so to speak." Then she asked, "Has it made any difference?"

"Not really," Miele said, "except for the fact that we are no longer treated as a minority."

"But enough of politics," Miele suggested. "Your mother told me about all the hours you have to spend in the air raid shelters. I've already sought refuge in a shelter twice in the short time that I've been here. How do you cope with all that?"

Hertha gave her a distressed look and said, “We just have to make the best of a bad situation. We go to the shelter, and more often than not, we hear the deafening roar of the antiaircraft guns. We cringe and take a deep breath whenever a bomb explodes nearby, and we thank the Lord every time we can go back to the apartment unscathed.

“Many times the alerts appear to be false alarms. The guns are silent, and the populace has been directed to the shelters, only because enemy aircraft are in the vicinity. Even those alerts, if occurring repeatedly, are unnerving. Having to get up night after night makes one quarrelsome and ill-tempered.

“I worry about Walther and the two older children. I worry about Walther, because he has to go to work regardless of how much sleep he gets; I worry about the children, because of the many lost school hours, which are never made up. I worry about how all this is affecting little Hannelore. In particular, I worry about Herbert who will be starting high school in two years. He has so much catching up to do, and I'm fearful that he will become discouraged.”

Miele noticed that Hertha had tears in her eyes as she related this. She took Hertha's hand and said,“I didn't realize how tough it is for you, and I didn't realize, until now, how lucky my family is to be spared all this misery. We don't even know what an alert is.” Miele stood up and said, “How about a cup of coffee? I'll go and brew some for us.”

Hertha nodded, while still dabbing her tears away.

While serving, after she returned with the coffeepot, Miele said, “I just had an idea.”

Hertha put her cup down and asked, “What would that be?”

“Why don't you let me take the children to the Sudetenland with me. They could stay as long as they like, and they would be out of harm's way,” Miele suggested, adding, “My daughters would be delighted to baby little Hannelore.”

Hertha gave her an incredulous look and said, "I can't do that. I can't just send my children away." Hertha was idly stirring her coffee and said, "No," and, shaking her head, she added, emphatically, "I just can't do that."

"Why not?" Miele asked. Without waiting for an answer, she continued, "The children probably wouldn't have to stay with us for very long, only until this mess is over. Look, France has fallen, and the word is that Hitler is partially demobilizing. If the British should call it quits, the war may be over soon."

"Do you really think that such a possibility exists?" Hertha asked.

"I certainly hope so," Miele commented.

"I'm afraid I don't share your confidence," Hertha said. Returning to the subject, she said, "Hannelore is just a baby; I can't send her away. Besides, I would feel that I am imposing on you."

"Why should you feel that you are imposing? I'm the one who made the suggestion. Look, your parents took me in when I had nowhere else to go. They made me feel like part of your family; you were like a young sister to me, during the eight years that I lived with you. I will be forever grateful to your parents, and I have often wished that in some way I could show my gratitude. If I can help you out, then, in some small measure, I could feel that I am reciprocating some of the kindness that your parents bestowed upon me."

"It's out of the question, Miele," Hertha said. "Things would have to get much worse, for me to send my youngest away. And that goes for Rosemarie too. I have to have her with me, because she does a lot of babysitting for me."

"You mentioned earlier that you are particularly concerned about Herbert. Why not have him stay with us? He could finish his elementary schooling by transferring into our school system and return to Hamburg in time to start his high school curriculum. I'm sure my son Peter would welcome having him stay with us, since Peter's siblings, those who are still at home, are all girls," Miele suggested.

"At the moment I am somewhat overwhelmed by your kind offer," Hertha said. "Coming out of the blue, I just don't know what to tell you right now. I'll need some time to think it over and to discuss it with Walther. But won't having another child around be an inconvenience?"

"I have a small army now," Miele said. "One, or even several more, would not inconvenience anyone."

"Mother told me that you have eight children in all. How many of them are still at home?" Hertha asked.

"If you have half an hour, I'll give you a complete rundown," Miele said. "My two children of my first marriage are Ellie and Hans. Ellie is twenty-nine, married, and living in Pirna. Hans is twenty-eight. He was drafted into the *Wehrmacht* [German army] at the start of the war, and he presently is in France. The children of my second marriage are Heinz, Ilse, Krista, Kaethe, Ruth, and Peter, and their respective ages are twenty-three, twenty, nineteen, sixteen, twelve, and eleven. Have you got all that, so far?" Miele asked.

Hertha nodded.

Miele continued, "Heinz was also drafted, shortly after Hans was. Heinz is in the *Luftwaffe* [German air force], and he is also in France at the present time. All the rest are still at home. As I indicated earlier, with the exception of Peter, all the rest are girls."

"How do you handle such a large family—do the children all sleep in bunk beds?" Hertha asked.

Miele laughed and said, "Oh no, they share two very large bedrooms. We have lots of room. Years ago, my husband Joseph bought a property just outside of Bodenbach that had been part of a small manor. The property included the manor house and three interconnected buildings that had functioned as barns and stables. Joseph had the barns and stables torn down and had buildings for a small paper-processing plant erected in their place. He then had the manor house renovated, and it became our home. It is a very lovely house—it even has a lookout tower that extends about fifteen feet above the roof of the house. Looking eastward from our property one can see the Elbe River flowing about a quarter of a mile away on its way northward."

"Well, Bodenbach and Hamburg have something in common, don't they?" Hertha asked.

"What would that be?"

"The Elbe River," Hertha said.

"Come to think of it, you're right," Miele said.

A commotion at the front door indicated that the two men and the children had returned from their little outing.

Grandmother Werner, feeling better after her nap, also rejoined the group. Addressing Hertha, she said, "You might as well stay for supper."

When the Klugs left later that evening, Miele called out to Hertha, "Remember what we talked about. I'll be going back home in about ten days."

Still later that evening, after assuring that the children were bedded down, Hertha returned to the kitchen where Walther was sitting at the table and reading the newspaper.

"Anything exciting happening?" Hertha asked.

"No." Walther answered. "Apparently we would have to suffer a major catastrophe before the OKW would change their comments of 'no damage' or 'minimal damage' when reporting on enemy air raid results. Even then, I suspect that they would stay with the same old line."

Hertha sat down opposite Walther. "Well, what do you think of Miele?" she asked.

"She struck me as well-mannered and debonair, exactly the way you described her to me from your most recent memory of her," Walther said while leafing through the paper.

"Yes, she hasn't changed a bit," Hertha said. "We had quite a discussion while you and father were out with the children."

"Oh? What did you talk about?"

"She told me how Germany changed, from what it was, to what it is now. After I told her of all the time that we spend in the shelter and of our concerns about Herbert, guess what she said," Hertha prompted him.

"That we should have stayed where we were," Walther ventured.

Not letting his taunt go unnoticed by giving him a disapproving glance, she said, "No, that would not be in character for her. Miele suggested that we let the children stay with her for a while."

"We can't send Hannelore away; she's way too young!"

"That's what I told her," Hertha said. "As a matter of fact, I told her that I didn't want to part with any of my children. She then suggested that by staying with her family, Herbert could finish his elementary schooling uninterrupted and return to Hamburg when the time came to register for high school."

"What about Rosemarie?" Walther asked.

"I told Miele that I wanted to have the girls stay with us as long as conditions don't take a turn for the worse. The school delays won't be that detrimental for Romi. She wants to quit school after the eighth grade anyway," Hertha said.

"So, what do you think?" Walther asked. He had put the paper aside and was loading his pipe.

"If our concerns for Herbert are realistic, which I think they are, we probably should take her up on her offer," Hertha said.

Walther struck a match and lit his pipe. "I don't know, Hertha," he said. "I feel like such a loser having to send my son away."

"I don't feel good about it either," she said. "But we have to realize that we have become victims of circumstance. Who could foresee this kind of predicament?" she asked.

"You're right. It could not be foreseen," he said but thought the handwriting was on the wall.

Walther looked at her and asked her, "Do you want him to go? Do you think that he'll *want* to go? We wouldn't want to force him."

"I think it would be good for him to go with Miele. No, I don't think he'll want to go. But I'll try to convince him that he should," Hertha said, while collating the newspaper that he had left in disarray.

"You might have a hard sell," Walther said. "How will you convince him?"

"I'll think of something."

The next afternoon, Hertha sent Rosemarie and her little sister to Mother Werner on some concocted errand, because she wanted to be alone with Herbert.

Once the girls had left, she called him into the kitchen and asked, "Well what do you think of the lady that we met at your grandmother's house last Sunday?"

"You mean Mrs. Lienhof?" he asked in return.

"Yes."

"She's OK, I guess." Herbert said.

"She and I had a long talk while you were out for a walk with your father," Hertha told him. "During our talk, I told her about your many school delays and about the concern they cause me. You know what she told me?" Hertha asked.

Without waiting for an answer, she said, "Miele said that you could stay with her for a while."

Herbert, who had been looking out the kitchen window at the courtyard below, spun around and exclaimed, "I don't want to go with her!"

Hertha beckoned him closer. She said, "Come, sit down next to me, and let us discuss this."

He complied, albeit halfheartedly.

"Look," Hertha continued, "You always tell us that you want to be an airline pilot when you grow up. That will require a lot of schooling—it will require a lot more, even after high school. With all the part-time schooling you are faced with at the present time and all the catching up you have to do in your German studies, chances are that your grades won't be up to snuff to enter high school in two years.

"I realize that your classmates are also being shortchanged, but they have been exposed to the German language all their life. Do you understand what I'm trying to say?" his mother asked him.

"I guess so," Herbert pouted.

"If you go with Miele, your classes will have continuity, and you will have a good chance to get caught up in your German subjects in time."

"But if I go, I'll miss all the friends I've made in class, and I'll also have to change schools again," Herbert responded.

"If you go, the chances are good that you will all start high school together. If you don't go, you may wind up starting a year after they do. In the first instance you will be separated from your classmates for about a year and a half; in the second instance you risk the possibility of being separated from them for all four years of high school," his mother said. She put her arm around him and looked at him in anticipation of a response.

"You mean, I have to pick the lesser of two evils, don't you?" he asked.

"I'm not sure that the word *evils* is an appropriate choice, but yes, I do mean that sometimes in life, you will be faced with alternatives neither of which will be to your liking," Hertha said. "But don't be weighing the pros and cons just yet," she continued. "There is another reason why I would like you to go."

"More reasons to send me away?" Herbert asked.

"Oh, honey, don't put it that way. I do have your best interest at heart," Hertha said, while fighting back the tears.

"The other reason is that I need you to act like a...how do you describe a soldier who is sent out to observe what lies ahead?"

"Do you mean like a reconnaissance patrol?" Herbert asked.

"Yes, a reconnaissance patrol," his mother said. "If the air raids get worse, I would also send Romi and little Hannelore to the Sudetenland, but before I could do so, I would need to know that they would not be unhappy there. How would I know? If you decide to go and if within three months I don't get a letter from you stating that you are extremely unhappy, I would know that it would be OK to send the girls, too. I'm pretty sure I would never receive such a letter because I know that Miele is a good person, and I expect that her husband is, too. The only problem I could foresee is the possibility of friction between you and the Lienhof children. If you were to advise me that this is the case, I would not send the girls, and I would have you return home immediately. Do you understand what I am saying?" Hertha asked.

"Yes, Mama."

"I know that my second reason for wanting you to go puts a lot of responsibility on your young shoulders. I also know that you won't invent a lot of reasons just so that you can come back home, because you are smart enough to realize that if you do, you possibly will put not only yourself but also your sisters unnecessarily in harm's way," Hertha said, as the tears started to well again.

"Why don't you and Papa go, too?" Herbert asked.

"Your father has to stay here because of his work, and you wouldn't want him to be all alone, would you?"

"No, Mama," he said. He looked at her and, when he saw how sad she looked, he gave her a hug.

"You can go back now to what you were doing," Hertha said. "Will you think it over?" she asked.

"I will, Mama."

Half an hour later, Herbert came back into the kitchen.

"I don't *want* to go, Mama. But I'll go."

✚ ✚ ✚

During the night following her talk with Herbert, Hertha awakened from a dream. In the dream, Herbert was going to stay with Miele, but in the dream Miele's home was far across the sea. Herbert had boarded a huge liner and was standing at the railing facing her. She was standing on the pier. Besides the two of them, no one else was present, either on the ship or on the pier. Herbert was gazing at his mother as the ship slipped away from the pier. As she lifted her hand to wave at him, he looked away. He did not wave back.

Chapter 15

One week later, Hertha and the children boarded a trolley to take them to the main railroad station where Miele and Herbert would be boarding a train for Dresden. Hertha and Miele had agreed to meet at the station half an hour before departure time. Looking out the trolley window, Herbert noticed the many young men in uniform: some in *Heer* (army) green, some in *Luftwaffe* grey, and some in *Kriegsmarine* (navy) blue. They all have to be away from home, too, he thought to himself.

His father had bid him farewell on the previous evening and had stressed that both parents felt that it was best for him to stay with the Lienhofs for a while. Herbert remembered his father expressing the hope that he would make his parents proud during his stay with the Lienhofs.

Suddenly he remembered the question he was going to ask his mother. "Mama, what should I call her?" he asked. When Hertha gave him a quizzical look, he rephrased his question, "What should I call Mrs. Lienhof? I can't just call her Miele."

"She probably wouldn't mind," his mother said, "but you're right. Addressing her as Miele would not be appropriate for you. As I told you before, we just call her Miele. Her real name is Emilia. Why don't you call her *Tante* [aunt] Emi?"

"Tante Emi?" he asked and then said, "OK."

The distance between the main station and the Klug apartment normally could be traversed on foot, but because they also were transporting the two suitcases that Herbert was taking with him, Hertha had elected the trolley ride. As they were getting off the trolley at the main station, Hertha was carrying one suitcase, while Herbert was toting the other one. Hand in hand, Romi and little Hannelore trailed behind.

✚✚✚

Hertha asked an attendant for directions to the train that would be leaving for Dresden within the next half hour, and she and the children soon found Miele standing on the designated platform. Miele asked Herbert, "Well, are you all ready to go?"

The boy just nodded.

Turning to Hertha, Miele said, "Remember, whenever you feel it to be a good time to have the girls stay with us, don't hesitate to send them. We have plenty of room, and they are always welcome." Looking down at Hannelore, she said, "Tell your mother to always remember that." Hannelore just turned away, pretending not to hear.

Hertha and Miele engaged in some small talk while the children observed the hustle and bustle of the train station. When the boarding announcement was made, Herbert kissed his mother on the cheek and hugged his older sister. He picked up little Hannelore and gave her a hug. As he was putting her down, Hannelore said, "I don't want you to go away."

"That makes two of us," he replied, but only loud enough for her to hear.

Miele and Herbert, luggage in hand, got on the train. After stowing the luggage in the compartment that Miele had selected, they went back into the car aisle to say last minute farewells to Hertha and the girls while leaning out of the open car window.

The train slowly left the station. As it picked up speed, Miele sat down in the compartment. Herbert did not join her immediately. He waited a while, because he did not want Tante Emi to see that he'd been crying.

✚✚✚

When Herbert went back into the compartment, he noted that he and Tante Emi had the compartment to themselves, even though quite a few people had boarded the train. Tante Emi beckoned him to sit beside her and said, "I'd like to show you some pictures of my family, so that you won't feel like a complete stranger when we arrive. Would you like that?" she asked.

Herbert did not say anything, but he did nod acquiescence. He watched as Tante Emi reached for her purse. She pulled out a little pocket album. "This is my husband," she said, "You can call him Uncle Joseph."

Herbert looked at a picture of a man who appeared to him to be somewhat older than his father. He was wearing glasses and had a receding hairline. Tante Emi next showed him pictures of her daughters Ilse, Krista, and Kaethe. Looking at the girls' pictures, Herbert couldn't help thinking that Tante Emi's kids looked pretty old. When she showed him her pictures of her daughter Ruth and her son Peter, he was somewhat relieved, because they appeared to be close to his age. "How old are they?" he asked. "Ruth is thirteen, and Peter is eleven," she told him.

"Oh."

Tante Emi then showed him two photos, each of them depicting a young man in uniform. "These are my sons Hans and Heinz," she said.

"Are they at home now?" Herbert asked.

"No, no, they presently are both in France," she said.

"Oh."

When she put the album back into her purse, he asked, "Are those all of your children?"

"No. I didn't show you a picture of my oldest daughter, because I didn't find it in my little album. Perhaps I lost it. My oldest daughter is married and lives with her family in another town not far from us."

"Oh."

Having looked at a map a few days earlier, Herbert knew that the train ride to Dresden would be even longer than the one he and his family had taken on their way to Kassel. He moved to the window seat, opposite the one that Tante Emi was occupying, for a better view outside. He watched the landscape as it appeared to rush by the window, although he had much less enthusiasm than that shown during the trip to Kassel. After a while, he noticed that the monotone of the train wheels traversing the rail joints was having a tranquilizing effect on Tante Emi; she was nodding off over a book she had been reading. As for Herbert, the unrelenting, repetitive monotone translated into further and further and further and further away from home.

About three hours after the train had left Hamburg, Tante Emi ordered some lunch from a passing steward.

"Would you like a *Bockwurst* and some potato salad?" she asked Herbert.

"What is a *Bockwurst*?" he asked.

"It is a smoked sausage," she replied.

"OK."

Tante Emi also ordered a lemonade for him, and she asked the steward for coffee or the best ersatz (synthetic) coffee available, for herself.

Remembering how the steward on the train to Kassel had pulled down the collapsible table top, Herbert lowered it into place.

"My, aren't you the accomplished traveler," Tante Emi said. Herbert gave a little smile and shrugged his shoulders. When the waiter returned with their tray, Tante Emi paid him twice—once with legal tender and once with the required ration coupons. Watching the transaction, Herbert, with a trace of anxiety asked, "Did Mama remember to give you my ration coupons?"

With a smile, Tante Emi said, "She gave me all your coupons; however, we won't have to use them today."

They ate in silence. Herbert liked the Bockwurst, but he would have preferred a hot dog.

The train arrived in Dresden late in the afternoon. Tante Emi and the boy had to wait about an hour before they were able to board a local train for the remainder of the journey.

When they got off the train in Bodenbach, Herbert noted that Tante Emi's whole clan was at the station to welcome her home. He could tell, because he remembered the faces from the pictures Tante Emi had shown him. Herbert performed a bow as Tante Emi introduced him to *Onkel* Joseph; he offered a lesser bow as Tante Emi introduced him to each one of the three older girls; as she introduced him to the two youngest children, Ruth and Peter, he dispensed with the bow and just said, "Hello." Herbert felt like half a dozen pairs of eyes were staring at him, which they were not. He looked up at Tante Emi, hoping that she would dispel what seemed to him to be an awkward moment. She did, by saying, "Our home is only a short distance from the station. After sitting all day, a little walking will do us good."

"OK," Herbert acknowledged.

Ilse and Kaethe each picked up one of his suitcases and started the homeward procession. They were followed by Krista and the two younger Lienhof children, while the elder Lienhofs brought up the rear, with Herbert silently trudging alongside of Tante Emi.

After they had walked for about fifteen minutes, Tante Emi, pointing to a house on the left side of the road, said, "That is our house." Herbert noticed that it was a huge L-shaped structure with the foot of the L being parallel with the road. He also observed that at the inside corner of the L, a tower rose far beyond the roof of the house. Herbert was impressed. They really do have lots of room, he thought.

✚ ✚ ✚

While the others entered the house, Tante Emi asked him, "Would you like to go up to the top of the tower?"

"OK."

From the entrance hall to the house she led him through a doorway and up a spiral staircase that wound its way to the top of the tower. At the top, she opened a portal that led onto the roof of the tower and beckoned him to step outside. As he stepped through the doorway, Tante Emi said, "You can see for miles in all directions from up here."

Herbert nodded in concurrence. Looking eastward, he saw a river flowing past, perhaps three quarters of a mile away.

"What river is that?" he asked.

"That is the Elbe," Tante Emi replied.

"Is it the same river that flows around Hamburg?"

"One and the same," she replied.

"Compared to its width around Hamburg, the river looks like a little trickle down here," Herbert remarked.

"Well, the little trickle, as you call it, is capable of barge traffic," she said with a laugh.

Herbert noticed that the circular tower was provided with a parapet around its flat roof. He envisioned knights in armor shooting arrows through the openings of the parapet and momentarily felt as though he had been transferred back in time by two or three hundred years.

"This property used to be part of a manor, and, at that time, this building was the manor house," Tante Emi said. "We did not buy all of the manor property, just the area containing this house with the garden on the other end and the three buildings you see directly below," she explained as she pointed southward.

Herbert looked in the indicated direction and noted that from their vantage point the three buildings were interconnected in the form of an inverted U. The building corresponding to the right side of the inverted U was in line with the foot of the L of the residence and separated from it by a huge gate. Except for the separation provided by the gate and an equivalent opening between the buildings at the garden end of the residence, the total building complex delineated a rectangle, with the inverted U of the interconnected buildings providing a huge courtyard.

"The three structures you see down there are Onkel Joseph's factory buildings," Tante Emi explained.

"Oh. Why is there a sand pile in the middle of the courtyard?"

"Onkel Joseph put the sand pile there when Ruth and Peter were younger so they could play in it. Peter still spends quite a bit of time down there."

"Oh."

We call our property the Lien Hof—a variation of Onkel Joseph's surname," Tante Emi said. "Well, we better go back down; supper will be ready any minute now."

✚✚✚

Supper was served in the dining room by the Lienhof's cook who had been introduced to Herbert as Bertha. Herbert observed that the dining room table could seat at least twelve. Onkel Joseph sat alone at the head of the table, and Peter and Ruth were seated to his left. Herbert was assigned the seat immediately to his right. Herbert wondered whether this seating arrangement was meant to ensure good behavior of the younger set during meals.

✚✚✚

After supper, Tante Emi took Herbert aside and said, "Come along. I will show you around, help you unpack, and show you where you can put your clothes."

She took him out of the dining room into the hallway that ran the length of the long house. Most of the rooms opened onto this hallway. Tante Emi showed him the large bathroom that the children utilized. Herbert was impressed with the bathtub, the shower stall, and the two sinks.

"You don't have to go to a bathhouse, do you?" he asked.

With a smile, Tante Emi just shook her head.

She showed him the location of two half baths and the family room, and then she took him to a large bedroom at the end of the hall. Herbert noticed three beds at the far end of the room and one near the entrance door.

"This will be your bed," she said, pointing to the one near the door.

"Who sleeps in the other beds?" he asked.

"The older girls sleep there."

"Oh."

While she helped him unpack and put his clothes in a dresser, she said, "Bedtime for the younger children is nine o'clock. Since it is almost that time now, why don't you take your pajamas and go take your bath now. Don't forget to throw your soiled clothes in the hamper. I'll finish up here in the meantime."

When he returned, she helped him with the covers and bade him good night. Turning off the light, she left the room. Herbert wondered why Ruth and Peter did not sleep in this bedroom. The room certainly was big enough to hold several more beds. Maybe they were scaredy-cats, who had to sleep close to mommy and daddy.

He did not dwell on the sleeping accommodations; his trepidations were about how he would fare during the next few days in a house full of strangers.

Chapter 16

Herbert was lethargic during his first few days in Bodenbach, even though the Lienhofs had treated him as one of the family from day one. He was overwhelmed by the way his everyday life had changed, and he was homesick.

On occasion, when his despondency seemed to become unbearable, he would briefly lock himself in one of the half-baths. When he looked out the window, the sight of the surrounding mountains only accentuated how far he had been displaced from the flat countryside of northern Germany, and he would sob and shed some tears. But he did so discreetly—he didn't want anyone to see or hear him crying.

After several days he finally realized that all his fretting would not change his predicament but could only result in annoyance to those around him. He also realized that his actions were not in line with his father's hope that he would make his parents proud.

+ + +

Instead of making excuses, Herbert would now accept Peter's invitations to go out and play. They would play board games, either on the tower roof or on the balcony that ran the length of the house, or they would play in the sand pile with Peter's toy cars and trucks and with those that Herbert had brought with him, or they would kick a soccer ball around in the courtyard.

While playing with Peter, Herbert had noticed on several occasions that Peter seemed to have a fixation about who might be the stronger of the two. Herbert knew he was a year older than Peter—he really didn't care who might be the stronger—and he remembered that he was a house guest.

For all these reasons he did not want to get into a scrap with Peter.

For what must have been the umpteenth time since Herbert's arrival, Peter one day again asked, "Who do you think would wind up on top if we were to have a wrestling match?"

Umpteen times minus one, Herbert had answered with a question of his own, "What difference would it make?" But this time he said, "Let's find out."

They went to the sand pile and sized each other up. They grappled momentarily. Then Herbert got a half nelson hold on Peter and floored him.

"Are you happy now?" Herbert asked.

Initially, Peter appeared stunned and then, deeply dejected. Herbert thought the boy would run to his mother, but he did not run, and he did not ask for a rematch.

On Sunday afternoons, weather permitting, Tante Emi and Onkel Joseph enjoyed walking along the mountain paths in the surrounding area and stopping at an inn for cake and coffee. Since the three older girls usually were out visiting friends on Sundays, these jaunts would leave the younger children without any supervision in the big house. This potential problem was resolved by having those youngsters, who were most likely to get into mischief, accompany the elder Lienhofs on their walks. This, of course, meant that the two boys, Peter and Herbert, had to go along. The boys objected that thirteen-year-old Ruth was exempt and they were not but to no avail.

Peter and Herbert disliked these excursions intensely, because they had to wear their Sunday best and therefore were constantly reminded to stay on the beaten path so as not to soil their good clothes. The only redeeming factor was the cake along the way.

✚✚✚

At the end of August, Herbert sent his mother a letter; he told her that he was fine, although he would rather be home.

Not having any untoward news to report, he felt she would know that his "reconnaissance" had turned out favorable for having his sisters join him in Bodenbach, if she were to so decide.

In September, Tante Emi registered Herbert for school. On his first day in school, Herbert was again introduced as the American, as he had been when he first started school in Hamburg. Herbert wondered whether the prolonged stares caused by his introduction would have been as prolonged if he had been introduced as a kid transferring from the neighboring town of Oberndorf.

Herbert's math teacher was also the school principal. On some school days when his SA[2] detachment would have a meeting that same evening, he would appear resplendent in his SA uniform: brown shirt with a swastika armband on the left sleeve, brown pants, and spit-polished black jackboots. Herbert noticed that whenever the teacher wore the uniform, his walk would change into a swagger, as if the uniform compelled the

2 SA is a contraction of *Sturm Abteilung* (Storm Troop). The SA was a paramilitary organization established in the formative days of the National Socialist Party to provide support to the Party.

change. But this change in demeanor did not alter Herbert's opinion that he was a good teacher and a fair one.

✚✚✚

Hamburg received a respite from the oncoming winter of 1940, when unusually mild weather, accompanied by clear skies, occurred in mid-November. Because of the clear skies, the respite for the populace unfortunately translated into an opportunity for the RAF (British Royal Air Force) to target cities in northwestern Germany.

On the night of 18 November 1940, Hamburg was once again under the bombs. The mild weather notwithstanding, Hertha and little Hannelore both had caught nasty colds. When the sirens sounded on that night, Hertha and Walther quickly dressed; then, Hertha went into the children's bedroom to help Hannelore put her clothes on. Seeing that her little daughter was sound asleep, Hertha quickly reversed her steps. As she came back into the foyer where Walther and Romi had already stacked their suitcases near the entrance door to the apartment, Walther asked, "Back already?"

"Walther, I gave Hannelore a mild sedative when I put her to bed. She slept through the raid alert, and I don't want to wake her up. Besides, I'm feeling somewhat wretched myself. I'm going to stay up here with her tonight. You and Romi can go downstairs," Hertha replied.

Walther thought for a moment, and then he said, "If you stay up here, we'll all stay up here. Let's go sit in the living room, but stay away from the window."

They sat in the living room and gauged the approach of the aircraft as the distant sound of antiaircraft gunnery gradually loudened to a thunderous intensity as the aircraft approached the inner city. The din of the flak, not at all muted as when they heard it in the backroom of the glazier store, added to their sense of foreboding. They tried to preoccupy themselves to put the noise out of mind. Walther and Romi leafed through magazines, while Hertha busied herself by darning socks.

About a half hour after the alert had sounded, the apprehensions turned into stark fear as three bomb explosions, in quick succession, drowned out the thunder of the guns and rocked the house. The second explosion smashed the windowpanes and brought down the heavy blackout curtain. The third hurled Romi out of her chair into a corner of the living room—both Hertha and Romi screamed.

"Are you all right?" Hertha asked, rushing to pick her older daughter up off the floor.

"I...I think so," Romi sobbed through tears.

Little Hannelore, dragging her security blanket, came crying into the living room. A voice from outside shouted, "Lights out, house number 16, first floor."

"Yeah, yeah," Walther mumbled as he reached for the light switch. After he turned off the switch, the living room was illuminated by the orange glow of the burning house across the street. "Damn fool!" Walther said. "The whole area is lit up by flames, and someone is worrying about light shining out of our window!"

He picked up Hannelore to console her and said, "Let's get out of this mess. Let's go sit in the kitchen, but don't turn the lights on before we close the door to the living room; otherwise that fool may start hollering again."

When they had settled down in the kitchen, Walther said, "We were very lucky that the blackout curtain contained the glass shards; otherwise, they would have whizzed around us like so many missiles."

The sound of fire engine sirens could be heard over the ebbing noise of the guns.

"Don't you think we should go downstairs after all?" Hertha asked.

"Nah. The flak noise is diminishing; besides, if we get hit by one of those things, we won't be any safer down there than we are up here."

As the all clear sounded, Walther looked out of the living room window. He saw that the firefighters were battling the blaze across the street and that two huge bomb craters were now blocking the street.

Walther heated some ersatz coffee, while Hertha tended to the girls in the children's bedroom. He poured himself a cup and added some skimmed milk. He would have preferred whole milk, but skimmed milk was all he could find. After he sat down at the kitchen table, Hertha came back into the kitchen with a writing pad and pen in hand. She sat down opposite him.

"Would you like some coffee?" he asked her.

Hertha declined by shaking her head.

"You're not going to start writing a letter at 2:30 A.M., are you?" he asked.

"Yes, I am"

"What's the rush?" he inquired.

She looked at him and said, "Walther, this last raid was the worst we have seen so far. I'm writing to Miele and asking her whether her offer to take the girls is still open. I want them out of here."

"Aren't you overreacting a little bit?" Walther asked."All we have seen is isolated homes or blocks of homes being destroyed here and there and, except for tonight, most of them have not been in the immediate vicinity. It seems to me that the odds are considerably in our favor that our house won't be hit."

"But it will get worse," Hertha said. "When the stakes are life or death, the odds cannot be high enough."

Walther thought about this a moment, and he had to admit that, even though the odds seemed favorable, sitting in the rear of the glazier store during an air raid was like playing Russian roulette, except that someone else was holding the gun to your head and spinning the cylinder.

"I want them out of here, Walther," she reiterated. "If anything were to happen to any of our children, I would never forgive myself."

Walther knew that she had made up her mind. He also knew that she was wrestling with her conscience for having put the children into this predicament.

"I suppose you're right," he said. "Write your letter, although I feel it could wait till morning. I'm going to try to get some shut-eye. I have to be up again in four hours."

✚ ✚ ✚

Herbert was very happy, when Tante Emi told him that his sisters would be coming to stay with them. Although he got along well with everyone in the Lienhof household, he thought his siblings' coming would be a lot of fun.

"When will they be arriving?" he asked.

"I will be picking them up in Dresden on the 29th of November—that's next week," Tante Emi said.

Sixteen-year-old Kaethe, Ruth, Peter, and Herbert were at the Bodenbach railroad station to greet Tante Emi and the Klug girls. When the train from Dresden arrived, the Lienhof children swarmed around their mother, and the Klug kids had their own little reunion. After the introductions had been made, the group started the walk to the Lien Hof. Observing his sisters, Herbert felt that they were as apprehensive as he had been, when he first arrived.

Chapter 17

After a few weeks Rosemarie and Hannelore became adjusted to their new surroundings. Rosemarie was enrolled in the same school that Ruth attended, and since they were the same age, they became classmates.

Hertha had told Tante Emi that Hannelore, who had just turned six, was not to be enrolled in school yet. Hertha wanted to hold her back a year because of her still limited German language capabilities.

Hannelore at first bemoaned the fact that she was all alone with Tante Emi, while all the other children were away at school. But she soon changed her attitude. She became friends with Bertha, the cook. Romi and Herbert were surprised that Hannelore would seek out Bertha. They soon realized that their little sister had some ulterior motives in befriending the cook. With rationing becoming more acute all the time, whom better to ally oneself with than the one closest to the larder?

Christmas of 1940 was the first time that any of the Klug children had spent the holiday away from home. Although they received packages from their parents and presents from the

Lienhofs, they longed to be home, and their holiday spirits were subdued.

Several days after Christmas, while Romi and Herbert were alone in the family room, Herbert asked Romi, "How do you like it here?"

"It's OK, I guess."

"Did you volunteer to come here?"

Romi gave him an incredulous look and said, "Are you kidding? I didn't want to leave. I didn't want to change schools again."

"Then how did Mama convince you to go?" he asked.

"She got really scared after one of the raids and wanted Hannelore and me in a safe place. She said Hannelore still needed someone to look after her, and I was elected to be that someone."

"You mean you had to come here to act like a permanent babysitter?" Herbert asked.

"Yeah, I guess so."

"But why? I was already here," he said.

Romi couldn't restrain herself from laughing. Then she said, "Mama learned a long time ago that you're not the world's best babysitter."

He looked at her with a contorted expression, but he did not argue her point.

They sat still for a while, each of them immersed in their own thoughts. After a while, Herbert asked, "What would we do if something happened to Mama and Papa?"

"Do you mean, if they were killed?"

Herbert raised his hands and shrugged his shoulders.

"Well, then we would be orphans," Romi replied.

"Yeah, I know, but where would we go?"

"We'd probably stay with Grandmother and Grandfather Werner," she said.

"What if something happened to them, too—where would we go?" he asked.

This time it was she who shrugged her shoulders.

"Do you think the Lienhofs would let us stay with them?" Herbert asked.

She shrugged her shoulders again and said, "I don't know."

The winter soon gave way to the spring of 1941.On a sunny afternoon, Kaethe said to the Klug children, "I'm going for a walk. Why don't you come along, OK?" A little later she asked Peter and Ruth whether they wanted to go, too. Peter acknowledged with, "OK."

Herbert was surprised—not by the invitation; he was surprised that his colloquial American "OK" was rubbing off on the German-speaking Lienhof kids!

Chapter 18

On a late afternoon in May, while most of his colleagues were already leaving for the day, Walther was still in his office. His eyes were directed toward the window, which opened onto a courtyard. The view provided a lovely scene of flourishing blossoms, but these manifestations of spring did not register with him. His gaze was not focused; he was deep in thought. Walther was worried.

The war was not winding down, as he had hoped it would. Just a month ago, German forces had invaded Yugoslavia and Greece. Rommel was in Africa, and several nights ago Hamburg was again raided, this time with what appeared to be the largest number of aircraft to hit the city since the start of the war.

Walther's main concern was the reports he had heard that the United States had agreed to a lend-lease contract with the British. He had never doubted that the sentiments of the U.S. would lie with Britain, and these reports seemed to validate his intuition of the eventual entry of the U.S. into the war. But such a move would affect him personally, since he was an American citizen. He was an alien in the land of his birth.

Walther emitted a sigh. He rued the day he had consented to their return. He knew that the only viable solution was for his family to go back to the United States while there was still time, but he also knew that he was engaging in wishful thinking. He did not have the means for such an endeavor, and more importantly, he had just found out that, even if she would, Hertha could not go back.

Chapter 19

Having played with the soccer ball in the courtyard, Herbert came into the house. He was hot and thirsty, and he was looking for a cool drink of water. As he approached the kitchen, he could hear the radio blaring: "Approximately twelve hundred aircraft have already been disabled, since the assault started early on this 22nd day of June, and some formations have already advanced forty miles...."

"What is happening?" Herbert asked Bertha as he entered the kitchen.

"German armies are attacking the Soviet Union," Bertha replied.

He turned her answer into a question, "German armies are attacking the Soviet Union? I thought Germany had some kind of pact with them."

Bertha just shrugged her shoulders without saying anything more.

After quenching his thirst, Herbert left the kitchen to go back outside. As he passed the elder Lienhofs' bedroom, he could hear Tante Emi crying behind the closed doors. He also heard the deep voice of Onkel Joseph trying to console her.

Between sobs, she was saying, "Just a year ago, Hans and Heinz had to take part in the French campaign, and now they will be sent off to Russia. Oh, how I hate this war! When is it ever going to end?"

Herbert decided to go back outside; to stay any longer would be to eavesdrop.

✚✚✚

When Walther returned from work on that day, he found Hertha distraught. As soon as he came into the door, she asked him, "Did you hear what that idiot did?"

Following her into the kitchen he asked, "What idiot?"

Her voice raised, she said, "That fool, Hitler, he—"

"Sh!" Walther admonished as he quickly reached for the window and pulled it shut. "If someone hears you talking that way, you'll be arrested. You know you can't say things like that."

"I don't care," Hertha said defiantly.

"You will, when they take you away," he admonished.

In a subdued tone she said, "I've been simmering all day, and I need to cool off." She reopened the window. "As I was saying, that idiot now is picking a fight with the Russians and—"

"I know," Walther interrupted. "I heard the news this morning, and I'm as disappointed as you are. Our hopes for an early end to this war have just gone down the drain."

"How can Hitler do this?" she asked. He signed a treaty with the Russians. I think his early successes have given him delusions of grandeur. I think he thinks himself to be invincible."

She started to cry. "Walther, I feel so guilty. I've felt nothing but self-condemnation, since we sent the children away. We wouldn't even be here, except for my insistence. I'm so sorry, and I hope that someday you can forgive me."

He took hold of her hand and tried to console her by saying, "Don't be too hard on yourself. Since I was unable to convince you that coming back to Germany was a bad move, I certainly have to share the blame."

"You're not just saying that to make me feel better, are you?" she asked.

"No, I meant what I said," he replied.

Wiping her tears away, Hertha said, "I probably was very naive when I thought the country would be the same as when I left it years ago," Hertha said.

"Your thinking probably was wishful rather than naive; however, at this point it does not make any difference. We will just have to make the best of a bad situation," Walther commented.

"Isn't there a way that we could go back even now, if not directly, then perhaps via a neutral country?" she asked and added, "After all, you are an American citizen."

"I can go back," he said, "and the children can go back. They can go back because they are regarded as American citizens, not only under American law but also under German law. German law assigns citizenship of minors to that of the father. Our problem is that you cannot go back."

"What do you mean? Why can't I go back?" Hertha asked.

"Soon after the war started, the borders were closed to German citizens wanting to leave the country, and you are a German citizen."

"You mean everybody but I can go?" she asked incredulously.

She started to cry again, and Walther once more tried to console her. He took some comfort in her apparent realization of having been misled about the new Germany, but coming at this time, her realization did nothing to change their circumstances.

Chapter 20

Kaethe, Ruth, Romi, and Hannelore were in the family room when Herbert entered. Romi and Ruth were playing a board game, and Hannelore was sitting on the floor, playing with cutout dolls. Just after Herbert had joined the girls, Romi and Ruth got into a squabble over one of the game rules. Kaethe, who had been reading a magazine, interceded and soon set them straight.

Of all the Lienhof siblings, Herbert most liked Kaethe. She was always friendly, always cheerful, and always willing to lend a helping hand. He also thought blond, blue-eyed Kaethe was the prettiest of the older Lienhof girls.

After Herbert watched the progress of the game for a while, he picked up a newspaper that he found lying on a coffee table. He knew that it would be a day old, because Onkel Joseph was fussy about the newspaper and had given Bertha strict orders not to remove it from his study until he was done with it.

Since Bertha could not be sure when this would be, she always waited until the following day before she placed it in the family room for others to read.

The paper was dated 6 August, 1941, and the headlines indicated that German forces had taken Smolensk and that approximately three hundred thousand Russian soldiers had been captured. Herbert could not help but be impressed by the rapid advances the Germans were making on the new eastern front.

Leafing through the paper, he noticed the crime section. Several people had received prison sentences for black market activities. Two individuals, convicted of political dissidence, had been sent to a concentration camp. A repeat rapist's punishment was to be castration.

Herbert did not know how a concentration camp differed from a jail. He assumed that it was a place intended to isolate dissidents from the general population, but he had no idea what kind of conditions might prevail in such a place. He felt that all the penalties he had just read were harsh, although he thought the last one perhaps fit the crime.

Herbert reached the last page that contained the death notices. He normally did not peruse them, but on this day he noticed the obituaries of several soldiers who had been killed on the eastern front. They all mentioned the sacrifice these men had made. Most of them read: "He made the supreme sacrifice for the Fuehrer and the Fatherland"; however, Herbert noticed that in some of the obituaries, the Fuehrer was conspicuous by his absence.

✚✚✚

The news that the United States had extended the lend-lease plan to Russia further convinced Walther that U.S. entry into the war was not far off. In mid-August his colleagues at work were already asking him how he would provide for his family once he was interned.

Shortly after hearing his colleague's remarks he discussed the issue with Hertha. One evening, over dinner, he said, "It's beginning to look like I'm going to have to do something drastic pretty soon."

"Drastic? What do you mean?" she asked.

Reiterating his view that the U.S. would soon be entering the war and mentioning the comments made by his co-workers, he said, "If the U.S. does enter the war, I will be in an untenable situation."

"Do you really think that you would be interned?" Hertha asked.

"That is the normal procedure, dear, but whether or not I am interned, I will be in an untenable situation unless I change my status."

"I don't follow you," she said.

"If I'm interned, we won't have any means of support, which is not a viable way to go. If I'm not interned and I'm given the opportunity to continue working, I would be helping the German effort in some measure, which, as an American citizen, is also not a viable way to go. It is a dilemma that can't be resolved without doing something drastic," Walther said.

"So what will you do?" Hertha asked.

"I'll have to renounce my American citizenship."

"That's not so drastic,"

"It is very drastic, Hertha. Changing one's allegiance is not like changing one's shirt," he countered.

"And it will be one more thing for which I am ultimately accountable," she said with a sigh.

Walther did not respond to her comment. "The thing that bothers me most about this course of action is that I will be turning the children into German nationals overnight. Do I have the right to do that?" he asked.

"You have the right to do what is best for the family. As you yourself have said, 'we will just have to make the best of a bad situation."

They looked at each other, and both noticed the anguish in the other's countenance.

+++

Renouncing his citizenship was painful for Walther, but it was perfunctory for the German officials involved. No residence tenure was required for Walther to regain German citizenship. Being native-born was a sufficient prerequisite. The whole process was completed in ten days.

A week later, in early September, Hertha greeted her husband with a worried look, as he came home from the office. "You have a letter from the *Reich Sicherheitsdienst* [Reich Intelligence Service]," Hertha told him.

"From the Sicherheitsdienst?" Walther asked. "I wonder what they want."

He knew that the Sicherheitsdienst came under the auspices of the SS[3], but he had no idea why they might be interested in him.

"You haven't been making any derogatory remarks about the government, have you?" Hertha asked.

"No! No! If that were the case, they would not be sending me a letter. They would just come and take me away," he replied.

Walther took a seat in the living room to read his mail. He was somewhat hesitant to open the envelope. By mid-1941, any correspondence from an SS agency was cause for apprehen-

[3] The SS, or *Schutz Staffel* (Guard Squadron), originated as Hitler's bodyguard. With time, it was expanded, and the Sicherheitsdienst, the Gestapo, and many other functions came under the jurisdiction of the SS. The SS itself consisted of two branches: the *Allgemeine* SS, (general SS), and the *Waffen* SS (combat SS). The Allgemeine SS was the political branch, whereas the Waffen SS was the military branch that was seeing action on all fronts.

sion. After he held the envelope up against the light, he finally opened it.

Coming back from the kitchen while drying her hands on her apron, Hertha anxiously asked, "What does it say?"

Walther held up one hand saying, "Give me a moment to read it." After a pause, he said, "I have been requested by a *Sturmbannfuehrer* Meyer to appear for an interview in his office."

"What is a Sturmbannfuehrer?"

"It is an SS rank, equivalent to an army major I think."

"What does he want?" Hertha asked.

"I have no idea."

"Are you going to go?" she asked.

"Honey, the man has not invited me—he has requested me to appear. I think I'll have to show up."

"When do you have to go?"

He looked at the letter again. "He wants to see me this coming Saturday at 6:00 P.M., and he wants me to bring this letter with me."

Walther was punctual on that late Saturday afternoon, when he arrived at the Sicherheitsdienst offices located in downtown Hamburg.

As he stepped out of the elevator on the designated floor, he found himself in a large foyer. Seated at a reception desk, a young man clad in the black uniform of the Allgemeine SS greeted him with, "Heil Hitler."

Walther took the man to be of sergeant's rank, or whatever the SS equivalent would be. Walther said, "Good afternoon, I'm here to see Sturmbannfuehrer Meyer." He handed the young man the letter.

Walther's assumed sergeant looked at the letter and said, "Ah, yes. Please have a seat. I will see whether the Herr Sturmbannfuehrer is available at the moment."

The receptionist returned after about five minutes, still holding the letter. "You can go in and see the Herr Sturmbannfuerer now," he said. "He is in suite 805 down the hall."

"Can I have my letter back?" Walther asked.

"I was told to hang on to it, sir," the receptionist replied.

"Oh."

+++

Walther paused at the entrance to suite 805. The door was open, but he didn't want to just walk in. A cursory glance revealed that suite 805 was rather well appointed. The floor was carpeted, and a sofa and several lounge chairs were set along the inside wall on the left. A massive desk was located on the right side of the room. Straight ahead, the windows of the outside wall afforded a view of downtown Hamburg. A pudgy looking man, apparently engrossed in some paperwork, was sitting behind the desk. The man wore the same kind of uniform as the receptionist, except that this man's epaulets were decorated with silver braiding.

After Walther finally rapped on the door frame to get his attention, the man at the desk looked up and beckoned him in. He stood and said, "Heil Hitler, I am Sturmbannfuehrer Meyer, and you must be Herr Klug."

Walther confirmed his initial assessment: he was short and fat—not at all the archetypical SS warrior conveyed by the recruitment posters. Walther said "Good afternoon. Yes, I am Herr Klug."

"Thank you for coming. Please have a seat," Meyer said, as he motioned to a leather chair opposite his desk chair.

After seating himself, Walther noticed the Reichs *Kriegsflagge* (Reich's war flag) standing at the left side of the desk, and when the Sturmbannfuehrer had returned to his seat, Walther also noticed the picture of Adolph Hitler that seemed to be peering at him over the left shoulder of the Sturmbannfuehrer.

"Herr Klug, I have some friends at the Immigration Service who advised me that you have recently returned from the United States," Meyer said.

"That is correct," Walther commented. "I returned with my family in June of 1939."

"So, how did you like it over there?"

"I liked it very much," Walther replied.

"Then why did you come back?" Meyer asked.

Walther felt that he did not owe this guy any explanations; however, he felt that Meyer probably already knew more about him than he let on. Consequently, Walther, all the while wondering what Meyer's motivations might be, decided to answer his questions in a straightforward manner.

"I left for several reasons: my wife was not happy there, and we ran into financial difficulties," Walther replied.

"Why was your wife unhappy?" Meyer asked.

"She never got over her homesickness for the old country."

"And when did you run into financial difficulties?"

"We were doing well until 1935, when I lost a well-paying job," Walther replied.

"In 1935?" Meyer asked.

Walther noticed that his last statement had evoked Meyer's interest.

"Were you already an American citizen in 1935?" Meyer asked.

"No."

"Then your layoff probably was a repercussion of the Jewish-led boycott of German imports that was going on at that time in the U.S. and Britain," Meyer concluded.

When Walther could not keep himself from laughing, Meyer gave Walther a reproving look. Walther felt that Hitler, looking over Meyer's shoulder, also gave him a reproachful glare.

"No," Walther said, "all that happened two years earlier. I suppose I was laid off because somebody in upper management wanted my job for some relative or friend. It happens all the time."

"Well, you have your theory, but I'll stick with mine," Meyer said with a sullen look. "What did you do after you were laid off?" he asked.

"With the Depression still in full swing, I had to accept a job at about half the pay rate of my former employment. Making ends meet became very difficult."

"You then became convinced that the great economic turn-around in Germany would resolve your financial problems," Meyer suggested.

"I was not convinced, but my wife became convinced, after a friend who worked as a steward on one of the German steamship lines painted what I considered an overly rosy picture of conditions in Germany," Walther said.

"Ah, this friend convinced your wife, who was already yearning to return to the old country. I see. Is your wife happy now?" Meyer asked.

Walther thought about his response; then he said, "She says that Germany is no longer the same country that she remembers from her youth, and she wishes that the war were over."

"Of course she doesn't recognize Germany. The Fuehrer has done many things that have resulted in radical changes. And we all hope that the war will end soon."

Walther was tempted to ask how the changes could be other

than radical when the whole government is being run by radicals, but he did not. After a brief pause the Sturmbannfuehrer asked, "How would you like to go back to America?"

Walther was momentarily stunned by the question and the only response he could think of was, "It's too late for that. I have renounced my American citizenship."

Meyer smiled and said, "I know—"

Walther interrupted him by saying, "How do you know?"

Meyer flashed his smile again and said, "I also have friends at the Naturalization Bureau." Meyer's smile contracted as he continued, "The renunciation of your American citizenship can always be revoked, or we can give you a new identity."

Walther suddenly knew why Meyer had made the appointment. The Sturmbannfuehrer wanted to recruit him into some cloak and dagger stuff—well, maybe just cloak stuff. Even so, Walther knew that he would have to disappoint him, since he also knew that he was not cut out for such an activity, but he would hear Meyer out first.

"You are about to ask me to go back to America undercover, are you not?" Walther queried.

"Yes, I am."

"But why? Germany is not at war with the United States."

"Once we beat the Russians and turn our attention back to the British, rest assured, we will be," Meyer said.

"What about my family?" Walther asked.

"We will take care of your family," Meyer replied.

"Who are we?"

"The Fatherland will take care of your family," Meyer answered.

Walther thought that there might be an opportunity here for his whole family to get back to the States. Of course, they would have to devise a way to lose themselves after they got back, so that Meyer and his cohorts could not track them down.

"Why can't I take my family with me?" Walther asked.

"You just told me that your wife was not happy there; besides, having your family with you might tend to distract you from your mission. Having your family stay here gives me the insurance that this will not happen."

Walther momentarily bristled when he heard Meyer's thinly veiled threat that he would hold his family hostage. After he had gathered himself he said, "Herr Sturmbannfuehrer, I would be wasting your time if we were to continue this discussion. I am not interested in your offer for the simple reason that I bear no animosity toward the United States. The country was good to me, and it was good to my family. I cannot turn my back on it as you would have me do."

Meyer looked at him and said, "I did not expect you to sign up at this very moment. Think about my suggestion as an open offer, and if you change your mind, let me know."

"You will be waiting a long time, Herr Sturmbannfuehrer," Walther commented.

Meyer shrugged. Then he said, "Incidentally, the conscription age limit has recently been raised from thirty-nine to forty-one. Were you aware of that?"

"No, I was not," Walther replied.

"I bring this up only to let you know that, in the event you should be drafted, my offer is still open."

"Don't tell me, Herr Sturmbannfuehrer, you also have friends at the draft board," Walther suggested.

Leaning back in his desk chair and smiling, Meyer said, "You are very astute, Mr. Klug, very astute." He signaled that the meeting was over by once again thanking Walther for stopping by. As Walther got up to leave, Meyer said, "I expect that we keep this meeting confidential. I will destroy the letter I sent you."

Walther, who was already walking toward the door, turned

around and nodded in assent. As he did so he once more noticed Hitler's countenance seemingly gazing at him from the picture. He felt the Fuehrer's expression had turned into a scowl—nah, it was just his imagination, he told himself. When he reached the door he said "Have a good evening, Herr Sturmbannfuehrer."

Meyer responded with a curt "Heil Hitler!"

✚ ✚ ✚

Hertha had a torrent of questions for Walther as she met him at the door. "How did it go? What did they want of you? Did you get a reprimand?"

"Whoa! Whoa! Whoa!" Walther exclaimed as he gave her a hug. "No, there was no reprimand, since I have done nothing to deserve a reprimand."

Following him into the living room, Hertha asked "Then what did they want?"

"I'll tell you in a moment, but first get me a cup of that nasty synthetic coffee, please. I need a pick me up, even if it's just a synthetic one." He sat down, while she rushed into the kitchen.

When she came back with a cup of steaming hot coffee, Walther prepared his pick me up to his liking to the extent that the wannabe substitutes, saccharin and the ubiquitous skimmed milk, would allow. After he took a sip, he patted the chair seat next to him and said, "Sit down here, and I will tell you what transpired." She followed his bidding and looked at him expectantly.

"Sturmbannfuehrer Meyer wants me to become a spy."

"He wants you to become what?" she asked incredulously.

"He offered to send me back to America to spy for him," Walther reiterated, and he proceeded to give her a rather full account of his meeting with Meyer.

When she heard that he would have to leave his family behind, she asked, "You wouldn't do that, would you?"

"Of course not," he replied. "I already told him that I am not interested in his offer under any conditions."

"How can they even think of splitting up a family like that?" she asked.

"That's the Party for you. They will stoop to any means to get what they want," he said.

Walther had not mentioned Meyer's remarks about the draft eligibility age, but he thought he had better prepare her for what he thought might be a real possibility.

He said, "Meyer also reminded me that the draft age has been increased from thirty-nine to forty-one. I'm wondering whether he might not be planning to give his friends at the draft board a call to induce them to give me 'preferred treatment,' that is, draft me at the earliest opportunity, in the hope that my being conscripted might change my mind about accepting his offer. He did indicate that the offer would still be open, even after I was drafted."

Walther sat in deep thought for a while. Then he said, "Or it could be his way of getting even for my refusal to accept his offer."

"Do you really think you will be drafted?" Hertha asked anxiously.

"I have very little doubt," he replied.

"But you have three children," she said.

"Age is the only factor of consequence," he countered.

"Can't you get a deferment because of your job?"

"No, our work is not critical to the war effort."

"How will we get along, once you are gone?" she asked in anguish."

"The same way as millions of others are having to get along," Walther said. After a pause he added "Remember that we returned to Germany of our own volition; no one forced us to come back."

With a sigh, Hertha put one hand over her eyes and said nothing. She could not respond to what he just said.

Chapter 21

Walther received his draft notice on 22 September, 1941. He was to report three days later. Late in the evening of 22 September, Hertha and Walther were out for a walk along the Alster shoreline. Hertha said, "Your Sturmbannfuehrer didn't waste any time to sic the draft board on you."

"Oh, I only said that as a conjecture. Perhaps he had nothing to do with it," Walther commented.

"I bet he did," Hertha ventured.

"Either way, it doesn't really matter," Walther said resignedly.

They strode along in silence for quite a while. "You'll be OK once I'm gone, won't you?" he asked.

"Yeah, I'll be OK. I'll be lonely for a while, and I'll just spend more time with my mother and father; however, it won't be for long. I have decided to recall the children from the Sudetenland."

Walther had noticed the dark clouds that were masking most of the sky. "We better start heading back," Walther suggested. "Those clouds, the blackout, and the fading light will soon leave us in complete darkness."

After they changed direction, he said, "I thought we were planning on letting them stay another year."

"We were planning on letting them stay a while longer, but the events of the last few weeks have impacted that planning. The kids are now considered German citizens, and they will have to abide by the rules that apply to all the other German kids," Hertha said.

"What do you mean?" he asked.

"Well, Romi who has finished the eighth grade of elementary school, must now spend a *Pflichtjahr* [compulsory year] on a farm. The Pflichtjahr is required of every German girl by law."

"Why do they have to spend a year on the farm?" Walther asked.

"I don't know," she said. "I suppose the idea is to make them more self-sufficient."

"Herbert will have to join the *Jungvolk* [subsidiary of the Hitler Youth that encompasses all boys between the ages of ten and fourteen]. Membership in the Jungvolk is also decreed by law—a law that took effect in 1939," she told him.

"What does seven-year-old Hannelore have to do?" Walther asked.

"Nothing yet, but give the Party time to think about it. Perhaps she'll have to be an air-raid warden," Hertha said derisively.

"Sh," Walther warned, "somebody might hear you."

Suddenly the air raid sirens started to wail. "Oh, not again," Hertha complained.

It was pitch dark now. They could barely see each other. Walther wished he had a walking stick that he could use to probe for obstructions that might lie directly ahead of them. He took Hertha by the arm as they slowly inched their way along the dirt path. The distant sound of aircraft engines became audible.

When Hertha tripped and fell, Walther lost hold of her arm. "Where are you?" he asked.

She was laughing and said, "Over here, in the bushes."

Grappling with his arms in the direction of her voice, Walther lost his balance and fell almost on top of her.

"Are you all right?"

"Yes, I'm all right," she said between laughter.

He kissed her and said, "Let's just stay here where we're hidden away from the rest of the world."

The thundering sound of antiaircraft fire quickly changed his mind. "Right now, that's not a good idea. C'mon, we have to get out of here." He picked her up and held her by the hand. The intermittent flashes of antiaircraft fire now allowed them to orient themselves. They moved along the dirt path as quickly as possible in the direction they had come. Once they got to the street, several flares, dropped by the aircraft, provided the illumination they needed to run all the way back to their apartment and their quasi-shelter. When they reached the shelter, they were still holding hands.

Walther picked up the conversation after the all clear had sounded, and they were back in their apartment. "Are you planning on recalling all the kids?"

"Yes," Hertha said. "Romi has to start her Pflichtjahr early next year, and I would like to spend some time with her before she has to leave. Hannelore has to start school. She is already a year behind. Having her start school in Bodenbach and then having her transfer a year later, when Herbert was scheduled to come back, just does not make sense, and if I recall the girls, I would not want to leave Herbert behind. He will start thinking that we have forsaken him altogether."

"You seem to have covered all eventualities," Walther said approvingly. "When do you plan on having them return?"

"I will write to Miele in the morning. I'd like to have them come home the first week in October," she replied.

Walther's draft notice had instructed him to report to the military barracks in Wandsbek. Hertha accompanied him on the subway ride to the barracks. They had to say their farewells at the gate, since Hertha was not allowed to enter the complex. "When will I see you again?" Hertha asked.

"We will have eight weeks of basic training, after which we'll get a few days leave before reporting to our assigned units," he replied.

After an emotional goodbye, Hertha cried uncontrollably, as she headed back to the subway station. She was still dabbing away the tears as the train left the station.

Chapter 22

Tante Emi had gathered the Klug children in the family room. Sitting in one of the lounge chairs, she asked them to seat themselves on the sofa.

"Children," she said, "I have just received a letter from your mother. She wants you to come back home. Isn't that a pleasant surprise for you?"

All three of them nodded in unison. Herbert asked, "How come? I thought that we were going to stay almost another year. Does she want all of us to come home?"

Hertha had told Tante Emi in her letter that Walther had been drafted and that the children would find her home alone. But she had also asked Tante Emi not to tell the children; she would break the news after their return. Therefore, Tante Emi answered Herbert's question by simply saying, "Yes, she wants all of you to return."

"When will we be leaving?" Romi asked.

"Your mother would like to pick you up when the daily train from Dresden arrives at the Hamburg station on 7 October; that would be a week from today."

"Will you be taking us?" Romi asked.

"No, unfortunately, I won't be able to leave at that time, but one of the girls and I will take you to Dresden, and we will put you on the train to Hamburg. All you have to do, once the train leaves Dresden, is to stay on the train until it doesn't go any further.

"Romi, since you are the oldest, here is what I want you to do: Decide what clothes the three of you will wear on the trip, remembering that you want to wear something that will keep you warm in October weather. Then, decide what clothes you will need the first few days once you're back home. Those clothes we will pack into the two suitcases that Herbert brought with him, and you will take them with you on the train. Since it would be difficult for you to handle all the luggage that you originally brought with you, I will pack all the remaining clothes into the three suitcases that you girls brought with you and send them to your mother by freight. Those suitcases should arrive in Hamburg a day or two after your return.

"Romi, after deciding what you will be taking with you, make sure that anything that needs to be laundered goes into the laundry hamper by tomorrow evening. I wouldn't want you going home looking like unkempt waifs. I'm putting you in charge, OK?"

"OK," Romi answered.

"What am I in charge of?" Herbert asked.

"You're in charge of helping Romi," Tante Emi said.

"Oh."

Tante Emi got out of her chair and said, "Well, I'm going to walk over to the station and check on the train schedules between here and Dresden."

As soon as Tante Emi had left, Romi jumped up and yelled, "Hurray! We're going home!" Hannelore was jumping up and down exclaiming, "I'm going home—going home to Mama!"

Herbert acknowledged their sentiments with a nod and a wide grin on his face.

Once their excitement wore off, Romi said, "We better get started right away and decide what we will be taking along. Herbert, let's check your stuff first; then, I will do mine and Hannelore's."

+++

Early, in the morning of 7 October, the Klug children said goodbye to Onkel Josef and to Ilse, who was getting ready for work in her father's laboratory. They also said goodbye to Ruth and Peter, before the two youngest Lienhofs left for school. Herbert asked Tante Emi to give Krista their regards, since she was away, studying at the university.

Although they were excited about going home, Romi and Herbert had mixed feelings when they were saying their goodbyes. On the prior evening Romi had reminded him that they would always be beholden to the Lienhofs for having treated them as their own and for having provided them with a wonderful home away from home. Herbert could only concur with his sister's assessment.

At about 1:00 P.M. they said goodbye to Bertha the cook. Bertha hugged Hannelore and handed her a small bag. "I prepared some sandwiches for you and your brother and sister to eat on the train."

Coming into the kitchen, Tante Emi said, "Kaethe will be going with us to Dresden. Be ready to leave in ten minutes. We'll meet you in the hallway."

After they had started their walk to the station, Herbert turned for a last look at the Lien Hof. He knew he would miss climbing the stairs to the top of the tower.

The local train arrived in Dresden one and one quarter hour before the express train to Hamburg was scheduled to depart. Tante Emi led Kaethe and the Klug children to the large waiting room and ordered some refreshments, and they whiled the time away with reminiscences of the children's stay.

When the public address system announced the boarding message for the Hamburg train, they made their way to the designated platform. Tante Emi stopped at a kiosk that had a sign that read "*Mutter und Kind.*"[4] Two ladies occupied the kiosk. After engaging one of the ladies in conversation, Tante Emi called Romi over and said, "This lady is Frau Voss. She will be on the train going to Hamburg. Her job is to look after children who are traveling alone. If you run into any problems, advise Frau Voss and she will help you. You can find her in the first compartment of the first car."

"OK," Romi said.

Tante Emi and Kaethe found a compartment for the children and stowed their suitcases in the overhead luggage bin.

When Tante Emi sat down, Kaethe asked, "Mama, don't you think we had better get off the train?"

"We'll have plenty of time when they announce the 'all aboard.' Besides, if we stay here a while, perhaps the kids won't have to share the compartment—at least for the first part of the trip," Tante Emi answered.

When the warning was sounded, the children kissed Tante Emi and Kaethe goodbye, and at Romi's prompting, Hannelore said to Tante Emi, "Thank you for everything."

Once Tante Emi and Kaethe were back on the platform, the children waved at them through the window, until the train started to pull out of the station.

[4] Mutter und Kind (mother and child) was an agency of the welfare system. One of the agency's tasks was to provide assistance to young mothers and to children traveling alone.

This time, Herbert did not mind the repetitive monotone of the wheels rolling over the rail joints, since each repetition now was bringing him closer to home. About three hours after they left Dresden, Romi opened the bag that Bertha had given to Hannelore, and the children munched the sandwiches. While they were eating, Frau Voss opened the door to the compartment and asked Romi how they were getting along. Romi assured her that they were just fine.

"It looks like you need something to go with those sandwiches," Frau Voss said. "Let me see what I can find."

A little later she came back with a soda pop for each of them.

Daylight receded, and soon they were enveloped in almost total darkness. Because of the blackout, the only lighting in the compartment was a blue light that barely made the contours of the compartment discernible. Prompted by what he felt was a spooky setting, Herbert soon went into his rendition of the opening line of "The Shadow," the syndicated radio show the children used to listen to in New York: "Who knows what evil lurks in the hearts of men? The shadow knows." And he then attempted to imitate the bloodcurdling laugh that followed the opening line.

"Herbert, stop that! You're scaring Hannelore," Romi cried out.

He repeated the bloodcurdling laugh.

"Herbert..."

"OK, OK."

Since, by now, it was even darker outside than it was in the train compartment, Romi and Hannelore soon fell asleep.

✚ ✚ ✚

Hertha arrived at the Hamburg main station at 9:30 P.M. to pick up the children. At 9:40 P.M. the air raid alert sounded, and all the platforms had to be cleared. Hertha approached a railroad employee and said, "I'm here to meet my children who are coming in on the train from Dresden, that is scheduled to arrive at 10:00 P.M. They will be concerned when they don't find me here to greet them."

"Don't worry, lady," the man said, "All the trains are stopped from entering the city while an alert is in progress. You'll have plenty of time to greet them on their arrival, after the all-clear sounds."

Hertha followed a crowd of people into one of the public air raid shelters that had sprung up since the start of the war. While sitting in the shelter she wondered what she should tell the children when they asked why their father wasn't present to pick them up. At this time, she could not tell them that his being drafted was a consequence of his own actions. She could not tell them that those actions had also affected their own status. She could not tell them that his actions were based on a premonition, namely, that war between Germany and the United States was imminent. She could not tell them any of this, because his premonition had not yet been fulfilled and, for all she knew, might never be. She knew that she would have to tell the children that they now were considered German nationals, but she wanted to do so in a way that would not cause resentment toward their father. If the true circumstances were known at this time, Romi might be resentful; she had often mentioned how glad she was that she was an American and therefore exempt from the Pflichtjahr. Hertha was not too concerned about Herbert. He would have to join the Jungvolk, but he probably would not mind too much, since all his classmates were already members.

I'll just have to come up with some prevarication, Hertha thought. Sometimes, a white lie is better than to open a can of worms. When the right time comes, I will tell them what really happened, and they will understand.

The girls were still asleep fifteen minutes before their scheduled arrival time in Hamburg, when the distant rumbling of antiaircraft fire awakened them.

"What is happening?" Romi asked.

"We are being greeted with fireworks," Herbert ventured.

"Don't be silly," Romi admonished.

"Take a look in the direction the train is moving," Herbert said.

When Romi looked, she could see searchlight beams scanning for their prey and antiaircraft shells exploding in the sky ahead. The exploding shells looked like miniature fireworks, only not as pretty.

The train continued on; the rumbling grew louder; the explosions of the shells grew brighter. The train soon stopped. The blue lamp was extinguished, and the children sat in complete darkness, except for the intermittent flashes of the exploding shells. Herbert and his sisters watched as the searchlight beams nervously traversed the sky. Herbert likened a searchlight beam to the finger of a child scanning a book page in search of a certain passage.

But the searchlight beam did not reflect the innocence of Herbert's comparison. Once it found a target it would stay focused by moving in unison with its prey. The shaft of light emitted by the parabolic mirror of the searchlight was a diabolic finger—its insistent pointing was a harbinger of death to a randomly found victim. When one of the fingers met with success, others, in a frenzy, would attempt to converge their shafts of light with the beam of the first, such that the beams would illuminate the intruder at their point of intersection. The resulting crisscross of light beams resembled a skewed set of crosshairs that became the target of the guns.

On several occasions, the children watched as aircraft were illuminated by multiple searchlights. They saw shells exploding in the vicinity of the intersecting beams, but in each case, the pilots apparently were able to evade the prying lights.

The chidren were frightened, and Hannelore started to cry. Romi put her on her lap and tried to console her. A few minutes later, the compartment door opened and the soothing voice of Frau Voss said, "Try not to be frightened, children. The train has stopped outside of the city, because Hamburg is under an air raid alert. As soon as the all clear sounds, we will be on our way. We will arrive at the main station about fifteen minutes after the train gets under way again."

The children heard the door shut.

Gradually, the sound of the guns diminished, and the probing fingers of the searchlights disappeared. A degree of encouragement was added, when the little blue light was turned on again. Hannelore stopped crying, and after several minutes, the train started to move.

As Frau Voss had predicted, the train arrived in the main station approximately fifteen minutes later. After the train had stopped, she came into the compartment to help the children retrieve their suitcases out of the overhead bin. "Come and see me if no one is here to pick you up," Frau Voss said as she left the compartment.

The children waited until the aisle of the car was clear of disembarking passengers. After they got into the aisle, they scanned the blacked-out platform through the car window for their mother.

"There she is!" Romi suddenly shouted.

"Where, where?" Hannelore asked. "I can't see her."

When Romi pointed her in the right direction, Hannelore exclaimed, "I see her! I see my Mama!"

✦✦✦

They had an emotional reunion. When Hertha asked about their trip, Romi said, "The train had to stop until the air raid was over before we could get into the station."

"Were you scared?" Hertha asked.

"Yeah, a little bit," Romi confessed.

Hannelore told her, "We had a compartment all to ourselves, all the way."

As they got ready to leave the platform, Herbert took a last look at the train. He could see Frau Voss looking at them through a car window. She waved and Herbert returned the gesture. "She really was looking out for us," he said to himself.

"Where is Papa?" Romi asked.

"He could not come. I'll tell you why when we get home," Hertha answered.

✦✦✦

After they got home, one of the first things Romi said was, "You were going to tell us why Papa couldn't meet us at the train station. Where is he?"

Hertha said to herself, oh, oh, here it comes. She had the children sit down around the kitchen table and said, "Your father was not at the train station because he has been drafted—he is now in the army."

"In the army...how can that be? He's an American citizen!" Romi burst out.

"According to present law, his renewed residence in Germany and the fact that he was born here apparently override his

American citizenship. He was called up two weeks ago, and he has just started basic training."

"Can we go see him?" Herbert asked.

"No, but he'll get to come home for a few days, after he completes his training," Hertha said, but thought, now for the hard part. She continued, "Since your father is now a German citizen, you children are also considered German."

"Aw, why did they have to do that?" Romi asked. "Now I'll have to do that stupid Pflichtjahr! You leave town for a while—you come back and find that your nationality has changed overnight—and you now are committed to spend a year on some stupid farm," Romi said with tearful eyes.

Her reaction was exactly as Hertha had expected, but Hertha was glad to hear her say: why did *they* have to do that. She would have said: why did *he* have to do that, if she knew what really transpired.

Hertha tried to console her older daughter. "A year on the farm won't be all that bad. Perhaps you'll even enjoy it."

The look Romi gave her mother clearly indicated that she was not convinced.

Hertha focused her attention on her son. "You will now have to join the Jungvolk," she said.

Herbert's response was a noncommital shrug of the shoulders.

"What do I have to do?" Hannelore asked.

"You have to stay home with your Mama," Hertha said as she hugged her baby.

Chapter 23

The first thing Hertha did, after the children's return, was to transfer Herbert back into the Hamburg school system and to enroll Hannelore for the first grade. Rosemarie, who had just finished the eighth grade of elementary school, had previously decided that she would not go to high school, because her mere total of two years of German schooling, interrupted midway by a school transfer, would put her at a significant disadvantage. To her mother she had said, "Most of the girls who go on to high school are the bright ones who plan to attend the university. With my background, there is no way that I could compete with them."

Now she was still bemoaning the fact that she would have to spend a year on a farm. "If I were at all undecided about going to high school, this compulsory farm service would make up my mind for me. In no way am I going to start high school, after losing a whole year milking cows or feeding pigs or doing whatever.

"It's not fair, Mama. How come only the girls have to do this, while the boys go their merry way?"

"I don't know," Hertha said. "I don't make the rules."

Hertha scarcely could blame her for feeling the way she did about high school and about the farm service.

Hannelore was also grumbling after her first few days in school. "Some of the kids make fun of me, because I don't speak German very well," she said to her mother.

"That's one of the reasons you are going to school, to learn to speak German well. As for the kids, just ask them how come they too are in the first grade, if they are so much smarter than you. I bet that will tone them down," Hertha suggested.

Herbert was the only one who was not complaining. "I'm back with my old classmates," he would tell anyone who would listen.

+++

In mid-October of 1941 Herbert joined the *Jungvolk.* He was disappointed at first, because he was thrown in with a group of ten-year-old neophytes. For the first few meetings parade drills were the order of the day. The group would assemble on one of the school athletic fields, and the assigned Jungvolk leader would have the thirty or so kids in his charge assemble in a formation of three deep and then put them through the paces of left turn, right turn, and about-face commands. Most of the kids caught on pretty fast; however, there were a few, who, after a left or right turn command was issued, often faced the opposite direction of the rest of the formation.

Marching in cadence was also a problem for some of the kids. Whenever they were marching in formation, Herbert knew there was a fifty-fifty chance that the kid behind him would consistently be colliding with his, Herbert's, heels as the instructor was yelling: left, two, three, four!

Incessant repetition was the only way toward improvement, but Herbert soon found the repetition to be boring.

On rainy days, the group would meet indoors and the instructor would recite recent German history. The lectures covered much the same material that Herbert's friend Ewald had espoused two years earlier. Since these meetings did not present anything new, they did not evoke Herbert's interest.

During the first meeting that Herbert attended, he noticed that many of the ten-year-old boys were already in uniform. Since the weather was exceptionally warm for October, they were still wearing the brown shirt and the black corduroy short pants of the summer uniform. Some of them had the sheathed knife, which had caught Herbert's fancy the first time he saw it, attached to their belt at the left hip.

Herbert reminded himself to remind his mother that he now would require not only the summer uniform but also the winter version.

When Herbert approached his mother about the uniforms, Hertha said, "Whoa! Whoa! Do you realize that all this has to come out of your clothing allotment?"

"I won't need anything else," Herbert ventured.

"I won't need anything else," Hertha mimicked. "What are you going to do for underwear? Wear your father's?" she asked. "You can have the shirt and the corduroy shorts for the summer. Now what do you need for the winter?"

"The winter uniform consists of long black pants, a black tunic, and a visored black cap," Herbert answered.

"Will any black tunic do?" Hertha asked.

"No, no! You have to buy this stuff in a uniform shop. The tunic is worn over the brown shirt. It comes together at the waist—"

"You mean it's gathered at the waist," she said.

"Yeah, gathered at the waist and tucked into the pants. The black pant legs come together…are gathered at the ankles and are tucked into the socks," Herbert said.

After Hertha spent several minutes mulling over his clothing allowance, she said, "You can have the tunic, but that is it. You can't have the long winter pants…the clothing allowance just won't reach," she told him.

"Aw, Mama," was all he could say.

"You have a pair of black sweat pants that will be almost indistinguishable from the winter uniform pants. You can wear them with your tunic."

"It won't be the same," he mumbled.

"It will be close enough," she countered. "If that's not good enough, then you will have to write a letter to the Fuehrer and tell him that your mother says that she needs a greater clothing allowance if he wants you all dressed up like a little soldier."

"Mama, I can't do that," Herbert protested. "Besides, he probably has more important things to do than worry about clothing allowances."

"If he worried more about clothing allowances, perhaps he wouldn't have time trying to outdo Napoleon," Hertha said.

"What do you mean, Mama?"

"Napoleon went to Russia, too…he got his butt kicked."

"Oh," Herbert said. After a pause he asked, "Can I at least have the scout knife?"

"You can have the knife if you promise not to cut yourself."

"I promise."

✚✚✚

The first time the air raid sirens sounded after the children returned from the Sudetenland, Herbert, with suitcase in hand, was leading the pack as they made their way downstairs from the apartment. He was headed for the back room of the glazier shop on the ground floor when Hertha yelled, "No, Herbert, we go to a different shelter now. Your father raised a fuss with the block warden about the inadequacy of that back room. We now have been assigned space in one of the public shelters that have been made available."

"So where do we go?" Herbert asked.

"Just head out the front door—I'll show you," his mother said.

The children followed Hertha as she turned north on the Iffland Strasse.

"Where are we going?" Romi asked.

"We're going to the Armgart Strasse school, it's about two blocks away," her mother answered.

The flak (antiaircraft) guns were already firing. Their fire was not aimed directly overhead, but it was close enough to induce Hertha to start running. The children followed on her heels. They ran two blocks down the Iffland Strasse and turned left onto Armgart Strasse. As they approached the school, Hertha stopped for a moment to catch her breath. She put down the two suitcases she was carrying; Herbert and Romi followed her example by putting down the suitcase each of them was carrying.

The increasing sound of flak bursts quickly served as an incentive for them to pick up their luggage and to enter the school basement. Once inside, the basement walls insulated them considerably from the noise of the flak guns. The Klugs found a place to sit and kept their belongings nearby. When Herbert looked around, he noticed small family groups throughout the basement. Each group was guarding the possessions it valued most or could not do without, in the event that something went awry.

Herbert wondered how much safer they were here than in the back room of the glazier shop; after all, they now were exposed to the rubble of six floors falling on them, instead of just three.

✚✚✚

In Walther's latest letter, he told Hertha that some delay had been incurred in his training schedule and that he therefore would not receive any furlough time before Christmas; however, he hoped he would be able to spend the holidays at home. He asked Hertha to tell the children that he was looking forward to seeing them soon.

When Hertha conveyed the message, Romi asked, "What will Papa have to do after his training; will he have to fight at the front?"

"I certainly hope not; after all, he is almost twice as old as most of the boys who are in the line," Hertha said.

After several weekly meetings of the Jungvolk, Herbert was transferred from the neophyte contingent to another group that was in his own age bracket. He was happy to see that some of his classmates were in that group. On clear days, the group would meet on an athletic field and engage in track and field sports such as running, jumping, and shot-putting. In inclement weather, activities were transferred to one of the school gymnasiums where the boys would, under supervision, try their mettle on the horizontal and parallel bars or on the gym horse. Many of the boys took the track and field sports quite seriously. By meeting prescribed minimum requirements in the 60-meter and the 100-meter dash and the long jump, they were awarded the coveted Jungvolk proficiency badge.

Herbert, who was the shortest in stature of the boys in his group, was neither fast in the dash nor long in the jump, but he enjoyed the camaraderie.

✚✚✚

Fall turned into winter. On the night of 30 November, the Klugs were again wakened by the air raid sirens. Nearby flak bursts were already assaulting their ears before they got out of the house to run to the shelter. As they got on the street, the flak bursts appeared directly overhead.

"Hold your suitcases over your heads," Hertha called out to the two older children to protect them from falling shrapnel. To Hannelore she yelled, "Put that book I gave you on your head." They did as they were told. Herbert thought they looked like hired safari porters as they ran after their mother.

✚✚✚

On 7 December, German radio reported the Japanese attack on the U.S. naval base at Pearl Harbor. At about the same time the OKW reported temperatures of -35 degrees Fahrenheit in the Moscow area, thereby indicating that the German advance toward the Russian capital had been stalled.

In the afternoon of 11 December, Hertha, on her way to do some shopping, stopped at her mother's apartment. "Have you heard the latest news?" Mother Werner asked.

"No, what is the latest news?" Hertha questioned in return.

"Hitler declared war on the United States!"

"He did what?" Hertha asked incredulously.

"Hitler declared war on the United States!" Mother Werner reiterated.

"He must think that the Japanese attack will prevent the U.S. from assisting the Russians and the British," Hertha said, "but my guess is that he will have another think coming. Well, Walther was saying all along that this would happen, although he probably expected that the U.S. would be the one to declare war."

"How is Walther?" Mother Werner asked.

"OK, I guess—I haven't heard from him for a week or so. He still expects to be home for Christmas."

"Are you staying for some coffee?" Mother Werner asked.

"No, thank you. I'm on my way to do some shopping. I just thought I'd stop to see how you're getting along."

After Hertha took her leave, she contemplated the significance of the news her mother had presented. If nothing else, the news meant that the war would be prolonged. According to Walther's thinking, it probably also meant that Hitler could not win this war. Serves him right, she thought.

Hertha noted how this reaction to the news emphasized her growing detachment toward Germany that had been building up in the past year. If Hitler lost, then Germany would lose another war. But she didn't care. This was not the Germany to which she had yearned to return. She was just longing to lead a normal life again.

Although welcoming a declaration of war ordinarily would appear perverse, she did welcome it, because it validated Walther's decision to renounce his citizenship. Until this news broke, his decision, which she knew he had made with a heavy heart and only in the interest of his family, had been for naught.

After she got home from shopping, Herbert, who had just returned from school, asked her whether she knew that Germany was now at war with the United States. Hertha told him she had heard the news from her mother. She reminded herself that she would now have to admit to the fib she told the children about the circumstances of Walther's conscription.

That evening, after Hannelore's bedtime curfew of 8:00 P.M., Hertha assembled the older children in the kitchen and asked them, "Remember how I told you that your father was drafted because German law considered him German because of his German birth and his renewed residence in Germany?"

The children both nodded. "Well," Hertha went on, "those were not the real reasons."

After giving her brother a quizzical look which triggered a shrug of his shoulders, Romi asked, "What was the real reason?"

"Your father felt that Germany would soon be at war with the United States. If that happened, he would be interned—"

"What does interned mean?" Romi asked.

"It means Papa would be held in some kind of a camp," Herbert said knowingly.

"That's right," Hertha concurred. "It also means that he would no longer be able to support us. With our well-being in mind, he therefore decided to voluntarily renounce his citizenship."

"Aw, why did he have to do that?" Romi asked beseechingly. "Couldn't we have gone back to the States?"

"You kids and your father probably could have gone back, but I would have had to stay."

"Why? You're our mother," Herbert asked.

"I'm a German national, and Germans have not been allowed to leave the country since shortly after the war started. Your father did not want to leave me behind." Hertha paused before she asked, "Would you children have left me behind?"

The children looked at her and said nothing. They both answered her by shaking their heads from side to side.

Romi sighed and said, "But now he had to join the army."

"That was a risk he had to take," her mother said. "It magnifies the sacrifice he made for us."

There was silence for a while, and Hertha felt that they understood.

Finally Romi asked, "Couldn't he have asked for special treatment when he was drafted—like, that I wouldn't have to spend a year on a farm?"

Hertha couldn't help laughing. Between chuckles, she said "No, dear. He could not."

Starting the last week in December, The *Winterhilfe*[4] urgently requested the populace to donate winter clothing, such as scarves, sweaters, and heavy jackets for distribution to the troops on the eastern front.

To many, this solicitation indicated that the government had not planned for an extended campaign in Russia.

Hertha had resourcefully managed the ration coupons such that a little extra would be available over the Christmas holidays, but Walther's ten-day furlough was the best Christmas present for all the members of the Klug family.

Not having seen him in uniform before, the children viewed him with some curiosity, when he arrived on 22 December. Romi told him that he looked very handsome.

Unlike New Year's Eve celebrations of the past, the Klug family was not looking forward to fireworks. They knew that fireworks were banned and that any noise or brilliant lighting effects would be courtesy of flak and RAF.

4 *Winterhilfe* was an agency of the welfare system. The agency's primary function was to solicit winter clothing for needy citizens.

Chapter 24

In mid-March of 1942, Rosemarie was confirmed in the St. Gertruden Lutheran church. One week later, she had to leave for the farm service. Hertha and Rosemarie's siblings accompanied her to the train station where they found several of Rosemarie's former classmates already assembled. The girls had been told that they would all be heading to the north German farm country near the Danish border and that each girl would be assigned to a distinct farm.

Herbert wondered why most of the girls seemed somewhat depressed until he remembered that none of them had volunteered for this trip. Rosemarie kissed her mother goodbye with tearful eyes and waved resignedly as the train slowly moved out of the station.

Hertha was reading the latest letter from Walther. He told her that he had completed his basic training and he now was enrolled in an English refresher course. Upon completion of the course, he would be sent to western Poland where he would be assigned to a POW camp as a translator. The camp was located in a town called Schildberg near the city of Poznan. He noted that he would be given a day's leave before his transfer, which was scheduled for the latter part of May. On the day of his leave, Hertha kept the children out of school so they could spend some time with their father. They enjoyed a pleasant day picnicking. Late in the evening, Hertha and the children accompanied Walther back to the barracks where they said their goodbyes.

✚ ✚ ✚

About two weeks later, Hertha received another letter from her husband. He indicated that he was getting settled in his new environment and that that environment was a POW camp for English officers and enlisted men—most of whom had been captured during the campaign in France.

In a somber tone, Walther wrote that the recent severe bombing of Cologne had him worried, because he felt that it was only a matter of time until Hamburg would also be subjected to such a massive attack. The tone of his letter became more upbeat when he told her that he had some good news: he would be allowed to live off base over the weekends. Walther therefore suggested that she and the children come to Schildberg while the children were out of school during the summer months of '42.

Walther wrote that he couldn't promise a nice apartment, but they would be out of harm's way, at least for summer.

Hertha, Hannelore, and Herbert boarded a train bound for Poznan on a morning in mid-June. During the long ride, Herbert noticed that many of the passengers were soldiers evidently on their way back to the eastern front, after being on furlough or convalescent leave. Quite a few wore the Winter Campaign Ribbon that had been awarded to those who had been in Russia during the worst of the previous severe winter months. Herbert had heard that some of the soldiers referred disparagingly to the award as the *Gefrierfleisch Orden* (frozen meat medal). To him, the award underscored the hardships these men had experienced while being so ill-prepared for the harsh Russian winter.

About eight hours after leaving Hamburg, the train arrived in Poznan in late afternoon. Walther was there to greet them and to accompany them the rest of the way on the local train to Schildberg.

"I was unable to find an apartment for you, because the authorities do not release apartments to transients. Only folks who can demonstrate that they don't have other housing facilities available are considered for apartments," Walther told Hertha.

"So where will we be staying?" Hertha asked.

"I was able to rent an attic room from a Polish forester," Walther replied.

"An attic room?" Hertha asked in a tone that couldn't conceal some apprehension. "Who lives in the house?"

"The forester and his wife and his daughter and her husband. The daughter has a two-year-old child."

"Do they speak German?"

"The forester, although a Polish citizen, has an ethnic German background and speaks some German, but the others do not."

"Uh,uh!" Hertha responded. "It will be interesting to find out just how we will communicate."

When they arrived in Schildberg, Walther suggested that they leave all but one or two suitcases in a baggage locker, since they would have to walk about a mile and a half to the forester's house.

After they left the station, they soon were on a dirt road that led out of town. The road wound its way through farm fields and along occasional stands of conifers that rose along the roadside. After a while a large wooded area came into view on the left side of the road. On the opposite side of the road stood a house and several sheds.

"That is your summer home up ahead," Walther announced.

When they reached the house, the forester came out to greet them. Walther introduced his family to the man, whom he addressed as Mr. Kosiaruk. The forester, who appeared to be in his mid-fifties, invited them inside where they met his wife, his daughter Marie, and his little two-year-old granddaughter Olga. Because of the language barrier, the introductions were a bit cumbersome, but Mr. Kosiaruk did his best to interpret what was said.

After a while, Mrs. Kosiaruk took them upstairs and showed them the attic room, where they would be staying. It was only about ten feet wide but long enough to accommodate one double and two single beds, with enough space left over for a closet, a table, and a couple of chairs. The table was located under a window that afforded a view of the dirt road they had just traveled.

Mrs. Kosiaruk wished to excuse herself to let them get settled a bit. Because she didn't know how to verbalize this in German, she just pointed at the suitcases and motioned her hands as though she were unpacking them.

Hertha nodded understanding.

After the forester's wife had left them, Hertha said, "How am I going to cook up here—there are no facilities."

"Mrs. Kosiaruk told her husband that you can share the kitchen with her."

"Then I will need some pots and pans, some dishes, and some cutlery. I don't want to impose on the woman anymore than I have to."

"I've been given another day off," Walther said.

"Tomorrow we can go into town and pick those things up. It will take a few days to get organized."

"I won't be able to speak Polish in a few days," Hertha said.

Walther reached into the pocket of his uniform jacket.

"Here," he said, as he handed her a little booklet. "It is a German-Polish dictionary. You can look up a key word or two before you try to converse with Mrs. Kosariuk, or you can let Herbert look them up for you."

"Wonderful," Hertha said somewhat derisively.

Sitting on one of the beds, Herbert asked, "Where is the toilet?"

"There is an outhouse across the yard," Walther replied. "An outhouse?" Herbert incredulously cried out.

His father looked at him. Shrugging his shoulders, Walther said, "Sitting in an outhouse beats sitting in an air raid shelter."

Herbert lowered his head and offered no further comment.

Addressing his family the next morning Walther said, "Let's go into town. I won't be able to show you many sites worth seeing, because there really aren't any, but I can show you a nice park where you can spend a lot of time this summer. Bring your bathing suits along."

Turning to Hertha he said, "We can pick up something for lunch at the commissary, where you also will be able to do a lot of your shopping."

Herbert was immediately smitten by the park. He noted it had a lake that contained a raft-like structure anchored a short distance away from a sandy beach area, bathhouses close to the beach area, and picnic tables spread over a green lawn.

"Can we go in the water right away?" Herbert asked his mother.

"No. We'll have some lunch first. After that, we'll put on our swimsuits and then you can go into the water."

While they were eating lunch at one of the picnic tables, Hertha commented, "We're the only ones here." Then she asked, "Why don't more folks take advantage of this nice park?"

"You have to remember that we are in Poland now. The park is off limits to the Poles," Walther answered.

"Why is that? Are we Germans afraid that they will contaminate the water?"

Walther shrugged and said, "I don't know why, dear."

Then he added, "At this time of day attendance usually is low; however, later in the afternoon some of the soldiers from the camp or from other units in the area may show up."

"Do any of them have family here?" Hertha asked.

"I only know of one or two who have occasional visitors."

"Can we go and put on our swimsuits now?" Herbert piped up after they had finished lunch.

"No, you shouldn't go in the water right after you have eaten. Let's wait a half hour or so," his mother said.

"Aw, gee!"

When they had changed to their swimsuits, Herbert watched his father swim out to the raft, while his mother attended to Hannelore in the shallow water of the lake. Herbert recalled the few swimming lessons he had had as part of his school's physical education program. He remembered that he was not afraid to delve into deep water in the pool, because he always stayed close to the side of the pool, and he could always grasp the railing that ran alongside the inside of the pool whenever he became unsure of himself. But this lake was different; there was no railing to grasp onto. He decided that practice in the shallow water was the order of the day, but he challenged himself then and there that he would be able to swim out to the raft before summer's end.

They left the park in late afternoon and stopped to buy the cooking utensils that Hertha needed. Since Walther had to report back to the camp by 6 P.M., he did not accompany his family back to the forester's home. "I'll see you Saturday," he said as he kissed Hertha goodbye.

On the way back to their attic room Herbert was carrying a bag with one of Hertha's purchases in it. When he looked inside the bag, he saw that it contained a porcelainized cooking pot.

Herbert remembered that when Hannelore was still very young and the family took the Brooklyn subway to the beach or some other outing he had always been elected to carry another porcelainized pot, and he had always taken great care to conceal the pot in a brown paper bag. Many times, while entering or exiting the subway car, his brown bag would bump one of the upright porcelainized bars that were located near the car doors to allow standing passengers a handhold to steady themselves whenever the train was accelerating or slowing down. The resulting collision of porcelain against porcelain, albeit slightly tempered by the paper bag, produced a loud clang which caused Herbert considerable embarrassment. He always felt that the loud clang drew the attention of all the occupants of the car, and when they saw the family with the little girl, they would instantly know that he was little Hannelore's potty bearer.

On one of these excursions, the content of the bag was fully revealed, because the bag tore and the potty headed toward the car floor. The potty did not merely plunk onto the floor; it fell with a torque component perpendicular to its vertical axis that caused it to wobble round and round after it hit the floor, thus evoking smiles from nearby passengers, before it finally came to rest.

When Herbert looked at his father with a "what do I do now" glance, the only response he got from Walther was, "Well, pick it up!"

Herbert bent over and retrieved the wayward pot; however, it got away from him one more time before he—now thoroughly mortified—was able to once more hide it in the remnants of the torn bag.

When they arrived back in their room, Hertha reviewed her purchases and said, "I only bought the most indispensable utensils, because I don't want to intrude on Mrs. Kosiaruk's kitchen regimen anymore than is absolutely necessary; therefore, you kids better be prepared to eat a lot of simple casseroles."

Herbert and Hannelore looked at each other and noncommittally shrugged their shoulders.

When their mother got to the last shopping bag she said, "Here are the shoes that your father bought for you. He wants you to wear them when you are tramping around in the woods, so you won't ruin your good leather shoes."

Herbert and Hannelore again looked at each other, but this time their faces reflected disdain. Herbert looked at the shoes that his mother had just given him. They were clogs. The tops were made of rough leather and the soles were made of wood. They seemed to weigh a ton.

"Do we really have to wear these things, Mama? I'll never be able to get up the stairs with these weights on my feet," Herbert groused.

"You're not supposed to wear them coming upstairs; you're supposed to wear them outside. Your father thinks it's a good idea, so I want you to give them a try."

"Aw, gee whiz!"

+++

On the following morning, Hannelore came running up the stairs and lamented to her mother, "Mama, I can't get to the bathroom."

"Why can't you get to the bathroom?" Hertha asked.

"The geese are in the yard, and they won't let me through," the little girl wailed.

"Herbert, escort your little sister to the outhouse. Wait until she comes back out; then, escort her back."

"OK."

Herbert sympathized with his sister. He had already noticed that the forester's gaggle of six or seven geese was often in the yard of the house, and they seemed to think that they owned the place. Being a city boy, he at first had been intimidated by all the honking and flapping of wings as the geese would approach in an apparent attack mode whenever he tried to cross the yard, but he soon found out that waving a stick at them would keep them at bay.

Herbert kept the stick handy and now picked it up to comply with his mother's bidding. When they came back, Hertha said, "I want you to escort her back and forth whenever she asks you."

"I won't have to do that. She can just borrow my stick," Herbert responded.

"Just do as you are told," Hertha admonished him.

"Aw, gee whiz."

✚✚✚

On the first Saturday of their stay, Walther took his wife and the children into the woods. Each of them had two small buckets that Walther had brought with him. "I'm going to show you where you can find a lot of blueberries. With a little patience you can also find some tasty mushrooms."

"What kind of mushrooms?" Herbert asked.

"I'll show you as soon as I can find one," Walther said, as he probed the ground under some trees. "Here's one," he noted, as he picked a mushroom. Calling to his wife and Hannelore to come and take a look, he said, "Take a look at this mushroom. Note the orange color, the funnel-shaped cap, and the gill-like ridges under the cap. This is the only mushroom you should be picking."

"Why, Papa?" Hannelore asked.

"Many kinds of mushrooms are poisonous, and this is the only edible mushroom with which I am familiar. It is a chanterelle. You want to remember to pick only chanterelles and not to mess with any of the others."

After spending several hours in the woods, they had several buckets full of blueberries and a nice haul of mushrooms.

✚ ✚ ✚

Hertha and Mrs. Kosariuk soon alleviated some of the language barrier by one or the other pointing at an object and reciting the name of the object in her native tongue, whereupon the other would reciprocate in her language. The little pocket dictionary was kept in the kitchen for access by either party.

Hertha soon was sharing the mushrooms and blueberries that she and the children were bringing out of the woods with Mrs. Kosariuk, and Mrs. Kosiaruk would reciprocate by giving Hertha some rabbit meat or even some venison to supplement her meager meat allotment whenever the forester returned from a successful hunt. The two women soon had a congenial relationship, and Hertha found out that she would not have to make good the threat of simple casseroles that she had announced to the children.

✚ ✚ ✚

"Mama, I can't wear these clogs," Herbert complained to his mother about two weeks after their arrival in Schildberg.

Hertha, who was busy making up the beds, looked up and asked, "Why can't you wear them?"

"They are giving me blisters. Come and take a look."

"Just give me a minute," his mother said.

"I've got a blister too," Hannelore whimpered.

Hertha confirmed that the boy indeed had a blister caused by the cover of the clog chafing against the upper part of the foot. "Well, if you can't wear them, you'll just have to go barefoot around here. I can't let you wear your good shoes all the time, because we've already used up your shoe allotments for the year. Let me see your foot," she said to Hannelore. After a quick inspection, she said, "That's not a blister; that's a mosquito bite."

"Do I still have to wear the clogs?" Hannelore anxiously asked.

"No. You'll probably wind up with a blister too, but you will have to go barefoot around here, like your brother."

The summer days of 1942 advanced into July and then into August. On a sunny mid-August day, Hertha and the children again were enjoying the park in Schildberg, where they had spent many hours in the last two months. Hertha and Hannelore were sitting on a blanket that Hertha had spread out on the lawn. Suddenly, Hertha heard her son yelling from the lake, "Mama, look where I am!"

When she turned toward the lake, she saw him standing on the float that was anchored about fifty yards from shore.

She was filled with apprehension, since she did not know whether he could make his way back, and she knew that her limited swimming capabilities would be of little help.

"Are you OK?" she hollered at him. He nodded his head.

"Can you come back on your own?" she queried. Again a nodding of the head. "Are you sure?" This time he didn't answer. He dove back into the water. She watched anxiously as he swam toward shore. He ran excitedly to where she and Hannelore were sitting and proclaimed, "I can swim all the way out to the raft!"

"You almost gave me a heart attack, young man," Hertha responded.

"Mama, I practiced my swimming all these weeks and made sure I could swim the distance to the raft in shallow water before I headed out to the raft. Today I knew I could do it!" Herbert explained.

"Nonetheless, I don't want you to swim out there again until Saturday, when your father is here. If he gives you a green light to swim out to the raft by yourself, you can do so to your heart's content. One more thing…" Hertha hesitated a moment and then she said, "Your perseverance made your mother proud." Herbert smiled at his mother and shrugged his shoulders, as if to say no big deal.

At the end of August, Hertha and the children had to return to Hamburg, since school would start in another week.

They decided to leave on a Saturday, so Walther would be able to accompany them on the local train back to Poznan.

When they said goodbye to the forester family, Mrs. Kosiaruk handed Hertha a bag of sandwiches for the trip. Hertha had to hold back the tears as she gave the forester's wife a hug and said, "*Do widzenia.*"

✚✚✚

There was another tearful farewell when they said goodbye to Walther at the Poznan railroad station. After the express train pulled out of the terminal and Hertha and the children had settled in, Hertha asked her son, "What will you remember most about your summer stay in Schildberg?"

Herbert replied, "Well, I'll remember that I learned how to swim there." After some thought, he added, "I'll also remember all the trips I made to the outhouse, and I will always remember that half the time I had to go was because you, Mama, said I had to go and escort Hannelore; the other half of the time I had to go was because I really had to go."

Both Hertha and Hannelore had to laugh at Herbert's response.

Chapter 25

After their return to Hamburg, Herbert was looking forward to going back to school, because he was about to start his first year in high school. He would not have to transfer to another school, since the high school section was located in the same complex as the elementary school he had attended.

The high school offered two foreign languages: English and Spanish. Since Herbert already was proficient in English, he opted for the Spanish classes. By the time the class had covered the first twenty pages of the textbook, the Spanish teacher was drafted. Since there were no other Spanish teachers among the teaching staff, Herbert decided to switch to English. For him, the English class would be an easy elective, which would allow him to concentrate more on his other subjects, his German language studies in particular.

Mr. Dongers was the English teacher. Herbert noted that he was a slight man of about fifty who always appeared to be wearing the same rumpled suit. Herbert had been slightly late for his English class on one or two occasions; therefore, he had been able to observe the English teacher, as he scurried just ahead of him down the hall toward the classroom. Mr. Dongers' gait suggested that he, himself, was always late, because it invariably exceeded double time.

Since school regulations required that classroom doors remained open until the session started, he would enter without slowing down, reach behind him with his right hand, and slam the door shut with a resounding crash. Herbert figured Mr. Dongers did this to disconcert the tardy students, who now would attract more attention to their late entry than if the door were open.

Mr. Dongers had interviewed Herbert when he requested a transfer to the English class; consequently, the teacher knew that he had been born in New York and that he was proficient in English.

When, on a test, Mr. Dongers marked Herbert's use of the word truck as an error, Herbert told him, "In America, we call it a truck; we don't use the term lorry."

"That may be so," Mr. Dongers said, "but I am not teaching American English. I am teaching the King's English."

"OK, I'll try to remember that," was Herbert's response.

"Then also remember that the American colloquialism OK also is not in the English language," the teacher remarked.

"OK…I mean, yes, sir."

Mr. Dongers was stricter than most teachers; therefore, he was not regarded as a favorite among students. One day, during recess prior to the English class, one of the students suggested that they should play a trick on Mr. Dongers. Another student proposed that they do something that might cure the teacher of his door-slamming habit.

Three or four boys soon were bandying ideas about. One of them pointed to the top of the heavy, wooden, collapsible map stand which was visible behind the now open entrance door.

While the rest of the class looked on, not applauding but not interfering, the boy who had pointed at the map stand fished a piece of string out of his pant pocket and tied the map stand to the inside knob of the class room door. Everyone took to their seats and silently awaited the teacher's arrival.

Had Mr. Dongers entered the classroom at a more leisurely pace he might have become suspicious, because the behavior of the class was completely out of context. He would have noted that instead of the somewhat unruly behavior, that was the norm during recess, everyone was in their seat and all eyes were focused on the classroom door.

Arriving in his usual double time cadence, his momentum prevented the classroom behavior to register before his hand reached behind him to slam the door shut. Simultaneous with the door closing, the heavy map stand crashed onto the floor, narrowly missing Mr. Dongers' head.

Mr. Dongers was momentarily shaken and speechless. When he saw the string tied to the map stand, he became livid with rage.

"Are you guys crazy?"

No response from the class.

"Who did this?"

No response from the class.

"Do you realize that that map stand almost hit me?"

No response from the class.

Mr. Dongers realized that no one was going to own up.

"There will be repercussions. I promise you, there will be repercussions," Mr. Dongers said as he started to stomp out of the room.

The fallen map stand blocked the door. One of the boys lifted it out of the way, and Mr. Dongers left in a huff.

There was silence in the classroom until someone said, "I wouldn't be surprised if some of us get expelled for this."

More silence, until Klaus Wolfert, the goalie of the class soccer team said, "If we all take the blame, no one will be expelled.

They can't expel the whole class!"

The class remained silent until Mr. Vogt, their homeroom teacher entered. He was visibly agitated. "Mr. Dongers told me what happened here. I'm surprised that you would do something like this, and I'm ashamed of you. Mr. Dongers told me that he no longer wants to have anything to do with this class. It took all the persuasion I could muster to get him to continue teaching this class; however, not today. Mr. Dongers also told me that no one would admit responsibility, so I will ask the responsible party to come clean—now."

The whole class rose as one.

Mr. Vogt did not seem surprised. "Very well," he said, "if you wish to share the guilt, you will share the punishment. You will select one out of your midst who will see Mr. Dongers in his office and apologize for the class. All physical education classes and all soccer games are cancelled for the remainder of the semester. In their stead we will institute a rigorous study of German grammar—there will be spot quizzes at least once a week." Mr. Vogt's edict elicited moans and groans from the class.

"You brought this on yourselves, fellows," Mr. Vogt said.

"Since we still have about twenty minutes of this session remaining, we can have a short German grammar quiz right away!"

At the next English session, Mr. Dongers did not slam the door; once he was at his desk, he asked one of the boys in the front row to close it.

✚✚✚

One weekend, in the fall of 1942, Herbert was scheduled to attend his first Jungvolk camp. The camp was located in one of Hamburg's suburbs which could be reached by commuter train.

When Herbert asked his mother whether he could go, she countered with a question of her own, "What will you be doing at this camp?"

"The main purpose of this camp outing is to give those boys, who are ready to take the tests for the Jungvolk sports proficiency badge or the marksmanship proficiency badge, an opportunity to do so," Herbert answered.

"I thought you told me that you couldn't run fast enough or jump far enough to compete for the sports badge."

"I'll be competing for the sharpshooter's badge, Mama."

"Well, I suppose you can go, but make sure you don't shoot yourself in the foot," she said.

"Mama, we don't use firearms; we use air rifles and air pistols. We don't shoot bullets. We shoot pellets—like BBs."

"Even a BB can give you a nasty boo-boo," his mother admonished.

Herbert laughed and mimicked his mother, "BBs can give you boo-boos—I think that's clever, Mama."

"I'm not trying to be clever; I just don't want you to get hurt," she said, "and, remember never to point a gun at one of your friends or at anyone else."

Rolling his eyes and giving his mother an impatient look, Herbert commented, "Our instructors tell us that at every practice session—I'll remember."

"Just make sure you do," his mother said.

"Does this mean that I may go?"

"You may go."

On the first day of camp, Herbert did well enough to earn his sharpshooter's badge. That evening, when he was back in the large barracks that housed the boys, he conveyed the good news to his friend and classmate Horst Drossen. Horst was in the camp to complete the requirements for the sports proficiency badge.

"How did you do today?" Herbert asked his friend.

"I did all right in the 60-meter and the 100-meter dashes and the shot put, but I didn't quite make it in the long jump. I'll have to try again tomorrow," Horst answered.

Herbert asked, "You've met the requirement at an earlier meet, haven't you?"

"Yes, but there weren't any sanctioned judges present to record my jump."

"Did you complete the swimming requirements?" Herbert asked.

"Yeah, I completed those a long time ago."

"What are you going to do tomorrow?" Horst asked.

"The swimming trials were completed today. Tomorrow the pool will be open to everyone. If it's not too crowded, I'll swim in the pool, otherwise, I'll head for the lake."

When taps sounded, Herbert climbed up to the upper tier of the two-tiered bunk bed that he and Horst were sharing.

"Get a good night's sleep, so you can complete your badge requirements tomorrow," Herbert said.

"Yeah," came the voice from below.

About two hours later loud screaming reverberated from the other end of the barracks and awoke most of the boys.

"What's going on?" Herbert asked as he called out to Horst while leaning over the side of the bunk bed.

"It sounds like someone is being visited by the Holy Ghost," Horst replied.

Herbert climbed down from the upper tier and sat down beside Horst who had risen and was sitting on his tier of the bed. "The Holy Ghost?" Herbert asked, "What's that?"

Horst did not answer right away. He was looking toward

one of the bunks located along the opposite wall and toward the end of the building. The intermittent movement of a flashlight beam provided the silhouettes of several boys scuffling on one of the upper tier bunks. Someone was screaming and yelling, "Hey, fellows, it won't happen again, I promise." Then, the same someone pleading, "Aw, guys, don't do that!" More screaming and scuffling.

Horst turned toward Herbert and said, "That guy *is* being visited by the Holy Ghost!"

"What is the Holy Ghost?" Herbert asked again.

"It is a group of guys from his unit who are exacting punishment for some misdeed that caused the whole unit to suffer."

"Like what?" Herbert asked.

Horst responded with a question, "What happens when your unit is doing parade drills and one guy continuously screws up?"

"You do it again," Herbert said.

"Who is you?" Horst asked.

"Well, the whole unit does it again," Herbert corrected himself.

"Exactly. What happens if someone is guilty of a screw up and won't come forward and accept responsibility?"

"The whole unit gets punished."

"Right. If your whole unit gets punished on your account, you set yourself up for a visit by a bunch of guys." Horst said.

"What do they do?"

"They visit you in the dead of night. They turn you on your stomach, pull down your pajama pants, and mete out the punishment."

"What is the punishment?" Herbert asked.

"They apply shoe polish to your buttocks—with a shoe brush."

"Does it hurt?" Herbert asked.

"I don't know. I've never been visited by the Holy Ghost, but I'm sure that it doesn't help one's self-esteem."

"But why is this procedure called a visit by the Holy Ghost?"

"Because the visit is intended to put you back on the straight and narrow," Horst explained.

"Oh."

Soon the flashlight extinguished, and the scuffling stopped. The screams turned to sobs. A little later, the water from a shower on the far end of the hall could be heard.

"I guess He's trying to wash the shoe polish off his butt," Horst commented.

"Will it come off?" Herbert asked.

"Yeah. In four or five days, if he has good soap. If he has to use the synthetic crap that passes for soap nowadays, it will take twice as long."

"Well, we better get back to sleep. I've got a big day tomorrow," Horst commented.

Herbert climbed back up to the upper tier of the bunk bed.

He stayed awake for a long time wondering whether he had screwed up sufficiently to warrant a visit by the Holy Ghost. After he finally told himself that he didn't think so, he fell asleep.

✚ ✚ ✚

Herbert sat next to Horst Drossen on the commuter train as it made its way back to Hamburg on Sunday evening.

"So, how did you like your first camp outing?" Horst inquired.

"It was fine," Herbert answered, "especially since I've earned my marksmanship badge."

"Have you been on any of the one-day outings?" Horst asked.

"No. Where do you go on those outings?"

"We go to open areas outside the city limits, and the outings are usually scheduled on Saturdays, so as not to interfere with school commitments."

"And what is the object of those outings?"

"Usually you take part in a war game."

"Why do you have to go all the way out to the country to play the game?" Herbert asked.

"Because the game involves fighting, and it probably wouldn't be a good idea to have Jungvolk boys fighting one another on the city streets."

"What do you mean when you say 'fighting one another'? Do you knock each other bloody? Does the team with the most guys left standing win?"

Horst broke out laughing. "No no," he said. He thought a moment and then continued, "Let me try to give you a rundown of how the game is played: The game is normally carried out at the *Jungzug* (platoon) level against another platoon. Since the whole concept of the game is really a seek-and-destroy mission, the two platoons must first enter the area at locations unbeknownst to each other. The respective entry points into the area are therefore determined by volunteer leaders of non-participating platoons who also act as observers and judges, and—"

"OK," Herbert interrupted, "so the two platoons are now in the predetermined area, but each platoon does not know the other's location. How do they go about finding the other platoon?"

"They send out reconnaissance squads."

"What happens if the reconnaissance squads are unsuccessful?" Herbert asked.

"They usually are successful," Horst commented. "As I mentioned before, the game area is predetermined and is small enough that eventual detection is almost assured. You can't go and hide your platoon in the next county."

"OK, tell me about the destroy part," Herbert suggested.

"Before the game starts, the volunteer observers, whom I mentioned earlier, hand out a strand of wool to each platoon member, which he ties around his left wrist. The color of the strand identifies the platoon to which he belongs. If one platoon is identified by a red strand, the opposing platoon will be identified by a strand of different color.

The strand around the platoon member's wrist becomes his life preserver. In combat, the opposing team will try to tear that wool strand off his wrist, thereby putting him out of the game."

"What if the strand does not break?" Herbert asked.

"Oh, it will break. It will tear off without ever coming close to breaking skin—that's why they use a soft wool strand."

"Oh."

"Only wrestling moves are allowed, no fistfights or anything else," Horst continued.

"How is that rule enforced?" Herbert asked.

"Three ways: 1. You are honor bound to observe the rule. 2. The observers are watching, and you lose points if you break the rule. 3. Also, if you break the rule, you might have midnight visitors the next time you attend camp."

"The Holy Ghost?" Herbert asked.

Horst just nodded in assent.

✦ ✦ ✦

Two weeks later Herbert came home from a Jungvolk meeting and excitedly waved two pieces of cloth at his mother. Each of the pieces had a chevron embossed on them. Excitedly he said, "I've been promoted, Mama!"

Hertha put down the newspaper she had been reading and said, "That's nice." She then asked him, "Will I have to address you as captain now?"

"No, Mama, the promotion does not make me a captain. It's equivalent to being a private first class in the army. It puts me…it puts me one notch above the run-of-the-mill guys."

"Oh, you're telling me that these chevrons will separate you from the, as you put it, run-of-the-mill guys," she said.

"Well, my Jungvolk leader seems to think so."

"I see," his mother said. "Just make sure you don't become swellheaded because of what your Jungvolk leader thinks."

"Don't you think that I'm above average, Mama?"

Pulling him towards her and giving him a hug, Hertha said, "To me, you've always been above average. As a matter of fact, I would have to put five or six chevrons on you to show the world how I feel about you. I just don't think that emblems should be necessary to categorize you in your group of friends, because your actions alone will always determine how your friends rank you."

"How can we have a chain of command without emblems?"

Herbert asked.

"At your young age, you shouldn't need a chain of command," his mother replied.

"Will you sew them on my uniforms for me?"

"Yes, I'll sew them on. How do I orient the V? Should it be upside down or on its side?"

"None of the above, Mama, it has to be right side up."

Teasingly, his mother asked him, "If I put it upside down, would that mean a negative promotion—like a demotion?"

Herbert grimaced and replied, "No, it would mean that I was too dumb to be promoted in the first place."

They both laughed.

✦✦✦

Hertha was worried. By mid-November temperatures had dropped below normal, and Herbert had outgrown his winter coat. While stopping by to see her mother, Hertha brought up the subject.

"Won't your clothing allotment cover a new coat for the boy?" Mrs. Werner asked her daughter.

"No, it won't," Hertha replied. "I had to buy new stuff for Rosemarie before she left in the spring; Herbert's uniforms were an extra outlay that I had not anticipated, and all three of them are outgrowing their clothes faster than the allotments permit. The Party just doesn't seem to take these things into account when they establish the allowances."

"Your father has an old winter coat hanging in the closet that he doesn't wear anymore. Let's take a look at that," she said as she shuffled off to fetch it.

When she returned, Hertha took a good look at the coat.

It was grey with a herringbone pattern. "Father has had this coat for a long time, hasn't he?" she asked her mother when she noted the frayed sleeves.

"You know your father; he won't throw anything out unless he has to," Mrs. Werner commented.

Hertha brooded over the coat some more. It will be too big for him around the shoulders and especially around the girth, she said to herself. Finally she sighed and said,

"Well, beggars can't be choosey—I'll take it, Mother."

Herbert didn't like the coat. "It's pretty old, isn't it?" he asked his mother.

"Oh, honey, it's the best I can do. If you'd take better care of your uniforms, we would be able to get you something else. If nothing else, the coat will keep you nice and warm over the winter." his mother told him.

Herbert tried the coat on and felt like he had put on a tent with sleeves. He thought his mother was right when she said it would keep him warm; but he wondered whether she had considered the possibility that he might sweat to death.

"Can you at least move the buttons, so I won't look so fat?" he asked.

"I'll try to make it fit a little better," his mother assured him.

Herbert didn't blame his mother. It wasn't her fault that the stupid clothing allotments were insufficient.

When Herbert wore the coat to school for the first time, one of the boys, within earshot of some of his class members, said, "I like your coat. Are frayed sleeves the newest style?"

The boys comment angered Herbert, but he controlled himself. He merely said, "Back in the United States I would not be wearing a coat with frayed sleeves. If I were back in the United States, my father could buy me half a dozen new coats, but in this country..." He had wanted to end his sentence with: he can't even get me one coat. But, remembering his father's warning about speaking out too freely, he did not.

The boy who had made the comment apparently got the drift, because, in a conciliatory tone, he said, "I'm sorry. I wasn't thinking."

"Forget it," Herbert replied.

Chapter 26

Toward the end of November 1942, the OKW reported that the German Sixth Army had been encircled at Stalingrad.

The official line was that they would be provided by air-lift until rescue forces would break the encirclement.

Entering the Christmas season, the holiday spirit of much of the populace was subdued, because 250,000 German troops were still trapped in the cauldron that Stalingrad had become. The relief effort appeared to be failing. The Christmas spirit for the Klug family was also subdued, mainly because Walther would not be home for the holidays.

In early February 1943 the OKW reported that Stalingrad had fallen and announced a three day period of national mourning. The German army had suffered its first major defeat of World War II.

+++

Several weeks later, Hertha and her two youngest children were at the Hamburg main railroad station waiting for the train that was bringing Rosemarie back home from her year-long sojourn at a farm in northern Germany. While they waited on the train platform in early afternoon, Herbert noticed that the station was bustling with activity. Most of the people crowding the various platforms wore the uniforms of one of the three service branches: *Luftwaffe, Kriegsmarine,* and *Heer.* He also saw some soldiers clad in the khaki colors of the *Afrika Korp.* Herbert wondered whether they would be returning to Africa, in view of the fact that Rommel had been forced into retreat after his early successes.

Military police, in groups of two, could be seen on all the platforms. They were disparagingly referred to as "chain dogs" by service personnel, because the breastplate that identified them as military police hung from a chain they wore around their necks. The chain dogs were randomly checking soldier's travel orders.

Looking up, he again noticed the sky through the grid-like structure of the arched roof of the station which had drawn his attention when his family first arrived from Cuxhaven. At the time, each grid had been closed with a pane of glass to guard against the elements, while maintaining an open air appearance. Now many of the grids had had their panes completely broken out or reduced to shards, due to the impact of flak or bomb fragments during the preceding months.

After a while, the train from Flensburg pulled into the station. Hertha was the first one to see Rosemarie, who was alighting from the train about two cars from where they were standing.

Hertha ran toward her daughter with Herbert, holding Hannelore by the hand, in pursuit. Hertha embraced her daughter and said, "Welcome home, dear!" Putting her daughter at arm's length, she said, "Here, let me take a look at you." Looking her daughter up and down, Hertha said, "My, you've come a long way toward turning into a young lady in the year that you have been gone."

Rosemarie smiled and gave her mother a kiss.

"Did you bring me anything?" Hannelore asked.

"I brought you all some nice smoked ham—straight from the farm," Rosemarie said, as she hugged her siblings.

"Did you have a good trip?" Hertha asked, as they prepared to leave the train station.

Rosemarie just nodded in response to her mother's question. Herbert picked up his sister's suitcase, and they headed for the trolley stop.

✚✚✚

After they returned to the apartment, Hertha placed a cake that she had baked on the kitchen table and prepared a pot of the ubiquitous synthetic coffee for the two older children and herself. While the children were seating themselves around the table and she was pouring a glass of skimmed milk for Hannelore, she said, "It's good to have you back home, honey." Then she asked, "You are glad to be back home, aren't you?"

"Yes, Mama, I'm very glad to be back home; as a matter of fact, if I had not been scheduled to come home at this time, I probably would have run away from that place."

"More trouble with the farmer's wife, eh?" Hertha queried.

"The trouble was a figment of her imagination, Mama! She kept harping about my talking to the two workers who had been assigned to help the farmer with his chores."

"You mean the two prisoners of war that you mentioned in your letters, don't you?"

"Yes Mama. I was only trying to treat them as I would any other human being. She treats the farm animals with more respect than she does those prisoners!"

"It sounds to me like things came to a head between the two of you," her mother suggested.

"Yes Mama, the situation did come to a head. One day, after she had again chided me for conversing with the prisoners, I got angry and I told her where I came from, folks do not treat one another in that way. When she sarcastically asked from where I did come, I told her that I was born in the United States and that I did not arrive in Germany until I was twelve years old. I told her that in the United States Germans, Poles, and Russians live amicably side by side."

"What did she say to that?" Herbert interrupted Romi.

"She didn't have a chance to say anything, because I wasn't finished yet. I told her that if the average German was anything like her, I would not want to remain in Germany once the war was over, that I would surely want to return to the United States."

"Uh, 'uh!" Hertha interjected, anticipating that the other shoe was about to fall.

Romi said nothing for a few moments. Then breaking into a sob, she asked, "Do you know what she told me? She told me that if I persisted in talking to them, I would be taking my meals with the prisoners in the bunkhouse rather than at the family dinner table." Romi's sobs broke into tears as she said this. "Mama, I wasn't making goo-goo eyes at them. I was merely trying to be friendly."

"So, what did you do?" Hertha asked.

"I took my meals in the bunkhouse."

Her mother reached across the table to hold her hands and said, "Good for you, honey, but you should have mentioned all this in your letters. I would have had a few choice words to offer that woman."

After Romi regained her composure she said, "It wouldn't have done any good. At best, she would have ignored you—at worst, she might have gotten the Party involved, which means that they probably would have charged you with abetting communicating with the enemy or some other crazy thing. I didn't want to take that risk."

"Honey, you shouldn't have worried about me; you had your own problems to face. But don't you think that she was trying to be conciliatory; after all, she did give you that ham to take home with you."

"She didn't give me that ham," Romi said resolutely. "The ham was given to me by the lady of the adjacent farm."

"Mama was right," Herbert chimed in.

"What are you talking about?" his mother asked.

"Well, you had her pegged right after the first time this problem came up in Romi's letters."

"What did I say?" Hertha asked.

"You called her an old bat."

Romi forced a smile and said, "Mama was right."

That evening, at 11:30 P.M., the air raid sirens sounded.

The children had gone to bed earlier, but Hertha was still up. She helped Hannelore get her clothes on, while the older two got dressed. When they were picking up their suitcases, Romi paused for a moment, and pointing at Hannelore, asked, "Mama, why does this little child have to run for her life on so many a night?"

Hertha was taken aback by the question, because she did not know whether Romi was referring to the cruelty of modern warfare or whether she was faulting her for the family's return to Germany. Either way she could not answer the question. Instead, she bypassed it by saying, "Hurry up children; we have to go."

As they were running toward the shelter in the school basement, Herbert commented, "Welcome back to the war, Romi."

✚ ✚ ✚

By March of 1943 Germany was well into the fourth year of war. Rationing was getting ever tighter, and on the home front the bombing raids were becoming more devastating.

At the beginning of the war, the RAF was sending twin-engine Bristol-Blenheim bombers over the German coastal cities. By mid 1942 the RAF was dispatching four-engine Lancaster and Stirling bombers that could strike deep into the German heartland with bomb loads that dwarfed those of the aircraft used in the earlier stages of the war.

As a consequence, the evacuation of school-age children from threatened urban centers, which was started earlier in the war, increased dramatically.

Children now were being evacuated not only to nearby outlying areas but also to areas beyond the German border.

Evacuation usually was done on a school class basis, with two teachers per class being assigned to accompany the students to their new environment. The teachers were given living quarters, and the students were distributed among families who, by prior arrangement, had agreed to take them in. Male classes with students between the ages of ten and fourteen also had two Jungvolk leaders assigned to them. The evacuees generally would remain in their assigned environment for six to seven months before returning home.

✚ ✚ ✚

One afternoon in mid-March of 1943, Herbert came home from school, and after he had joined his mother in the kitchen, he told her, "Mr. Vogt told us today that our class has been selected to be evacuated to Hungary."

"To Hungary? Why all the way to Hungary?" Hertha interjected as she interrupted her cooking chores and sat down beside him.

"I don't know. Maybe the government is running out of places to send kids."

"Yes, but Hungary—you won't be able to understand them. In case you have forgotten, people in Hungary speak Hungarian," his mother reminded him.

"Well, we can quickly pick up important expressions such as good morning, good night, please, and thank you. I only hope that the Hungarians don't have the rationing that we have, because in that case, learning to tell them that I am hungry would be a useless exercise," Herbert commented.

Hertha had to laugh. "Honey, I'm sure you won't be going hungry. Although Hungary is allied with Germany, the country has essentially been untouched by the war. I would guess that they do not have any rationing at all," she said.

"I hope you are right, Mama." He then told her, "One of my classmates talked to a boy whose class just returned from Hungary. They were evacuated to a place near Lake Balaton. They were housed on big estates and were allowed to ride horses and stuff like that."

"And you would like that?" Hertha asked her son.

Herbert looked at her and shrugged his shoulders.

His mother mimicked his shrug and asked, "Does that mean yes?"

This time he nodded and said "I suppose so, but I'm just getting used to being back home, after having been with the Lienhofs for almost a year and a half."

Hertha gave him a hug and said, "I realize that it was tough for you kids to be away from home for so long, and I am sorry." She hesitated for a moment and then said, "Your mother picked a bad time to come back here."

Herbert didn't know what to reply, so he just shrugged some more.

"Are most of your classmates anxious to go?" Hertha asked.

Herbert nodded.

"What would happen if you don't go with them?" his mother asked.

"I would have to transfer to another school, because Mr. Vogt and another teacher are going with the class, and the school doesn't have replacement teachers available for a handful of students that decides not to go."

"You like Mr. Vogt, don't you?" Hertha asked.

"Yeah, he's a good guy."

"Given your choice, would you rather go with your classmates and Mr. Vogt or transfer to another school?"

"I'd rather go with my classmates."

"Well, then it's settled," Hertha said. "When is all this supposed to happen?"

"Sometime in May."

"And what do I have to do?" she asked.

"You have to let Mr. Vogt know that I have your permission to go."

"I'll let him know in a day or two," his mother said, and, "Right now I have to concentrate on getting dinner ready. You can stick around and give me a hand if you like."

"Do I have to?"

"No, you don't have to."

✚ ✚ ✚

On a Monday evening, while the Klugs were having dinner, Herbert advised his mother and sisters that the Jungvolk had another exercise planned for the following Saturday.

"Will this be another weekend outing?" his mother asked.

"No, it will only run through Saturday," Herbert answered.

"What is the purpose of the exercise?" Romi asked.

"Three guys from my platoon will be acting as would-be saboteurs, while all the guys from another platoon will try to keep us from planting a simulated bomb on a predetermined objective, known to both platoons. I have been selected to be one of the three guys," Herbert said.

"Three guys against a whole platoon does not seem fair," Romi countered.

"It's fair enough. We get ten points each time one of our guys is successful; the guys from the other platoon get points according to how soon they can intercept us on any one of three predetermined routes to the objective, and we have to traverse the route on foot. Whoever gets the most points wins," Herbert explained.

"What is the objective?" Romi asked him.

"Our objective is the canal bridge on the Muehlendamm, and we have to plant the simulated bomb while remaining undetected."

"Well, that shouldn't be too difficult. Just go there after dark. With the blackout, nobody will see you," Romi ventured.

"The exercise has to be carried out during daylight hours, smarty-pants," Herbert informed her.

"In that case I wish you lots of luck," Romi offered.

"My Jungvolk leader thinks we might have a good chance, if we can come up with some good disguises."

Romi perked up immediately, "A disguise—that's it!"

After a moment's thought she cried out, "I have just what you need for a good disguise," as she jumped up while nearly upsetting her dinner plate. She was halfway to the children's bedroom when Hertha intervened, "Romi, come back and finish your dinner. Don't get yourself all in a tizzy over this silly exercise."

Romi was still excited as she reluctantly sat back down.

"Mama, don't you see? I've thought of a good disguise for him. With some of my old things, we can dress him up as a girl!" she exclaimed.

Herbert rolled his eyes as he heard his sister's suggestion. "I don't want to be disguised as a girl—it will never work."

"But it will!" Romi said. "You don't shave yet. Your cheeks are still as smooth as a baby's butt. You won't look like Miss America, but I can make you look like a girl.

"Your disguise will be perfect, because I think it will be unexpected."

"Yeah," little Hannelore chimed in. With a giggle, she added, "I'll be able to tell everyone that you are my other sister."

Herbert gave his kid sister a sullen look.

Hertha looked at her son and said, "I think her idea might just work. Just how are you thinking of planting your simulated bomb without being detected? Surely the defenders will have someone close to the bridge in the event that you should get that far. And by the way, what is this simulated bomb?"

"It's just a marked brick. I'm thinking of putting the brick into a paper bag and adding some groceries on top.

"Once on the bridge, I will feign that the bag got away from me and let some of the groceries drop out. While picking up the groceries and putting them back into the bag, I will surreptitiously retrieve the brick, and place it under the bridge railing," Herbert explained.

"Whoa! Whoa!" Hertha said. "I don't have any groceries to play games with; as a matter of fact, I don't have enough groceries to feed you with. I'll tell you what, I'll give you some turnips that you can put in your bag. We have plenty of those at the moment."

Hertha paused for a moment. Then she said, "I think your plan is a good one, and I also think Romi's idea has merit."

Addressing her son, she said, "Why don't you give it a try?"

Herbert frowned and fiddled with his coffee cup for a while, but he finally said, "Oh, all right."

Romi announced her approval with a loud, "Yeah!"

Holding up her hands, Hertha said, "Let's not get too excited now. We'll work on this tomorrow afternoon, after you kids get home from school."

+++

When Herbert returned home from school the following afternoon, Romi had already laid out the clothing that would constitute his disguise. When he looked down on his bed, he saw a blouse and skirt, a jacket and scarf, and a pair of white stockings.

Romi greeted him with, "Try these things on, so that we can see how they will fit."

"Do I have to do that right now?" Herbert asked.

"The sooner, the better," she said. "Remember that you'll have to come up with an alternate plan if this does not work out."

Herbert took another look at the items Romi had laid out. "What is the scarf for? It isn't that cold out."

"We will use the scarf to hide your short hair by wrapping it around your head to form a turban."

When he gave her an incredulous look, she said, "Don't worry. Because of the scarcity of ladies hats nowadays, a lot of women are wearing scarves around their heads. You will be right in style. As a matter of fact, scarves are the current rage. Try these things on while I hunt for some shoes in the hall closet."

When she came back, he had put on the skirt and blouse and the thigh length white stockings.

"How do I hold these stockings up?"

"Oh, I forgot something," Romi answered.

Herbert scowled as she rummaged around in one of the vanity drawers on the girl's side of the children's bedroom.

"Here, this will hold them up," she said, as she handed him a stocking girdle.

"What's this?" he asked.

"It's a girdle."

"I'm not going to wear a girdle!" he cried out.

Herbert's outburst was loud enough for Hertha to stick her head into the doorway to inquire what was going on.

"She says I have to wear a girdle," Herbert wailed.

"What's so bad about that? We women wear them all the time."

"That's different, Mama," the boy said.

"Well, I suppose it is," his mother acknowledged. After some thought, she said, "I have some large rubber bands that you can use to hold those stockings up. Will that be OK?"

"Yeah."

When he sat down on his bed and attempted to put Romi's low-heeled shoes on, they turned out to be too small.

"Mama, I think you wear a half size larger shoe than I do. Do you have an old pair that he can try on?"

Hertha soon came back with a pair of her shoes. She sat down next to him on the bed while he tried them on.

"These fit pretty good," he said, still sitting on the bed.

"Well, get up now, and let's see you walk," his mother suggested.

Herbert stumbled along the length of the bedroom several times until Romi said, "Herbert, you're a girl now. Girls don't march; they take smaller steps. You have to take smaller steps."

After he tried this several times, Romi said, "OK, you're going to have to practice that between now and Saturday. Now let's put your turban on."

Herbert sat quietly, except for an occasional, "Ouch!" when she poked him with a bobby pin. When Romi was finished, she stepped back to evaluate her handiwork. "I think he looks cute," she said to her mother.

"On Saturday I'll apply just a little bit of lip rouge, and he'll look even cuter."

Herbert's demeanor suggested that he still did not fully share her enthusiasm.

After Romi got him all dolled up on Saturday morning, his mother said, "If you were to look into a mirror and ask, 'Mirror, mirror, on the wall, who has the best disguise of all?' it would reply, 'You do.'"

"I hope the mirror is right, Mama." he retorted. As he kissed her goodbye, he asked, "Why the reference to a fairy tale?"

"Because I can't believe that what you are going to do is for real," she answered.

Herbert shrugged and left.

As she closed the door behind him, Romi said, "If he for any reason stops concentrating on his walking, he is a dead duck."

"I was thinking the same thing," Hertha responded.

Take short steps, take short steps, Herbert kept repeating as he walked to the entry point of his predetermined route to the bridge. He was on the lookout for members of the opposing platoon who would be in uniform and bent on intercepting him.

On the second block into his route he saw two Jungvolk boys on the opposite side of the street dribbling a soccer ball back and forth. The boys looked up briefly as Herbert approached, but they did not challenge him. Herbert's confidence grew after this first encounter. Only eight more blocks to go, he told himself.

About half way into his route, he saw three uniformed boys up ahead. With some misgiving, he realized that they were on the same side of the street. He decided not to cross over to the other side since that might evoke suspicion, but he became very apprehensive. He remembered what Romi had told him if someone were to address him: Don't open your mouth—you will give yourself away. Just show your condescension by giving your head a haughty tilt away from the speaker. He remembered her demonstration of a haughty tilt of the head. As he passed the three boys, they came up with some remarks. Not even listening to what they were saying, Herbert gave his head the haughtiest tilt he could muster. He immediately wondered whether his reaction had been overdone, since it was not at all a normal response for him, but the ensuing silence put him at ease and increased his confidence level by another notch.

Herbert passed another two boys in uniform without any trouble, before the little bridge came into view.

As he approached the bridge, he saw two Jungvolk boys leaning against the railing at the center of the bridge.

Also on the bridge, walking toward him, was an elderly lady. Now comes the hard part, he thought. He was almost on the bridge when the elderly lady was about to walk past him, but she stopped and asked him the way to the Schroeder Strasse. Herbert was nonplussed since he couldn't very well respond with a haughty tilt of the head.

Just when he had finished giving her the directions while trying to keep his voice about an octave higher than normal, he heard one of the boys on the bridge yell, "Let's get him!"

Hearing the commotion behind her, the elderly lady turned around and saw two Jungvolk boys assaulting the young girl to whom she had just spoken. She retraced her steps screaming,

"You louts, leave that girl alone," and started to pound the two boys with her handbag. None of the combatants paid any heed to the elderly lady as she continued to flog the two boys. Herbert was successful in tearing off one boy's life preserver—the woolen strand around his left wrist—thereby neutralizing him, but he was soon overcome by the other boy, even though his assailant's head was bearing the brunt of the lady's handbag.

To reassure the elderly lady, one of the boys tore Herbert's scarf off of his head and said, "See, he's not a girl." The lady shook her head. As she walked away, she could be heard muttering, "What is this younger generation coming to?"

Herbert had dropped his bag at the beginning of the confrontation, and his turnips were scattered all over the bridge. He asked the two boys, "What gave me away? Was it my walk?"

The taller of the two looked at him and said, "The old lady was your downfall. When you were done talking to her, you bowed. Girls don't bow, girls curtsy."

During the tussle, Herbert had been knocked down to the pavement, and the rubber band on his right leg had broken.

Now the back of his skirt was muddy, and the stocking was draped around his ankle.

When he got home, his mother and sisters immediately knew that he had run into trouble. After he had given them the particulars, Hertha said, "I think the old woman was the most sensible of the lot of you." Then she asked, "Were any of the other boys successful?"

"Nah, we got skunked."

"Gee," Romi said, "you came so close. Next time—"

Herbert cut her off with, "Forget it. There will not be a next time; I absolutely refuse to learn how to curtsy."

Chapter 27

In mid-April of 1943, Herbert was a confirmand in the Lutheran church where Romi had been confirmed about a year earlier.

He had grumbled a lot about having to attend the Sunday school classes, but he remembered how his mother had insisted, and had said, "Although I do not attend church very often, I want you to be confirmed to enable you to apply for church membership in the future, should you so choose. Confirmation is a prerequisite for membership, and if you are not confirmed now, you probably never will be."

Several weeks later, Herbert excitedly told his mother that his class would be evacuated to Hungary about the middle of May.

"That won't give us much time to get your stuff together," Hertha said.

Herbert shrugged and then said, "Guess what, Mama. We won't be taking the train all the way to Hungary."

"What are the powers that be going to do? Are they going to have you march into Hungary on foot?"

"No! No! No! We will get off the train at Passau in Bavaria and stay there overnight. The next morning we will board a riverboat that will take us from Passau all the way to the Hungarian capital of Budapest. Our teacher, Mr. Vogt, says that we will spend two days on the boat."

"Will you boys stay on the boat overnight?"

"No, the boat will dock in Vienna at the end of the first day, and we will spend the night at some youth hostel."

"Will all the boys leave the boat in Budapest?"

"Yeah."

"Does that mean that you all will be staying in, or in the vicinity of, Budapest?" his mother asked.

"No. From Budapest we will be sent to different parts of the country on a class basis."

"What part will be your class' destination?"

Herbert drew up his shoulders and said, "I don't know. I hope it will be one of those where we will be able to do some horseback riding."

"I can understand that you would like that, but just remember that you are not going there to be doing a lot of horsing around."

"I'll remember, Mama."

+++

On an afternoon several days later, Hertha suggested that Hannelore pay her grandmother a visit. Hertha's suggestion was a pretext, because she wanted to talk to the two older children alone.

When Hannelore had left, Hertha called the children into the kitchen. "What's up, Mama? Did you get another letter from Papa?" Romi asked, after they had seated themselves around the kitchen table.

"No," Hertha said. "I want to tell you about the bad news Miss Brund just received."

"You mean the old spinster lady that lives in the other apartment on this floor? What happened? Did someone die?" Herbert inquired.

Hertha appeared lost in thought when she said, "No, no one died. Miss Brund told me that her nephew, who is half Jewish, got his notice for deportation to the East. I believe he has already left."

"Why is he being deported?" Romi asked.

"Apparently it is part of Hitler's grand plan. When Tante Emi was here to visit your grandmother in 1940, she told me that Hitler had instituted many restrictions against the Jews way back in 1935, and now, it seems, he is deporting them."

"Where is the East?" Herbert asked.

"Rumor has it that it is the eastern part of Poland."

"Is that where Papa is stationed?" Herbert asked.

"No. Your father is stationed in western Poland, the part of Germany that was ceded to Poland after the First World War and that again became part of Germany after the Polish campaign in 1939."

"Didn't the German people object when all these restrictions were imposed on the Jews?" Romi asked.

"I guess they could no longer object. By then, I suppose Hitler was already governing with an iron fist." After a pause, Hertha continued, "If they could not object then, they certainly cannot object now—if they do, they too are likely to disappear."

"What happens to the Jews after they are deported?" Romi asked.

"According to the Party line, they are being resettled," Hertha replied. She shrugged and added, "That is all that anybody hears."

They sat in silence for a while. Then Hertha said, "Poor Miss Brund—she was so sad when she told me what had happened. I want you to be as kind to her as you possibly can, and don't tell your little sister about this; she is already exposed to all the fear she can handle whenever the air raid sirens sound."

✦ ✦ ✦

The main railroad station, as usual, was bustling with activity, when Hertha and the children arrived on the day of Herbert's departure to Hungary. Although they had been told on which station platform Herbert was to report, that information became superfluous, since the milling throng of about three hundred Jungvolk boys on one of the platforms immediately pointed out the assembly area.

The various teachers had spaced themselves along the platform. Each of them held up a sign which bore the name of the school they were representing to guide the boys to their respective class assembly area.

When they reached Mr. Vogt, Hertha said, "Good morning, Mr. Vogt. Have you got all your charges assembled?"

Mr. Vogt smiled and replied, "Good morning Mrs. Klug. Except for one or two strays, I believe they are all here."

"Won't the boarding be somewhat chaotic, once the train has pulled into the station?" Hertha asked.

"Not at all, Mrs. Klug. We have made arrangements with the railroad people beforehand. They have reserved three carriages for the evacuees and have told us exactly where the three carriages will come to a stop. Therefore, to effect a smooth boarding process, all we teachers had to do was to space ourselves along the platform according to previously arranged carriage assignments. My class has been assigned the first four compartments of the second carriage. I would be very much surprised if the carriage door is not within one meter of where I expect it to be, once the train has come to a halt."

"That is wonderful, Mr. Vogt," Hertha exclaimed.

She and her children then stood aside to let several other parents, who had gathered close by, exchange a few words with the teacher.

As they stood there, Herbert felt a certain ambivalence.

He was not all that eager to be leaving home again, yet he was somewhat excited about visiting another country with his classmates.

After the train had pulled into the station, Herbert kissed his mother and sisters goodbye and boarded the train along with the other boys. Herbert's friend, Karl Rothman, was just ahead of him as they entered the car.

"Just let's place our suitcases on two adjacent seats and then we'll go back out to the aisle until the train pulls out of the station."

Since incoming traffic was coming from both ends of the car where the doors were located, Herbert said, "We need to head toward the center of the car where traffic will be minimal."

Having reached the center of the car, Herbert opened the aisle window and yelled, "Mama, we are over here!"

Hertha and the girls heard him and moved close to the window. Karl had also called out to his parents.

The boys engaged in small talk with the respective parents, then, amidst well wishes, the train started to ease out of the station. Herbert noticed the tears in his mother's eyes. She stood still, while Romi and Hannelore moved alongside the train until it began to pick up speed, and soon they were out of sight.

Herbert and Karl remained at the window, while the other boys, who had shared it, retreated to their compartment.

Soon someone from the adjacent compartment cried out, "Hey, we're blowing away in here. Close that window!"

Karl responded with, "Close the compartment door if the breeze is bothering you."

The rumbling of the closing door ended the interchange.

"Are you excited?" Karl asked Herbert.

Herbert shrugged.

"I'm excited," Karl announced. "I've lived in Hamburg all my life, and this will be my first extended trip away from home."

Herbert looked at his friend. He is as short in stature as I am, Herbert thought. He wondered whether being the smallest guys in their class had anything to do with their becoming good friends. In grade school they had been called Max and Moritz after the two ne'er-do-well boy characters in a German comic periodical. He, Herbert, was thought to resemble Max because Max had dark hair and brown eyes, while Karl was thought to look like the blond and blue-eyed Moritz. Additionally, Herbert's frame was in keeping with Max's stockier build, while Karl's physique resembled that of the skinny Moritz.

"How fast do you think this train is going?" Karl asked as the north German countryside seemed to whisk by.

"Probably between eighty and eighty-five kilometers per hour," Herbert replied.

"I hope we'll get to stay on one of those estates where they have a lot of horses," Karl said.

"Yeah, me too."

With some trepidation Karl said, "I've never been on horseback before."

"Don't worry. I'll teach you how."

Surprised, Karl asked, "Do you know how to ride a horse?"

"I've ridden a horse on a merry-go-round."

They both laughed.

After they had been at the aisle window for about two hours, Mr. Vogt stopped by and said, "You two better go back into your compartment. You'll be getting some sandwiches and something to drink pretty soon."

The boys went back to the compartment that they were sharing with eight other guys from their class. Herbert hoisted the suitcases he and Karl had left on the seats into the luggage bin.

"Where have you guys been?" someone asked.

"We were taking in the scenery," Karl answered.

When a train steward brought sandwich packs and soft drinks, he was greeted with boisterous approval, but the noise quickly abated as the boys focused on their lunch.

After lunch, Herbert turned to Karl and said, "You told me once that you know how to play chess."

Karl nodded concurrence.

"This would be a good opportunity to teach me how to play," Herbert suggested.

"How are we going to do that? We don't have a chess set; besides, with the train rocking back and forth, the chess pieces will be jumping all over the place."

Herbert smiled and said, "I'll show you how we can do that."

He got up and pulled his suitcase out of the overhead luggage bin. After he had set the suitcase on his lap, he opened it and pulled out a box about the size of a small book.

Herbert waved the little box at Karl and said, "My mother bought this for me. It is a travel set."

Opening the box he said, "See, it has the required checkered squares, and the chess pieces are stored in the rectangular recesses on opposite ends of the box."

Karl took a look and immediately noticed that each square had a hole in its center and that the bottom of each piece was provided with a pin that fit the hole in the squares.

"Hey, that's pretty neat," he exclaimed.

"Watch," Herbert said, I'll show you something even neater."

He placed three pieces on three of the squares and closed the box. He turned the box upside down and rattled it back and forth. Then turning the box right side up again, he removed the cover. The three pieces were still in place and all the unused pieces were still in their respective recesses.

"See," Herbert said, "you can start a game, then close the lid and send the box to China and back. Once the box is back, you can resume the game. All the pieces will still be in place!"

Herbert's demonstration had evoked the interest of several of the other boys in the compartment.

"Let's see your game," someone said. "Pass it around."

"I'll pass the box around, but I'll hold on to the chess pieces. By the time the game gets passed around, one of you clowns is liable to have dropped it, and I might wind up missing some of the game pieces," Herbert responded.

When the box was returned to him, Herbert said, "OK, Karl, show me how it's done."

The following hour was spent with Karl explaining the rudiments of the game.

"Let's start a game," Karl suggested after he had shown Herbert how the various pieces were allowed to move.

The two boys sitting opposite Karl and Herbert immediately started to kibitz.

"Move your knight out," one of them would say.

"No, no. Get your bishop into action," the other one would advise.

Herbert would accept the advice of the kibitzers when they were in agreement, but he alternated between them whenever they disagreed. He and the kibitzers promptly lost the first two games.

During the third game, Herbert concluded that Horst Drossen, one of the kibitzers, was the sharper of the two; consequently, he followed his prompting only. Karl was almost forced into a draw, but he prevailed, thereby winning his third game in a row.

Pulling the remaining game pieces off the playing board and putting them into their respective storage recesses, Herbert put the cover back on the box and said to Karl, "Well, I now know of a good pastime for us on a rainy afternoon."

"What would that be?"

Herbert laughed as he put the chess set back into his suitcase and said, "You'll have the opportunity to teach me how to play this game."

"Yeah, we can do that," Karl responded, as Herbert lofted his suitcase back into the luggage bin.

"Want to go back out into the aisle a while?" Karl asked.

Herbert nodded.

Looking out the aisle window, the boys noted the long shadows of late afternoon and the rolling hills that had replaced the north German flatlands.

From the far end of the car they heard the opening and closing of the teacher's compartment door, and they saw Mr. Vogt approaching. When he joined them at the window, Karl asked, "Where are we now?"

"We are in Bavaria. Those hills you are looking at are the foothills of the Alps. We should be stopping in Regensburg any minute now."

About fifteen minutes later, the train eased into the Regensburg main station.

When the train left the station, it did not accelerate in the normal manner, but moved forward at a slow pace.

After about five minutes, the train stopped and then started up again, in the opposite direction!

"Did the engineer forget something in Regensburg?" Karl asked of no one in particular, just before the train stopped again.

Mr. Vogt said, "No, no. The train we were on is the mainliner to Munich. Since our destination is Passau, not Munich, our cars had to be decoupled and will be switched to a local line. At the moment, we have been shunted onto a siding."

About fifteen minutes later, some jostling felt in the three evacuee cars indicated that the cars had been coupled to the local train. Shortly thereafter, the reconstituted train began to move off the siding.

It was almost dark when the train pulled into the Passau railroad station. The train intercom advised that the evacuees were to take their luggage and to load it onto the two trucks that were parked in the station square and to assemble on a class basis in march formation in the square.

When Herbert and Karl had stowed their suitcases on one of the trucks, they tried to locate their assembly area, as were several hundred other boys.

"There's Gunther, our Jungvolk leader, on the other side of the square," Karl said. "He is beckoning us to join him."

"Why are you assembling us way over here?" Herbert asked.

"Because it would take us at least twice as long if we were to try to position ourselves amidst that chaos at the station entrance. We'll assemble here and then wait until we're told where to fall in when it is time to move out."

A Party member in SA uniform had been assigned to show the recent arrivals the way to the military barracks where they would be spending the night. He apparently was impressed with the way Gunther had assembled his group in the least amount of time. The SA man walked up to Gunther and said, "I'd like your group to head up the column. Tell the other Jungvolk leaders the order you want them to fall in when you start to move out."

With Gunther and the SA man leading, the column soon got underway. Herbert was marching alongside Karl at the tail end of the first group.

"What happened to the teachers?" Herbert asked Karl.

"Didn't you notice when we put our luggage on the trucks?" Karl asked. "They got to ride in the three cars that were parked behind the trucks."

Having marched about a mile, the column arrived at the

military barracks. Two classes were to share each of the five buildings the SA man assigned to the boys.

Before he let the Jungvolk leaders dismiss them, he pointed to a nearby large building and said, "The commissary is over there. Dinner will be dished out starting in about an hour. I suggest that you go over there two classes at a time in fifteen minute intervals so that we don't overwhelm the help by having about three hundred guys queuing up all at once. I'll leave it up to the Jungvolk leaders to determine who goes when."

After dinner, Karl and Herbert and Horst Drossen headed back to their barrack.

"I hope I don't get seasick on that boat tomorrow," Herbert worried out loud.

"You won't get seasick on a river boat," Horst reassured him.

"I got seasick on the steamer that brought me to Germany," Herbert said.

"You were crossing an ocean then," Horst declared. "Trust me, you won't get seasick."

Back at their barrack, they chatted until a wall-speaker intoned a warning that the lights would be extinguished in another ten minutes, whereupon they eased themselves into their respective bunk beds.

Herbert was one of the first to make use of the shower stalls the next morning. Upon viewing the single faucet, he surmised that he probably would not want to dawdle while showering that morning. His conjecture was correct; the water was ice cold. Knowing that his body would never adjust to the water temperature, he quickly cleansed himself, all the while prancing from one foot to the other. When he was done, he turned the water off and dried his goose-bumped body. Still shivering, he made sure that he wrapped his towel around his waist because he thought he might be exposed to howls of laughter if any of the incoming boys noticed that the cold water had shrunk a certain body part to almost nothing.

+++

After the boys had breakfast, they were told to load their luggage pieces back onto the two trucks and then were marched to the boat landings alongside the Danube River.

As they approached the river, they could see that five boats were tied up at the landings. Once the column had stopped and the at ease order was issued, the boys waited for the next instructions.

"It looks like we'll be split up two classes per boat, the same way we were split up among the five barracks last night," Karl commented.

"Yeah, it would be standing room only, if we were all squeezed onto just one of those boats," Herbert commented.

He noted that all five boats were of similar construction. They all had large aft decks that were provided with tables and chairs, similar to sightseeing boats. The decks were made rainproof by overhanging tarpaulins, which were attached to the top of poles that stood about seven foot high along the perimeter of the aft decks.

The Jungvolk leaders soon advised their classes which boat they would be boarding. Gunther also told his charges that, if they could not under any circumstances wear the same underwear two days in a row, they should open their luggage and stuff an extra pair in their pants pocket before the luggage was stored in the hold of the boat. When he got some quizzical looks from some of the boys, he told them that, once in the hold, they would not see their suitcases again until they disembarked in Budapest.

Because of Gunther's underlying sarcasm, opening a suitcase now would risk appearing prissy; therefore, none of the suitcases were opened before they went into the hold.

As the boarding process was completed for any boat, that boat would cast off independently of the others.

✚ ✚ ✚

Karl, Herbert, and Horst sat on the aft deck area for a while but soon got up to explore the rest of the boat.

They wound up at the bow of the boat, from where they watched patches of forest alternating with cultivated fields seemingly glide by on either side of the river as the boat moved downstream.

"How far could we go in this tub?" Herbert asked.

"We could go almost anywhere in the world, assuming that the boat is seaworthy," Karl piped up.

"How is that possible?" Herbert queried.

"Well, the river runs into the Black Sea, and from there you could reach the Mediterranean and then the Atlantic Ocean. You could also reach any of the Soviet Republics that border on the Black Sea, if you could dodge the Russian Black Sea fleet," Karl answered.

"Could we link up with some of the German forces that are now in Russia?" Horst asked.

"Sure. We could go to the Crimea," Karl asserted.

"We would not only have to dodge the fleet but also have to convince the Russians to occasionally sell us some diesel fuel, wouldn't we?" Horst asked with a smirk.

"Look, Herbert asked a hypothetical question, and I am giving him a hypothetical answer," Karl countered. "This boat could even take us to the Volga River deep inside Russia."

"By what route?" Herbert asked.

Karl continued his geographical mini lecture with, "We would have to turn into the Sea of Asov and then cruise the river Don to its source, which is a huge reservoir—I forgot the name of it—whose northernmost shore connects with the Volga via a canal."

"How do you know all this?" Herbert asked.

"I have a big map on the wall of my bedroom that I use to track the advance of the German forces by sticking pins into the map to demarcate the front lines. I therefore have become fairly familiar with the area. When we first found out that a boat trip would be involved, I studied the map to trace our route along the Danube, and I then just studied the map some more to see how far the boat could take us."

"Do you also track the retreats?" Horst asked.

"I don't have to track retreats. The pinholes to the east of the current front lines show me the areas that had to be evacuated," Karl answered.

"Why did you bother with all the rigamarole of finding out how far the boat could take us?" Horst wondered aloud.

"I don't know, but I think it might be of interest to you to know where you would be once you reached the Volga," Karl answered.

"A long ways from home?" Horst asked sarcastically.

"The entry point to the Volga would be about twenty miles from Stalingrad," Karl concluded.

The mere mention of the city immediately triggered Herbert's memory back to about three months earlier when the surrender of what remained of the German Sixth Army had been made known. Although the OKW report had not gone into details, the three-day national mourning period, which was instituted almost immediately after the report was issued, indicated that a near cataclysmic event had taken place.

Herbert looked at his friends. Their silence made him

feel that they too had been reminded of what had happened months earlier.

Horst said, "If you were to go there now, you probably would be about two hundred miles behind enemy lines."

Herbert tried to redirect their thoughts by saying, "Have you guys noticed how muddy this river is?"

"Did you expect otherwise?" Horst asked.

"Yeah, according to Johann Strauss, aptly described as the Waltz King, it is supposed to be blue, and he lived in Vienna, which is a long way downstream from where we are now," Herbert replied.

"Maybe he didn't always live in Austria. Perhaps he lived way upstream in Germany at one time. Or maybe he was colorblind," Karl ventured.

His two friends gave him a derisive look, and all three of them laughed.

"Maybe he just used poetic license," Horst guessed.

"Karl knows all about navigating a boat across Europe, and you appear to know quite a bit about Johann Strauss. How did you learn about him?" Horst asked.

"My mother used to sing some of his songs when I was a little kid. I think she was homesick a lot while she was in America. It was her idea, to which my father grudgingly acquiesced, that prompted our coming to Germany just before the war started—not that she expected war to break out. She just thought that Germany would still be the same as it had been when she was a young lady, but she noticed huge changes immediately after her arrival," Herbert recalled.

"Germany has not changed that much," Horst declared. Your mother probably remembers the Kaiser; now we have a Fuehrer. That is not such a big difference."

Herbert smiled and said, "But there is a big difference. In the Kaiser's day the people could express themselves."

"We can express ourselves," Horst countered.

"Yeah, as long as you follow the Party line. In America I could stand on a street corner and shout, 'Roosevelt is a stupid oaf,' and only those who would be in agreement with my statement would stick around to hear what else I might have to say. All others would simply walk away. They might be shaking their heads as they walked away, but they would still simply walk away." Herbert argued.

"I too can stand on any street corner and shout that Roosevelt is a stupid oaf," Horst said.

"Yes, but could you shout something disparaging about the Fuehrer?" Herbert asked.

Taken somewhat aback, Horst said, "I could say something disparaging about the Fuehrer, if I were in the company of true friends."

"See what I mean?" Herbert responded.

"We are in the midst of a war. It would be unpatriotic to disparage the head of state during war," Horst replied.

"Germany was not at war when my mother first noted the change," Herbert said.

Horst answered with a shrug.

Before he could say anything else, a loudspeaker, blaring that sandwiches were available on the aft deck, brought the conversation to a close.

+++

After their arrival at the military barracks in Passau the night before, Herbert had asked Mr. Vogt to store his little chess set for safekeeping in the briefcase that the teacher always carried with him. After they had eaten and had downed a soft drink, Herbert retrieved the chess set from Mr. Vogt and invited Karl and Horst to play a few games.

They left the relatively noisy aft deck and found a more secluded spot with several chairs toward the front end of the boat. Horst played opposite Karl in the first game, which Horst lost. Herbert was unable to break his string of consecutive losses as he played the second and third games against Karl and Horst respectively. When they had completed the third game, it was late afternoon.

+++

The three friends left their chairs and walked past the aft deck to the stern of the boat. In the distance, they could see two of the other four boats that had left Passau in the morning as part of their flotilla. Upstream traffic had been light in the Passau area, but now barge traffic heading west had increased considerably. Herbert and Horst were observing the boat's wake while Karl was spitting into the river.

"I knew it was poetic license," Horst said.

"What are you talking about?" Herbert asked.

"The Danube…I'm talking about the so-called blue Danube. It is as muddy here as it was in Passau."

"Well, don't ever tell my mother. She would be very disappointed," Herbert responded

Karl quit spitting and turned around. "Hey! I think I can see the skyline of Vienna up ahead."

Fifteen minutes later, they could see the giant Ferris wheel from a distance. The well known landmark confirmed that they were indeed approaching Vienna.

+++

Staying overnight in Vienna followed the same routine as the previous night. The boys were marched to a youth hostel where they were assigned bedding and then fed. Most of the boys enjoyed the Wiener schnitzel as much as they had enjoyed the *Knoedel* (dumplings) in Passau.

On the second morning afloat, the weather seemed to promise a repeat of the almost cloudless sky of the day before. About two hours after cast off, a voice transmitted over the intercom intoned that the boat would be leaving Austria just before the boat reached the town of Bratislava, which was just coming into view on the left bank of the river.

The loudspeaker message continued by saying that upon leaving Austria the river became the boundary line between Slovakia and Hungary, with Slovakia on the left and Hungary on the right bank. Both banks would not be part of Hungary until just before the river made its sharp turn to the south on its way to Budapest, about four hours hence.

The boat crew brought out deck chairs which they distributed along the forward decks. Since there were not nearly enough deck chairs for all of the boys, the chairs were all quickly occupied.

"Sit on the foot end, and we'll trade places later on," Karl told Herbert, after he and Horst had been able to grab two adjacent chairs.

Two hours later, when the loudspeaker announced that lunch would be available on the aft deck, the three friends quickly made their way aft to insure a place at the front of the line. When lunch was served, they grabbed their sandwiches and drinks and immediately headed back to the forward part of the boat, where they were able to grab three deck chairs that were side by side.

Having eaten lunch, they stripped to the waist and basked in the midday sun while they watched the rolling hills give way to the flatlands of the Danube basin.

Mr. Vogt, the teacher, soon came along and admonished the boys in his charge with, "Don't be staying in the sun too long.

I have some boric acid in my medical kit, but I don't have enough for all of you."

Grudgingly, the boys put their shirts back on.

It was about 4:00 P.M. when their boat docked in Budapest, the second of the five boats that had left Passau two days earlier. The boys were told to leave their luggage on board, because their suitcases would be forwarded to the railroad station. After the boys had disembarked, they had to wait for the other three boats to arrive.

Horst and Herbert utilized the waiting period to walk along the boat landing. "Do you have any idea what all the signs around here are trying to tell us?" Herbert asked.

Horst looked around, and pointing at one that depicted a lightning stroke under its inscription said, "That one probably says: Danger, high voltage. As for the rest of them, I don't have a clue."

"How are we ever going to be able to communicate with the people we will be staying with, if all they understand is Hungarian?" Herbert asked.

Horst drew up his shoulders and said, "Maybe Mr. Vogt will give us a crash course."

"He doesn't know Hungarian," Herbert commented.

"Exactly. That's why I called it a crash course. It would be a disaster."

Herbert noticed Horst's smirk and responded with, "Smartass." They both chuckled.

The two boys had a good vantage point from where they were on the landing. It offered an excellent view of the Hungarian capital which had a population about the same size as their hometown Hamburg. They could see the two bridges that spanned the Danube. Their boat had crossed under the northernmost bridge to reach the landing which was approximately equidistant between the bridges.

"There sure is a lot more river traffic here than there was further upstream, even at Vienna. And look how wide the river has become," Horst observed.

"Yeah, but not nearly as wide as the Elbe is at Hamburg," Herbert countered.

"You're not getting homesick already, are you?" Horst asked.

"Nah."

Half an hour later, Horst declared, "Hey, we better get back to the assembly area. The last boat just arrived."

Mr. Vogt told his charges that their group of ten classes would now be split up. Two of the classes would remain in the Budapest vicinity, while the remaining eight would march in formation to the railroad station and entrain to get to their final destination.

The Jungvolk leaders had the boys line up in march formation according to class, with a separation of about three strides between classes. As they paraded down one of Budapest's main thoroughfares, they drew quite a few stares from the local populace.

"They probably think we're future SS guys," Karl commented to Herbert.

Because of their short stature, the two boys were marching side by side at the rear end of their class.

"When they look at you two, they probably will think that you're two dwarfs from another planet," a voice from the first row of the following class commented.

Herbert balled his fist with middle finger extended and let his finger point toward the voice from behind in cadence with the next rearward motion of his right hand. He kept his hand down lest the local folks would construe his gesture as being meant for them.

✚✚✚

Before the formation was dismissed at the railroad station, the boys were told where to pick up their luggage, and each class was advised of its departure platform. The luggage of the approximately three hundred boys had been deposited somewhat willy-nilly in an improvised baggage area in the terminal; therefore, it took a while before each boy was able to retrieve his belongings.

As Mr. Vogt's class assembled on their assigned platform, the boys soon became aware that their class alone had been directed to this particular location.

"How come we are the only class that is assembling here?" Klaus Wolfert asked Mr. Vogt.

"This is where we part company." Mr.Vogt replied, adding, "Apparently we are the only ones heading south. The train that we will be boarding will be headed for Pecs. It will be a local train, meaning that it will stop at every station along its route."

An "uh-uh!" here and an "uh-uh!" there could be heard from some of the boys who interpreted what the teacher just said as a possibility that they might well wind up somewhere in the boonies.

"And we will be getting off the train at a town called Bonyhad. It will take us about two hours to get there," Mr.Vogt continued. Then, addressing one of the two Jungvolk leaders, he said, "Gunther, I'll be relying on you and your sidekick to get the boys off the train as soon as possible when the train stops at Bonyhad and to verify by head count that no one has been lost in the shuffle."

Gunther nodded assent.

As the train came squeaking into the station, Karl commented, "Man, where did they pick up this junker?"

"What's your problem?" Herbert asked in turn. "It looks just like one of our commuter trains back in Hamburg with each compartment having its own set of doors and with the two staggered running boards along the sides of the cars."

"Yeah, but they are of much later vintage. These cars must date back to the first world war."

"They probably are old German cars that you guys sold to the Hungarians so you could pay your reparations after the war," Herbert suggested.

"You really think so?" Karl asked.

"Sure. If you can find a second class compartment, try to get into it, and run your hand between the upholstered seat and backrest; I think you just might find a couple of pre-World War I gold marks."

Karl gave Herbert a derisive look and said, "And I think not that you just might be but that you are a complete idiot."

Their one-on-one banter ended with both boys bursting into laughter.

✚ ✚ ✚

Once the train had left Budapest's suburbs, the boys' interest was centered on what could be seen through the train windows.

"There's a big horse ranch over there. Look at all the horses grazing in that pasture," someone cried out.

"Looks like we're headed in the right direction," Detlev Wolfert exclaimed, and he demonstrated his exuberance by getting up out of his seat and performing an impromptu jig.

Detlev was the nonidentical twin of Klaus, the class's soccer goalie. Not knowing that they were twins, one would never have guessed it. While both were of athletic build, Klaus was tall, slim, and dark-haired, whereas Detlev was short, stocky, and blond. He was the class' ace soccer forward.

Through the first three stops the train made after leaving Budapest, many horses, most grazing in the pastures and some prancing along the pasture enclosures, could be seen. Since the boys' destination was only two stops away, they became confident that they would be staying in horse-raising country.

As the old train labored toward the fourth stop, the pastures along the wayside became almost devoid of horses.

The few horses that could be seen were sharing the grazing areas with some sheep and an occasional cow or two.

In a foreboding murmur, someone uttered, "I think we should have gotten off at the last stop."

Looking out the train windows while the train was at its fourth stop, the boys began to realize that they were definitely migrating toward the poorer cousins in the Magyar pecking order. The village houses surrounding the station had a somewhat squalid appearance. On some of them, the peeling white wash bared the straw imbedded loam construction of the walls. The lack of maintenance certainly did not suggest affluence but rather that upkeep costs had to be relegated to the bottom of the shopping list. The real shock was not so much the appearance of the town, but the well that could be seen offset from every home. The well meant that they would have to do without indoor plumbing, and—horror of horrors—the absence of indoor plumbing meant that they would be using an outhouse in the very near future.

One of the more optimistic boys suggested, "Those houses probably belong to the sharecroppers that work for the estate. We just can't see the estate from here."

His supposition provoked only blank stares from the other nine boys in the compartment.

The train started up again and lumbered toward Bonyhad.

Mr. Vogt left the teacher's compartment and stopped at all three compartments the boys were occupying to remind them that they had to get off at the next stop. He then again alerted Gunther that he would need a quick head count from him.

After the railroad cars came to a halt and the engineer released the brakes, the sound of the escaping air gave the impression that the old engine was giving a sigh of relief.

The boys tumbled out of the cars, and Gunther quickly reported that he had accounted for all the boys.

Mr. Vogt's concern for the boys had left him little chance to think of anything else.

All of a sudden he cried out, "Where is the other teacher? Where is Mr. Bohnke?"

Gunther immediately hopped back on the train. He soon reappeared helping the not quite awake Mr. Bohnke out of the car and down the running boards. Gunther's action elicited a loud hurray from everyone except Mr. Bohnke. Luckily the old engine had to take on some water at this stop; otherwise, Mr. Bohnke would have been, all alone, on his way to Pecs.

When everyone, with suitcase in hand, had exited the station and was standing on the dirt road that ran parallel to the train tracks, a man on the other side of the road jumped off his farm wagon. The wagon was hitched to an old swaybacked mare. Having had a front row seat to watch the boys leave the train and the incidence with Mr. Bohnke, he evidently came to the conclusion that Mr. Vogt was the man in charge.

He walked up to Mr. Vogt and introduced himself as Mr. Muller, and said, *"Ich bin hier um Sie im Namen der Einwohner der Ortschaft Graboc zu empfangen."* ["I am here to welcome you as the representative of the residents of the township of Graboc."] Everyone's ears pricked up! The man was speaking fluent German!

Mr. Muller told Mr. Vogt that all the luggage could be loaded on his wagon and that the teachers could ride with him. He indicated that Graboc was about three miles down the road.

Gunther ordered the boys to line up in formation, and the boys started marching down the road. The old mare, pulling the wagon but dictating her own cadence, followed the column.

As they left Bonyhad, Horst said, "This town doesn't look any more promising than the one we saw on the previous stop."

"I think it looks even worse," came a murmur from someone else.

Marching beside Herbert on the dirt road, Karl asked him,

"Do you think we have reached the ass of the world?"

"If we haven't, I'm sure it's along this road somewhere and in the direction in which we are marching," Herbert answered. "But be grateful for the little things," he continued, "At least, we know that there is one guy in town with whom we can converse."

"You mean the guy on the wagon?" Karl asked.

Herbert nodded in assent.

About halfway to their destination, a farm wagon, going the other way, passed the column of boys.

"Did you see that?" Karl asked perplexedly.

"Did I see what?" Herbert countered.

"Did you see the wagon that just passed us?"

"Yeah, but I didn't pay much attention."

"Didn't you notice what was pulling it?"

"No."

"It was being drawn by a…by a cow!"

The formation trudged onward, with most of the boys engrossed in their own thoughts. As they neared the village of Graboc, renewed interest in their surroundings animated them, but all they could see appeared to be a rerun of what they had seen in Bonyhad: They saw the straw embedded loam house walls, a well in every yard, and the inevitable outhouse.

Some smart-aleck quipped, "The privies are all located approximately west of the living quarters; therefore, the prevalent winds around here must be out of the east."

Entering the village square, the boys noted that their sponsors had brought their entire families to the square where they would select which boy, or boys, would stay with them.

Already knowing that they had been shunted into one of the poorer areas of Hungary, the boys, now seeing their sponsors for the first time, felt that they had been transferred backward in time!

At first glance, Herbert felt like he was reviewing a pictorial presentation which he had seen in an American magazine. The presentation had featured the Amish farmers of the Midwest.

In dress, the sponsor families resembled Amish folk. The men all wore a white shirt with dark pants and jacket. On their heads they had a black hat with a brim. The women were also darkly clothed: They wore a blouse and a skirt that reached to the ankles. Their heads were covered with a kerchief.

The kids of the sponsor parents were dressed in an identical manner, and they all looked like little men and little women.

Mr. Muller guided the old mare to the center of the square, and the teachers climbed off the wagon, while Mr. Muller, now standing in the back of the wagon, started to address the crowd. The boys assumed that he was addressing only them, because his first few statements essentially were a duplicate of his greeting at Bonyhad and, more important, because he was still speaking German.

Provoking snickers from some of the new arrivals and several sponsors' kids, the old swaybacked mare seemed to show her disdain for the whole proceeding by farting loudly during his opening statements, but the speaker carried on unabashed.

After he had welcomed them once more, Mr. Muller told them that the town's residents were of ethnic German descent, and that they were farmers who were working their own small holdings. While he was relating this, several of the newcomers exchanged glances of surprise, because some of the townspeople were nodding in assent to what the speaker was saying, thereby indicating that at least some of them understood him.

When Mr. Muller told the new arrivals that the townsfolk, a long time ago, had decided to retain the German language among themselves, the cat was out of the bag; they all were proficient in the German language. A sigh of relief seemed to ripple through the newcomers, and they broke out in applause, including the teachers—they would not have to learn another tongue to make themselves understood in their new environment.

"Starting with myself, we will now have the sponsors select which boy they would like to stay with them," Mr. Muller announced.

He selected two boys from the front row of the column; Klaus Wolfert was one of them.

Reading a name from a piece of paper that he had pulled out his pocket, Mr. Muller invited another farmer to make his selection, who also picked two boys from the front of the column.

Looking at his list, Mr. Muller called out the next name. This farmer selected one boy, again from the front of the column.

"You know where this is heading, don't you?" Herbert whispered to Karl.

"What do you mean?" Karl asked in return.

"Well, our formations are assembled with the tallest guys up front and the shortest guys on the tail end.

Since the farmers' choices seem to favor the front end, we are going to wind up standing here all by ourselves before it is all over."

"So what?" Karl whispered.

Herbert shrugged.

"How come the first two got to pick two boys each?" Karl asked.

"There probably are only twenty-eight sponsors, so the two farmers with the largest farms got to pick two boys, since our class totals thirty boys," Herbert surmised.

"What if there are only twenty-six sponsors?" Karl asked.

Herbert almost laughed out loud. He said, "We will be excluded from the raffle, and we will be standing in this square all alone, after everyone else has gone home."

Karl gave him a worried look.

The selection process did not unfold exactly as Herbert had predicted; however, he and Karl did wind up to be the last boys to be chosen.

Mr. Muller called out the next name on his list, "Johann Borkenau."

A man, about five foot ten, with a black moustache responded and started to walk toward the remaining two boys. He approached Herbert and, putting his hand on the boy's shoulder, he said "I am Johann Borkenau. Now tell me your name." After Herbert responded, the man asked, "Would you like to stay with my family?"

Herbert nodded.

"Then come and meet them," Mr. Borkenau suggested.

Before responding, Herbert looked at the somewhat forlorn Karl and in a low tone tried to encourage his friend and said, "Don't worry. I'm sure that there are twenty-eight."

Herbert walked with Mr. Borkenau to the side of the square where the crowd of sponsors, now swelled by the boys already chosen, was assembled.

Mr. Borkenau walked up to a woman who was about five foot tall, therefore about Herbert's height, and proudly said, "This is my wife Marie. Marie, this is Herbert."

The woman had blue eyes like her husband. A strand of hair that had strayed from under her kerchief told him that she was brunette. He guessed her to be about the same age as her husband, about thirty. Even with the concealing effect of the kerchief, Herbert could tell that she was a very pretty lady. He bowed and said, "How do you do."

"And these are our children, Helga and Robert," Mr. Borkenau proclaimed, pointing to the girl and boy standing next to his wife. "Helga is eleven years old, and Robert is four years younger."

Herbert acknowledged the introduction by giving both of the blond and blue-eyed children a nod of recognition.

During the introductions, Herbert had heard Mr. Muller call out one more farmer's name. When he now turned around, he saw the farmer walking back toward the crowd with Karl in tow.

Having gone through his list, Mr. Muller invited Mr. Vogt to say a few words. Mr. Vogt climbed back on the wagon and thanked the farmers and their families for taking the boys in. He vouched for their good behavior during their stay in Graboc.

Mr. Muller then addressed the farmers one more time, stating, "Since our order of business has been concluded, we can all go home now. Thank you all for your patience."

The crowd slowly started to disperse.

Mr. Borkenau accompanied Herbert back to the wagon, where Herbert retrieved his suitcases.

Mr. Borkenau took them, saying, "I'll carry those."

As they walked back to Marie and the children, Mr. Borkenau said, "Our house is only a short distance from here."

Having walked two blocks, they entered a small house. The entry door opened into a foyer. To the left of the foyer was a kitchen area which was not walled off from the foyer. Herbert noticed an older, somewhat heavy-set, woman busy over a wood burning stove. Mr. Borkenau put down Herbert's suitcases and introduced her as Mrs. Schneider, his mother-in-law.

Mr. Borkenau then showed him the living room which was to the left of the kitchen and pointing toward a door in the living room, he said, "Our bedrooms are in the back of the house through that door."

He then led Herbert back to the foyer, picked up the suitcases and said, "Your room is over here, to the right of the foyer." As he led Herbert inside, the boy noted that there were two beds in the room.

"Who else sleeps in here?" he asked.

"Nobody else," Mr. Borkenau answered.

"Where does your mother-in-law sleep?"

"Mrs. Schneider doesn't sleep here. She is a widow lady, and she has her own home not far from here," Mr. Borkenau explained.

"Oh," Herbert said, hoping that he had been able stifle his sigh of relief.

Mr. Borkenau pointed to a basin and suggested that Herbert get some water out of the bucket in the foyer, so that he could refresh himself before they had supper. As he left the room he told Herbert, "Whoever empties the bucket, goes to the well to replenish it."

✚ ✚ ✚

Having fetched the bucket, Herbert poured some water into the wash basin and replaced the bucket in the foyer.

Guess I lucked out, Herbert thought; the bucket is still half full, so I'll be able to defer admitting my ignorance of operating a well to another time.

It was getting dark. He looked for a wall switch or a lamp. Since he could find neither, he did his best by washing in the waning light.

He was just finishing up when there was a tentative knock on the door.

"Come in," Herbert responded.

Mrs. Schneider stuck her head through the doorway and said, "We're ready to start dinner."

"OK, I'll be right there."

✚✚✚

As Herbert left his room he could see that there was light in the living room. When he saw the source of the light, he stared in disbelief. The light was coming from a kerosene lamp!

Because he had not eaten anything since a snack was served on the boat, he soon put the lamp out of his mind and enjoyed a dinner of potatoes and spinach and the biggest slice of ham he had had in a long time. Everyone had a glass of wine with their dinner.

"Is this a special occasion?" Herbert asked Mr. Borkenau.

"It is special in that you have arrived today; otherwise, no," Mr. Borkenau answered. "What made you think it to be special?" he then asked.

Herbert pointed at his wine glass.

"The wine?" Mr. Borkenau asked, and then added, "The wine does not denote a special occasion. We have wine with our dinner every day."

✚✚✚

After dinner, Mr. Borkenau asked, "The boy who was standing next to you when we first met, is he your friend?"

Herbert nodded.

"He is staying with the family that lives in the second house around the corner from here. If you like, you can go over there and visit him," Mr. Borkenau offered.

"OK," Herbert responded.

"OK? What is 'OK'?" Mr. Borkenau asked.

"It means…it means oh, yes," the boy answered.

"Oh," Mr. Borkenau acknowledged, looking a little puzzled.

When Herbert got up to leave, Mr. Borkenau said, "Just turn right when you leave, and go to the corner. The second house from the corner is where you will find him. Come back as late as you like; we don't lock our doors."

+++

Herbert felt a little tipsy as he walked the short distance, but he soon found Karl sitting on the porch of the house.

"Hey, how are you doing?" Herbert asked his friend.

"Great, like in g-r-a-t-e," Karl answered.

"Did you have a good dinner?" Herbert inquired.

"I had a good dinner, not by candlelight, but by kerosene lamp. And I had some wine. Like a dope, I drank two glasses of the stuff, and now I have a headache."

"We'll have to get used to the wine. My sponsor says that they drink it all the time," Herbert commented. Then he asked, "What do the kerosene lamps tell you?"

"They tell me that this dump does not have any electricity," Karl opined.

Both boys laughed.

"Tell me, what would you have done if they had run out of sponsors?" Herbert teased.

"I would have asked Mr. Vogt to get me a return ticket for home. And you know what? I would have been the only one to come out a winner," Karl surmised.

Herbert shrugged.

They talked a while longer. When Herbert got up to leave, he said, "Get some sleep. Tomorrow, once you're rid of your mini-hangover, you'll see things in a different light."

"No, I won't. The light will still be from a wick, and I'll still see cow-drawn wagons!

Herbert returned to his new home. Mr. Borkenau and his wife were still up and sitting in the living room. Herbert stuck his head in the doorway to wish them a good night.

Mr. Borkenau responded by pointing to the kerosene lamp and saying, "One of these and a box of matches are in your room."

"OK, Mr. Borkenau."

"You can dispense with the Borkenau," his sponsor said. "Just address us by our first names, Johann and Marie."

"OK, Mr…OK, Johann."

Herbert did not try to light the lamp in his room, mainly because he thought he might do something dumb and start a fire. He thought waiting for daylight and then practicing with the lamp would be a better idea.

He left the door to his room open a bit, while he changed into his pajamas. After closing the door, he felt his way to the bed and under the covers.

The lack of electricity preoccupied his mind. Without it, there would not be any radio. He also remembered that he had not seen any telephone lines during their march into town. Dozing off, he felt that, except for mail, they had been cut off from the outside world.

Chapter 28

Shortly before 8:00 A.M. the following morning, the boys assembled in the schoolhouse, which Mr. Muller had pointed out to them the day before as being available for their classroom work. It was nothing more than a one room house containing a sufficient number of tables and chairs for a class of thirty and a desk for the teacher.

When Herbert entered the schoolroom among the early arrivals that morning, he noted that Mr. Vogt was already seated at his desk. After selecting a seat and while waiting for the rest of the class to arrive, Herbert contemplated his teacher. Mr. Vogt was of slim build and somewhat less than six foot height. Herbert estimated the teacher's age to be nearing forty. His graying blond hair circumscribed the bald spot on the top of his head like a wreath. His sparkling blue eyes and his ready smile, combined with his easy manner, gave Mr. Vogt the attributes of what is often defined as a sunny disposition. On this morning, he was casually dressed in shirt and slacks and a sport jacket.

Herbert had seen Mr. Vogt dressed otherwise. On occasion, back in Hamburg, Mr. Vogt had conducted his class wearing an S.A. uniform. Herbert often wondered whether Mr. Vogt was an ardent Nazi or whether he was forced to be a *Mitgaenger* (follower), in order to retain his teaching position.

But one day, after Mr. Vogt assigned the class to memorize an old German poem, Herbert wondered no longer. The first stanza of the poem, "Die Gedanken sind frei," thought to be attributable to German poet Joseph von Eichendorff, 1788–1857 and loosely translated into English by the author, results in the following:

Thoughts are free.
Who of their presence knows?
They pass and flee
Like evening shadows.
They are known to no one,
Immune to the hunter's gun.
Thoughts are free.
Thoughts are free.

✦ ✦ ✦

Once all the boys were accounted for, Mr. Vogt asked, "Well, are you adjusting to your new environment?"

"It's hard to adjust overnight when it seems as though the clock has been turned back by about sixty years," one of the boys remarked.

"Yeah. This place reminds me of my grandfather's boyhood stories," another boy added. "He always told me of all the shortcomings he had to endure, like having to walk a mile to school and having to put up with other stuff."

Mr. Vogt laughed and said, "You won't have to walk a mile to school."

"No, but the other stuff—hauling water out of a well and using an outhouse—applies."

"Mr. Bohnke had the right idea when he didn't want to hop right off the train in Bonyhad," someone else proclaimed, eliciting laughter.

After the laughter had died down, Mr. Vogt said, "I realize conditions here are somewhat primitive. We will just have to make the best of a less than ideal situation."

"Can't we get a transfer to another place?" another student asked.

Mr. Vogt smiled and shook his head. "No," he said. "The townspeople committed to sponsor us a long time ago, and the evacuation authority accepted their offer."

Mr. Vogt scanned the class and then said, "Look, you should be happy that you won't be cellar dwellers for the next seven months and that you will be able to pursue your studies unimpeded by school delays caused by the air raids.

"You have a lot of catching up to do, and I intend for you to do just that. By dispensing with your summer vacation and by adding an extra hour to your daily class schedule, you will be able to cover most of a semester's requirement, thereby giving you an outside chance to graduate in 1945 rather than in 1946."

Wild applause greeted Mr. Vogt's comment.

After a pause, he asked, "Now, are there any other questions?"

Horst Drossen raised his hand and asked, "Are we expected to help the sponsors with the farm work?"

"Absolutely not," Mr. Vogt responded. "Your sponsors receive a stipend from the German government for taking you in. They are being paid for letting you stay with them. As a matter of fact, you boys too will be getting an allowance."

"How much?" someone asked.

"Two and a half Pengo per month."

"What will two and a half Pengo buy?" Karl Rothman asked.

Laughing, Mr. Vogt responded with, "Probably not a whole lot."

He then suggested, "Let's get back to Horst's question. Once you are caught up with your homework, there is no reason why you shouldn't volunteer to help your sponsors out now and then, if for no other reason than to get to know them better."

Mr. Vogt looked at the class over the rims of his glasses and said, "I'm sure many more questions will come up, but let's defer them to another time. Right now let's pick up our geometry from where we left off in Hamburg."

+++

A week after Herbert had left for Hungary, Hertha received a letter from Walther suggesting that she and the girls come to Schildberg over the summer months to get them out of the danger zone that Hamburg had become. He added that they would not be staying with the forester family, since he had been able to get a short term apartment rental for them. Hertha could sense his excitement when he informed her about the apartment.

After Hertha read the letter to the girls, she asked them what they thought about their father's suggestion.

Romi said, "If we won't be hearing the guns blasting two or three nights a week, by all means, let's go!"

Hannelore concurred with, "Let's go! I want to be with my Papa!"

+++

Two weeks later, Walther met them at the station in Poznan. The girls watched as their parents embraced; then, it was their turn to give their father a hug.

Noticing the chevrons on her father's jacket, Romi said, "You're looking pretty good, Corporal Klug. If this war lasts long enough, you'll probably wind up being a general."

Walther laughed. "We don't need another Hundred Year War, Rosemarie," he said, mimicking her formality by addressing her by her given name.

✚✚✚

In the latter part of July, 1943, Hamburg had experienced unusually hot summer weather. The temperature had exceeded 80 degrees under clear skies.

Mr. and Mrs. Werner took advantage of the evening breezes by sitting on their balcony. The entrance from the kitchen led onto the left half of the balcony which was an open area with a wooden fence along its perimeter. The right half of the balcony was partially enclosed by two windowed walls along its perimeter and was roofed to provide shelter from the elements. At this time of year, flowers were in full bloom in the boxes that were attached to the fence in the open area.

On the evening of 24 July, Mrs. Werner came out of the kitchen to join her husband on the balcony. She was carrying a coffee pot and a tray with two coffee cups.

"Emil, would you like to have a cup of real coffee? I don't have any cream, so you will have to drink it black," she said.

"Where did you get the coffee, Johanna?" her husband asked.

"Oh, I have a little bit put aside for a special treat now and then, and I have another treat for you," she said as she scurried back into the kitchen.

"When she came back with a small cake she said, "I also splurged a little with our ration coupons."

"Johanna, you're a doll," Emil said as she poured him a cup of coffee.

She seated herself next to him, and they indulged themselves in their repast, which was really part of the following week's ration.

"I wonder whether Hertha and the girls have acclimated themselves to their new environment in the Warthegau," Johanna mused.

"What is the name of the town where they are staying for the summer?" he asked.

"Schildberg," she replied.

"Schildberg—I never heard of it," her husband commented.

"Well, it's probably just a little one-horse town in the middle of nowhere," Johanna supposed.

"Hertha's letter did say that Walther had been able to find an apartment for them, did it not?" Emil queried.

"Yes."

"Then why don't they just stay there instead of coming back to Hamburg in August?" he asked. "Staying there would be a lot safer for them," he added.

"Yes, but the apartment lease probably is just a makeshift arrangement. Besides, Hertha feels that they have to come back so that Hannelore can resume her schooling," Johanna said.

"Couldn't she go to school there?" he asked.

"Like I said, Schildberg surely is just a small town, and Hertha probably feels that the quality of education would be inferior to that which Hamburg can provide."

"Well, she's probably right in that assumption," he said.

When Johanna picked up the dishes and carried them back inside, Emil followed her. He wanted to read the newspaper a while, but, because of the blackout regulations, reading on the balcony was not an option.

Busying herself at the kitchen sink, Johanna said, "I sure hope the British will continue the respite they have given us. We have had only several minor raids so far this month, the so-called nuisance raids, where the Brits send over half a dozen planes to harass the populace by getting them out of bed at night or by forcing them to seek shelter during the day."

"Looking up from his paper, her husband said, "I certainly share your hope, but I don't think it will be long before they are done with whatever they are blowing up right now; then, they will be back."

"You are so encouraging, Emil," his wife replied.

"I'm just trying to be realistic, Johanna."

Johanna sat down opposite him at the kitchen table to share the newspaper. After a while she said, "It's too hot in here. I think I'll go back out on the balcony. Do you want to come along?"

Looking at his pocket watch and noticing that the time was almost 11:30 P.M., he replied, "No, I think I'll hit the hay."

Johanna stayed on the balcony for about another half hour. She was just about to go inside when the air raid sirens sounded.

"Emil, wake up!" she shouted as she ran inside.

"Yeah, yeah."

The Werner's apartment was located on the top floor of a two-storied building. The landlady, a fifty-five-year-old widow, was the sole occupant of the lower floor since her two sons had been drafted into the service; therefore, she and the Werners now were the only ones to occupy the cellar when the air raid sirens issued an alert.

After Emil quickly dressed, he and his wife trudged down to the vestibule of the building and from there down another staircase into the cellar.

"Good evening, Mrs. Schmundt," Johanna greeted the landlady as she and her husband entered the cellar.

"Well, it was a good evening until now," Mrs. Schmundt countered. Then she asked, "How are the Werners?"

"We were fine until the alert sounded," Emil commented.

They all sat down in the decrepit easy chairs that Mrs. Schmundt supplied back in 1940, after the initial air raids had occurred.

The drab surroundings of the cellar affected Johanna anew every time she entered: The pile of coal remaining under the coal chute from the previous heating season, the water seeping from one of the walls and pooling briefly on the floor before draining through a crack in the floor to who knows where, the dingy light bulb at the center of the ceiling, not illuminating but only accentuating the starkness of the cellar, and the occasional mouse scurrying across the floor all affected her sensibilities and made her shiver. In order to ease her discomfort, she tried to engage the landlady in conversation.

"Have you heard from either of your boys recently?" Johanna asked.

The answer was a terse "No."

Johanna did not pursue the issue any further. She knew that the landlady was worried sick about her sons. They were both on the eastern front, the most dreaded posting at that stage of the war.

About 12:30 A.M. the distant rumble of the flak became audible in the cellar. The rumbling noise gradually increased in intensity as the aircraft approached the city. Soon the staccato sound of the nearby guns drowned out the more distant rumble. The already earsplitting racket then was intensified by the cacophony of exploding bombs.

The concussions of the initial bomb explosions sent tremors through the house that caused chunks of ceiling plaster to drop on the cellar occupants and mortar dust to pollute the air they were breathing.

Johanna was shaking with fear. "Dear God, is this how I am going to die?" she sobbed.

Her husband and Mrs. Schmundt tried to calm her, although they too were trembling. Transfixed with fear, all three of them turned to prayer beseeching the Lord to spare them.

The sound of the antiaircraft guns continued unabated; however, after the initial bombs had fallen, the intensity of the sound of exploding bombs gradually diminished, thereby suggesting that the bombs were impacting farther away. With renewed hope, the Werners and Mrs. Schmundt brushed the plaster dust off their clothing and out of their hair.

The air raid lasted about one hour. As the firing of the nearby guns ceased and the rumbling of the distant guns faded, the sirens of emergency vehicles became prevalent.

Soon the all clear sounded.

Before leaving the cellar, Mrs. Schmundt said, "I think this may have been the heaviest raid we have seen to date." After a pause, she added, "Perhaps you should be thinking about going to the public shelter from now on. You would be a lot safer there than in this cellar."

"The nearest public shelter is about half a mile away," Emil replied, "and we are both pushing seventy. It would be difficult for us to walk that far and completely out of the question if we had to run."

Mrs. Schmundt nodded and said, "All these trips to a shelter are hard on everyone, but I can see where they would be even tougher for the older folks."

"You got that right," Emil acknowledged.

After they climbed the stairs back to the vestibule, they did not go back to their respective apartments immediately but walked out onto the street. Johanna started to cry again, when she saw the two houses burning on the other end of their block and several fire engines engaging in an apparently lost cause.

Toward the northwest the sky was a deep red from the many fires that had been ignited in that part of the city.

"Oh, what have they done to my Hamburg?" Johanna implored between sobs.

While Emil tried to console his wife, a neighbor man from across the street strolled over and said, "It looks like the British are trying to put us in a festive mood in spite of the carnage they have just perpetrated."

With a perplexed look, Mrs. Schmundt asked, "What on earth are you talking about, Mr. Henzel?"

"Look at the street Mrs. Schmundt. Don't you see all the Lametta (tinsel) lying in the street?" he countered.

Because her eyes were still accommodating to the darkness, Mrs. Schmundt had not noticed anything untoward. When she took a closer look, she saw the many strips of tinsel strewn about the street.

"How do you know the strips came from the airplanes?" she asked.

"Well, they certainly came from above. Look at the trees over there. You can see tinsel hanging from the branches," Mr. Henzel replied.

"Why would they throw that stuff out of the airplanes?" Mrs. Schmundt queried.

"I don't know. I've talked to several people, and they do not know. Nobody seems to know."

The Werners had overheard the conversation. When Emil stooped to pick up one of the strands, Johanna shouted,

"Don't touch it, Emil!"

"Why in the world not?" her husband asked, as he straightened up.

"Do you know what it's for?" his wife asked him.

"Well, no."

"Then I wouldn't touch it," she suggested.

"Your wife's caution is well put," Mr. Henzel volunteered, as he added, "Some folks seem to think that the strips have been impregnated with poison. I, myself, find that to be a little far-fetched."

"Then why are they dropping this stuff on us?" asked Mrs. Schmundt.

"I don't know, Mrs. Schmundt. As I said before, nobody seems to know," Mr. Henzel reiterated.

Mrs. Schmundt threw up her hands and said, "So what's another little worry in our everyday life. You know what? I'm going to bed. Good night, Mr. Henzel."

"Good night all," Mr. Henzel countered as he walked back across the street.

The Werners followed their landlady back into the house. As they started up the stairs to their apartment, Mrs. Schmundt said, "I'll be gone for a week visiting my daughter who lives in a small town just north of Hamburg. The cellar door will be unlocked, as always."

"When will you be leaving?" Johanna asked.

"Later on this morning."

"Have a good trip, Mrs. Schmundt, and have a good night, or what's left of it," Emil said.

"You too," the voice at the bottom of the stairs responded.

It was after 2:00 A.M. when the Werners got to bed.

In the afternoon of 25 July, Johanna surprised her husband with another cup of real coffee.

"I thought you were saving this for a special occasion," Emil commented, as he sat down at the kitchen table.

"Come out here and take a look," she said, beckoning him to follow her out onto the balcony. Pointing to the northwest, she said, "Look at the columns of smoke that are still rising over there. That part of the city is still burning after last night's attack." She then said, "Surviving an air raid, in my mind, is fast becoming a special occasion. It no longer makes any sense to plan beyond the latest survival."

"I suppose you are right," Emil said, taking her hand and walking her back into the kitchen.

They had just sat down again when the air raid sirens started their insufferable wailing.

Emil looked at his wife and said, "This probably will be just a nuisance raid. I don't think we will have to go down to the cellar." He continued to indulge himself in the treat she had offered him. When distant heavy flak firing could be heard, he had second thoughts. He rushed out onto the balcony and directed his sight toward the sound of the distant guns. He could not see any aircraft, but he could discern the contrails of a formation approaching at high altitude from the southwest.

"Quick, get ready to go to the cellar," he yelled at his wife as he came back inside, adding, "The Americans are coming!"

"The Americans are coming? How do you know that the Americans are coming?" Johanna asked.

"Honey, the British heavy bombers only show themselves at night—let's go!"

Shortly after they had settled themselves in their cellar chairs, they could hear bomb explosions toward the southwest. After that, the formations seemed to pass directly overhead, because the flak noise reached a crescendo and then soon started to die out. Half an hour after the alert had been issued, the all clear sounded.

Emil had reached for his wife's hand when the bomb explosions became audible; he was still holding her hand when the all clear was heard.

"Does this mean that we will have to be running down here day and night?" Mrs. Werner asked.

"I don't know," Mr. Werner replied, "but we will find out soon enough."

On the morning of 26 July, Johanna was up at 8:00 A.M. and left the house an hour later to go shopping. About 10:00 A.M., air raid sirens sounded again.

Emil, in his pajamas, was in the middle of shaving when he heard the alert. Again hoping that the British were engaging in a nuisance raid, he continued to whittle away at his stubble. When he heard distant flak firing and viewed the sky to the southwest from the balcony, he knew he was in for a repeat performance of the previous afternoon. As on the day before, he saw the white trails of condensed water vapor of a formation of aircraft flying at high level.

The direction of the contrails indicated that the formation was again headed toward the city. Uh, uh, he thought, the Americans are back!

Emil shifted into double time. He ran back into the apartment, wiped the remaining shaving cream off his face, dispensed with trimming his moustache, and threw on some clothes.

He was more than slightly winded when he arrived in the cellar. Sitting there by himself, he worried about Johanna, but he soon consoled himself that she probably had sought refuge in one of the public shelters.

The raid ran its course in the same manner as the one of the previous afternoon. It lasted no longer than half an hour.

"I was near the main railroad station when the alert was given, so I had to go to a public shelter," Johanna said when she got home.

"I figured as much," her husband replied. "What kind of scuttlebutt was making the rounds in the shelter?" he then asked.

"Everyone was wondering about the tinsel strips that the Brits dropped the night before last, but no one could explain the why and wherefore. Everyone also seemed to know that the Americans are orchestrating the daylight raids."

"They only had to read the morning paper to find that out," Emil commented. He picked up the paper and said, "It says right here, 'In the afternoon of 25 July, Hamburg was subjected to its first raid by American bomber formations.' Of course, it also says 'Damage to harbor installations was minimal.'"

He sighed. Speaking more than to his wife, he continued, "The British come in the blanket of night. They drop their marker flares over residential areas and then drop their bombs into the areas targeted by the flares. The Americans, on the other hand, come during daylight hours, because they are looking for selected industrial targets. They don't always hit those targets, but at least they try."

"Emil, there is nothing we can do about any of that. Let's concentrate on something we can do, like having lunch," his wife suggested.

Emil smiled at his wife and said, "I'd like that very much."

In the afternoon of 27 July, the sirens warned of another attack, but it turned out to be a nuisance raid. Not hearing any flak, the Werners did not venture down into the cellar.

Hoping for a peaceful night they went to bed early, but the sirens wakened them just before midnight. Carrying their suitcases, they wearily made their way down to the cellar.

The raid started in the same manner as that of the raid three nights earlier. First, the rumble of the distant guns was heard. The rumbling noise increased in intensity as the aircraft neared the city, and the staccato sound of the nearby guns again overwhelmed the more distant rumble. The already earsplitting racket again was intensified by the cacophony of exploding bombs.

The discord of the guns and the din of exploding bombs continued unabated. Huddled in the cellar, the elderly couple looked at each other wide-eyed with fear.

About fifteen minutes after the first bombs had fallen, Emil sniffed the air. "I smell smoke, Johanna," was his terse comment.

"What did you say?" Johanna asked. "I can't hear you."

"I said that I smell smoke!" he bellowed.

She repeatedly drew in some air and shouted, "Oh dear! I can smell it, too. What are we going to do, Emil?"

"I'm going upstairs to take a look," he hollered as he got up from his chair.

Just as he uttered those words, an explosion rocked the house. The coal chute window was blown into the cellar; its blackout-proofed glass panels shattered as the window frame fell to the cellar floor. Most of the ceiling plaster fell and engulfed the Werners in debris. The dingy ceiling bulb brightened briefly and then extinguished.

The cellar was in complete darkness except for the intermittent reflections of the muzzle flashes of the guns that were now admitted through the open coal chute.

Ridding himself of the ceiling plaster that had fallen on him and the plaster dust that had settled inside his collar, Emil, his voice still at an elevated level, asked, "Are you alright, Johanna?"

There was no answer. He inched over to her chair and repeated his question.

Through sobs, she said, "Yes, I'm all right. Just help me to get this mess off my clothes."

As he assisted her, he said, "I've got to check where the smoke is coming from. I've got to do it now!"

"Don't leave me here alone, Emil," she implored.

"You will be safer—"

"I can't stay down here by myself!" she cried out.

"Well, come up to the vestibule with me. You can stay there while I check the upstairs."

He felt for her hand and helped her out of the chair.

"Grab your suitcases and let's go!" he exhorted.

As they felt their way toward the cellar stairs, he cautioned, "Be wary of broken glass."

When they reached the vestibule, he tried the light switch several times; the vestibule remained pitch-black.

"Stay here while I go upstairs," Emil said, "and stay away from the entrance door."

She nodded. "Please hurry back," she entreated.

In total darkness, he groped for the banister that would guide him up the stairwell to their apartment door.

"Be careful!" she shouted, wondering whether he could hear her over the din coming from the world outside.

Johanna stayed away from the entrance door as her husband had suggested, but when she heard several loud whooshing sounds, she could not contain her curiosity. She moved to the door and pulled back the blackout curtain.

The burning house across the street illuminated the scene. Women, children, and mostly elderly men were running toward the large street intersection two houses away from the Werner residence. She saw the incendiary stick bombs that had caused the whooshing sound as they came hurtling from above. They now were lying on the cobblestoned street.

Having ignited after impact, their burning charge of magnesium produced a brilliant white flame, which seemed to proclaim their evil intent. Johanna flinched at the sight. When she saw the body of a man lying in the street, she screamed!

✚ ✚ ✚

When Emil had reached the top of the stairs, he unlocked the apartment door. As he opened it, he was inundated by pungent smoke. Looking down the long hallway, he immediately saw that the balcony and the kitchen were already engulfed in flames. The sight of the flames temporarily paralyzed him; however, the acrid smoke soon urged him into action.

We have only one option, he thought. We have to get out of here quickly, but first I must save my instrument.

He rushed into the living room and put his cherished clarinet into its case. He picked up the case and was about to leave, when he noticed the living room wall adjacent to the kitchen. The wallpaper was blistering at a rapid rate and discoloring to an ever darker brown. Suddenly, the wall burst into flame. "If I don't leave now, I won't make it back to the stairs," he said.

He lunged down the hall and back to the stairway. The flames raging in the back of the house now illuminated the stairway through the open doorway. They also illuminated Johanna, who lay on the floor at the front door.

Maneuvering down the steps as quickly as he could, Emil shouted, "Johanna! Johanna! What happened?"

She did not respond.

"Johanna, we have to get out of here—the whole house will soon be in flames!" he exclaimed as he cradled her head in his hands.

She did not respond.

He checked her pulse and then gently slapped her cheeks.

"Wake up Johanna, wake up!"

She finally opened her eyes.

"Oh, Emil, I must have fainted."

The crash of falling timber upstairs emphasized the gravity of the situation.

"Johanna, we have to get out of here," he repeated as he helped her up.

"Emil, I don't want to go out there."

He looked back at the stairway. Flames were already licking at the apartment doorway. Do you want to stay here?" he asked, pointing at the apartment entrance.

Johanna sighed. "All right, let's go," she said as she picked up two suitcases.

Emil stuck the clarinet case under one arm and picked up the remaining suitcases. They stepped outside.

Emil saw the flames coming out of the lower stories of the house directly across the street. He saw the body directly in front of the house. He looked to the left and saw a large bomb crater in the street several houses away. A chill went through him when he saw the bodies, or what was left of them, lying near the crater. Looking beyond the crater, he could see that most of the houses on the block were ablaze.

The noise level was several decibels greater than what it had been in the cellar. The duet of firing guns and exploding bombs was now accompanied by the droning sound of many aircraft. To hear one another, voices had to be raised to an elevated level.

"Come on," he shouted at his wife, "we have to go toward the intersection."

They moved along with other folk who had been forced out of their shelter.

Burdened with the two suitcases, Johanna had to stop and set them done to catch her breath, although the intersection was only a short distance away.

"Emil, let's rest a moment," she yelled to her husband.

Having always been ensconced in the cellar during previous night raids, she was transfixed with horror by what she saw.

The serenity of the starlit sky was being violated by red flares hovering to mark the target area for the bombers, by searchlights desperately scanning for their prey, and by flak shells exploding in kaleidoscopic images. Under this canopy of mayhem, explosive bombs loudly proclaimed their destructive effect, while scores of incendiaries silently ignited whole housing blocks.

Johanna's mood changed from weary to agitated when she saw several tinsel strips land on her husband's jacket. She quickly brushed them off with her handbag.

Turning toward her, her husband asked, "What are you doing?"

"They are dropping that tinsel again. Some of it landed on your jacket."

"I don't think that stuff will cause us any physical harm," he commented.

"Better safe than sorry," she admonished. "Do I have any on me?" she asked as she slowly turned in a circle.

He shook his head.

Just as they were about to pick up their suitcases, they heard a voice behind them holler, "Ma'am, this is not the time to be dancing in the street."

Johanna turned around and saw that a Hitler Youth, dressed in his brown shirt and short corduroy pants, had approached them. She took him to be about fifteen years old.

"Here, let me help you with those suitcases," he said. Then he asked, "Where are you going?"

"We just escaped from our burning house. We have no idea where we should be going!" Emil exclaimed.

"Well, you can't stay here!" the boy countered. "Let me take you to the park just a block from here. It should provide a firebreak."

He picked up Johanna's luggage and headed toward the intersection.

With both her hands suddenly free, Johanna turned to her husband and said "Let me help you with those suitcases."

"I can handle them," he said, "but it would be a big help if you can take my clarinet case."

Johanna pulled the case from under his left arm.

When the youth reached the intersection, he turned right, into the Iffland Strasse. All the houses, along the sidewalk they were on, were aflame. Looking back at the Werners, the boy pointed to the conflagration and shouted, "We want to stay as far away from that as we can. Let's cross over to the open area on the other side of the street."

The Werners followed him. Both Emil and Johanna were out of breath when they finally reached the park. The Hitler Youth led them to one of the big trees.

"Stay close to the tree; it will offer some protection from flak splinters. You folks really should have something to protect your heads from the shrapnel," the boy said.

"Everybody seems to be forgetting that we are not soldiers," Johanna replied, adding, "How come you are not wearing a helmet?"

"Well…I'm not a soldier either."

Johanna immediately regretted having taken her frustration out on the boy. In a conciliatory tone she asked, "Why aren't you with your family?"

"My family is all right. We live in one of the suburbs. My unit was ordered into the city to help out where we could."

"Aren't you afraid?" Johanna asked.

The boy drew up his shoulders.

"What is your name?" Johanna asked him.

"My name is Hermann."

Johanna completed the introductions with, "Well, we are the Werners."

The boy nodded in acknowledgment.

"We want to thank you for your help, Hermann," Johanna said. "You certainly have proven to be more dependable than our fire department. I have yet to see a single fire engine!"

"Perhaps they are overwhelmed. Perhaps the streets are

blocked, and they can't get through." Hermann conjectured.

"Your first assessment probably is correct," Emil interjected, adding, "They surely must be overwhelmed. I'm not even sure that they were done putting out all the fires that were started three nights ago."

The burning houses illuminated the park in an orange hue sporadically superimposed by the incandescent muzzle flashes of the nearby guns.

Johanna observed the many people who had sought refuge in the park. She saw several older couples, a few young couples, and many women. Some of the younger couples and most of the women were accompanied by children. Most of the younger children were crying. She guessed that the many women with children were having to fend for themselves because the husbands had been called into the service.

When Johanna noticed the burnt patches of grass where incendiaries had expended themselves, she shivered.

Suddenly the whizzing sound of falling shrapnel spurred Hermann into renewed action. "We have to find a safer place," he confided to Emil.

"Where will we go?" Emil asked.

"Let's go to the other side of the park and across the street to the Lohmuehlen Krankenhaus. The hospital has a below ground air raid shelter. Perhaps you can stay there."

He picked up Johanna's suitcases and started out toward the other side of the park. The Werners, as well as several other folks, followed him.

As Hermann and his small contingent approached the hospital, they saw numerous ambulances, their emergency beacons flashing, lined up on the ramp to the emergency room. The drivers were waiting their turn to unload casualties of the raid. Hermann led his group to the main entrance and down a flight of stairs to the air raid shelter, but when they reached the shelter entrance, an air raid warden immediately waved them off.

"I'm sorry, but I cannot admit anyone else into the shelter. All of our ambulatory patients are in there, and we have taken outsiders in to the extent that the shelter is now overcrowded," the warden told Hermann.

"I can't ask them to go back outside," the boy responded.

"Nobody is asking you to do that," the warden said. "Take them back upstairs. Don't go to the main entrance; that area is all glass enclosed. Take them to one of the inside hallways where there aren't any windows. You'll find some benches in the hallways. They can stay there until the all-clear," adding in a lowered voice that only Hermann could hear, "or until we take a hit."

"Your fifty-fifty odds are not very encouraging," Hermann said to the warden.

The warden responded to the boy's sarcasm with, "Hey, they've hit almost everything else tonight."

After Hermann took his charges back up the stairs, he pointed out several hallways where they could wait for the all-clear. The group that had followed Hermann and the Werners dispersed. He then led the Werners to an empty bench.

"You will be safer here than in the park," Hermann said to the Werners. After a brief pause, he continued, "Well I'd better get back outside."

"What will you be doing back outside?" Johanna asked.

"I'll be looking for some poor souls that need some help; I'm sure there are many out there."

"You're a brave young man, Hermann," Johanna said. "Do be careful."

"I will."

"Thank you for your help," Emil called out as the boy left.

Johanna turned to Emil and asked, "Well, where do we go from here?"

Emil shrugged and replied, "I have no idea."

+++

Emil looked at his pocket watch. It was now 1:30 A.M. After he replaced the watch, he looked up and saw a soldier coming down the hall. Noticing the soldier's red collar emblems and his shoulder insignias, Emil knew that the man was a first lieutenant with an antiaircraft unit. Emil also noticed that the soldier's tunic was stained with blood at the right shoulder. The man sat down next to Emil.

"What happened to you, officer?" Emil asked.

"I got in the way of a bomb fragment."

"Shouldn't you be seeing a doctor?" Emil asked

"I've already seen a doctor," the soldier replied, as he pulled aside his tunic and bared a bloody bandage. "The doctor told me I would have to wait a while before he could remove the fragment, because he is presently overwhelmed with casualties, most of them being burn victims. At the moment, those casualties need the doctor more than I do."

"It seems like this raid is as bad as the one we had three nights ago," Emil suggested.

"This raid is much worse. Whole city districts are aflame, and the British have again provided our radar with false echoes which have put our air defenses at a severe disadvantage. Many of our guns and searchlights are directed by radar."

"How do the Brits affect our radar?"

The flak soldier looked at Emil and said, "A week ago I would not have been allowed to talk about what I'm going to tell you. We have had a radar deterrent in our inventory for a long time, but we never used it for fear that the enemy would copy it and use it against our own radar installations. But now, since the British have come out with an almost identical version, the cat is out of the bag." He then pulled something out of his tunic pocket and opened his hand. Emil looked incredulously at the tinsel strips the soldier held in his hand. "We saw that stuff falling to the ground three nights ago! You're telling me that those little strips cause radar interference?" Emil asked incredulously.

"Not the little strips by themselves," the soldier said.

"The strips are wrapped in bundles when they are dropped out of the aircraft and the bundled strips provide a false echo to our radar. You can imagine the many false echoes that are received when each aircraft drops the bundles in thirty second intervals over the target area. On their way down, the bundles disintegrate and the individual strips fall silently to the ground."

Emil looked at the soldier with some disbelief. "I'm not an expert, but I can tell the difference between the sound of exploding bombs and flak bursts. The flak was very heavy during these last two night raids. Are you telling me that they were shooting blind?"

"That is exactly what I am telling you. We estimate that the bundles dropped by each aircraft provide ten echoes for that aircraft on the radar screen. At the rate that the echoes were appearing on the radar screen during the raid three nights ago, the British would have had to field five thousand bombers for the echoes to be true targets, but we know that even the British do not have that many aircraft available. Yes, we were, and still are, shooting blind! We are shooting barrages to fill the sky with shrapnel at the altitude of the bombers!"

"Did you hear that, Johanna? The mystery of the tinsel has been solved!" Emil exclaimed.

"Yes, yes, I heard."

The trio sat silent for a while.

"What does this foretell for future raids?" Emil asked.

The soldier drew up his shoulders and said, "We'll look for a way to tweak the radar to make it less susceptible to false echoes. In the meantime, we will bring in a lot more searchlights. The searchlights won't go out of style, because the British bomber formations usually only come on clear nights."

Emil pondered the soldier's response for a moment and then commented, "All those counter measures won't change our predicament."

"You lost your home?"

"Yes," Emil answered.

"I'm sorry."

About 2:00 A.M. the antiaircraft firing started to diminish, and fifteen minutes later the all-clear sounded. Immediately thereafter, the hospital intercom announced that all those who needed to be evacuated should report to the main entrance area.

"I guess that means us," Emil said as he turned to Johanna.

"Unfortunately, it does," she commented.

Emil turned to the soldier and said, "As you heard, it's time for us to leave. How is that shoulder doing?"

"I feel a dull pain, but I can live with it."

"Well, we wish you a speedy recovery and better luck in the future," Emil said.

"Good luck to you," the soldier reciprocated.

The Werners picked up their luggage and trudged toward the assembly area.

The main entrance area presented a calamitous scene. It was filled with gurneys bearing as yet untreated victims of the many fires. Lying on the gurneys were adults and children. The adults were moaning; the children were crying. The smell of burnt flesh pervaded the air. Johanna and Emil exchanged glances through tearful eyes.

"We have to go over there," Emil said, as he pointed to an attendant who was holding up an improvised sign that had "evacuees" scrawled on it. They joined a group of people already assembled.

"We will wait another five minutes for stragglers; if none arrive, Hans here will lead you to the supply building which is adjacent to this one," the attendant said while pointing to another attendant who had joined him. "At the supply building you will find several Wehrmacht trucks that will take you to a nearby athletic field. Once you reach the athletic field, you will transfer to busses that will take you out of the city."

"Where will the busses take us?" someone asked.

The attendant holding the sign thought for a moment then he said, "They will take you away from the greatest disaster that has ever befallen this city."

There weren't any more questions.

After no one else showed up during the attendant's grace period, he said, "Hans, show these folks where they have to go."

As the evacuees left the hospital, they noticed that the surrounding fires had turned the night's darkness to near daylight. Johanna looked toward the east and saw an inferno. Flames were licking the sky, and black clouds of smoke were billowing thousands of feet into the air.

"Imagine the poor souls who were caught up in that," Johanna wailed and started to sob.

"Try not to dwell on those poor souls. They are beyond help," Emil replied.

The trucks had backed up to the loading dock of the supply building for easy access to the truck beds.

"Board the trucks as quickly as you can," Hans bade his charges.

Once all were aboard, he waved his hand and wished them well before he started back toward the hospital.

Progress of the convoy of four trucks was slow because the drivers had to circumvent bomb craters and maneuver deftly through debris that littered the streets. The trip normally would have required ten minutes, but on this night it took over half an hour.

The athletic field seemed to have been transformed into a huge bus depot, and refugees were streaming toward this makeshift depot from all directions. Emil asked someone who seemed to be in charge, "Which bus should we get on?"

"It doesn't make any difference. They will all be heading north to temporary evacuation centers."

"Thank you." Turning to Johanna, he said, "We might as well get on this one." Before boarding, he put their luggage into the storage compartment, but he held onto his clarinet case. As they entered the bus, the driver handed Emil a clipboard, "Please enter your names and former address."

"What for?" Emil asked.

"Police orders—they are maintaining a record of who was evacuated."

Once all the seats were taken, the bus driver circumspectly maneuvered the bus in low gear through rubble-strewn streets until he reached a main artery leading out of the city; then, he accelerated in a northerly direction.

Emil looked at his wife sitting beside him. Grateful that she had been able to doze off, he reclined in his seat and closed his eyes.

Top: Walther and the children in 1939

Bottom row, left to right:
Herbert, Romi and Walther four and a half years later

Hertha's ID card issued in June 0f 1942 and validated through 1947

BALTIC SEA
NORTH SEA
BUESUM
CUXHAVEN
NORDHOLZ
HAMBURG
BREMERHAVEN
[SCHNEIDENM
BREMEN
CELLE
BERLIN
HANOVER
MAGDEBURG
ROTTERDAM
KASSEL
LEIPZIG
COLOGNE
ERFURT
DRESDEN
SIEGEN
BRUSSELS
DECIN
[TETSCHEN]
TREUEN
PRAGUE
GERMANY
CZECH REPUBL
PASSAU
FRANCE
AUSTR
SWITZERLAND
ITALY
ADRIATIC SEA
LIGURIAN SEA

BYDGOSZCZ [BROMBERG]
SZUBIN [ALTBURGUND]
BIALYSTOK
WARSAW
POLAND
OSTRZESZOW
[SCHILDBERG]
SLOVAKIA
BRATISLAVA
BUDAPEST
HUNGARY
BONYHAD
PECS
POST-WAR
NORTH
CENTRAL
EUROPE

Chapter 29

On Friday, 30 July, Herbert's class was surprised when the associate teacher, Mr. Bohnke, called the class to order. When one of the boys asked about Mr. Vogt's whereabouts, Mr. Bohnke told the class that Mr. Vogt had to go to Bonyhad to pick up several telegrams addressed to him.

On Monday, 2 August, Mr. Vogt addressed the class and told them that he had some bad news.

"Hamburg was subjected to severe air raids in the early morning hours of both 25 July and 28 July. Damage was severe, and the casualty count was high.

"The saddest news I have is from relatives of Horst Damm, who have advised me that his mother was killed in one of those raids."

Mr. Vogt noticed a mixture of regret and foreboding ripple through the class—regret for their classmate and foreboding for their own loved ones.

After scanning the classroom, one of the boys asked, "Where is Horst now?"

"He is already on his way back to Hamburg," the teacher answered.

"Will we all be going home?" another boy asked.

Mr. Vogt shook his head. "No, no. The only reason we came here was to get out from under the raids; besides, logistically it would be impossible to return now."

Mr. Vogt gave the class a few minutes to come to grips with what he had just told them and to let them talk among themselves.

When the teacher continued to address the class, he said, "We will not be doing our normal classroom work today. I have brought postcards—enough for all of you—so that you can write a short note to your parents to urge them to let you know as soon as possible how they fared during the raid."

"What good will that do, if our home has been destroyed?" someone piped up.

Mr. Vogt had anticipated the question. "In those cases the cards will come back marked undeliverable. Hopefully, in all such cases your parents temporarily will have found new quarters either in the city or elsewhere. In either case, I am sure your parents will immediately correspond with you without the urging of your card." Then he added, "The undeliverable cards that I am worried about are those that are not followed shortly by news from your parents."

The teacher looked at the class and asked, "Do you understand what I am saying?"

The class nodded in assent.

"Anyone whose card comes back marked undeliverable will let me know immediately. If we don't hear from your parents within ten days of receipt of such cards, I will send Mr. Bohnke back to Hamburg to make the necessary inquiries; I sincerely hope this will not be necessary."

"Were the raids really that bad?" Horst Drossen asked.

"They were that bad," Mr. Vogt replied. Then he said, "I will distribute the postcards now. After you have completed your message, bring them back to me. I will then have each of you cosign a letter of condolence that I have written to Horst Damm. After that you are dismissed."

Although Herbert knew that his parents and siblings were not in Hamburg, he too sent a card. He sent his card to his grandparents, Mr. and Mrs. Werner. Herbert also wrote a letter to his mother, asking whether they had heard from the grandparents.

✚✚✚

The severity of the raid in the early morning hours of 28 July had been such that even the OKW could not ignore it. The OKW issued a statement that Hamburg had been subjected to considerable damage.

Walther was granted emergency leave to look after his affairs; however, his travel papers were not issued until 3 August. He and Hertha boarded the first available train for their journey back to Hamburg. During the train ride, Walther commented, "I sure hope we can bring Hannelore's doll back, as she requested."

"Why is that so important?" Hertha asked.

"If we can't bring the doll back, we probably won't be able to bring anything else back!" Walther replied.

After they arrived at the Hamburg main station, they soon found out that the British had staged two more early morning raids: one on 30 July, the other on 3 August.

As they walked along the Steindamm towards the Werner's residence, the many gutted houses on either side of the avenue were portentous of what might lie ahead. Folks were clearing debris from the street and some of the luckier ones were retrieving some of their possessions from homes that had been merely damaged, but were no longer habitable.

"Oh, my God!" Hertha cried out as she saw the ruins of the Werner's dwelling from afar. As they drew nearer, she cried when she saw that the house had collapsed onto itself and spilled its brick facade into the street.

"Oh, Walther! You don't suppose...you don't suppose that they are buried under that rubble?" she uttered amidst sobs.

Walther reached out and put his arms around her and held her close. When she looked up at him, she could see that he, too, had tears in his eyes.

After regaining his composure, he said, "This house burned to the ground; it was not hit by an explosive bomb.

"Incendiaries probably crashed through the roof and set the house ablaze. Without intervention, the house will then burn from the top down. I'm sure that your parents had enough time to get out." As he said this, he was hoping that she would not realize that the Werner's apartment had been on the top floor.

"Do you really think so?"

"I really do," he lied.

"How can we find out?" Hertha asked.

Walther had noticed that two houses in the middle of the block remained essentially unscathed. "Let's see if we can find someone over there whom we can ask about your parents," he replied as he gestured toward the houses.

As they approached the first house, they saw a man who was replacing several window panes.

When the man turned to look at them, Walther said, "Looks like you got away with minimal damage."

Smiling wryly, the man said, "Luck of the draw, I guess... perhaps I should say we were lucky that our number was not drawn."

Walther nodded and then asked, "Do you know what happened to the folks who lived in house number 1A?" He pointed down the block, as he added, "1A is...was located near the intersection to the Iffland Strasse."

"Sorry, I don't. I don't even know the folks who lived in 1A. Perhaps someone over there can help you," the man said as he gestured toward the other house. Walther thanked him and nodded in acknowledgment when the man wished them luck.

After they had entered the vestibule of the other house, Walther pushed the doorbell for the ground floor. An elderly woman opened the door.

"Good afternoon," Walther said, "We are trying to determine the whereabouts of the Werners who lived—"

"I know the Werners…" she hesitated when she saw Hertha's apprehensive look, "but I don't know what happened to them."

Hertha again burst into tears. "How do we find out?" she sobbed.

"I understand that the police are keeping records of the folks that are being evacuated. You might inquire at police headquarters whether their names are listed. The headquarters itself was hit, but they are operating out of temporary quarters. You'll have to ask around, because I don't know where those temporary quarters are located," the elderly woman volunteered.

"Well, thank you very much for your time. We will do as you suggested," Walther replied.

They were about to leave, when the woman said, "My husband and I were very lucky. If it had not been for the tenant man who lives upstairs, this house would have burned to the ground, too. That brave soul elected to stay in the attic during the raid of the 28th. Two incendiaries crashed through the roof while he was up there. Somehow he managed to pick them up with a long-handled shovel and to pitch them through the attic window before they could do much damage. We are keeping the shovel as a memento. The blade has holes burned through it from the few seconds the incendiaries rested on it."

"Your tenant is indeed a brave soul," Walther said as they bade her farewell.

He led his wife away in the same direction they had come to spare her another look at the rubble of the Werner residence.

"Are you all right?" he asked.

She answered with a halfhearted nod.

They walked in silence.

What do I tell Hertha in the event that the Werner's names do not show up on an evacuation list, Walther asked himself. Even though this would not mean that they did not survive the raid, what do I tell her to convince her that all is not lost? What do I tell her to give her hope and to assuage the agony of not knowing until we hopefully will receive news of their survival? Should I tell her that they probably were able to escape the city on their own? Should I intimate that a good Samaritan conceivably led them out of harm's way? Should I suggest that perhaps they were not even at home? Which scenario do I propose to lessen the devastating impact of their names not being on the evacuation list? I need more time to think this through, Walther concluded and said, "Let's go to the Iffland Strasse to find out how we have fared before we make our inquiry at the police station."

She answered with another spiritless nod.

+++

When they turned a corner into the Iffland Strasse, Hertha clutched Walther's arm and gasped, "Oh, my God!"

They could see from afar the huge void where their apartment house had stood, as well as the remaining outer walls of the adjacent buildings. Tears were running down Hertha's cheeks when she said, "We put so much work into that place, and it was all for naught. Now we have lost everything, and I suppose, when everything is said and done, I am the one who is accountable."

"No, no," Walther replied, adding, "no one in their wildest dreams could have imagined that something like this would happen." He put his arm around her while they stared at the devastation that had replaced their home.

"Come," he finally said, "there is no sense in going any closer. Let's find someone who can tell us where the temporary police headquarters are located so that we can find out your parents' whereabouts."

+++

A long queue of people stood outside the temporary police headquarters. "Wait here, while I go inside and talk to the desk sergeant," Walther told his wife.

When he came back out, he motioned toward the line of people and said, "We have to go to the end of the line. All those folks also are trying to locate missing persons."

"Whatever," Hertha laconically replied, and then in a subdued voice added, "Standing in line has become a national pastime; now even matters of life and death can't be resolved unless one first stands in line."

The queue slowly inched forward. It was a somber procession. Knowing what a missing name might imply, everyone dreaded the possibility of not finding the names of their loved ones on the list.

After the queue had moved forward sufficiently to where Walther could recognize the folks who had been considerably ahead of them in line leave the headquarters, he felt that the look of despair on some of the faces singled out those folks who had not found the names of their loved ones on the list.

Finally it was their turn to talk to one of the attendant officers standing behind a long counter.

"We're looking for a Mr. and Mrs. Werner, my wife's parents," Walther told the police officer.

"In which city district did they live?" the officer asked.

"Hohenfelde," Walther replied.

The officer turned and pulled a loose-leaf binder out of a cubbyhole. "These lists were compiled by the evacuation people. Since they are not in alphabetical order, this will take a little time," he said as he started to scan the lists.

"Werner, Werner," the officer mumbled. Then he asked, "Is that first vowel an e?"

Walther nodded in assent.

"Werner, Werner," the officer mumbled again as he continued his search. "Here we go. I have a Mr. Werner listed—"

"Thank God!" Hertha exclaimed exuberantly.

The officer completed his sentence with, "a Mr. Georg Werner."

Hertha's exuberance collapsed back into despair. Between sobs she cried out, "No, no, we're looking for Emil and Johanna Werner."

The policeman lifted both hands and said, "Try to calm down, lady. I haven't searched the whole list."

They waited while he ran his finger down several pages of the list of names. Suddenly he looked up and said to Hertha, "Your parents were evacuated in the early morning hours of 28 July."

Hertha gave a sigh of relief. She clutched Walther by the arm and exclaimed, "They're alive!.They were able to get out!" Turning to the officer, she asked, "Where are they now?"

The officer shook his head and said, "I don't know. The only thing the list tells us is that these folks were evacuated. We do not know where they wound up."

"Well, I'm sure we will hear from them soon," Hertha said and addressing the officer added, "Thank you for your help. You have restored our peace of mind."

Before they left, Walther asked the policeman about the conditions of the city's transit system.

"There isn't any. At the moment, the whole system is down," he replied and then asked, "You're presently from out of town, yes?"

Walther nodded.

"Well, if you plan on going anywhere in the city you'd best plan on going there on foot. Also, the worst hit districts of the city have been cordoned off. You cannot go there."

Walther acknowledged the policeman's statement with another nod.

As Walther and Hertha left the temporary headquarters, he said, "We won't be able to stop and see your friend Ihde, as you had planned. It would take us hours to get there on foot."

"So where do we go from here?" Hertha asked.

"Since all the neighbors whom we knew here in Hamburg are now…are now elsewhere, there is no reason to stick around, other than to get a statement from the housing authority that we have lost our home. It looks like you will have to stay in Schildberg for the foreseeable future, and we will need that statement to convince our landlady to extend our apartment lease indefinitely. After that, we will head back to the main railroad station and make arrangements for our return trip."

Chapter 30

Romi and little Hannelore rushed to greet their parents upon their return.

"We missed you a lot," Romi said.

"I missed my Mama and my Papa," Hannelore chimed in.

"Well, we missed you, too," Hertha countered as she gave both another hug.

"Grandmother Werner's house got hit, didn't it?" Romi surmised.

"It was completely destroyed, but how did you know?" Hertha asked.

"There is a letter for you from Grandmother Werner—it has a different return address. You also have a letter from Herbert. Did you get to see the Werners while you were there?"

"No. As a matter of fact, we feared for the worst when we saw the ruins of their house. We finally went to the police and found out that they had been evacuated, but the police did not know their destination," Hertha replied.

"Did you bring back my dolly?" Hannelore asked.

Walther and Hertha exchanged a quick glance. When Walther saw Hertha trying to control her tears, he answered the question. "We couldn't bring back your dolly, Hannelore," he said. He looked at the little girl and her older sister and added, "We have lost our home too."

"Is my dolly broken?" Hannelore asked as she started to cry.

Her father nodded.

"Are all my dollies broken?" she wailed. Walther nodded again. He tried to console her by saying, "We'll try to get you new dolls."

"They won't be the same," she responded between sobs.

Rosemarie was also lamenting. "How am I going to replace all my clothes? Couldn't anything be salvaged?"

"There was nothing left to salvage," Hertha told her. "We will get you new stuff, as soon as we get the necessary clothing allotment."

"As Hannelore put it: It won't be the same. Just don't get me that synthetic fiber clothing that is now being offered," Romi admonished. "That stuff is a bunch of crap."

"Romi, that's not a nice way for a young lady to express herself," Hertha chided.

"Maybe not, but that new stuff itches when you wear it, shrinks when you wash it, and falls apart in no time at all."

"Well, let's look at the bright side," Hertha said. "If you and Hannelore and I had been in Hamburg instead of here, looking for new clothing might not have been an option; we might have all been killed. Even though the bright side is still a bad situation, we will just have to make the best of it." She sighed as she looked sympathetically at her two daughters and said, "But enough of that for now. Let's have a little lunch, after which, we will read the letters from Grandmother Werner and Herbert."

✚ ✚ ✚

After Hertha opened the letter from her mother, she read it aloud to Walther and the girls. She had to interrupt herself several times to wipe away the tears, as she read her mother's description of having fled the burning city.

Grandmother Werner indicated that they presently were in a temporary evacuation camp and that they had no idea when and where they would be allocated a more permanent residence.

Hertha then read the letter from Herbert to them. When she put the letter down, she said, "Looks like I'll have to get busy and write three letters just as soon as possible."

"Why three letters?" Walther asked.

"The third letter will be to Miele Lienhof—better known as Tante Emi to you girls," she said, glancing at Romi and Hannelore and then adding, "Miele told me years ago that if my parents ever were in need, she would want to help them out. We can't take them in, since we are already cramped for space. I'm sure Miele's offer was sincere. I'm sure she will take them in. The letter to Miele is the most urgent; therefore, I will write to her before I answer the other two."

Mr. Vogt had received another telegram on 4 August advising him of the additional heavy raids on Hamburg in the early morning hours of 30 July and 3 August.

The following morning he told the class that he wanted them to repeat the exercise of sending postcards to their parents in another effort to ascertain that the parents were all right.

Six of the cards issued during the prior exercise had been returned marked "undeliverable," but only four of the boys who had received the returned cards had been contacted by their parents. The remaining two boys who had received "undeliverable" notices anxiously awaited the next mail call in hopes of hearing from their parents. The anxiety extended to about half of the remaining class whose cards had not been returned, but who had not yet received news from their parents.

"I want everyone whose parents still may have been in Hamburg between 30 July and 3 August to send a second card," Mr. Vogt said before adding, "This is not a redundant exercise. You must realize that these last two raids put us right back to where we were when we received notice of the first two."

Within the next two weeks all the boys had received confirmation that their parents were unscathed, and no additional "undeliverable" cards were received.

✚✚✚

Herbert's mood changed from relief to dejection while he read his mother's letter. He was relieved that his grandparents had been able to escape the fiery city, but he felt despondent when his mother told him that their home also had been destroyed.

He was primarily disappointed that he would never be able to test-fly the model sailplane that he had built in shop-class during his last year in grade school. The model had a wingspan of just over one meter, and he had placed it out of harm's way, just before leaving for Hungary, by hanging it over his bed in the children's room.

When Herbert told Mr. Vogt that his home had been destroyed, Mr. Vogt said, "I'm sorry to hear that. Are your parents all right?"

"Yes. My mother and my sisters were with my father in the former Polish territory when the raids occurred."

"The former Polish territory?" Mr. Vogt asked with surprise. "Why there?"

"My father is stationed there."

"I see," Mr. Vogt acknowledged. "Is that where you will be staying after we leave here?"

The boy hunched his shoulders and said, "Even if we could find another place to stay in Hamburg, I don't think my father would want us to return there."

Mr. Vogt looked at him and said, "Including Horst Damm, seven of you boys have lost your home. Makes you sort of wonder just how much of the city is left, doesn't it?"

Herbert nodded.

"When the time comes, I'll make the necessary arrangements for you to return to your parents. But you will first have to come to Hamburg with us. My responsibilities toward you do not end until I have brought you all back to Hamburg. After that, you will be on your own," Mr. Vogt said. Then he asked, "Do you feel you will find your way all by yourself?"

Herbert shrugged and said, "It will just be another eight-hour train ride."

✦ ✦ ✦

Life returned to normal, as normal as life could be for big-city boys who had been relegated to the boondocks. The boys adapted to the shortcomings of not having indoor plumbing and electricity. They did not mind hauling water from the well. And they accepted using the outhouse, because there was no other option.

Food was plentiful; therefore, there was no need for rationing. Breakfast consisted of pieces of bread contained in a bowl of coffee with cream or milk. Along with the "cereal," slices of smoked bacon were available. Lunch featured smoked bacon or ham sandwiches served with coffee or milk.

Dinner was served in the evening. Ample helpings of meat, potatoes, and vegetables reminded the boys of prewar times. A bottle of wine was a ubiquitous feature of the dinner table-setting.

Shortly after the boys had arrived in Graboc, Mr. Vogt urged them to go easy on the wine, stating that he was very much averse to teaching a classroom full of lushes. Apparently the boys were heeding his urging. To date, no one had been hung over when reporting for class.

By mid-July most of the boys were saving wear and tear of their shoes by walking around in batschkas, which were calf-length wool stockings with a patch of canvas sewn across the sole and heel. Batschkas were the footwear of choice of the local populace, except when they were wearing their Sunday best.

One afternoon Horst Drossen and Herbert visited Karl at his sponsor's place. With no particular agenda, they walked around in the farmyard and eventually wound up in the cow shed.

"Wow, your farmer must be one of the better heeled ones," Horst remarked after he had counted eight cows. "My farmer has only two."

"That's all my farmer has—two cows," Herbert said.

"Do your sponsors have any horses?" Karl asked.

Horst and Herbert both shook their heads.

"My sponsor has two horses, but they are old draft horses, not riding horses." Karl related.

As they walked along the cow stalls, Herbert said, "In America cowboys ride these critters."

"They ride cows?" Horst asked incredulously.

"No, no. They don't ride the cows; the cows are too docile. They ride the bulls."

"What's so great about that?" Horst asked.

"Have you ever ridden a bull?" Herbert asked as they stopped at one of the stalls.

Horst shook his head.

"Well, if you ever do, you will soon find out that the bull does not like it. The bull will buck and kick up his hind legs in an effort to get you off his back. He won't quit until he has thrown you. Once he has thrown you, he may even turn around and try to gore you."

"So why do the cowboys do it?" Karl asked.

"They do it as a contest, which usually is part of an exhibition called a rodeo. The cowboys accumulate points according to how long they can stay astride the bull. The one with the most points wins a prize," Herbert explained.

"What else do they do at a rod…a rodeo?" Horst asked.

"Well, among other things, they have bronco-riding and calf-lassoing contests."

"What's a bronco?" Karl asked.

"It's an untamed horse," Herbert answered.

"I can see trying to ride an untamed horse, but I don't know about riding a bull," Horst said and then asked, "Have you ever ridden a bull?"

"Hey, I'm not a cowboy," Herbert responded.

"Have you ever ridden a cow?" Horst asked.

"No."

"I don't think cows are as docile as you think they are," Horst ventured.

"Yeah, they are," Herbert countered.

"Well, we could debate the issue from now until doomsday. I'm willing to bet a month's allowance that if you were to mount one of these cows, she would let you know that she doesn't like it," Horst challenged.

Herbert thought, a month's allowance was enough to buy a ticket to one of the occasional German movies that were shown in Bonyhad.

"OK, you're on," he told Horst.

Herbert climbed one of the fences that separated the stalls and eased himself onto one of the cows. The cow just turned her head backward while continuing to chew her cud. "See, I told you they are submissive," Herbert cried out triumphantly.

A moment later, the cow started to kick up her hind legs. After Herbert felt his head impact a roof beam, he lost his balance and fell to the floor of the stall.

Horst and Karl broke out laughing.

Herbert, somewhat dazed, got up and felt his way toward the exit of the stall. Just before he got out, the sudden warmth engulfing his right foot through his batschka told him that he had stepped into a freshly baked "cow pie."

His friends responded with renewed laughter.

Still laughing, Horst said. "That cow sure was docile—about as docile as a pugnacious pit bull!"

✦✦✦

By mid-August, the grape harvest was in full swing. One afternoon Johann asked Herbert whether he would like to go out to the vineyards with the family to help with the harvest.

"Sure, I'll go along," Herbert responded.

"We'll be harnessing the cows to the wagon and taking them into some hilly terrain. I'll need someone to brake the wagon on the downhill slopes during our return trip. I don't want the loaded wagon to bear down on the cows and force them to run. Dairy cows don't like to run; besides, it is hard on them," Johann told him.

After the baskets were loaded onto the wagon, Marie, the children, and her mother Mrs. Schneider started to walk ahead, while Johann got ready to follow in the wagon.

Herbert jumped up onto the wagon and seated himself next to Johann on the driver's seat. "Where is the brake handle that you want me to operate on our way back," Herbert asked.

"Brake handle? There is no brake handle," Johann replied.

"How do I apply the brakes if there is no brake handle?"

"Take a look at the back of the wagon. The brake is in the back."

Herbert looked and saw a plank of wood about a foot wide, three foot long, and perhaps two inches thick, lying in the back of the wagon. One end of the plank was tied to the wagon by a short heavy rope. "Is that piece of wood back there what you use to brake the wagon?" Herbert asked.

Johann nodded.

"It's not heavy enough to cause any substantial drag," Herbert reckoned.

Johann laughed and said, "Of course it isn't. On our way back we will drop the plank and let it drag behind the wagon. When I ask you to brake, you will hold onto the wagon and stand on the plank. You will be surprised how quickly you will slow us down. We call it our brake board.

"Now, why don't you jump off and walk with Marie and the children. We don't want to strain the cows anymore than we have to."

No electricity, no indoor plumbing, and no brakes, Herbert thought as he scrambled to catch up with Marie and the children. I wonder if they still write with a quill?

His thoughts ran along those lines until he realized how fortunate he was that these people had taken him in. He was well fed, and was far away from the air raids.

As they walked along, they came upon several gypsy children who were standing along the roadside. The sight of the children in their ragged clothing and the ramshackle huts wherein they lived reinforced Herbert's feeling of being very lucky.

Once they had reached the vineyards, they spent the rest of the afternoon picking grapes, putting them into the baskets, and loading the baskets onto the wagon.

"What are you going to do with all these grapes?" Herbert asked Marie. "It will take weeks to eat them all."

"Most of them will be used to make wine. We will put them in the stone vats that you may have seen in one of our sheds. Johann has been busy getting the vats ready during the past few days."

"What happens after the grapes are in the vats?" Herbert asked.

"We climb into the vats and mash the grapes."

"How do you do that?"

"We mash them with our feet."

"With your feet?" he asked while giving her an incredulous look.

She laughed and reiterated, "Yes, with our feet. Next to each vat is a basin. We fill the basin with water and wash our feet before we climb into the vat."

"Oh."

After the wagon had been loaded, Herbert remembered that they had traversed several hills on the way to the vineyards; therefore, braking would be required when they reached the downward slopes of those hills on the way back. To be prepared for Johann's command for braking action, he lowered the brake board onto the ground at the start of the return trip.

On the modest down slopes, Herbert found that he could effect sufficient braking merely by walking such that his left foot came down on the ground while his right foot impinged on the brake board. On more severe slopes, he found that sufficient braking required that he put his full weight on the board.

"More brake," Johann yelled on two occasions when Herbert's full weight was already on the board. The first time this happened, Marie deftly jumped on the board behind the boy, maintaining her balance by holding onto his waist.

On the second occasion, Marie's mother joined him on the board. She did not hold onto his hips; she put her arms under his and laced them across his chest. Her grip was so tight that he had difficulty breathing. Herbert thought, that by stepping backward and tweaking her toes, she surely would release her grip, but he immediately discarded that notion, not only because the woman might fall and be injured but also because he would be left skidding down the steep slope behind an out of control load of grapes. He frantically held onto the wagon until they reached the bottom of the hill.

"That was a tough one, wasn't it?" Johann shouted back at them.

You don't know how tough, Herbert thought.

On a Sunday morning Herbert got up a little earlier than usual. As he stepped out of his room into the foyer, he did a double take, and he could feel the blood rush to his head. He knew his entire face was turning red as a pomegranate, as he saw that Marie had set up a basin in the foyer and was washing her hair. She was stripped to the waist!

Herbert stood there dumbfounded for a moment. He quickly averted his eyes and was ready to mumble an apology, before slipping back into his room, when she said, "You're up early this morning. Go, sit down in the living room. Breakfast will be ready in a little bit."

Her tone of voice seems completely unfazed, almost as if she runs around like that all the time, his befuddled mind told him. But I can't go in there, he thought, from my assigned seat at the table, she'll still be in full view!

He searched his memory to determine how he had handled a similar situation in the past, but he found none. With his head still feeling like it had been stuck into a sauna, he told himself to do something. Finally, guided by her apparent nonchalance, he decided to react in like manner, while simultaneously wondering how to demonstrate such nonchalance.

Herbert's eye caught the foyer bucket. Ah, there is my escape route, he thought. Out loud, he said, "Uh, uh, I better go to the well and replenish the bucket."

"You don't have to do that; it's still a quarter full," Marie replied.

"I might as well fill it up," he said, "I still need the practice." In his bewildered state, he reached for the bucket and promptly let it slip out of his hand, thereby allowing the contents to spill on the floor.

"Now you do have to replenish the bucket," Marie said with a laugh.

"Idiot," he chastised himself under his breath, "you couldn't have picked a worse time to act like such a klutz!" He grabbed a mop from the corner of the foyer and began to mop up. Noticing that the water was flowing toward Marie's basin, he slowly mopped toward her.

"Just put the mop down and go fetch the water," she said. "I'll take care of that as soon as I am finished here."

Herbert gratefully accepted what he considered a reprieve.

He dropped the mop, grabbed the bucket, and headed for the door.

He had not completely composed himself when he reached the well. Gee whiz, he thought, back home Romi would yell, "You can't come in right now," if he approached the children's bedroom when she was in her underwear. Hannelore, then all of seven years old, would mimic her sister's "You can't come in right now." Here, the lady of the house stands half naked, and she doesn't say boo!

Herbert took his time to lower the well bucket, to pull it back up, and to transfer the water to his hand held bucket.

He dawdled intentionally to ensure that Marie had completed her toilette by the time he came back into the house. As he came back in, he noticed that he had come back too soon. Marie was still standing at the basin, and she was conversing with her two children. Herbert placed the water bucket in its corner and headed back to his room. He sat on his bed and thought, Different folks, different strokes. With just a twinge of disappointment he realized that she thought of him as one of the kids. He waited until a splash of water signified that the basin had been emptied into the farm yard; then, he waited another five minutes, before he walked to the door.

As he opened the door to join the family at the breakfast table, he resolved to just crack the door and to take a peek the next time he decided to get up early.

In mid-September, Herbert received another letter from his mother. He read that Emi Lienhof had traveled to northern Germany to pick up his grandparents who, at the time, were still housed in temporary evacuation shelters. She had taken them back to the Sudetenland with her, where they would be staying with the Lienhofs for the foreseeable future. Tante Emi is a good soul, Herbert thought.

His mother also told him that, upon his return from Hungary, he was to join her and his sisters in Altburgund, since they now had no place else to go.

Since Graboc did not have electricity, telephone lines, or a newspaper, local news was announced by the town crier. He would walk through the village streets in the early evening hours and make his announcements at prearranged locations.

Since he did not operate on a timetable, he had a small drum attached to his waist with which to evoke the villagers' attention at each location by performing a drumroll before proceeding with his "newscast."

The town crier received his inputs from two sources: the village elder and the Roman Catholic parish priest.

Primarily, the village elder's inputs advised the farmers of the going prices of various staples at the farmer's markets and of special events that were scheduled to take place in nearby towns. The priest's inputs were mainly concerned with the announcement of any newborn infant, wedding, illness, or death notice. Because all the villagers were parish members, the news service covered all from the cradle to the grave.

After the nightmare of losing their home in Hamburg, Hertha and the girls spent a quiet summer in Schildberg.

On a Saturday toward the end of September, Romi, with Hannelore in tow, went on an errand to the local drugstore for her mother. Romi was reluctant to go, because she would be having another encounter with Kezimi, the store clerk. He was a young Polish fellow who was also a photographer. Although always friendly, he had badgered her on every one of her prior visits to the store to allow him to take her picture. She had declined, since to do so might be interpreted as fraternizing with a Polish national which was strictly prohibited. Riding on his bike, he had even followed her on the street in several instances and had begged her to let him take a photograph of her.

As expected, Kezimi was behind the counter when they entered the store.

"You made it just in time, Rosemarie," Kezimi said in broken German, as he rushed toward them on the other side of the counter. "I was just getting ready to close up. How are you?"

"I'm fine."

"And how is Hannelore?" he asked the little one.

"Fine."

Turning back to Romi, he asked, "What can I do for you?"

"My mother sent me for some aspirin. She is having a bad headache."

"Aspirin it is," Kezimi replied.

He handed her a packet and after giving Romi her change, he said, "I hope your mother will be feeling better, and..."

Romi, busy with her purse, asked, "And what?"

As she looked up he had answered her question without another word. He had reached under the counter and retrieved his camera. He was holding it up by its strap, and he was smiling and nodding his head in the hope of getting a positive response from her.

"No, Kezimi," she said. "Both, for your sake and for mine, let's not go into that again." She took Hannelore by the hand and headed for the door.

The girls were walking past the city park on their way home when Kezimi slowly passed them on his bicycle. He rode past them in an effort to cover up the fact that he was about to engage in forbidden conversation with German nationals. On his first pass, he said, "I think a picture of you would make a wonderful present for your father's birthday."

Since there was very little traffic on the street, he could make a wide turn in the direction from which he came and slowly come back for another pass. As he slowly rode by once more in the direction the girls were walking, Romi asked, "How do you know it will soon be my father's birthday?"

"Your mother bought a birthday card the other day."

Another wide turn. On the next pass, Romi asked, "How do you know it was for my father?"

"It was addressed 'To my darling husband.'"

Kezimi turned again, and in order to give her time to think, he delayed his next pass for several minutes.

As he again rode by, Romi said, "You can take a picture of me and my sister, if you promise not to bug me anymore after this."

Kezimi made another turn. Passing again, he said, "I promise."

"Hannelore and I will go into the park, and we will take a seat on one of the benches. Then you can take our picture."

Kezimi rode around for a while; then, he followed them into the park. After he took several pictures, he said, "Thank you, young ladies. You can pick up your copy at the store in two days. I'm sure your birthday present will make your father very happy!"

Two days later, Romi picked up her pictures at the drugstore. On her way home she heard someone behind her yell, "Hey, you!"

Romi turned around and saw a buxom BDM[5] leader approaching her.

"I saw you two days ago with that Pole in the park. Don't you know that you are not supposed to fraternize with his kind?"

"I wasn't fraternizing. I merely let him take a picture of us for my father's birthday."

5 BDM is the abbreviation for *Bund Deutscher Maedchen*, the female arm of the Hitler Youth.

"You could have gone to a German photographer, instead of seeking out a Pole."

"I didn't seek him out. He volunteered to take the pictures; besides, what difference does it make? Whether German or Pole, I'm still dealing with a human being."

Romi's comment infuriated the BDM girl. "I'll show you what the difference is. This is the difference when you fraternize with a Pole," she shrieked as she lifted her arm and slapped Romi across the face.

Romi reeled backward. Her first instinct was to defend herself, but she decided that she had better not, because she knew that the girl's father was a policeman.

The enraged BDM girl shouted, "I'm going to report your fraternizing to the authorities!"

Still somewhat stunned, Romi replied, "Go ahead and report me, and don't forget to mention in your report that you conducted yourself like a bar bouncer!"

Chapter 31

About the time Romi ran into the BDM girl, Herbert, trying to get comfortable, was sliding around in his classroom seat. He had been sitting on one cheek for four days now because he had a large boil on the other one. After the day's last session he decided to ask Mr. Vogt for help.

"I can take care of a boil for you," Mr. Vogt said, after Herbert had approached him after class. "Come and see me in my quarters in about an hour."

"So, where is this boil that has been troubling you?"

"It's on my cheek."

Mr. Vogt scanned Herbert's face from one side to the other. "I don't see a boil," the teacher remarked.

"It's on my lower cheek."

"Your lower cheek, eh? Well then you better drop your pants and your drawers, so I can take a look at it."

After Herbert had complied, Mr. Vogt said, "Wow, that's a lulu."

"Can you give me some pills or some ointment to make it go away?"

"That thing is not going to react to pills or ointment. We're going to have to do a little surgery."

Herbert's head spun around as he gasped, "Surgery?"

Mr. Vogt laughed and said, "It won't be surgery that requires a hospital and an operating table. We will lance it and squeeze all the pus out. It won't be as bad as you think."

Mr. Vogt took some gauze and a roll of surgical tape out of a desk drawer. From another drawer, he retrieved a small box. He took a scalpel out of the box and sterilized it with a piece of gauze that he had wetted with alcohol.

"Lean on the back of that chair," Mr. Vogt said.

"Ow!" was Herbert's reaction as the scalpel pierced his skin.

"Ow!" as Mr. Vogt squeezed.

"Ow! Ow!" as Mr. Vogt squeezed some more.

"We're all done." Mr. Vogt said. "Now we can apply some ointment and dress the wound. Are you OK?" he asked.

Herbert nodded.

"Leave that dressing on for a couple of days. If you still have discomfort at that time, come back; then we will squeeze some more."

He acknowledged the teacher's comment with another nod, but thought, easy for you to say, since you'll again be the squeezer, and I'll still be the "squeezee."

As he left, he said, "Thank you, Doctor Vogt."

+ + +

Romi cried when she told her mother about the incident with the BDM girl.

"Did you say something to incite her?" Hertha asked.

"No! All I said was that I was not fraternizing. Kezimi had asked me on several occasions to let him take a photograph of me, and when he said that a picture would be a nice birthday present for Papa, I had to agree," Romi sobbed.

"How did he know that your father's birthday is coming up?"

"He remembered the birthday card that you recently bought."

"Well, don't you worry about it. Your father will have something to say about this!"

+++

When Walther arrived at the apartment to stay for the remainder of the week-end, Romi reiterated the story to him.

"Don't worry your pretty little head about this; there won't be a report."

"How do you know?" Romi asked.

"A buddy of mine was close by on his bike. He witnessed the incident and told me about it. He was going to intervene, but when he heard you yell something about her behaving like a bouncer, he knew that you were perfectly capable of handling the situation. He told me that he would step forward as a witness, if necessary."

"Oh, thank God." Romi said with a sigh.

"Is this girl the policeman's daughter?" Walther asked.

Romi nodded.

"Well, I'm going to talk to him and, I'm going to tell him to make sure that his daughter keeps her hands to herself. Don't worry, there won't be a report."

During lunch that day, Walther had a bombshell of his own. "I've just been advised that I'm being transferred to another POW camp in a small town near the city of Bydgoszcz," he announced.

"Oh, Walther! We've just settled in here," Hertha lamented. Does this mean that we won't see you on week-ends anymore? Will we have to stay here by ourselves? When is this going to happen?" she asked in an anguished voice.

"Whoa! Whoa!" One question at a time," Walther responded. "The transfer is effective as of 1 October, so I'll have to leave in about three weeks. I'll still be able to stay with you on week-ends, but it is too far to commute back here. I'll have to find another apartment; then, you can join me."

✚✚✚

One week after his departure, Hertha received a letter stating that he had found an apartment. In another week she and the girls were on their way to meet him at the Bydgoszcz railroad station.

Walther was waiting on the platform when the train arrived. After the greetings, he turned to Hertha and said, "We have to take a local train for a fifteen minute ride to Altburgund where I am stationed. The town was formerly known as Szubin, but it was renamed after the Warthegau was reclaimed by Germany."

Picking up two of the suitcases, Walther nodded toward the adjacent platform and said, "We have to go over there to catch our train."

Looking for an overhead crosswalk, Hertha asked, "How do we get over there?"

"Well, we just make sure nothing is coming; then, we cross the tracks. Don't worry, they don't have electric trains here; there is no third rail," Walther replied reassuringly.

Once the Klugs were on the local train, they shared a compartment with an elderly gentleman. Walther described the apartment he had rented. He told Hertha that it consisted of a large furnished room with kitchen and a bathroom.

"That's not a lot of room," Hertha remarked.

"I know. But with the many bombing victims and the many ethnic Germans that Hitler has recalled into Germany, the housing authority has become very stingy when allocating space."

He also told them that there was a downside—the toilet was in an outhouse. Hertha and the girls all rolled their eyes in unison.

After the old gentleman got off at the first stop, they were alone in the train compartment.

Walther leaned toward Hertha and in a low voice said, "You will have to be careful when you talk to the landlady. She is German, and she appears to be a dyed-in-the-wool Nazi."

Hertha covered her eyes with her hand and groaned, "I knew that there would be a another catch!"

He tried to placate her, "Now, now, don't get upset. You will be dealing with her only once a month when she collects the rent."

✚✚✚

Hertha was not exuberant when she saw the apartment. She noticed that the kitchen was without kitchenware; however, this did not bother her, since she had the utensils and cutlery that she had brought when they came from Hamburg early in the summer. As she gave the furnished room a once-over, Hertha suddenly said, "Well, we'll have to do something about that."

"Do something about what? What's the matter?" her husband asked.

"This is the matter," Hertha said as she took the picture of Adolph Hitler off its hook, turned it around, and replaced it with the backing facing the room. I don't want to be looking at that guy all the time, and I don't want him to be looking at me!"

"Remember what I told you about the landlady," Walther said. "Will you remember to adjust the picture when she comes to pick up the rent? The picture is in full view as soon as one enters the apartment. Unfortunately, as we just found out with Romi, there are some overly zealous people around who can cause trouble over what they deem an infraction, no matter how absurd it might appear to us." Hertha walked over to the apartment entrance door. After a brief examination she said, "Ah, yes." She turned to Walther with an impish smile and said, "When the doorbell rings, I'll look through the peephole to see who it is. If it is the landlady, I'll quickly turn the picture around before I let her in." Mockingly, she added, "I may even greet her with a loud 'Heil Hitler!' when I let her in."

"Hertha, aren't you forgetting that we are merely renting and that the woman probably has another key to gain entrance anytime she wants to do so?" Walther asked.

"Just because we are renting does not mean we have to give up our rights to privacy. I will have the lock changed," Hertha replied.

"But you will advise the landlady of the change," Walther suggestively said.

"Yes, I will tell her that I just do not feel comfortable with the possibility that a former tenant might still have a duplicate key to the apartment."

"Well, if you feel that strongly about it, go ahead," Walther commented.

"Walther, I am not trying to make trouble, but I do feel that strongly about it," his wife replied.

Walther was silent for a moment. Addressing his younger daughter, he said, "Hannelore, what we have been talking about concerns just the family. We don't want to be talking about it to anyone else. Do you understand?"

"Yes, Papa."

Chapter 32

Just before class on a mid-November morning, Mr. Vogt proclaimed, "I have good news! We will be going home on the fifth of December!"

His announcement was followed by loud cheering from the class. After the cheers died down, someone asked, "Will we get another boat ride on the Danube?"

"No, no, I don't think you would want to sit on that open boat deck in the early part of December. We will entrain in Bonyhad at noon and go back to Budapest, where we will change to an express train that will take us to Vienna. In Vienna, we will change trains again, this time to another express train that will take us all the way back to Hamburg."

"When will we arrive in Hamburg?" Horst Drossen asked.

"We should arrive about 10:00 P.M. on 6 December."

After a short pause, someone else asked, "It sounds like the trip will take over a day and a half. "Why so long?"

"Well, it's close to 1250 kilometers from here to Hamburg, as the crow flies; in actuality, it will be quite a bit more; also, we will have layovers both in Budapest and in Vienna."

"Will we stay overnight in either of these places?" Herbert asked.

"No, both layovers will only be three hours each," Mr. Vogt replied.

Mr. Vogt gave the class a few minutes to settle down. Then he said, "I have more news."

The class' attention again focused on the teacher.

"When you get back to Hamburg, you will be required to volunteer to either enroll in a Hitler Youth leadership school or join the Luftwaffe Auxiliary that recently has been organized as part of the air defense effort."

Mr. Vogt's latest announcement hit like a bombshell. The normal tranquility of the classroom turned into a clamor of voices as the boys discussed with one another what they had just heard. The teacher gave them free rein to absorb what he had just told them.

As the class quieted down, Detlev Wolfert asked, "What other choices do we have?"

"There are no other choices," the teacher replied, thereby renewing the clamor.

"Having to select one or the other isn't really volunteering," Horst Drossen commented.

"I suppose that is correct, but that doesn't change the fact that you will have to choose one or the other," Mr. Vogt replied, as he thought, I don't want to tell them my true feelings about the subject, namely that many experienced soldiers of the air defense system probably are being called to the eastern front to utilize their expertise to disable tanks on the ground rather than to disable aircraft over the homeland. As a consequence, the air defense system is facing a manpower shortage. The Hitler Youth thing is just a ruse to give the appearance of choice. If all the boys were to choose the leadership school, the Hitler Youth would not be able to place them all, and they do not intend to. They will accept a few and tell the rest that they have to exercise the remaining option.

"Who made up these rules?" someone asked.

"Don't look at me," Mr. Vogt said with a smile, as he held up his hands in a protective gesture.

"What would be our task if we choose the Luftwaffe Auxiliary?" Karl Rothman asked.

"I don't know," Mr. Vogt replied. "You probably will help man the guns, operate the searchlights, or work in the communications system. That's what the folks of the ground based air defense do."

"I wouldn't want to have to operate one of the searchlights; they stand out as excellent targets, especially at night," someone mused.

The class snickered.

"They usually are not turned on during the day, dummy," someone else replied. More snickers from the class.

"What will happen to our schooling?" Klaus Wolfert asked.

"Those of you that select the leadership training will go to another school in Hamburg, since our school was destroyed during the July raids. Those who select the Luftwaffe Auxiliary will receive continued schooling at their base," Mr. Vogt replied.

"If most of us decide to join the Luftwaffe Auxiliary, would you go with us?" one of the boys asked.

"I would do that," the teacher responded. He looked at the class and realized that the news he had given them probably had shattered their attention span for the rest of the day; therefore, he announced, "Class is dismissed for today, but I want you to think about the decision you will have to make after we return to Hamburg."

That afternoon, Horst Drossen, Karl Rothmann, and Herbert took a walk along the unpaved road that led to Bonyhad. "Well, it looks like we will have to make a decision pretty soon," Horst Drossen commented.

"I only have one choice," Karl remarked.

"Why do you say that?" Horst asked.

"Because the leadership school looks for strong athletic types. that leaves me out. I don't have any of the proficiency badges that some of the guys have."

"I guess that makes two of us," Herbert acknowledged.

"Hey, maybe you could tell the students at the Hitler Youth leadership school about rodeos and other American idiosyncrasies," Horst suggested with a laugh.

"Yeah, right! And then be picked up for disseminating foreign propaganda. Will you guys visit me while I'm in a concentration camp?"

Both Horst and Karl laughed.

"Even if I thought I could qualify for the leadership school, I wouldn't want to attend," Herbert remarked.

Horst Drossen asked, "Why not?"

"My family now lives in the area of Poland that was re-annexed to Germany after the Polish campaign. Some of the ethnic Germans who stayed there after the area became Polish following the First World War now think it is time to demand redress of the Poles for grievances suffered, either real or imaginary, under Polish rule. They tend to lord it over the Poles, and it is not an environment in which I wish to take part," Herbert replied and added, "I wish you guys hadn't started a war right after I came to this country; then, none of these choices would be necessary."

"Hey, this war was forced upon us. Any nation with a sense of honor, faced with the demands of a Versailles Treaty, would have done the same thing," Karl admonished.

Horst averted an impasse by asking, "You're torn between two conflicting allegiances, aren't you?"

Hunching his shoulders, Herbert muttered, "I suppose so."

After the boys turned around to go back to their village, not much was said. Each boy was immersed in his own thoughts.

When Herbert got back to his sponsors' home, he went to his room. He sat on his bed and thought, I'm not the caliber of person sought by the Hitler Youth leadership school; besides, I'm not interested in doing something like that. I certainly don't want to spend time on a parade ground teaching kids how to march in formation. Then he thought about the remaining choice. He cringed at the possibility of having to fire a gun at American planes. I might be shooting at some of the older boys with whom I used to play stickball, he said to himself.

Chapter 33

Ten days before the class was to return home, Herbert began feeling ill. He had headaches, accompanied by nausea.

After feeling like this for four days, he noticed that his skin was taking on a yellowish pallor; his eyeballs, too, had a yellow tinge. He decided to ask Mr. Vogt for help.

"I've noticed that you seemed to be a little under the weather these last few days," the teacher told him after class, "but after seeing you today, I have become a little concerned. Your coloring indicates that you might have a touch of hepatitis."

"Is that something bad?"

"It is something that needs to be treated right away."

After some hesitation, Mr. Vogt added, "We're going to have to get you to a doctor immediately for some testing."

An hour later, Herbert was sitting next to Mr. Vogt on the driver's seat of a horse-drawn wagon that the teacher had borrowed from one of the farmers. Mr. Vogt had brought a blanket, which he wrapped around the boy before they started their trip to Bonyhad.

At the doctor's office, they spent about a half hour in the waiting room before the doctor could see them. When the doctor became available, Mr. Vogt, speaking German, started to tell the reason for their visit. The doctor immediately put up his hands in a halting motion. He then called in his receptionist and spoke a few words to her. The receptionist, in turn, told Mr. Vogt that she would have to translate, since the doctor was unfamiliar with the German language. Herbert thought, oh, great, a German teacher and a Hungarian doctor trying to analyze what's ailing a kid from Brooklyn!

After the doctor gave Herbert a cursory examination, he took Mr. Vogt aside and told him, via the receptionist, that the boy obviously had some type of hepatitis and that he would have to conduct liver function tests to determine the cause. He advised the teacher to bring the boy back on the following day, because he could not perform the tests on a moment's notice. He also indicated that a blood sample, which was part of the tests, would have to be sent to the medical university in Pecs; therefore the results would not be available until about three days hence. Nodding toward the boy, the doctor suggested he be kept isolated as much as possible until the results of the test were known. The doctor also indicated to the teacher that the boy would have to be hospitalized if the cause was viral.

"What was all the whispering about between you and the doctor?" Herbert asked Mr. Vogt on the way back to Graboc.

"The doctor seems to think that you have hepatitis, but he won't know how to treat it until he runs some tests, which he will do tomorrow."

"What...what is this hepatitis?" Herbert asked

"It has something to do with the liver."

"Did he give you some medication for me to take?"

"He can't give you any medication until he is sure of what kind of hepatitis you have. He asked me to tell your sponsor family to avoid close contact with you and to keep your eating utensils separated from all the others, and I am excusing you from classes for the next few days."

"Why?"

"Because if the hepatitis is caused by a virus, it will be infectious."

"Will the doctor be able to give me some medication for that?"

Mr. Vogt didn't answer immediately. When he did, he said, "If it is viral, you won't be going home with us. You will have to be hospitalized."

"Hospitalized? I don't want to be left in a Hungarian hospital," Herbert replied somewhat contentiously.

"You wouldn't want to make all your classmates sick, would you?" the teacher asked.

"No."

"Don't be giving up hope just yet," Mr. Vogt said. "For all we know, your jaundice may not be infectious at all."

"Aw, gee whiz," Herbert responded, unconvinced, and in English, because he couldn't think of a German equivalent.

"What did you say?" the teacher asked.

"Nothing."

When they were back in Graboc, Mr. Vogt drove the wagon to the Borkenau home. He accompanied Herbert inside, and he cautioned the Borkenaus to quarantine the boy, at least until the test results were known.

"I'll see you in the morning, when I'll take you back to the doctor to have the tests performed."

Herbert nodded in acknowledgment.

✚✚✚

After Herbert returned from the doctor on the following day, Marie brought Herbert's lunch into his room.

"You probably should just set it down by the door, because the doctor doesn't want anyone to come near me. He's afraid that I could make others sick."

While she set the lunch on his desk, she said, "If I made myself scarce every time someone is sick in this house, I would soon be somewhat of a stranger to my own family. When we signed up to take you in, we promised to take care of you to the best of our ability, and your becoming ill does not relieve us of that promise." Marie smiled and as she left, she added, "Try to eat something. Maybe it will make you feel better."

Herbert sat down at the desk. Because he wasn't hungry, he poked around at his food before forcing himself to take a few bites. A wave of nausea caused him to lay down the fork. He reached for his mother's letter, which he had received about a week earlier. He reread the letter that told him about his father's transfer—and the family's subsequent move—to a town named Altburgund. When the letter mentioned that his little sister would have to change schools after having attended school in Schildberg for several weeks only, he thought, poor Hannelore.

Once he had reread the letter, he said to himself I had better put the envelope in a safe place. Without the return address, I'll have a hard time finding my family.

After folding the envelope, he got up and placed it in a pocket of his uniform tunic, and he put the letter, which also contained the address, in one of his suitcases as an extra precaution.

Sitting down again, he pondered his own situation. Maybe being sick would make me ineligible for either of the two choices Mr. Vogt had mentioned, he thought. But what good would that do? I would be stuck in a Podunk type of town, and my schooling would be interrupted. I can't imagine Altburgund having a viable high school system. I have to go with the Luftwaffe Auxiliary, he told himself. Most of my classmates are opting for the Luftwaffe Auxiliary. They sense an opportunity to inflict retribution on the English for dropping bombs willy-nilly into populated areas of their city, and I share their feelings. After all, my home was destroyed, too, he thought.

Still musing, he said to himself, their decision is an easy one; my decision is a bit more complex. I'm an American by birth, and I'm German because German law says I am. To which side do I really belong? He was overcome by another wave of nausea. He wasn't sure whether it was caused by his sickness or by despair over the ambiguity of his situation.

Chapter 34

During the fourth day of Herbert's quarantine, Mr. Vogt stopped by at the Borkenau home. As he walked into Herbert's room he said, "I have good news. Your jaundice is not infectious."

"Hurray!" Herbert shouted from his bed where he was lying fully clothed.

The teacher took off his coat and asked, "How are you feeling?"

"I've been a lot better," the boy answered.

"Well, I have something that will help you out." He retrieved a bottle of pills out of his coat pocket and handed it to Herbert. "The good doctor said that you are to take three pills a day—morning, noon, and evening. He thinks you should show significant improvement in seven to ten days."

"Thank you, Mr. Vogt."

The teacher nodded and said, "You do realize that we are leaving two days from now. Do you feel up to the trip?"

"I'll be all right."

"Well, you take care of yourself," the teacher said as he put his coat back on. "We won't have any more classes before we leave. Get all the rest that you can between now and then."

+ + +

All the sponsor families accompanied their respective charges to the town square on departure day to see them off. Also present was the old mare. Appearing as disdainful as on the day the boys had arrived, she was again hitched to a wagon that would carry their luggage.

Some tears appeared while the goodbyes were said. As Herbert wished Johann and Marie well and thanked them for their hospitality, Marie gave him some food for the trip. He said goodbye to the children, Helga and Robert. When he looked at the girl, he thought, you're going to turn out to be as pretty as your mother.

Just as the Jungvolk leader gave the command to line up in formation, Mr. Vogt beckoned to Herbert. "Don't be taking your place in the lineup, I want you to ride on the luggage wagon with Mr. Bohnke and me."

As the boys marched out of the town square, the sponsor families waved and the boys waved back.

A tug at his sleeve woke Herbert up. "Come on, get up!" Detlev Wolfert yelled in his ear. "We're in Budapest, and we have to change trains."

I must have fallen asleep right after we boarded the train in Bonyhad, Herbert thought as he sluggishly got out of his seat.

He felt weary; therefore, he was glad that this time they would not be marching through the Budapest streets; all they had to do was to while away some time during the layover and then to board at another platform.

The Vienna bound train had four compartments—three for the boys and one for the teachers—reserved for Mr. Vogt's class. As Herbert boarded the train, Mr. Vogt was standing in the aisle. He pulled Herbert aside and said, "Come with me."

He led the boy to the teacher's compartment where Mr. Bohnke had already taken a seat. "You can stay here with us. Even though we may have to accommodate several boys from the other three compartments, there will still be enough room for you to stretch out. I want you to get as much rest as possible. We will do the same thing when we change trains again in Vienna. Is that understood?"

"Yes, sir."

"Are you remembering to take your pills?"

"Yes, sir."

The train rolled into the Hamburg main station at about 12:30 A.M. The boys retrieved their luggage out of the overhead bins and headed toward the exits. The parents of most of the boys were on the platform to greet them. Herbert stood aside until the crowd thinned out. Finally, only he and Mr. Vogt were left on the platform.

"How are you holding up?" Mr. Vogt asked.

"I'm starting to feel better."

"Good," Mr. Vogt said, while reaching in his pocket for a notepad and pencil. "I'm going to give you my telephone number. If you run into any trouble, go to the nearest police station and ask someone to call this number, collect." He tore the sheet off the pad and handed it to the boy.

"I don't think I'll have any problems; however, thank you, Mr. Vogt."

"Well, if you do, you'll have someone to turn to, but I hope everything will go well," the teacher said.

As Herbert was about to leave, he asked, "Mr. Vogt, do you have any idea how many of my classmates are opting for the Luftwaffe Auxiliary, and are you really going with them to wherever they will be based?"

"According to the inputs I have received, about ninety percent are opting for the Luftwaffe Auxiliary, and yes, I will be going with them.

"Will you be joining us?" the teacher asked.

"I think so, Mr. Vogt."

"Well, perhaps I'll be seeing you soon. Give my regards to your parents, and ask your mother to take you to see a doctor right after you arrive home."

After Mr. Vogt left, Herbert picked up his two suitcases and headed for the mezzanine where the waiting room was located. He sat down at a table and retrieved his sandwich bag, which he had tucked in his tunic. While he ate one of the three remaining sandwiches, he noticed that most of the people in the waiting room were soldiers. He guessed that the soldiers who were loners were on their way home and just starting their furlough, whereas most of those accompanied by civilians were returning to their units.

From the mezzanine, the boy had a good view of most of the station. As he had done on previous occasions, he glanced at the grid-like structure of the station roof. Hardly any of the grids still contained the glass panes that were intended to protect the station from the elements. Herbert thought, if that roof is any indication of how the war is going, Germany is in deep doo-doo.

Herbert glanced at the big wall clock in the waiting room. It was 2:00 A.M. Only six and a half more hours until my train leaves, Herbert thought.

Since he had slept most of the day, he was not at all tired, although he did feel weak. He moved his suitcases under the table such that he could rest one leg on each, because he didn't want someone to walk off with them, in the event he dozed off.

He sat and watched the clock. It didn't seem to want to move at all. Finally, at 3:30 A.M., he couldn't sit still any longer. He got up and picked up his luggage and walked downstairs onto the concourse. Once on the concourse, Herbert sought a spot outside of the main traffic flow. He put down his suitcases and sat down on one of them to watch the world go by.

Herbert observed a constant bustle to and from the various platforms of mostly uniformed people coming from and going to who knows where. The chain dogs were diligently spot-checking the soldiers and asking to see their papers. A Luftwaffe major came into the concourse carrying a canvas bag. Herbert saw the Knights Cross on his neck. The boy wondered how long ago the major had received his decoration. He said to himself, assuming he's a fighter pilot, a year ago twenty kills would have earned him the decoration, but now, the ante has gone up to about forty.

After what seemed like an eternity, Herbert decided it was time to seek out his platform. As the train rolled into the station, he noticed the quad twenty millimeter antiaircraft gun that was emplaced on a flat car immediately following the coal tender. Almost simultaneously, he also noticed that the train was already crowded. Oh, crap! he said to himself, I forgot that most of the long distance routes originating or terminating in Hamburg do so at the Altona station. Forget about a window seat, he thought, I'll be lucky to just get on the train!

Trying to reach the center of the car, Herbert alternately moved forward through the aisle by pushing when the crowd was disinclined to make way or by feigning ineptness and nudging a toe or two, when that approach was more likely to stimulate folks to let him pass. He finally found a spot at an aisle window where he could put his suitcases down. He set them down upended to conserve floor space.

The train moved slowly out of the station. When it did not accelerate after moving out of the station, Herbert turned toward the window and saw in the pre-dawn light that the train was passing entire sections of the city that had been reduced to rubble. Debris-littered streets that led into these areas were still cordoned off. That is why we are moving so slowly, he thought, and this section of track has probably seen only temporary repair.

Looking through the window with repugnance, all kinds of thoughts surged through his head: This looks as bad as the newsreel pictures I saw of Stalingrad about a year ago—I wonder how many bodies are still lying under those ruins—surely, they could not all be retrieved—estimates are that tens of thousands died—would Mama and the girls have survived if they had been in Hamburg when this happened? When my classmates see this, they'll know that opting for the Luftwaffe Auxiliary is the right thing to do.

Herbert felt overwhelmed. He had never before witnessed such destruction. As the train started to accelerate, he turned away from the window and sat down on one of his suitcases.

After even more passengers had boarded at the first two stops, Herbert observed the packed mass of humanity standing in the aisle. He thought, if someone faints, no one will notice, because there is no room to keel over.

+++

"This is insane!" someone cried out. Herbert looked up and saw a soldier opening a compartment door and stacking luggage from the aisle atop the luggage already in the compartment bins. "We need a little breathing room out here," the soldier shouted.

Someone in the compartment countered, "All that extra luggage is likely to fall on top of us!"

"Then put it at your feet, between the seat rows."

"We won't be able to get up to move around." someone else in the compartment hollered.

The soldier laughed and said, "No one is going to move around much until it is time to get off this train."

Other soldiers joined in to stack most of the aisle luggage into the compartment bins. One beckoned Herbert to hand over his suitcases.

"Can I keep one of them to sit on?" the boy asked.

The soldier nodded.

The luggage transfer allowed the standees to relocate a bit. A young girl now stood close to where Herbert was sitting on his suitcase. He noted that she was wearing an RAD[6] uniform and that she was very pretty.

After a while, Herbert got up. Eliciting some disapproving looks from his nearest neighbors, Herbert flipped his suitcase out of the upended position. After sitting down again on one side of the suitcase, he tugged the girl's sleeve and said, "You're welcome to share my suitcase if you like."

The girl looked at him and gave him a worried look. "You look sick, what's wrong with you?" she asked. Herbert laughed and said, "Oh, I have some kind of jaundice, but it isn't catching."

"How do you know it isn't catching?"

6 RAD is an abbreviation of *Reichs Arbeits Dienst,* the German Labor Service in which all German youth had to serve at the age of seventeen.

"Because I've been to a doctor. All I have to do is take some pills to make it go away."

"You sure?"

Herbert nodded, and the girl hesitantly sat down.

"My name is Elke, what's yours?"

"I'm Herbert."

"Where are you going?" she asked him.

"To Bydgoszcz."

"What's in...what do you call it?"

"Bydgoszcz, my family lives in a little town nearby. We lost our home in Hamburg."

"Is that where you are coming from now—from Hamburg?"

"Yes, but I was there only to change trains. I'm on my way home from Hungary."

"From Hungary?" she asked with surprise. "What were you doing in Hungary?"

"My school class was evacuated because of the bombings."

"Oh. My family lost their home, too," she said. They are now sharing an apartment with another family back in Bremen. It's not an ideal situation, but at least they have a roof over their heads."

"Where are you going, Elke?"

"I have to report to my unit in Schneidemuehl."

"Well, you'll be getting off the train much sooner than I will. What will you be doing in Schneidemuehl?"

"I don't know, dig trenches, maybe."

"Dig trenches?" he asked with surprise. "The front lines are still as far away as Ukraine. You won't be digging trenches!" Lowering his voice, he said, "You want to be careful when you talk like that. Someone might report you as a defeatist."

Elke laughed and said, "Well, maybe I'll be filling in trenches."

"I don't believe that either, but at least it sounds much more optimistic."

They both laughed.

After a while, they sat, each immersed in his or her own thoughts. The lulling effect of the swaying train car soon caused Elke to doze off. Her head would briefly fall toward his shoulder, only to be pulled back again. Eventually, her head found a resting place. Herbert didn't mind.

After Elke left the train at Schneidemuehl, Herbert noticed that the remaining occupants of the car, by far, were soldiers; not many civilians remained. The train terminated in Bialystok, in the easternmost part of Poland. From there the soldiers would continue on to the eastern front. Some of them seemed not more than one or two years older than he was.

"There he is!" Hannelore yelled, as Herbert got off the local train in Altburgund. His mother and sisters rushed to greet him.

When his mother got a good look at him she said, "Oh my, what's the matter with you?"

"I contracted some kind of jaundice about a week before we were to leave Hungary. Mr. Vogt took me to a doctor who gave me some medication. The good news is that it is not serious and not contagious, but Mr. Vogt suggested that I see a doctor as soon as I got home."

"You must be hungry," his mother said. "We'll have some lunch; then, I'll take you to the doctor's office."

"I'm not hungry," Herbert replied.

"Did you have a good trip?" Romi asked.

"It was OK until I got on the train in Hamburg; then, I had to squat on one of my suitcases in the train aisle."

"How did you like Hungary?" his mother asked.

"The people that took me in were real nice, but the way of life was very primitive. Can you imagine having to do without running water and electricity?"

Romi said, "Wait until you see our itty-bitty apartment. It doesn't offer any modern conveniences either."

✚✚✚

While his mother and the girls had some lunch, Herbert, still not hungry, surveyed the apartment. It was really only one big room and a kitchen. The room had to serve the dual purpose of living room and bedroom. It was sparsely furnished with two couches, a double-tiered bunk bed, and a small table. One of the couches could be pulled out to serve as a double bed.

"You sure don't have a lot of room here," he hollered into the kitchen.

"We make do as best we can," his mother replied.

"Where will I be sleeping?" Herbert asked.

"You'll be sleeping on the smaller couch," his mother said.

He inspected the picture hanging with its backing facing the room. "Why is the Fuehrer facing the wall?" he asked.

"That's the way I want him to face," was his mother's answer.

Hearing his mother's emphatic response, Herbert quickly put the picture back the way he had found it.

✚✚✚

That afternoon his mother took Herbert to see a doctor. Although they had to wait a while, the doctor was able to accommodate them without a prior appointment. Herbert gave the doctor a translated transcript of the Hungarian doctor's findings, which Mr. Vogt had given the boy after they arrived at the Hamburg main station. After the doctor read the transcript, he ordered a refill of the medication that Herbert was already taking, and he assured Hertha that her son should be fully recovered within a week's time.

✚✚✚

Herbert was going to tell his mother soon after he arrived that he would be leaving for Hamburg again in a few weeks, but he knew that the news would upset her; therefore, he decided to put it off until his father would be home for the weekend and to tell both his parents at the same time.

After his father arrived on the following Saturday, Herbert waited for a fitting time to talk to his parents. The opportunity presented itself that afternoon. Romi had taken Hannelore along to do some grocery shopping, and his parents were sitting at the kitchen table engaged in small talk. Herbert sat down with them and told them of the announcement Mr. Vogt had made to the class shortly before they left Hungary.

"You're telling us that you and your classmates have to choose between the Hitler Youth leadership school and the Luftwaffe Auxiliary, now that you have returned from Hungary," Walther commented as he looked at his son.

"Yes, Papa."

Walther looked at his wife who was shaking her head.

"So you are being given a limited choice—an either/or situation. Which are you going to choose?"

Herbert wanted to say that he would not have to choose at all if he had not been made a German by decree, but he did not. Instead, he said, "I'm not interested in the leadership school, especially since I would be posted here in former Polish territory. I conceivably could be tasked with keeping Polish kids out of the swimming pools. I wouldn't want to get involved in that sort of thing."

"Well, I don't think you'd be called upon to do that, but I see your point," his father said, as he watched his wife brush away the tears. "Did Mr. Vogt have any idea what you would be doing in the Auxiliary?" he asked.

"Whatever the ground based air defense system does: man

the guns, the search lights, and the communications system," Herbert responded.

"As I see it, the Hitler Youth leadership thing, for the most part is a sham, to allow the authorities to deny that mere boys are being drafted into the Luftwaffe Auxiliary," Walther said.

"It doesn't really matter. Since the leadership school is not an option for me, the Luftwaffe Auxiliary is the only choice I have, but I don't mind."

"Why is that?" his father asked.

"Most of my classmates have already opted for the Luftwaffe. I'll be able to stay with them and, as I told you, Mr. Vogt will be going with us. I'll be able to continue my schooling in some manner."

"Are there any other reasons?" Walther asked.

Without hesitation, Herbert said, "Papa, as I left Hamburg to come here, I looked out the train window and saw what the British had done to Hamburg. I've never seen anything like it before."

"Your mother and I were there a few days after the raids took place. We saw what was done," his father interjected.

"Yeah, well, what they did by far exceeds the boundaries of civilized warfare."

"Civilized warfare is an oxymoron. It does not exist," Walther replied. "From what I've heard, we have caused a lot of destruction, too. Look at Russia, for example."

"In Russia, two opposing armies are fighting it out, and stuff is bound to get broken, but there was no army in Hamburg," Herbert countered.

"Did we not do the same thing to the English about two years earlier?" his father asked.

"I don't think the Germans ever had the resources to cause the havoc that Hamburg was subjected to in just three or four night attacks.

"Papa, while I was sitting for hours in the waiting room of the Hamburg station on my way here, I overheard a conversation between two soldiers. One of them apparently had been in Hamburg during the raids. He told the other soldier that on 28 July a vast number of explosive bombs and incendiaries were dropped on the city. The incendiaries resulted in many fires. The strong updrafts of the fires initiated a vicious cycle that caused air from areas surrounding the fires to feed and merge the fires, whereby the updrafts became even stronger. Ever increasing amounts of air were sucked in by the updrafts to merge more fires. The velocity of the air currents feeding the fires reached 150 miles per hour—that is hurricane force. Glowing embers, picked up by these man-made winds, started new fires. Temperatures rose to unbearable levels. Folks who were forced to leave their shelters were swept up by these cyclonic currents and incinerated. He said that thousands died in the fires; thousands more died of carbon monoxide poisoning." Herbert looked at his father and asked, "Papa, if you had the option of joining an outfit that might help to prevent something like that from happening again, wouldn't you take it?"

"I don't have that option."

"Well, I do! And that's another reason why I'm choosing the Luftwaffe Auxiliary; besides, they busted all my stuff!"

Walther sighed and said, "I was hoping, that after you came back from Hungary, we could all stay here in comparative safety."

Hertha put her arm around her husband and said, "He has decided what is best for him. He doesn't have a good choice."

"Will you be stationed in Hamburg?" his father asked.

"I don't know where I will be stationed," Herbert answered.

"When will you have to leave?" Walther asked.

"I have to report to the induction center on December 28."

✚✚✚

During supper that evening, Hertha said, "If you are stationed in Hamburg, perhaps you will get a weekend pass now and then. In that case you could visit my friend Ihde Johte. I'm sure she would be glad to see you. I just received a postcard from her. Their home was not damaged during the July attacks."

"I didn't know that the Johtes also came to Germany," Herbert replied.

"Of course you did. We even visited them in Hamburg, back in 1940." Hertha reminded him.

"Well, I probably forgot."

+++

Two weeks after Herbert had arrived, the doctor took him off the medication and gave him a clean bill of health. The Klug family spent a quiet Christmas in 1943. Hertha, having hoarded some flour and other necessary ingredients, surprised the family with two cakes over the holidays, but the holiday spirit was moderated by the fact that Herbert would be leaving again in two days.

+++

Herbert shivered. He was sitting alone in an unheated compartment of the local train that was taking him back to Bydgoszcz where he would board the express train back to Hamburg. It's been four and a half years since I came to Germany, he thought, and of those years, I have already spent two years away from home. Now I have to leave again for who knows how long. He tried to glance out the car window, but his breath immediately fogged the window. He did not try to clear the window—there was nothing to see in the predawn darkness. Tears welled in his eyes. He let them flow freely down his cheeks—there was no one to see the tears.

Chapter 35

Herbert arrived back in Hamburg at 3:00 A.M. on the morning of 28 December. He whiled away about three hours in the station waiting room and arrived at the induction center well before the 7:30 A.M. deadline. Since members of several classes of different schools were assembling, he did not find his classmates immediately. When he did, he was greeted with "Good to see you" and "How are things in the Warthegau?"

The boys were lined up according to class before the induction procedure commenced. Physical examination and registration were scheduled for the first day. Uniforms were to be issued on the following day.

Everyone in Mr. Vogt's class passed the physical except Karl Rothman. When Herbert found out that Karl had been disqualified, he thought, I'll miss him. He is my best friend. Herbert also contemplated the fact that Karl's departure would make him the shortest guy in his class.

+++

After the physical examination, the boys lined up at several tables where the registration process would take place.

Herbert's conflicting allegiances were never more acute as when he faced the *Unteroffizier* (sergeant) sitting on the other side of one of the registration tables.

"Name?" the Unteroffizier asked.

"Herbert Klug."

"Current residence?"

"Altburgund, Warthegau."

"You lost your home in Hamburg?"

"Yes."

"Born in Hamburg?" the man behind the table asked.

"No. I was born in New York."

The Unteroffizier gave the boy a surprised look.

Herbert thought, I've got to find out from this guy whether I really don't have a choice.

After some hesitation, he blurted, "I'm an American citizen."

"Really," the Unteroffizier commented with a smirk. "Tell me, what makes you think you are an American citizen?"

"It is my birthright; I was born on American soil."

"Your parents, they are also American citizens?"

"No, they are both German."

"Aha, your parents are German, and it appears to me that you are still a minor. Is that correct?" he tauntingly asked.

"I'm fifteen."

The Unteroffizier gave Herbert a long look and said, "Let me tell you something. While you are in Germany, the only rights you have are granted by German law, and German law says that minors have the same citizenship as the father. Once you are twenty-one, maybe—and I do mean maybe—you can select one or the other. Until then, consider yourself German. Do you understand?"

"Yes, sir."

The Unteroffizier asked Herbert several more questions to complete his dossier; then, without giving the boy another look, he shouted, "Next!"

That night the boys were housed in nearby barracks, and the next morning they were led to the quartermaster depot to receive their uniforms. They were outfitted with dress uniforms, fatigues, underwear, socks, two blankets, a pair of boots, a mess kit, a steel helmet, a gas mask, and a duffel bag.

After Herbert received his supplies, he stuffed everything into his duffel bag except for the dress uniform and the helmet. He went to one side of the supply room and tried on the uniform—it was way too big. He went back to the supply corporal to ask for a smaller size.

"You already have the smallest size in my inventory," the corporal declared.

"Yeah, but look how this jacket fits; the sleeves are too long. Look at the pants. If I'm not real careful, I'll trip over them."

"Well, roll them over, or have your mother alter them," the supply corporal suggested.

"My mother is five hundred kilometers away from here."

"Well, then you better start taking some sewing classes."

Herbert muttered some profanities and trudged back to his duffel bag. He thought, the regular Luftwaffe probably would have rejected me, since they don't carry my size.

He tried on the steel helmet. It was the one item in his inventory that fit, only because the liner was adjustable.

Once the boys were issued their uniforms, they were told that they were on their own until 2 January, when they were to assemble at the Stellingen subway station to entrain for the trip to their basic training area. They also were told to leave their civilian clothes at home. Those that could not go home during the interim were issued a cardboard box in which to pack their civilian clothes. The boxes were to be delivered to the postal service of the induction center for shipment back home.

When Herbert had returned to the barracks from the postal service, he asked himself, "What am I going to do about my uniforms?"

After pondering for a while, he remembered that his mother had given him the address of the Johtes before he left.

He thought, Aunt Ihde is a seamstress. I'll ask her whether she can alter my uniforms for me, but how do I get from here to there without looking like a circus clown?

Having given the matter some more thought, he went to the post exchange and bought a small travelers sewing kit. He wasn't interested in the needles and the yarn that came with the kit; he only wanted the pins that were included.

When he returned to his assigned barrack, Herbert followed the Unteroffizier's suggestion and created a cuffed pair of pants by turning up each pant leg to form a cuff. He carefully pinned each cuff in place. He shortened the jacket sleeves by putting the cuffs on the inside and also pinning them.

To assess his handiwork, Herbert changed from his fatigues to his modified dress uniform, and viewed himself in the full-length mirror located at one end of the barrack. He thought, well, it's not—what is that French expression that I'm trying to recall—haute couture. It certainly isn't haute couture.

Taking another look, he shrugged and thought, it will have to do, for now.

✚ ✚ ✚

Herbert piled all his new belongings into his duffel bag and headed for the subway station for his trip to the Johtes. During the short journey he tried to ignore the occasional pin pricks to his lower arms caused by the modified jacket sleeves.

"Well, look who's here!" Ihde Johte exclaimed when she saw Herbert standing in the doorway. "Come on in." Turning her head toward an adjacent room Ihde called out, "Come and see who's here."

After a moment, Ihde's daughter Annalisa walked into the room. Herbert remembered that the blond, blue-eyed girl, who was his junior by a year, used to play with his sisters when the families visited one another back in Brooklyn. He and the girl exchanged greetings.

"Your mother wrote to me and told me that your whole class was being inducted into the Luftwaffe Auxiliary. I've sort of been expecting you," Ihde said. "Let me look at you."

Giving his uniform an appraising glance, she could not restrain a chuckle and asked, "Who is your tailor?"

Herbert laughed and said, "I know, it's too big. The guy at the quartermaster depot said it was the smallest size available. Aunt Ihde, one of the reasons I stopped by is that I am hoping that you could alter it for me."

"Were there any other reasons?" she asked.

"I thought it would be nice to see you again, and..."

"And what?"

"I didn't have anywhere else to go."

"Oh, you poor boy, let me give you a hug." After she released him, she asked, "How much time do I have to get this done?"

"I have to report for transport to basic training on 2 January."

"Oh, that will give me plenty of time," Ihde responded. "If you can change into something else, I can get started right away."

"I'll put on my fatigues, but..."

"But what? Oh...Annalisa, show Herbert where the bathroom is."

+++

Two days later, Ihde had altered his dress uniform.

"You can put your dress uniform back on and give me your fatigues, so I can alter them," she told Herbert.

After he had changed, she said, "Let me look at you." She scrutinized her handiwork and added, "At least, you now look like you were issued the right size."

As she started working on his fatigues, Ihde said, "I'll be able to get a good start on these today, and I'll be able to finish them tomorrow." She looked at him and asked, "Will you be staying up with us tonight to celebrate New Year's Eve?"

"Nah, I don't think so."

"What's the matter? Are you homesick, or are you fretting about what lies ahead?"

"A little bit of both, I guess."

"Well, that's understandable."

Herbert broke the ensuing silence with, "Aunt Ihde, I want to thank you for helping me out like this."

"Don't mention it. Your mother would have done the same if the roles had been reversed."

Chapter 36

Six classes from various schools assembled at the suburban train station in Stellingen early on the morning of 2 January; a Luftwaffe noncommissioned officer was on hand to receive the boys. He instructed them to attach the shoulder straps to their duffel bags, so they could be carried as a backpack. He then had the boys line up in formations according to class.

"We won't be boarding a train here; we will be boarding at the marshalling yards about five kilometers down the road. Unfortunately, the train's departure time has been advanced from what we were previously told; therefore we will have to cover the distance in double time because the train will not wait for us," the noncom told them.

"Oh, great, we're going to have to march five kilometers just for the privilege of hopping unto a freight train," Detlev Wolfert mumbled to Herbert.

"How do you know that it will be a freight train?"

"You don't go to the marshalling yards to board a passenger train."

Detlev attached the shoulder straps to his duffel bag and swung it on his back. Herbert attempted to do likewise, but the weight of the bag nearly knocked him over.

"Here, let me help you with that," Detlev said as he picked up the bag and held it while Herbert slipped into the shoulder straps.

"Thanks," Herbert said, adding, "if I stand up straight this thing will knock me on my ass."

Detlev laughed and said, "Just stay stooped forward a bit. Who knows, with your eyes glued to the ground, you may even find a couple of coins during our march to the marshalling yards."

"Yeah, but I'll fall on my face if I try to pick them up."

They both laughed.

+ + +

Thirty minutes later, the boys, somewhat winded, arrived at the rail yards. A railroad official pointed out to the Luftwaffe noncom which one of the trains the boys were to board and the six cars that had been reserved for their transport. The noncom then assigned each class to one of the cars.

Klaus Wolfert was the first one of Mr. Vogt's class to heave his duffel bag and to hoist himself into the car.

"Hey, this isn't all bad," he shouted to his classmates.

"We've got a small potbellied stove in here, which is already fired up. There's enough firewood to last us a while."

One by one, the boys climbed into the car. The floor of the car was lined with straw, except for the area around the potbellied stove. They placed their duffel bags along the walls of the car, so they could sit on them while resting their backs against the wall.

Once all the boys had boarded, the noncom called for their attention and said, "You're on your own now. Make sure that you leave the sliding door open a crack. Those stoves are not always vented as well as they should be. Have a good trip."

"Where is this train taking us?" one of the boys asked.

"You are going to Buesum to receive your basic training," the noncom replied as he waved and then left.

"Where the hell is Buesum?" someone asked.

"It's a small town on the North Sea coast about sixty or seventy miles northwest of here," someone answered.

Shortly thereafter, the train whistle blew and they were underway.

+++

The train apparently had a very low priority, since it repeatedly was shunted onto sidings to make way for other traffic; however, the stops did afford the opportunity for the boys to jump off the train to relieve themselves.

Some of the waiting periods lasted over half an hour. As a result, the boys did not arrive in Buesum until late afternoon. They were met at the rail yard by half a dozen Luftwaffe noncoms who marched them to the nearby training base where each class was assigned a barrack that would be their home for the next eight weeks.

Reveille was sounded at 6:00 A.M. the following day, and by 7:30 A.M. the boys were on the parade ground. The noncoms, one per class, had them perform the usual parade ground drills. Two hours later, all six classes assembled in one formation to listen to an address by the base commander. When the base commander, a Luftwaffe major, arrived, he said, "I want to welcome you to our training base. The noncommissioned officers who have taken you through the parade ground drills this morning have already told me that any more of that would be a waste of time, because you already know all that stuff. We therefore can start your equipment training almost immediately. A few of you will be trained in radio communications, and some of you will be trained to operate a searchlight. Most of you will train to become members of a gun crew.

"You will get your assignments tomorrow morning, and after an introductory session tomorrow, you will have hands-on equipment training in the mornings and theory and maintenance classes in the afternoons.

"Are there any questions, so far?" the major asked.

"Will we receive training on the eighty-eight millimeter heavy flak gun?"

The major smiled and commented, "No, you won't be starting with one of the biggies. You will train to become proficient with the thirty-seven millimeter gun, which is medium flak used mainly to defend against low-flying aircraft. In about six weeks you will have an opportunity to show your stuff by firing live ammunition at an aircraft-towed target. Are there any further questions?"

As there were none, the base commander continued, "Since you have done so well today, you can have the rest of the day off. You may want to utilize the time to write to your mother and perhaps to a young lady who may be pining for you back home."

His last remark elicited several chuckles. Turning to one of the noncoms, the major said, "You can dismiss them."

The following morning, Mr. Vogt's class of thirty found out that twenty-four had been assigned to train as gun crew members; four would train as searchlight team members, while the remaining two would receive instructions in radio communications. Herbert's name was among those designated to become gun crew members.

For the introductory session, the gun crew trainees were marched to the gun sites which were located on an earthen embankment parallel to the North Sea shore line and approximately a half mile from the shoreline. Six guns were aligned along the embankment, and each of the six classes was assigned to one of the guns.

Waiting for them at each gun site was a noncom who would be their hands-on training instructor. Each noncom held the rank of Unteroffizier.

The sergeant assigned to Mr. Vogt's class introduced himself as Unteroffizier Reinicke. Herbert thought him to be in his early forties, old enough to be his father.

While the boys were still assembled in marching order, in columns of three, Unteroffizier Reinicke said, "I want you to give me a headcount alternating between the first column and the last column for a count of eight." Seeing the perplexed looks of the boys after he requested the unorthodox headcount, Unteroffizier Reinicke reiterated, "I want you to give me a headcount alternating between the first column and the last column, that is, four odd numbers from the front of the formation and four even numbers from the rear of the formation."

"Why is he doing that?" Herbert asked his neighbor.

"He doesn't want to wind up with a gun crew composed of all the little shits."

"No talking back there," the Unteroffizier growled and reiterated, "Give me a count from one through eight." After someone yelled eight, Unteroffizier Reinicke said, "Numbers one through eight break rank and step forward." He gave one of the boys who had stepped forward a piece of paper and a pencil and said, "Write down the names of one through eight and return the list to me. You are gun crew number one."

He repeated another countdown of the remaining formation and designated those of the second countdown as gun crew number two and the remaining eight boys as gun crew number three.

After the Unteroffizier had collected his three pieces of paper, he said, "You now know to which crew you have been assigned, and I have the names of the members of each crew. There will be no deviations, no switching from one crew to another."

The boys, having broken rank, were now milling about a bit. Unteroffizier Reinicke said, "I want you to gather round on the parapet that has been built around the gun emplacement. I will go into the emplacement and tell you a little bit about the gun."

Once he was standing beside the gun, he lifted off the tarpaulin and said, "This is a thirty-seven millimeter flak gun. It has been in the inventory since the start of the war. Early on, it was used not only as an air defense weapon but also as an anti-tank weapon against light tanks. I emphasize the word light, because with tanks becoming ever heavier, it soon became useless as a tank adversary. Troops in the field soon referred to it as the 'door knocker.' Now, unless the gun scores a lucky hit through a visor, or manages to damage a tank track, any other hit merely lets the tank crew know that somebody is outside; consequently, in the field, it has been relegated to general troop support. Any questions, so far?"

"How is this thing moved around in the field?" one of the boys asked.

"In the field, the gun base is not mounted on a concrete block, as it is here, it is positioned on a self-propelled chassis."

"Oh."

"I digressed a little bit, but now let's get down to business," the Unteroffizier continued. "The gun and the attached platform, through a system of down gearing, are connected to a stationary ring gear in the gun base to turn the gun about its vertical axis. A hand-wheel initiates the action. The field of fire in azimuth is 360 degrees, which means that the gun will turn round and round, like a merry-go-round, as long as someone keeps cranking the hand-wheel. Have you got all that?"

The feeble response caused the Unteroffizier to say, "Let me show you." He pointed to one of two collinear mounted hand-wheels just above a seat on the right side of the gun.

"This hand-wheel on the left side is the one that turns the gun." He climbed into the seat and started to crank. The gun turned. "If I keep on cranking, I will come full circle, although not as quickly as a merry-go-round."

Unteroffizier Reinicke got out of the seat and said, "There will be times when you will want to turn the gun a lot faster. You and your buddies then will grab the gun platform on the left side of the gun and quickly spin the gun around." While demonstrating, he noted, "With several guys pushing on the platform, the gun will turn even faster."

"Why would you want to turn the gun around so quickly?" someone asked.

"Suppose you are shooting at an approaching target at some altitude, and you don't score any hits. You would want to take another crack at the target while it is moving away, wouldn't you?" Unteroffizier Reinicke answered. After a pause he said, "It doesn't make much sense with a low-flying aircraft. A low-flying aircraft will be long gone by the time you turn the gun around. Your best bet in such a case is to aim your shots just a bit ahead of the approaching plane and to wait for the aircraft to make another pass, if you missed."

"But won't the aircraft pilot be shooting, too?" someone else asked.

"That could well be, but that's just one of the drawbacks of the job," was the Unteroffiziers laconic reply. The murmurs that echoed through his audience told Unteroffizier Reinicke that they were paying attention.

"There is one more thing I want to make you aware of when you have to turn the gun rapidly." He again pushed on the platform and asked, "What else is turning?" There was no response. "Don't be looking at me, look at the hand-wheel," he shouted, as he again pushed on the gun platform.

"The hand-wheel is spinning like crazy," one of the boys yelled.

"That's right. It is spinning so fast that the guy in the seat better have his hands off the wheel, unless he doesn't mind several broken fingers; therefore, the command to rapidly turn the gun should only be given by the guy occupying the seat. Have you got that?" Most of the boys responded by nodding their heads.

"So, what do you think the other wheel does?" Unteroffizier Reinicke pointed at one of several raised hands.

"I suppose it controls the elevation of the gun barrel," the boy responded.

"Very good," the Unteroffizier commented. "The gun barrel can be elevated from zero to eighty-five degrees. The range of the gun at that elevation is about two thousand meters. The barrel can't go lower than the horizontal position. Why do you think that is?" Hearing no response, he said, "It is restricted from going any lower, so you guys can't fire into your own gun emplacement."

"We're not that dumb," one boy commented.

The Unteroffizier laughed and said, "I certainly hope not! So, who do you think sits in that right hand seat?" he asked.

"The sight gunner," one of the boys answered.

"That is absolutely correct. Now, I want you to regroup according to crew designations crew number one on the north side of the embankment, crew number two on the south side, crew number three on the east side," the Unteroffizier ordered.

After the boys had positioned themselves, he asked, "So, who wants to be a sight gunner?"

Almost all raised their hand.

He studied crew number one for a moment and asked the name of one of the boys who had his hand raised. After making an entry on the name lists he had exacted from the boys, he said, "You will be the sight gunner." He selected the sight gunners for the other two gun crews in similar fashion.

Noticing the apparent disappointment of some of the boys who had raised their hand, the Unteroffizier said, "Look, I have to start somewhere. The assignments I make today may well be temporary. You will all be trained in each of the crew positions sufficiently such that any one of you can switch to any other position, should the need arise. Besides, the final call will be up to the gun commanders of the batteries to which you will be assigned once your training has been completed.

"Incidentally, the sight gunner is designated K1, an abbreviation of *Kanonier 1* (cannoneer 1). Let us now take a look at another position. The guy that sits in the seat at the back of the gun is the K2. He will be busy when the battery shoots a barrage or when the target is not within line of sight during ground support. During these operations, he essentially aims the gun. In these instances, the gun commander first orders operation in automatic mode. I should mention that the gun design in itself is a semi-automatic system, whereby, among other things, the recoil gases are utilized to evict the empty magazine out of the breech and to pull a loaded one in. In automatic mode the traverse and elevation are controlled by two electric motors in the base of the gun. The motors are powered by a generator located either in the gun emplacement or in the command post. Upon receiving the automatic mode command, the K2 configures the gun for that mode by pressing a button. He then receives traverse and elevation inputs from the command post via a headset and enters those values into the now fully automatic system via a keyboard."

"How often will we be shooting a barrage at enemy aircraft?" someone asked.

"The heavy flak had to do just that last summer, when the RAF dropped aluminum strips all over the city of Hamburg, thereby causing false echoes to our radar directed guns. But the thirty-seven millimeter guns have never been used in that fashion, simply because the bomber formations are always well out of reach," the Unteroffizier answered.

"Then why do we need a K2?" the same boy asked and added, "He won't have anything to do!"

"Hey, you can take that up with your battery commander after you leave here. I have been tasked with training a full complement of thirty-seven millimeter gun crews, and that is what I am doing," the Unteroffizier blurted with some annoyance. After a brief pause, he said, "I will now assign the K2 positions for each gun." This time he did not ask who might be interested in the assignment. Instead, he merely pointed to a boy in each crew, asked for his name, and recorded it.

"You three are assigned the K2 position for your respective guns," he announced.

"I knew you would get the K2 job," Detlev Wolfert said to Herbert in a low voice.

"How did you know?"

"The first two that he picked were the shortest guys in their group, and you have that distinction for our group. He's just trying to give you little guys a cushy job."

"I don't need him to give me a cushy job," Herbert said with a frown.

Noting his friends misgivings, Detlev tried to placate him by saying, "Well, maybe he's doing that because there isn't enough legroom for the bigger guys in the K2 seat."

"Yeah, right," Herbert replied.

The Unteroffizier glanced at them and asked, "Would it be asking too much for your attention before I continue?"

The boys shut up.

"There are three guys that get to ride around on the gun," the Unteroffizier said. "You have already been introduced to the first two, namely the K1 and the K2. The third guy is the K3. He is stationed on the platform, and his job is to load a magazine containing six projectiles into the breech of the gun. He is supported by two ammunition handlers: one accepts the spent magazine to have it replenished, while the other one hands him the next magazine to be loaded. Who wants to be the gun loader?"

The boys sensed that once the loader position was assigned, the remaining tasks would be grunt work; therefore, all those that had not yet been given an assignment raised a hand. The Unteroffizier again picked three guys and registered their names.

"There is a method to his madness," Detlev confided to Herbert. "He picked the three whom he thinks are the strongest."

"Well, we have assigned the three most important gun positions," the Unteroffizier commented.

"The remaining positions, K4 through K8 handle ammunition or are deployed as aircraft lookouts. We won't go into detail about these positions at this time. Each of you will receive exposure to them during your training.

"I want to reiterate that today's selections essentially are merely a starting point and that each of you will receive training in each position in the next several weeks. The final decision as to who does what, after you leave here, will be made by your gun commander, once you have a permanent assignment. I've noticed that some of you are starting to stamp your feet even though it is a pleasant January morning, so let's do a little hands-on stuff to warm you up. I will show you how to remove the gun barrel, which you will have to do during your maintenance procedure and how to replace it," the Unteroffizier said.

He opened the door to a small bunker that had been built into one side of the emplacement and pulled out two tripods. He placed them about four feet apart from one another on the bunker side of the emplacement.

"Crew number one, come on down," he ordered. He separated them into two groups of four. "I want the first group of four to remove the barrel after I show you how to disable the locking mechanism; then, while they are catching their breath, the other four can put the barrel back in place."

The Unteroffizier cranked the gun barrel into the horizontal position and showed them how to unlock the barrel.

Addressing the first four, he said, "Now, with two guys on the muzzle end and the other two on the gun chassis end, I want you to pull the barrel out of the chassis, and set it on those tripods. You want to be careful; that barrel weighs a couple of hundred pounds."

Once the barrel rested on the tripods, the Unteroffizier said, "If we were doing a maintenance procedure, you would first remove the muzzle protector." With an impish grin, he proclaimed, "Some guys call it the big condom." When his remark elicited only isolated guffaws, he smiled and thought, some of these guys probably don't even know what a condom is.

Redirecting his attention to his audience, the Unteroffizier said, "After removing the muzzle protector, you would run a wire brush at the end of a long handle through the barrel to clean it. You could run it through either way from the muzzle end or from the chassis end, whichever way strikes your fancy. For lubrication, you then would wet a long-handled sponge with oil and run it through the barrel.

"Now, the second group can mount the barrel back into the chassis. You will have to be careful that the notch on the end of the barrel coincides with the chassis groove; otherwise, the barrel won't go in."

With the barrel back in place, the Unteroffizier showed them how to implement the barrel lock. He then invited the other two crews to run through the procedure.

When the last crew had completed the task, the Unteroffizier said, "There is another instance when the barrel has to be changed. Does anyone know when that would be?" Hearing no response, he said, "When you have to fire eight or ten magazines in quick succession, the barrel will get very hot. If it overheats, a shell might explode while still in the barrel. The exploding shell will rupture the barrel and all kinds of nasty stuff will whiz around in your gun emplacement. So what do we do?"

"Use asbestos gloves," someone suggested.

"That's a good idea, but the barrel will be red-hot, and the gloves won't protect your other body parts, if the barrel should get away from you. What we have to do is to handle the barrel with tongs."

The Unteroffizier went back to the bunker, and after some rustling he came up with two pairs of tongs. The tongs had handles that were about three feet long. He showed the boys that, unlike most tongs, these did not grip when the handles were almost parallel to one another; they gripped when the handles were in line with one another. He asked one of the boys to assist him in a demonstration. With the tongs in the open position, he placed the grips of the tongs under the barrel. The Unteroffizier held one handle and asked the boy to go to the other side of the barrel and to grab the other handle. Turning to his audience he said, "As we lift the handles, the grips will enclose the barrel. Once the handles are in line, the grips are clenching the barrel, and as you can see, he and I are standing a safe two and a half feet on either side of what normally would be a be a very hot gun barrel. There is no weight bearing down on us now, but if we had another set of tongs on the muzzle end and if we were to pull the barrel out, the barrel weight would keep the grips closed."

The Unteroffizier dismissed the boy that had assisted him in the demonstration and said, "So, let's run through the exercise, while we pretend that we are changing a hot barrel."

Herbert's crew was the first one to be called into the gun emplacement, and he was in the group of four that were to remove the barrel using the tongs. He was on the chassis end of the barrel.

After the Unteroffizier once again disabled the locking lever, he positioned himself close to Herbert. "Before the barrel comes out of the gun, you will have to lift a bit on the tongs handles; otherwise, the grips will just slide along the barrel. The gun barrel started to move out of the chassis as they lifted and exerted a slight pull forward. As the barrel left the chassis, the tongs handles on the chassis side, although in-line, were slanted toward the ground on Herbert's side, because he was much shorter than the guy on the other side of the barrel. He held on, but the Unteroffizier quickly grabbed the tongs handle and elbowed him out of the way.

"Let's get this thing onto the tripod," the Unteroffizier shouted. Once the barrel was secured, the Unteroffizier said, "I forgot to tell you that unless the tongs handles are horizontal when they receive the weight, the guy whose handle is closer to the ground will bear a disproportionate part of the weight." Pointing toward Herbert, he said, "I think he would have managed, but I didn't want to take a chance. The solution is simple: Have either two short guys or two tall guys working the tongs. Better yet, let the four biggest guys effect the barrel change."

The remaining boys of Herbert's crew replaced the barrel without incidence, and the crew returned to their assigned place on the embankment.

"I told you that he was looking out for you," Detlev said.

"Yeah, yeah."

After the other crews had performed the exercise, Unteroffizier Reinicke observed, "It looks like the other gun crews are getting ready to return to the barracks for lunch." Pointing to one of the boys, he said, "Line your class up in formation and we'll do the same."

Herbert was tired by day's end, but when taps sounded he could not sleep. He thought, I struck out during the gun position assignments, and I fouled out during the hot barrel practice. I wound up with a big fat zero on the scoreboard. I'm not sure I belong here, but what choice do I have? If I were to wash out of the Luftwaffe Auxiliary, my schooling would suffer, because I would have to enroll in some backwater school in that backwater town of Altburgund. He yawned, and before he drifted off to sleep, he thought, I'll just have to somehow show them that I can pull my own weight.

Chapter 37

Hertha was preparing another meager evening meal for the girls and herself. She sighed and thought, potato soup with some turnips thrown in that seems to have become our standard fare. Walther occasionally can supplement our rations by buying a few eggs or a little meat from some farmers he has befriended in the outskirts of town; however, I am always in a state of anxiety whenever he goes on one of those foraging trips. Obtaining food without ration cards is considered to be black market activity, and if the participants are caught, the consequences are severe for both buyer and seller.

Hertha sighed again and looked at the wall clock. It was 6:00 P.M. "Romi should have been home by now," she said to Hannelore who grudgingly was doing her homework at the kitchen table.

"Dinner is almost ready," she told her younger daughter.

"Do you want to eat now, or shall we wait till Romi comes home?"

"Let's wait until she comes home," Hannelore answered as she slammed her notebook shut.

"Have you finished your homework?"

"No, I thought you wanted me to clear the table."

"Not until we're ready to eat. You might as well get as much done as you can, because you know that you will have to stick with your homework assignment, either before or after dinner, until you have completed it." Hannelore expressed her displeasure with a pout, but she reopened the notebook.

Romi got home about half an hour later. She gave her mother a hug and greeted Hannelore with, "How are you doing, short stuff?" Hannelore mumbled something about homework overload.

Hertha looked at her daughter, who would be celebrating her seventeenth birthday in a few weeks' time and thought, my God, she looks so frail and so tired. She asked Romi, "How come you are so late today?"

"There was an error in my tally, and I had to stay until it was resolved. I guess I hit the wrong button on the adding machine at some time during the day."

"You look weary. Is the job getting to be too much for you?"

"It's all right," Romi said, and, "I don't mind working at the bank, but, as you know, a bank job was never my first choice. When the authorities advised me that I either had to get a job or go to trade school, I told them I was interested in learning textile design. I took the teller job, because they told me that my first choice was not available.

"I get along well with my co-workers, Germans and Poles alike, but...but the incidentals of the job bother me."

"Like what?" her mother asked.

"Like the train rides I have to take to Bydgoszcz twice a week to go to the classes my boss has ordered me to attend. Since I don't intend to make banking my life's work, I could care less about interest rates and foreign currencies. The trip back and forth is often interrupted because the train has to get onto the main line to get to Bydgoszcz. All other main line traffic seems to take precedence; therefore, I miss half of my class occasionally because the train can't get into Bydgoszcz, or I may spend my own time on a stalled train, because the train can't leave Bydgoszcz.

"I just hate having to go to those classes, Mama."

"Is anything else bothering you?"

"Mama, this whole milieu that we find ourselves in bothers me.

"The bank offers a savings program to the kids in the German school system. Once a week I have to go to the two schools to pick up the deposits. After I got back to the bank after my latest trip, the boss who, of course, is a Party member called me into his office and said to me, 'I understand that you didn't wear a swastika on your coat when you visited the schools.'

"I asked him why I should be wearing a swastika and told him that all I'm doing is picking up the deposits.

"Do you know what he said, Mama? He said, 'If you don't wear a swastika, the children might think you are Polish.'

"I was with a Polish male co-worker, Mama. What was the swastika supposed to do? Make him look inferior? Make me look superior? Pinning a Nazi emblem on my coat surely isn't going to make me a better person.

"I've seen ethnic German kids lollygagging in front of a dairy store, and when a Polish kid would come out carrying a milk container, they would grab the container and dump it! What kind of craziness is that?

"Last summer, the Party called up all the young people in town—how the Party keeps track of us is beyond me—to help unload a train that had brought ethnic German refugees from the Ukraine into town. The train was a freight train, and the people must have been on it for weeks. They were unkempt and dirty, and they smelled bad. Little babies wore only a little shirt and no diaper.

"Apparently they arrived before shelter was made available for all of them. Many had no place to go. Even now, some are still quartered in the station waiting room.

"They roam around town with nothing to do. They defecate in the street. They have nothing but the shirt on their back. They will go into a store, pick something up, and leave without paying. When they are challenged by the storekeeper, they invariably respond with 'Hitler called, Hitler pays!'" With a hint of a smile, Romi said, "I can't blame them for their attitude.

"Mama, I have never seen such abject poverty. We, in our one room apartment with a straw mattress on the bed, are living in luxury compared to those people." She started to cry. Little Hannelore, who had paid their discussion little mind up to now, reached over and patted Romi's hand.

With tears running down her cheeks, Romi lamented, "I wish we had never come here. I wish we had stayed in Hamburg!"

"If we had stayed in Hamburg, we might all be dead now," her mother responded.

"Then why didn't we stay in New York?"

Hertha bristled. Staring at Romi, she thought, don't you start reproving me, too. I've heard enough reproaches, however veiled, from your father.

Seeing her mother's countenance, Romi immediately knew that she had hit a raw nerve. Me and my big mouth, she said to herself.

Hertha softened her look and said, "We cannot change the past; therefore, it makes little sense to rummage through the why and wherefore." Trying to console her daughter, she added, albeit without conviction, "Surely the worst is behind us."

That evening, after the girls had gone to bed, Hertha sat alone in the kitchen. It was her turn to cry as she thought, my daughter is not just tired; she seems close to a nervous breakdown.

✦✦✦

Herbert's class was in its third week of hands-on training in the mornings and gun theory, aircraft identification, and maintenance training in the afternoons.

Herbert liked the theory and aircraft identification classes, and he took copious notes. He had to improvise to study his notes after the training classes, because he couldn't concentrate during the noisy barrack atmosphere before the lights out order, and he couldn't turn on a table lamp lest he would incur the wrath of a noncom making a cursory inspection after the lights out order.

Herbert resolved his problem by first going to the commissary and buying a flashlight and a backup of spare batteries. He then literally went undercover and studied his notes, the gun manual, and the aircraft identification booklet under his blankets. Herbert soon was able to identify the various German, British, and American aircraft, which were in service at the time, by recognizing their silhouettes when viewed from the front, side, or bottom.

As a consequence of his persistent study, Herbert soon was able to respond to questions asked by the theory instructor when no other hands were raised. After several such instances, on many occasions, the instructor no longer posed the question to the class, but, pointing at Herbert, would say, "Let's ask the flak professor for an answer."

One morning, after Herbert had answered a question posed by the instructor, Manfred Romke, who was sitting next to Herbert and who was the K1 of the gun crew Herbert had been assigned to, commented, "Wow, you must have some kind of photographic memory."

"Nah, I don't have that gift; I just study this stuff more than you guys do." To himself he said, I'm not doing this to make you guys look bad. I'm doing it in the hopes I won't wash out; otherwise, I'll be presented with a one way ticket back to Dullsville, better known as Altburgund.

+++

The training facility was located outside the town of Buesum but close enough that the boys could hear the blare of the town's air raid sirens whenever an alert was sounded. During morning alerts, when the boys were at the gun emplacements, they would hear the roar of the coastal guns and on cloudless days see the serenity of the clear blue skies being violated by the contrails of the bomber formations and the dark puffs of smoke of the exploding flak shells. When the bombers passed overhead in the middle of the night, hardly any of the boys would part the blackout curtain to watch the searchlights nervously scanning the sky and the radar directed guns displaying their deadly fireworks; they had seen it all before.

+++

After six weeks of training, the base commander made good his promise: An airborne target would be available for half an hour, and the aircraft would make three passes to give all three crews training at each gun a chance to fire with live ammunition. All six guns stationed on the embankment along the North Sea coast would take part in the exercise.

When Mr. Vogt's class had assembled on the parapet of their gun emplacement for the target practice, Unteroffizier Reinicke said, "I have taught you all I know. Today you are on your own. There will be no guidance from me; however, I will give you my evaluation of your efforts when we are done. Each crew will only get to shoot during one pass, and you will have to move quickly to change crews between passes. The aircraft will be coming in from the north. It will fly on a steady course half way between here and the coastline at an altitude of 150 meters. After each pass, the aircraft will make a wide turn inland and then return for the next pass. You will only fire while the aircraft is passing between here and the shoreline.

"Are you ready?" the Unteroffzier asked the boys. A sufficient number of nodding heads convinced the Unteroffizier that they thought they were. "When I say, 'Go!' crew number one will take their positions in the gun emplacement!" he said and then added, "I beseech all of you guys; please, do not shoot down the airplane!"

"Go!"

Shortly thereafter, the aircraft with target in tow arrived and soon commenced its first pass.

The gun responded as the K1's foot depressed the firing pedal: BOOM! BOOM!

The boys of the two crews waiting their turn stood on the parapet at the rear of gun and watched the action. Some of them put their hands over their ears; all of them watched the flames curling around the muzzle-flash damper with each shot. They anticipated the third shot, because they knew that every third round of the magazine was a tracer. BOOM! The tracer's trajectory indicated that the K1's aim was a little high and somewhat behind the target.

BOOM! BOOM! BOOM! The K1 kept the pedal depressed and emptied the magazine just as the aircraft started its wide turn.

After each of the first two passes, there was somewhat of a scramble as the next crew took control of the gun.

When the aircraft had completed the third pass, the Unteroffizier said, "You guys did better than I expected, but the K1s had the same problem that all fledgling K1s seem to have. You do well with the azimuth hand-wheel, but you seem to forget about the elevation wheel. When an aircraft makes a lateral approach, as this one did, you have to keep on raising the gun barrel ever so slightly as the aircraft comes closer; otherwise your shots will just whiz by beneath the target. But you will learn with experience.

"As I said, you guys did pretty good, and the base commander will be happy that one of the other guns did get a piece of the target."

"I think the target is way too small," one of the boys called out.

"I agree that it's not very big," Unteroffizier Reinicke said, and with a mischievous grin, he added, "Hey, I proposed to the base commander that the aircraft should tow a blimp for you guys, but he wouldn't buy my suggestion."

Chapter 38

The truck convoy left Buesum at 6:00 A.M. on a cold morning in mid-February. It was transporting the boys to a Luftwaffe base on the outskirts of Hamburg. The boys had been loaded per class, with each class being assigned two trucks. When the convoy reached the base, the boys were told to go to the commissary to get some breakfast and to line up class-wise alongside the trucks an hour later.

After the boys had positioned themselves, a Luftwaffe lieutenant told them that the convoy would now split up and they would be taken to their assigned batteries.

About an hour later, the two trucks that were transporting Mr. Vogt's class turned onto a dirt road. "I can see our gun emplacements!" someone at the back end of the lead truck yelled. The boys farther forward in the truck were denied the view because of the truck tarpaulin. Some of them quickly moved to the back to catch a glimpse of their new home.

The battery was located on a field with each gun surrounded by a parapet just like the guns at the training base in Buesum were. The guns, half hidden by their tarps, were approximately one hundred yards from one another and placed such that each was at the juncture of two of the sides of an equilateral triangle. Close to each gun was a barrack. Two more barracks and a larger brick building were located at the north end of the field. Turf had been removed to create paths between the guns and the buildings, and the paths were covered with wooden lattices to maintain the integrity of the paths during inclement weather.

The trucks continued on the dirt road until they reached the brick building. An Unterofffizier came out of the building and ordered them to disembark and to line up in formation.

"Attention!" the Unteroffizier ordered as an *Oberwachtmeister* (master sergeant) and three additional Unteroffiziere exited the building.

"At ease," the Oberwachtmeister commanded. "I am Oberwachtmeister Lange. I will be your battery commander. Assisting me are my gun commanders: Unteroffiziere Kimmel, Latner, and Pfahl." He pointed to each of the noncoms as he introduced them. "Unteroffizier Junger is my liaison noncom," he added as he nodded toward the man who had ordered the boys to line up.

The boys noticed that, with the exception of Unteroffizier Pfahl, all the noncoms including the battery commander were men in their late thirties or early forties. Unteroffizier Pfahl stood out not only because he appeared to be about twenty-five, but also because he had been awarded the Iron Cross, First Class[7]. His uniform jacket also bore the wound badge and the winter campaign ribbon, which had been awarded to those who were on the eastern front during the severe winter of 1941.

The Oberwachtmeister scrutinized the rank and file assembled in front of him and said, "I want to welcome you to our battery. You have just come from seven weeks of training, and some of you undoubtedly think that you now know all there is to know about the thirty-seven millimeter gun and how to handle it. We will go through some exercises to find out whether such confidence is warranted. If it is not, we will continue

7 A medal, equivalent to the Silver Star in the American forces.

training until it is. I want to make sure that you will give a good account of yourselves whenever an enemy plane comes within range of our guns. Are there any questions?"

One of the boys raised his hand and asked, "When will our teacher, Mr. Vogt, be joining us?"

"Ah, yes, the teacher..." the Oberwachtmeister said with some impatience. "Mr. Vogt will join us in about a week. In the barrack next to this building we have provided living quarters for your teacher as well as an area that will serve as your classroom. Our field kitchen is in the other barrack.

"I wish to stress that your first responsibility is to me. It is not to your teacher! At night as well as during the day, you will have to be at the guns during every alert, and be advised that our alert usually precedes the warning given the populace, and their all clear may come long before we stand down. You will lose two hours of class time whenever your guard duty shift coincides with class time, because we have to maintain guard duty around the clock.

"Any interruptions in your class schedules and your schooling in general will have to be addressed by your teacher and by you, yourself. When your class schedule falls behind, your teacher may well have to schedule classes on those days when we tend to relax a little bit around here, namely Saturdays and Sundays. Your schooling is of no concern to me, because such concern would interfere with how I have to do my job. I reiterate that your first responsibility is to me, and I want that to be understood." Hearing no objections—he certainly did not expect to hear any—the Oberwachtmeister said, "Junger, have them regroup according to the gun crew assignments they were given in Buesum."

After the boys had reorganized, the battery commander said, "Kimmel, you take gun crew number one; Pfahl, you take gun crew number two; and Latner, you take the rest."

Turning his attention back to the boys, he said, "I am maintaining the crew assignments as they were made in Buesum by the training instructor, because I believe that he had good reason for making his selections. If, in the course of our continued training, we find that some changes are desirable, we will initiate them at such time.

"The Unteroffiziere will now show you to your barracks. After you have changed into your fatigues, we will start our first training session in...in an hour. Unteroffizier Junger, you can dismiss them."

✚✚✚

Unteroffizier Kimmel took his crew to their barrack. He told them to pick a bunk and to select one of the lockers that stood along one of the walls. He showed them where two rifles were kept under lock and key and a great coat was hung on a nearby post all of which were to be used for guard duty.

"Who has the key for the rifles?" one of the boys asked.

"I do," the noncom replied. "You will find it in my upper right hand desk drawer—woe to whomever does not return the key! My quarters are in the room at the front end of the barrack. The great coat that you see hanging near the rifles is to be used by you communally when you are pulling guard duty during the winter months."

"Where is the toilet?" another boy asked.

Raising his hand and pointing with his thumb the noncom said, "It's on the other end of the barrack. You'll also find a sink and a shower stall back there." He sat down at one of the tables while the boys stowed their gear into the lockers. When the boys were almost done, he said, "You better start changing into your fatigues; the boss man does not like to be kept waiting."

✚✚✚

It was almost 4:00 AM in the morning. Herbert had wakened the boy in the gun number two barrack who was scheduled to relieve him from his first guard duty assignment. When Horst Drossen came out of his barrack, Herbert asked him, "How do you like your noncom?"

"He's great, but I don't think he'll be around for long."

"Why is that?"

"He recently completed a convalescent furlough."

"Was he wounded on the eastern front?" Herbert interrupted.

"Yeah."

"Oh...is that where he was awarded the Iron Cross?"

"I suppose so. He told us he was drafted just before the Russian campaign started. He doesn't talk about it, but I imagine he singlehandedly knocked out one or two Russian T34 tanks either with an eighty-eight millimeter gun or with a Panzerfaust[8]. It had to be something extraordinary—they don't just give that medal away!"

"Wow! Well, I'm going to get some shuteye," Herbert said.

"How do you like your noncom?" Horst inquired.

"He's OK. He tells us his expertise is range-finding rather than commanding a gun. But I'm sure he knows more about the guns than he lets on."

Horst nodded. "Well, see you later," he said.

"Yeah."

The first few weeks were tough on the boys. They soon found out that their battery commander was a stickler for perfection, which he tried to instill with countless drills done over and over

8 Bazooka

again. At times, even the noncoms would raise their eyebrows when the battery commander would repeat, "Let's go through that exercise one more time and this time without any hiccups!"

Five or six weeks later the Oberwachtmeister probably realized that the constant goading was doing more harm than good, and he finally let up on the boys.

As promised, Mr. Vogt had joined them one week after their arrival, and their classes were resumed.

During those first weeks, the boys experienced several alerts. Most of them lasted about an hour and a half, and they were a mix of daylight and nighttime intrusions by small numbers of aircraft. The daylight incursions mostly were reconnaissance flights, whereas the nighttime flights apparently were designed to scare the populace into their shelters at the sound of the alarms. The scare usually was underscored by dropping several bomb loads on the city.

The heavy flak did not bother with the daylight intruders and took action at night only when several searchlights coned one of the aircraft. On several occasions, a huge explosion seen within such a cone indicated that that particular intruder would not be coming back.

Chapter 39

In early March, Romi called her supervisor at the bank and told him she would not be coming in to work because she had come down with a cold.

She told her mother that she felt very weak.

"Well, you've been lethargic for some time now, and you hardly eat at all," her mother responded.

"I just don't have any appetite, Mama!"

Hertha went to the pharmacy and obtained over the counter cold remedies. A week later, Romi's condition had worsened. She had developed a severe cough.

"The over the counter pills and lozenges are not doing the job," Hertha finally said. "I'm going to make an appointment for you to see our doctor!"

Two days later they went to the doctor's office in Altburgund.

"How long has she been this way?" the doctor asked as he scanned Romi's personal data which the nurse had given him.

"She has been listless for quite a while, but this cold, or flu, did not start until about a week ago," Hertha answered.

"I see, and ...." He was interrupted by one of Romi's coughing spells. "How long has that been going on?" he asked.

"About three days," Romi answered.

The doctor nodded as he got up from behind his desk and called the nurse into his office. "Erika, please take this young lady to the examination room. I'll be there in a few minutes."

After they departed, the doctor said, "Rosemarie is seventeen, about five foot one, but she barely weighs ninety pounds."

"We are all malnourished nowadays," Hertha commented.

"Yes, but your daughter is malnourished to the extreme."

"She hadn't been eating properly even before she caught this cold. She keeps telling me that she isn't hungry."

"I'm concerned about that cough," the doctor said.

"Do you think Rosemarie has something more than a flu attack?"

"I certainly hope not; but we will have to wait until I have examined her before I can answer your question," the doctor replied. "If you will excuse me, we should know a lot more in twenty or thirty minutes."

Hertha was left in the doctor's office by herself. She wondered why Romi's coughing spell should be of such interest to the doctor. She thought, my kids have had many bouts with influenza over the years, and the majority of them entailed a cough. His apparent concern certainly has not been reassuring; I am now more worried about Romi's condition than when we came in here.

Hertha's troubled state of mind made the minutes appear to tick by ever so slowly. Finally, the doctor came back into the office.

"I have good news for you, Mrs. Klug. I performed a Mantoux test on your daughter, and the results are negative!"

"So what is the good news?" Hertha asked, "I don't even know what a...a Man..."

"A Mantoux test," the doctor interjected. "The test requires that the patient be given an injection to determine the presence of tuberculosis."

"Tuberculosis? What on earth made you think that my daughter has tuberculosis?"

"I have diagnosed tuberculosis on several occasions during the past months. Most of the cases involved ethnic Germans that had arrived from the east. I also am aware that the young folks in town have been called upon to help these people upon arrival. Since I assumed that Rosemarie was among those youngsters, I felt she might be at risk. I did not mention this when you first came in because I wanted to spare you the anguish such a supposition would have provoked."

"I appreciate your consideration," Hertha replied.

"I believe that physically your daughter is afflicted with a bad case of the flu; however, I also believe that your daughter is suffering from some kind of psychoneurosis," the doctor commented.

"Are you now telling me that my daughter is crazy?"

"No, no," the doctor said with a smile. "I said psychoneurosis, not psychosis. Psychoneurosis is an anxiety brought about by everyday experiences which might make a person feel anxious or resentful. Can you think of any such experience that might explain Rosemarie's anxieties?"

Hertha looked at the doctor and thought, can I tell you about the run-in with the BDM girl? Can I tell you about the nonsense of having to wear a swastika emblem when she picks up the school children's savings deposits? To what extent can I trust you, dear doctor?

Finally, Hertha said, "She is working as a bank teller only because there aren't any facilities around here that would allow her to learn textile design. She took the job, because she really didn't have any other choice, and yes, certain aspects of the job bother her a lot."

"Certain aspects?" the doctor asked in an attempt to cause her to be more specific.

Hertha thought, that's as specific as I'm going to be and reiterated, "Certain aspects bother her."

"Do you feel that these 'certain aspects' are causing your daughter's anxieties?"

"I do."

The doctor nodded and asked, "Are you dependent on your daughter's income from the bank?"

Hertha said, "No. She is working, because she was told to work!"

The doctor nodded and said, "Well, then we must get your daughter out of that environment. I will give you a disposition that states that Rosemarie is unfit to carry on her job for the foreseeable future. I will also...." He was interrupted when Rosemarie came back into the office and sat down beside her mother. "I will also prescribe additional food coupons for her, so that she can regain some of the weight she has lost. If at all possible, I would suggest that you take your daughter out of this environment perhaps to the mountains where she can rest up a bit."

Turning to Romi, he said, "It looks like you just have a bad case of the flu, but as a precautionary measure, I am asking your mother to take you to a specialist in Bydgoszcz for a chest x-ray."

"The injection that you gave me, what was it for?" Romi asked.

"The injection confirmed that you just have the flu," the doctor answered.

"Are we all done?" Hertha asked.

"Yes. Please stop by sometime tomorrow, and I will give you

the appointment with the specialist in Bydgoszcz."

Hertha nodded and thanked the doctor.

"What else did the doctor tell you while I was in the examination room?" Romi asked her mother after they had left the doctor's office.

"I told him that your job at the bank was causing you considerable stress."

"So, what did he say?"

"He felt that the job was the major cause for your anxieties, and he gave me a letter that excuses you from having to work."

"Oh, good! I won't have to travel back and forth to Bydgoszcz any more, and what's more important, I won't have to put up with those silly regulations any more.

"The doctor seemed evasive when I asked him about the injection. I never heard of an injection being required to determine whether someone has the flu."

"The doctor diagnosed several people with tuberculosis recently. He wanted to make sure that you had not been exposed to it," Hertha said.

"Then I tested negative, is that correct?"

"Yes honey, thank God, you don't have TB!"

Several days later, Hertha and Romi went to see the specialist in Bydgoszcz. While on the train, Hertha noticed that several people in the compartment moved away from them when Romi had one of her coughing spells; some even moved to another compartment.

After Romi had undergone another examination and x-ray testing, the doctor told Hertha that Romi's lungs were clear. He said that she did have a mild respiratory tract infection due to the influenza. He prescribed medication and told Hertha to make sure that Romi got a lot of rest.

✚✚✚

Herbert also took ill in March. He had headaches and a runny nose, and he finally asked Unteroffizier Kimmel where to report for sick call. Unteroffizier Kimmel referred him to Unteroffizier Junger, who told him he would have to go to the flak bunker to see a doctor.

"I've heard about the three or four flak bunkers that are located in the greater Hamburg area, but I have never seen one," Herbert said, and then asked, "How do I identify it?"

"Just take the trolley southbound until you see a massive concrete structure. You can't miss it. Go to room 209 and sign in at the receptionist's desk; then, wait until the doctor calls you in."

✚✚✚

As Herbert left the encampment, he reminded himself: Unteroffizier Junger told me to take the southbound trolley. He boarded the second car of the trolley. Since he wasn't sure just where he was going, he stayed on the forward platform of the car to ensure the best possible overview of his surroundings. About twenty minutes later, he saw a massive dark-grey concrete structure and thought that must be the place to which Unteroffizier Junger was referring. It was even bigger than Herbert had imagined. He thought, that thing must cover two city blocks, and it appears to be about ten stories high.

He knew that the bunkers were not only built to accommodate the 105 millimeter guns on the roof, but also to provide refuge for the populace during an air raid.

After he got off the trolley, he looked at the monstrous building in awe. The building had not one window. This place must be capable of housing thousands of people, he thought. Herbert directed his scan toward the top of the building. At what he estimated to be the eighth floor level, he saw the platforms that extended from the building at its corners. The platforms provided space for the emplacement of light antiaircraft guns. He could see the gun barrels pointing toward the sky at the three corner platforms within his field of vision. From his vantage point, he could not see the 105-millimeter guns on the rooftop, but he knew they were there.

As Herbert walked into the building, he noticed that the floors, the ceiling, the walls, and the stairs that were located on one side of the building, all consisted of reinforced concrete. Everything, except the large elevator and the stair banister, was solid concrete. Since he had to go to the second floor, Herbert chose the staircase. As he walked up the stairs, his footsteps echoed off the walls and ceiling as though he were in a large tomb. He soon found room 209 and gave the receptionist the sick call ticket that Unteroffizier Junger had given him. Herbert noticed that he was third in line to see the doctor. He sat down to wait his turn.

When the receptionist gave Herbert the green light, he entered the doctor's office. The doctor was sitting behind his desk and wearing a white coat over his uniform, but Herbert could discern that the doctor's rank was that of a Luftwaffe captain by observing his nameplate on the desk. In one corner of the room, a phonograph was playing an operatic aria.

"What can I do for you, young fellow?" the doctor asked.

"I have a runny nose, and I've been having a lot of headaches these last few days. I think I have the flu," Herbert answered.

"Well, take off your tunic, and I will check you out."

While Herbert was busy complying with the doctor's request, the stylus of the phonograph reached the end of the recording, and the music was replaced by a soft clicking sound. "Excuse me for a moment," the doctor said as he walked over to the phonograph to change the record. "Do you like my music?" he asked.

"Yes, sir," Herbert replied, adding emphasis by nodding his head.

"Did you recognize that last piece?"

Herbert nodded again and said, "I believe that was 'Musetta's Waltz,' from *La Boheme.*"

"Very good," the doctor declared, as he replaced the record with another one.

"Do you know who composed it?"

"Giacomo Puccini."

"Excellent!" the doctor commented as he returned to start his examination. He stuck a tongue depressor in Herbert's mouth and asked, "Do you recognize that aria?"

Herbert's response was limited to "Uh huh!" because of the tongue depressor.

"So, what is it?" the doctor asked after he completed the throat examination.

"It's from *Madame Butterfly*. I know it as 'One Fine Day,'" Herbert replied. He pronounced the title in English, because he did not know the German version.

"Right again!" the doctor exclaimed. "Do you like Wagner?"

"He's all right," Herbert answered.

"Ah! You prefer Puccini over Wagner. Sounds to me like you will be a lover rather than a warrior, once you are several years older!"

"Right now, I am merely hoping that I will live to be several years older," Herbert commented.

The doctor nodded and then asked, "I'm wondering why you know the music by the English titles?"

"Because my parents' record labels were in English."

The doctor chuckled and said, "I meant why did your parents buy the English labels? Before the war, when you still could buy the records here, they would be labeled in German."

"My parents did not buy the records here; they bought them in New York."

"Oh? Were you born in the United States?"

Herbert nodded as the doctor reached for his stethoscope.

"How do you like living in Germany?" the doctor asked while performing the auscultation.

"It's all right."

"I see. Being at war makes any place less desirable," the doctor said without expecting a response. He probed some more and then said, "I can't find anything wrong with you, except for a light case of the flu. I will prescribe some pills that my receptionist can give you on your way out."

Herbert put his tunic back on and thanked the doctor.

The doctor had final words of advice, "Remember to listen to some music once in a while. It will soften the effects of the bumps in the road that you will encounter every now and then."

As Herbert walked back down the concrete stairs, he reflected upon what else the doctor had said. Herbert thought, he said that in a few years I most likely would be a lover rather than a warrior, thereby implying that presently I am neither. Herbert shrugged and with a smile said to himself, at least he did not use the term coined by the populace and used occasionally to describe the Luftwaffe Auxiliary. He did not refer to me as "baby flak."

Chapter 40

During the first few months of 1944, the Hamburg area was subjected to occasional nuisance raids with small numbers of aircraft getting the populace out of bed at night or having them scramble for shelter during the day. The many air raid alerts during that time belied the actual number of nuisance raids because the alerts would sound any time the bomber formations were close to the greater Hamburg area. Since the ground defenses could not predict which city the nearby bomber formations would be targeting, the alert would sound if there were any chance that Hamburg might be the objective.

The boys of Mr. Vogt's class had to man the guns every time the alert sounded, but they managed to attend classes to a reasonable degree. Normally, Mr. Vogt would stay in the encampment with them during the weekdays and leave for home on Friday afternoon; however, if the class fell behind in its schedule, he would stay and order a Saturday morning or even an afternoon session to make up for lost time.

There were times during class when one of the boys would have to nudge his neighbor to keep him from falling asleep, but all in all, the class was able to stay on schedule.

In mid April, Herbert received a letter from his mother advising him of Romi's recent sickness and that she and the girls would be visiting the Lienhofs in Bodenbach for a month. His mother indicated that the primary reason for going was to give Romi a chance to fully recuperate from her illness and that they would be in Bodenbach during the month of May. She added that his father would be joining them in mid-May, since he had been granted a two-week furlough. She wondered whether there was any chance that he could also get away and join them during that time period.

Herbert did some quick calculations. I have accrued two days per month furlough time, he thought, and I have accumulated three weekend passes. That should give me about twelve days. I'll ask Unteroffizier Junger whether he can let me go in mid-May.

After Unteroffizier Junger perused the battery's furlough and pass calendar, he indicated that the battery might be able to get along without Herbert's presence for ten days starting on 15 May. Herbert broke out in a smile and said, "Thank you, Herr Unteroffizier!"

Herbert returned to his barrack and quickly wrote a letter to his mother. He advised her that his arrival date in Bodenbach would probably be 16 May.

It was 5:30 A.M. when Herbert left the battery encampment.

He remembered that the the long distance routes out of Hamburg did not originate at the main station; therefore, he took the trolley to the subway line which would take him to the suburb of Altona.

The Altona station was similar to the Hamburg main station. Like the main station, its roof was arched and of a grid-like structure, and like the roof of the main station, the glass panes of most of the individual grids had been shattered or blown out.

As Herbert was walking through the concourse toward his

departure platform, he was stopped by one of the military policemen.

"Where are you going, young fellow?" the chain dog inquired.

"I'm on furlough, and I'm on my way to the Sudetenland for a reunion with my family."

"Let me see your travel orders."

Herbert put down his satchel and reached into his tunic pocket for the envelope that Unteroffizier Junger had given him. While groping for the travel orders, Herbert's ration cards and the five twenty Mark bills, which represented almost all of the compensation he had received for the past four months, fell to the concourse floor. He stooped over to pick up the elusive papers. As he straightened up, the chain dog's tilted head and arched eyebrows were registering impatience. Herbert handed him the travel orders, and stuffed the retrieved ration cards and the bills back into the envelope.

The chain dog took his time perusing Herbert's papers. Herbert thought, c'mon, let's not be playing tit for tat. I have to catch a train!

Finally, the chain dog said, "You can go," as he handed the boy his travel papers. Herbert put the travel orders back into the envelope and picked up his satchel. He hurried toward the front of the train that extended beyond the enclosed part of the station in the hope that it would not yet be crowded.

Herbert found an empty compartment. He quickly placed his satchel in the overhead bin and occupied one of the two window seats. After he sat down, he thought, I better organize my papers a little more so that they won't scatter all over the place as they did when the chain dog stopped me.

He put the travel orders in one breast pocket, the ration cards in the other breast pocket, and the money in his pants pocket.

Well, I'm all set, he mused with a sense of self reliance. An elderly couple and a soldier seated themselves in the compartment before the train left the station. Herbert again saw some of the vast areas of devastation attributable to the raids of July 1943. After the train left the city limits, he enjoyed the changing panorama of the country scenes. When the train stopped in Magdeburg and in Leipzig, Herbert observed that these two cities also had been subjected to considerable destruction from the air.

About five hours after leaving Hamburg, the train arrived in Dresden. Herbert got off to transfer to a local line for the short remaining trip to Bodenbach. Scanning the departures sign in the station, he noticed that he would have a three hour layover. Since it was a pleasant day, Herbert decided to do some sightseeing. He wasn't burdened by his satchel, because it only contained two dress shirts and several changes of underwear. To see as much as possible in the short period of time available, Herbert elected to ride the trolleys. From afar, he saw the Church of Our Lady, the Zwinger palace, and the Opera House. After he returned to the train station about two hours later, his main impression of the city was that it seemed to have been completely spared by the British bombers. He assumed that at the time the city was still out of their range.

Herbert rang the bell at the former manor house a second time. When Kaethe opened the door, she did not recognize him immediately, but after some scrutiny she cried out, "You're Herbert!"

Herbert nodded and gave her a hug and a kiss on the cheek. He looked at her and thought, you're even prettier than I remembered.

"C'mon in!" Kaethe urged as she turned her head and yelled, "Mother, Ruth, Peter! Come and see who is here!"

There were more hugs and kisses as they responded to Kaethe's call. "What kind of outfit did they put you in?" Tante Emi asked Herbert.

"I'm with the flak in Hamburg."

Tante Emi shook her head and said, "It's bad enough when they commit the young men to go to war; now they even commit the children." She shook her head again and said, "We're just getting ready to have some cake and coffee. Why don't you join us?"

"OK."

"Ah, I remember that expression," Kaethe said. "Believe it or not, we've been using it around here ever since you left."

✚ ✚ ✚

Over coffee and cake in the Lienhof dining room, Tante Emi asked, "Wasn't your whole class evacuated to Hungary for some time?"

"Yes. We were there for seven months, and we returned to Hamburg last December."

"When did you have to report to the flak?" she asked.

"I had to report to the induction center in Hamburg on 28 December of '43."

"That didn't give you much time to share with your family," Kaethe commented.

Herbert just hunched his soldiers.

"Have you been shooting back?" Peter asked.

"No. We have shot only some practice rounds. The bombers fly at an altitude that is out of our range. When the heavy flak rounds explode directly overhead, we seek refuge in a little bunker that is built into the earthen mound surrounding our gun to keep from getting hit by shrapnel coming back down. During daylight raids, one guy, of course, has to stay outside to maintain a lookout for low-flying aircraft."

"How do you decide who stays outside?" Kaethe asked.

"We take turns."

After he finished his cake, Tante Emi said, "Well, you must be anxious to see your parents, and we shouldn't keep you any longer. They are sharing the apartment down by the garden with your grandparents. I hope I'm not giving away a surprise when I tell you..." She hesitated for a moment and then continued, "Your father arrived here yesterday."

"No, no. It is not a surprise. My mother mentioned in one of her letters that he would be here," Herbert replied.

As Tante Emi walked him to the door, she said, "While you are here, our home is your home. Stop in any time."

"Thank you, Tante Emi."

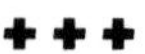

Herbert had a joyous reunion with his family and the Werners. One of the first things his father asked was, "How could you get away so soon? I had to wait a whole year before I could get a furlough."

"I saved up most of my weekend passes; therefore, I was able to apply for a ten-day leave."

Hertha surveyed his uniform and said, "It seems to fit pretty well. I was afraid that it might be too big."

"It was, by several sizes," Herbert responded.

"So, what did you do?" his mother asked

"I went to Aunt Ihde. She essentially reconstructed not only my uniform, but also my fatigues for me."

"Well, bless her heart. She is a good soul."

"When I thanked her, she said that you would have done likewise if the roles had been reversed."

"I certainly would have given it a try, but I'm afraid I'm not nearly as good a seamstress as she."

The mild mid-May weather, enticing the crocuses and gladiolas to bloom and the trees to renew their foliage, also enhanced the joy of the family's reunion. They could spend time outdoors and marvel at nature's renewal.

One afternoon Herbert asked Romi whether she would like to go up to the roof of the Lien Hof tower to view the surrounding countryside from that vantage point. When she replied affirmatively, they walked along the courtyard to the tower which could be accessed either from ground level, or from the first floor of the Lienhof's house. Only the first floor entrance from the house was provided with a lock.

They walked up the spiral staircase, as they had so many times in the summer of 1941, and enjoyed the panorama that the view from the top of the tower afforded.

"In one of her recent letters, Mama wrote that you had been very sick," Herbert said.

Romi turned from viewing the Elbe river and replied, "Yeah, I had a bad case of the flu. I also had a bad cough, which lingered until recently."

"How are you feeling now?"

"Pretty good. The doctor prescribed extra rations for me, to beef me up. He also made me quit my job because he thought that aspects of it were causing me anxieties, which they were.

"Once my flu symptoms were gone, Mama always made me go with her whenever she had any kind of errand to run. It didn't matter where she was going, whether it was to the grocery, the post office, or wherever, she always asked me to tag along. I was still coughing like crazy at the time. At first I didn't mind, since I was no longer working. I thought that she was asking me along because she felt that the fresh air would do me good; however, her insistence that I should go with her every time she left the house soon made me feel that there was another reason, but I couldn't figure out what it was."

"Why didn't you ask her?"

"I did, but all she would say was that I would find out soon enough."

"Well, did you?"

"Yes, but not right away. One day while we were shopping, I stopped to look into a store window. Mama was a couple of steps ahead of me when a lady approached her and told her how sorry she was that I had contracted TB. I quickly turned away from the window to tell that woman that I didn't have any such thing, but Mama's hand, extended toward me, told me to keep quiet. Mama then thanked the woman for her concern and added that the doctors were doing all they could for me."

"Why would she do that?" Herbert asked.

"I asked the same question, but she again said that I would find out soon enough.

"Four weeks later, she handed me two clippings taken from the local newspaper. One was six weeks old and announced that all girls born in 1927 would receive notice to report for induction into the Labor Service within the next thirty days. The more recent clipping only reported that the Altburgund contingent for the Labor Service had arrived at their training camp.

"After I read the clippings, a little bulb lit up in my head, and I asked Mama whether her intent had been to spread the rumor that I had TB. She said 'I never told anyone that you had TB, and I didn't start the gossip. I merely recognized that the least little stimulus could provoke a rumor among the town folk, and that your coughing would provide the stimulus for them to believe that you had TB.' She then added, 'I did it to keep you out of the Labor Service and perhaps even out of the army.'"

"Wow!" Herbert exclaimed. After a moment he said, "That wouldn't have worked in a bigger city."

"What do you mean?" Romi asked.

"In the bigger cities the authorities don't go by hearsay! They would dig a little deeper."

"Well, can I help it that I wound up in a one-horse town with one-horse authorities who don't dig?"

Herbert looked at his sister, and they both broke out laughing.

"You know what's even funnier?" Romi asked.

"No, what?"

"Mama already told me that when we get back to Altburgund, I won't have to accompany her on all her errands, but when I do accompany her, I will have to feign a cough to keep the rumor alive!"

They both had another good laugh.

On another afternoon, Herbert and his mother took a walk along the Elbe River. When they reached the bridge that separated Bodenbach from the neighboring town of Tetschen, she said, "They have a movie theater in Tetschen," and added, "Would you like to go see a movie?"

Herbert nodded and said, "OK."

Hertha asked for two tickets at the box office.

"How old is he?" the attendant asked, pointing at Herbert.

"He just turned sixteen. Why do you ask?"

"The main feature is for mature audiences only. He would have to be eighteen for me to be allowed to admit him," the attendant answered.

"Don't you see his uniform? Can't you see that he has already been drafted into the flak?" Hertha countered with some irritation. "Come now, ma'am, please give me two tickets."

"I'm sorry, but I can't admit him."

Herbert noticed that his mother's irritation was yielding to indignation.

"No one asked whether he was mature enough when he was told to report to the induction center. But when he wants to see a movie, that issue becomes of paramount importance," Hertha blurted out.

Herbert thought, folks behind us in line are asking what is going on, and Mama's indignation is turning into rage.

"I'm sorry Ma'am, but rules are rules," the attendant insisted.

"That is what is the matter with you people." Herbert tugged at his mother's sleeve and said, "It's all right, Mama. We don't have to see the movie."

Passersby were starting to wonder what the ruckus was about, because the volume of Hertha's voice seemed to be attuned to her feeling of displeasure.

She brushed Herbert's hand aside and continued, "You people are given a rule and you are expected to follow it blindly, whether it makes any sense or not. Can't you see how absurd it is to ask him to stick his neck out for you; then, deny him the admission to a movie?"

"Mama, please don't get so upset. This issue isn't worth arguing over," Herbert counseled as he urged her away from the box office.

He noticed the tears in her eyes when she said, "Those people make me so mad!"

"I'd much rather spend more time with you than sit in a movie theater," Herbert said as they slowly walked back toward the bridge.

+++

The days seemed to flow by much faster than usual, and soon Herbert had to leave again. He said goodbye to the Lienhofs; then, accompanied by his family, he headed back to the railroad station. As he got on the train, Herbert noticed the tears in his mother's and his sisters' eyes. He had to turn away and blink several times in order not to show his own.

Once the train had left the station, Herbert recalled Romi's story about her "deferral" and the incident at the movie theater. He said to himself, Mama sure can be a tough cookie, when someone gets her dander up.

Chapter 41

When Herbert returned from his furlough in late May, the eastern front was reeling from the start of the Soviet summer offensive. The Germans desperately were attempting to hold on to the last remnants of Russian soil they had occupied, and on 6 June, news of the Normandy invasion was announced.

On 18 June, B-17 Flying Fortresses staged another major daylight raid against Hamburg. Their targets, apparently, were the harbor facilities to the north of the boys' base; however, the bombers overshot the targets, and the bombs fell in the city center.

As Herbert watched a pall of smoke rise above the inner city, he recalled his mother's words while she was pointing out the various sites of Hamburg when they first arrived on the train from Cuxhaven, and when she said, "…and that one with the green steeple is the St. Jacobi Kirche."

He thought, Mama, the green steeple now is bright red. No, it wasn't repainted. It is bright red because it is burning, Mama. It is completely engulfed in flames, and now it is…it is caving in! Mama, the one with the green steeple is no more.

✦ ✦ ✦

On 20 June, the B-17s were back, again in force. The boys of gun No.1 were in the bunker, because the heavy flak shells were detonating directly overhead. Unteroffizier Kimmel was busy inspecting the gun, and Herbert was providing the lookout for low-flying aircraft.

While scanning all around, he exercised caution to not incline his head upward anymore than necessary, because several pieces of shrapnel had already bounced off his helmet. Suddenly, a wailing sound, intermixed with the flak din, did cause him to look straight up. He felt a chill along his spine when he saw the B-17. It had already lost considerable altitude and now was spiraling downward about its vertical axis. The starboard wing of the aircraft had been severed between the two engines. The port engines were still running and were desperately trying to keep the aircraft aloft. Akin to an air raid siren, the aircraft emitted a wailing sound in its death throes that increased and diminished in frequency with every cycle of the spiral. Herbert likened it to the sound of a wounded animal.

"Jump, you guys! Jump!" he instinctively yelled at the top of his voice in English.

No one jumped.

The stricken aircraft soon assumed an ever more nose-down position and plowed into a field about one half mile from the flak position. The ensuing multiple explosions indicated that the bombardier had been unable to release his bomb load.

Hearing the bomb bursts, some of the boys came out of the bunker. "We couldn't hear you over the flak noise. What were you yelling about?" Klaus Wolfert asked.

"Never mind, I was...I was just doing some...some wishful thinking, aloud," Herbert responded.

+ + +

One morning in early July, Unteroffizier Kimmel told Herbert to report to Unteroffizier Junger. When he arrived at the battery command building, Unteroffizier Junger said, "I'm sending one of our *Hiwis*[9] on loan to our sister battery. I want you to take him there. Check out a rifle before you go."

"Yes, sir!" Herbert responded. "Which one are you sending?"

"Vlacheslav, he's been there before."

Herbert rolled his eyes when he heard the name and asked, "Which one is he? We address them all as Ivan."

"He's the big guy."

Herbert nodded and left. He went back to his barrack and checked out a rifle; then he went to the field kitchen and looked for the tallest of the three Hiwis working there. Knowing that he would not be able to converse with the man, Herbert first got the man's attention and then tried to convey to the Russian what he wanted of him by letting his hands do the talking. He repeatedly pointed at the Russian and then himself.

The Russian nodded.

Herbert then extended his index and middle fingers and walked them across a tabletop to communicate that the two of them were going somewhere.

Again, the Russian nodded.

Finally, extending his arm and pointing in the direction of the sister battery, Herbert said, "Boom boom."

The Hiwi gave him a toothy smile and nodded once more. When he mimicked Herbert's routine exactly, Herbert knew that he had made himself understood.

"Let's go, Ivan," he said. They left the flak base and headed for the trolley stop. Herbert motioned the Hiwi to lead the way up the three steps onto the rear platform of the trolley and

9 German contraction of *Hilfswillige,* Russian POWs who volunteered to work for the Germans.

indicated to him that they would stay on the platform rather than entering the passenger compartment. As the trolley made its stops, Herbert noticed that most of the boarding passengers did a double take when they saw the POW who towered over the baby flak with the shouldered rifle. Some of the newcomers appeared restive to Herbert after they had seated themselves in the car and stared at him and the Hiwi.

When the trolley reached their destination, Herbert again motioned the Hiwi to go first. As he started to follow, he tripped and would have fallen if he had not managed to grasp an exit side-rail with his left hand. In the process, the rifle strap slid off his right shoulder and the rifle clattered down the steps onto the sidewalk.

He noticed that several passengers had risen from their seats to investigate the unexpected commotion. Many noses suddenly were pressed against the trolley windows for a better look-see.

"The prisoner has the gun!" a woman cried out.

Herbert pulled himself out of his crouched position and walked down the remaining two steps onto the sidewalk. He saw that the Hiwi had indeed picked up the rifle. He was holding it by the stock with the business end pointing toward Herbert. When Herbert extended his hand and said, "Give me the rifle, Ivan," the Hiwi first turned the gun around and then handed it to him.

Some applause emanated from the car, and Herbert heard a lady say, "The kid seemed to be completely unconcerned."

As the two passed along the car for the short walk to the sister battery, Herbert waved at the noses still pressed against the windows, and the Hiwi gave them his toothy smile. Herbert thought, for your information, lady, I was unconcerned only because I knew that I had forgotten to load the rifle!

✚ ✚ ✚

When Walther arrived at the apartment to stay for the weekend sometime in mid-July, he announced, "I have bad news. I'm being transferred to Berlin."

"That's not such bad news," Hertha replied. "The girls and I will just have to try to find a place to stay in Berlin."

"No, you won't!" Walther admonished.

"What do you mean, 'No you won't!'?" Hertha asked.

"Hertha, Berlin is under attack from the air almost on a daily basis. You and the girls will be much safer staying here for the time being."

His wife groaned and asked, "How long is 'for the time being'?"

"Hertha," Walther replied, "one doesn't dare say it openly, but things are falling apart. Hitler and Goebbels keep ranting about the new weapons, but what have they got to show for it? Nothing, but the V-1. The British are already calling it the doodlebug, which hardly heralds intimidation. I expect that in four to six months the Russians will have occupied this area. I want you to promise me that, once the Russians reach Warsaw, you will leave here and head west! You must not stay any longer than that!"

"But where will we go?"

"At such time, I will meet you in Berlin, and I can make temporary arrangements for you to stay with the mother of a buddy of mine until we figure out where you go from there."

"Why can't we just stay with her?"

"Hertha, this lady only has a two-room apartment. Any refuge she can provide would have to be of a very temporary nature, and for all that I know, she, herself, may be in need of new living quarters any day now; besides, I don't want you to stay in Berlin any longer than necessary."

"But where will we go?" Hertha repeated.

"How about the Sudetenland?" Walther suggested.

"No! I feel that we have imposed on the Lienhofs way too much already!"

"How about your cousin Hedwig on your father's side of the family? Doesn't she live in a small town near the city of Plauen in the Vogtland? You probably would be safe there. Plauen is well west of the Elbe river," Walther called to mind.

"That's an idea," his wife replied. "I'm going to get a letter off today yet to find out whether, if necessary, she would be able to help us out."

✚✚✚

About the same time that Walther broke the news of his transfer to his wife, the flak battery was being relocated to another part of Wilhelmsburg. At the new site, the three guns were located along an embankment parallel to a marshalling yard. The guns had to be mounted on twenty-foot-high towers to avoid the possibility of the guns inadvertently firing into a nearby workers housing block when the gun elevation was at zero degrees.

While the boys had remained in their gun emplacements at the old location during high altitude raids that put them at immediate risk, they now were each assigned a foxhole at the base of their gun tower where they could seek cover during such raid conditions.

On 20 July news of the failed attempt to assassinate Hitler was broadcast on the radio. Some of Herbert's classmates felt that the army officers involved had broken their oath to the Fuehrer; others showed little reaction.

In the early morning hours of 29 July, British bombers again visited Hamburg. German sources estimated the number of bombers to be three hundred. The German populace dubbed the attack to be an "anniversary raid" of the 1943 raids.

A day later, Unteroffizier Pfahl was ordered back to his

unit on the eastern front. He was replaced by an Unteroffizier named Knabe. Several days after Unteroffizier Knabe arrived, Detlev told Herbert, "You want to be careful of what you say in the new arrival's presence. He worked for the Gestapo before he was relegated to the flak."

Herbert thought big deal. If he were more than a minor cog in that organization, he wouldn't have been sent to the flak. Or would he?

Chapter 42

The Americans returned for another daylight raid on 4 August. Since the flight path of the oncoming bombers would take them directly over the flak base, the boys were ordered into the foxholes. Herbert scrambled to his hole, which, like all the others, was lined with an oil drum to keep the hole from caving in. The bottom of the drum was pierced in several spots to allow rain water to drain off.

Herbert watched the oncoming bombers. When he saw the lead aircraft release a smoke marker, he scrunched deeper into his foxhole. Immediately thereafter, the din of the exploding bombs was ear-splitting, and he quickly removed his helmet and covered his ears with his hands. The uproar lasted only about fifteen seconds, but to him those seconds seemed like an eternity. When he could again hear the flak, he righted himself. After climbing out of the foxhole, he could see that parts of the nearby housing block had been reduced to rubble and the remainder was aflame.

The bombers gave no respite. On 6 August they were back.

The boys again were ordered to take cover. When peering out of his foxhole toward the droning of the engines above, Herbert saw a group of approximately eighteen aircraft approaching on a line that would take them directly over the flak base. Another group, of approximately the same number of planes, followed close behind. He could barely see the high-flying bombers, but their contrails, as always on a clear day, gave them away.

Herbert did a quick calculation and thought, with bombs of 500 pounds usually being on the menu, those guys are likely ready to lay down a bomb carpet of 360 of those babies.

This time he did not wait to see a smoke marker; he immediately slunk down in his hole. Again the bomb bursts deafened the flak thunder. Herbert knew the bombs were falling nearby when he felt an upward tug of his helmet strap against his chin. He quickly released the strap. He knew that they were falling even nearer when he looked up and saw dirt flying over the foxhole. When the outgoing pressure waves and the returning suction waves of the bomb blasts caused the drum liner of his hole to move in an up and down motion, akin to a piston in an engine cylinder, he felt as though he were on the rim of an erupting volcano. He had difficulty breathing, and paralyzed with fear, he instinctively cried out, "Mama!"

After the liner motion stopped and dirt no longer flew overhead and flak noise again had the upper hand, Herbert remained crouched in his foxhole. He was still trembling. After the shock wore off, he wiped the sweat off his brow and wondered about his involuntary outburst with a sense of embarrassment.

He didn't leave the foxhole until he heard some of his buddies talking nearby. As he climbed out, he thought, they couldn't have heard me over the noise; I'm glad I didn't pee in my pants that would have been a dead giveaway. Herbert noticed that the bombs had played havoc with the marshalling yards. Some of the bombs had exploded within the perimeter of the flak base but without causing any damage. His foxhole was about twenty yards from the center of the nearest crater.

He could tell by its size that it had been dug by a 500-pound bomb.

+++

In mid August, Oberwachtmeister Lange was replaced by a Leutnant Bautz. The boys figured the twenty-something lieutenant to be a ninety-day wonder of the German officer training system. His uniform was always immaculate, and the shine of his boots was such that if he broke his shaving mirror, one of the boots would have been an adequate replacement. At first, the boys made sundry comments about his dapper appearance, but the comments diminished as they realized that under all the dapperness there was an affable guy. They soon found out that the lieutenant was a soccer enthusiast. On weekends, circumstances permitting, he would set up a soccer match. Everyone got a chance to play, including the lieutenant.

+++

One afternoon, while the boys of gun number one were performing gun maintenance, the commander of gun number two, Unteroffizier Knabe, stopped by. He took Herbert aside and said, "I understand that you were born in the United States."

"Yes, sir, I was," Herbert replied.

"Do you plan on going back to the United States after the war is over?"

Herbert remembered Detlev telling him that this guy had worked for the Gestapo and wondered whether his interest was more than casual. Herbert hunched his shoulders and said, "I don't know yet."

"I don't know yet," the Unteroffizier mockingly repeated Herbert's comment. "Don't you prefer living in Germany?"

"I haven't experienced Germany in peacetime long enough to make a meaningful comparison. After I was here for three months, the war broke out. Since then, I was evacuated to the Sudetenland for a year and a half and to Hungary for seven months. In 1943, the family home took a direct hit, and I have been hungry for a good part of the time since my arrival. Now, I am here."

"Now I am here," the Unteroffizier again mocked. "You make it sound as though it were an imposition for you to be here. Your parents are German, are they not?"

"Yes."

"Well, then you are German, too! You should be proud to be a part of this fight. Mr. Roosevelt will rue the day he picked a fight with us. We may be seeing some minor setbacks right now, but once we get the new weapons the Fuehrer has promised us, things will turn around, and even the U.S.A. won't go unscathed."

Herbert used the second person pronominal when he shot back, "I believe it was your Fuehrer who made the declaration of war."

"What choice did he…'YOUR FUEHRER'?" the Unteroffizier cried out loud enough to get some of Herbert's classmates to look up from what they were doing. "What do you mean when you say 'your Fuehrer'? Whose side are you on?"

"You already told me whose side I'm on, Herr Unteroffizier," Herbert replied.

"Well, make sure you don't forget it!"

"Yes, sir!"

Still irritated, Unteroffizier Knabe dismissed the boy with a wave of his hand.

Chapter 43

Hamburg experienced several daylight nuisance raids in the latter part of August. During one of those raids, the boys got their first chance to fire at an enemy aircraft.

"P-38 at ten o'clock!" Detlev Wolfert had yelled.

The boys were taken by surprise, and by the time they had taken their gun positions, the aircraft, on a lateral fly-by, was just passing the battery emplacement when they were ready to shoot. They emptied one magazine at the aircraft but were wide of the mark.

"That guy must have been moving about three or four times as fast as the towed target that we practiced on in basic training," one of the boys cried out.

"Don't feel bad," Unteroffizier Kimmel remarked. "We were the only gun that fired. The other two crews apparently did not see the aircraft soon enough."

Two days later, a similar incident occurred—again a P-38 was sighted—this time all three guns fired, but all three were wide of the target.

+++

The next morning Leutnant Bautz addressed the battery personnel in the classroom barrack.

"Well, you all have had the opportunity to fire your first shots at the enemy. Gun number one is to be congratulated for being prepared on both occasions. They detected the aircraft in time in the first instance to take action, while the rest of you were asleep. In the future, I want you to perform a more diligent lookout.

"We didn't score any hits, but I don't want you guys to feel dejected. You are definitely at a disadvantage against those low-flying fighter bombers. Why? Because they are so fast and your guns are not maneuverable enough. How many of the K1s actually got either of these aircraft in their gun sight?"

Only one of the three raised his hand.

"Did you actually get a shot off while the aircraft was in your sight?"

Without commitment, the boy shrugged his shoulders.

The lieutenant seated himself on Mr. Vogt's desk and said, "The trouble with a lateral fly-by is that the K1 cannot crank the gun in azimuth fast enough to track the aircraft. Your best bet in such a situation is to estimate the trajectory of the aircraft while sighting ahead of the aircraft and then hope that it will fly into your gun sight. Firing any more than one or two shots under those conditions will be a waste of ammo, because the aircraft will be in your sight for only an instant, and you won't be able to track it thereafter.

"So, what do you do when the aircraft is making a direct approach or a nearly direct approach?"

One boy raised his hand and said, "Our training instructor in Buesum told us to aim slightly ahead of the aircraft."

"That is good advice once you are experienced and you are well camouflaged. I have requisitioned additional netting; however, even when well camouflaged, I suggest you take a similar approach to the lateral fly-by until you are more experienced—turn the gun barrel quickly in the direction the aircraft is flying and try to capture it in your gun sight once it has overflown your position. If you shoot while the aircraft is approaching, you risk detection, but if you wait until the aircraft has passed your position, the pilot may not even realize that he has been shot at if he doesn't have a rear view mirror. If the aircraft is already shooting during a direct approach, I want you to do nothing other than hit the deck!

"Because of your gun's poor maneuverability, you can only be effective either during the aircraft's approach or when it has overflown your position. We would be foolish not to go with the approach that provides the lesser risk."

Leutnant Bautz scanned his audience and said, "I want you to think about what I have said and act accordingly."

Nodding toward Unteroffizier Junger he said, "You can dismiss them."

Unteroffizier Junger hollered, "Attention!" as the lieutenant picked up his briefcase, followed by "At ease!" once he had left.

In mid-September Herbert was granted another ten-day furlough. This time he went to Altburgund to visit his mother and sisters. Rosemarie seemed much more relaxed than when he had seen her last. Hannelore, who had turned ten years old two months earlier, proudly told him that in only three years she would be a teenager.

"It's too bad that you won't be able to see your father this time around. I believe I told you in one of my letters that your father has been transferred to Berlin," Hertha commented, shortly after his arrival.

"Yes, you did, Mama. Where is he stationed in Berlin?"

"He wrote that he is in one of the suburbs and that his barracks are just a short walk from the terminal of one of the subway lines. Why do you ask?"

"Well, I have a five-hour layover in Berlin on my way back. Perhaps I'll have a chance to see him."

"Oh, that would be wonderful!" his mother exclaimed.

After a short pause, she said, "I had hoped that the girls and I could have gone with him to Berlin, but he thought it would be too dangerous."

"I would agree with him, Mama. Staying here makes a lot more sense than ducking bombs in Berlin."

"Your father thought it only a matter of time before we would have to leave here, too. He emphatically told me that we have to leave here before the Soviets arrive and that once they take Warsaw, we should get out of here."

"Well, they still have quite a way to go," Herbert responded in an effort to ease his mother's concern.

"Yes, but they seem to be getting closer every day," she replied.

Herbert spent a relaxing week with his mother and sisters. When it was time to leave, his mother accompanied him to the railroad station.

"Have you got the note with your father's address?" she asked, as he boarded the train.

Herbert nodded. As the train left the station, Herbert waved his hand through an open window until she was out of view.

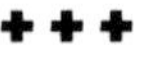

After arriving at the Berlin station from which the train for Hamburg would be leaving, Herbert studied the wall chart of the Berlin subway system to find out which line he would have to take to visit his father.

He boarded the subway, but at the third stop the air raid sirens started to wail, and everybody was ordered out of the train and into a public shelter.

Herbert thought, why do those guys have to arrive at such an inopportune time? He quickly realized the absurdity of his question when he realized that there is no opportune time when one is on the receiving end of an air raid.

Forty-five minutes later, he was back on the subway.

He had no trouble finding his father's barracks. He went into what appeared to be the headquarters building and told the soldier at the receiving desk that he would like to see Corporal Klug.

"Wait in there," the soldier said as he pointed toward the visitor's room, adding, "I'll see if I can get hold of him."

While Herbert waited, he leafed through a magazine that he found on one of the tables in the room.

"Well, look who's here!" Walther exclaimed as he stood in the doorway.

Herbert got up and gave his father a hug. "How are you, Papa?"

"I'm OK. This sure is a surprise. What brings you here?"

"I'm returning from furlough. Since I have a layover before my train leaves for Hamburg, I thought I'd stop by to see you. Mama and the girls send their love."

His father steered him away from the door toward a table at one corner of the room. After they sat down he asked, "How is your mother?"

"She is worried that she and the girls will have to leave Altburgund soon, and I'm wondering: where will they go?"

"I've talked to your mother about that. I told her to come here first; after that, I would help them to make arrangements for them to go to the Vogtland to stay with one of your mother's cousins. Your mother has already corresponded with her, and the cousin has offered to take them in, should the need arise."

"Why wait? Why don't they just leave now?" Herbert asked.

Walther, his voice low, said, "That crazy *Gauleiter*[10] of the Warthegau still thinks that the Russian advance can be stopped. He has banned any evacuation out of his Gau!"

"Then how will they get out?!" Herbert cried out.

"Shh!" Walther admonished, pressing an index finger to his lips. Then he said, "When push comes to shove, they'll get out—the local authorities will take matters into their own hands!"

Herbert noticed that his father seemed preoccupied. They talked a while longer until Walther said, "You caught me at a bad time. I just received word from my parents that my youngest sister was killed in an air raid in Kassel two weeks ago."

"I'm sorry to hear that, Papa. If I remember correctly, she was only twenty-four years old."

"She didn't quite make it to twenty-four," his father said as he turned his gaze from his son to hide the tears.

"I'm so sorry, Papa," Herbert reiterated as he too tried to control his emotions. Not knowing what to do to relieve his father's distress, he said, "I'd better go…I have a train to catch." He took leave of his father and headed back to the subway station.

On the train headed back to Hamburg, Herbert worried. He worried about his father being stationed in Berlin; he worried about his mother and sisters being in a pseudo trap in Altburgund. He was not at all elated about having to go back to Hamburg. Instead, he was filled with a sense of foreboding.

He thought, maybe I should have taken a train headed south toward the Swiss border. With some luck I might be able to

10 Province governor.

scoot across. He chuckled to himself and reconsidered, idiot, you're forgetting where you are. The first time someone checks your papers you'd be in deep doo-doo. Even if you could manage to get across, the authorities here would resort to the *Sippenhaft*[11]. No way can I risk having a family member sent to a concentration camp!

[11] Doctrine of shared accountability of family for the transgressions committed by any one member.

Chapter 44

After Herbert returned from his leave toward the end of September, he found out that Leutnant Bautz had been transferred to front-line duty and replaced by an Oberwachtmeister named Besler. Herbert guessed him to be somewhere between his late forties and early fifties.

"How do you like the new battery commander?" he asked Klaus Wolfert.

"He seems to be real easygoing. He takes sort of a patriarchal approach toward us boys, and we already refer to him as Papa Besler, but only when he is out of hearing range."

Hamburg's citizens experienced another heavy daylight raid on 6 October. According to German estimates, several hundred aircraft attacked the city. Industrial and transportation facilities suffered heavy damage.

Additionally, three nighttime nuisance raids occurred during the time frame of 12 October through 16 October.

Several days later, after roll call, Oberwachtmeister Besler said, "I have important news for you. Our battery is being reassigned to an airfield on the North Sea coast."

As his words echoed through the ranks, Oberwachtmeister Besler raised one hand and said, "Before you get all excited, let me tell you everything I know; after that, I will try to answer any questions you may have.

"The airfield is located near a small town named Nordholz, which is situated along the rail line that connects Cuxhaven with Bremerhaven. Formerly servicing Me-109s, the airfield now is home to Me-110 and Ju-188 night fighters. We will be moving out in the early morning the day after tomorrow. Except for guard duty, you are all relieved of your normal functions. I want you to spend the rest of the day and tomorrow to pack all your stuff. Make sure you don't forget anything I won't grant any special leave to come back to pick up something that was left behind.

"Your teacher, Mr. Vogt, has consented to go with you even though he will have to travel an additional 120 miles to commute between our base and his home on weekends.

"Immediately after we leave, a replacement contingent of Luftwaffe Auxiliaries will take over here. I believe it is one of the classes that trained with you in Buesum. As I speak, an engineering unit is mounting thirty-seven millimeter guns in their emplacements at the airfield." The Oberwachtmeister paused for a moment to let his comments sink in. Then he said, "That is the good news. The bad news is that we won't have any barracks to move into once we get there. The same engineering unit that is mounting the guns will be putting up the barracks, but the gun emplacements take precedence. I've been told that it may be three to four weeks before we can move in." After a pause, he asked, "Are there any questions?"

One of the boys raised his hand and asked, "Where will we stay in the meantime?"

"You will be quartered in tents," the battery commander replied.

Mutters of discontent reverberated through the formation. Another boy lifted his hand and asked, "How can we perform properly if we have to sleep in a tent this time of year?"

Oberwachtmeister Besler looked at the boy for a moment and answered, "I've talked to several guys who have seen action on the eastern front. They told me they had to perform for weeks at a time and in midwinter without any respite except for occasional catnaps in the trenches."

There were no further questions.

The boys experienced a sense of deja vu during the transport to the airfield. Their trip was another ride in a freight car equipped with a potbellied stove. As the train came to a stop at a rail siding just outside the Nordholz station, the boys got their first look at the airfield. They saw two intersecting runways when they looked eastward. The orientation of the runways implied that the prevailing winds ranged out of either the northwest and north-northwest or the southeast and south-southeast, but the boys knew that for this part of the country the winds usually were out of the northwest. Toward the eastern perimeter of the airfield stood several brick buildings.

The boys disembarked and were met by a reception committee consisting of the Oberwachtmeister and the four Unteroffiziere.

"How did they get here so fast?" Herbert asked Klaus Wolfert while one of the Unteroffiziere ordered them into formation.

"They probably traveled like normal people do. They came by passenger train. You have to remember that rank has its privileges," Klaus answered.

After the boys were assembled, the Oberwachtmeister addressed them, "Welcome to your new surroundings. Our gun emplacements are on the southwest corner of the airfield. Unteroffizier Junger will lead you there. Once you arrive, your gun commander will issue two tents per gun crew and will show you how to erect them. Your normal duties will commence as soon as the tents are up. Be assured that these arrangements are temporary. The engineering unit has started work on your barracks, and you should be able to move into your permanent lodgings in two to three weeks." The Oberwachtmeister scanned the formation and asked, "Are there any questions?" Hearing no response, he said, "Unteroffizier Junger, lead them to the gun emplacements."

✚✚✚

The three guns were located on an embankment that ran in a northerly direction along the western perimeter of the airfield. The guns stood in line on the embankment at approximately fifty-yard intervals. The southernmost gun had been designated as gun number one and therefore would be manned by Unteroffizier Kimmel's crew.

After the crew of gun number one arrived at their gun emplacement, Unteroffizier Kimmel designated where to pitch the tents adjacent to the gun site, and he then assisted the the boys in setting them up.

Upon their arrival, Herbert had noticed what appeared to be a circus caravan located just beyond the number three gun position. The dilapidated appearance of the caravan and the wooden spokes of its wheels suggested it had been around for some time and but for salvage by the Luftwaffe would now be resting on a scrap heap.

"What's with the trailer?" Herbert asked the Unteroffizier.

"It will serve as the battery command post, until the barracks are built."

"Who gets to stay in the trailer?"

"The battery commander and the Unteroffizere will occupy it."

"Oh." Herbert said. He recalled Klaus Wolfert's remark about rank having its privileges.

Once the tents had been set up, the Unteroffizier said, "You can rest for half an hour and take a look around.

"After that, we will check the gun emplacement to make sure that everything is in order."

"Where do we go for chow?" Detlef Wolfert asked the Unteroffizier.

"We will eat right here."

Detlev scanned the area, shrugged his shoulders, and said,"I don't see a field kitchen."

"The food will be prepared by the Luftwaffe commissary. Two guys from each gun, carrying provision backpacks, will have to haul the food over here for every meal."

"Oh," Detlev responded. Then he asked, "Where is the commissary?"

The Unteroffizier pointed eastward and said, "It is part of the building complex at the other side of the field. All the Luftwaffe facilities are over there: the administration building, the personnel quarters, and, as I've just told you, the commissary."

"We'll only have to haul our own food until our barracks are up, isn't that right?" another boy commented.

"Wrong!" Unteroffizier Kimmel countered. "The barracks won't be supplied with running water; therefore, we won't be able to set up kitchen facilities on this side of the field. You'll be hauling provisions for as long as we are stationed here."

As on command, all eight faces of Unteroffizier Kimmel's crew registered incredulity.

"If there is no running water, where can we take a shower or go to the john?" Herbert asked.

The Unteroffizier pointed again. This time he pointed to a row of buildings that were located along the southern perimeter of the airfield just below the embankment on which they were standing. "That is a navy compound," he said. "We have made arrangements with them such that we can share their shower and toilet facilities."

"You mean that every time we want to take a shower or have to go to the john we have to walk all the way over there?" Herbert asked.

The Unterofffizier hunched his shoulders and said, "I don't care if you pee in the bushes, but yes, for everything else you will have to go over there." He looked at the eight frowning faces that were staring at him and said, "Let's go and check out our gun emplacement."

As the boys fell in line to follow the Unteroffizier, one of the quicker minds muttered:

"If you're prone to the runs,
This gig is not for you.
Unless you really move your buns,
You'll never make it to the loo!"

✚ ✚ ✚

The first two nights of sleeping in the tents were tolerable. The following nights were not. The temperature dropped severely, and the skies, almost continuously, wept a frigid rain.

Herbert shared a tent with the Wolfert twins and Manfred Romke, the K1 of their gun. They slept in their fatigues and covered themselves with the blankets they had been issued by the quartermaster depot in Hamburg. During the third night, Herbert was awaked by water dripping on his face. Raising his upper body with his elbow, he looked around. Darkness was starting to give way to dawn, and he could just distinguish that Detlev was already sitting up.

“The tent’s leaking,” Herbert observed.

“No shit?” Detlev commented.

Their brief interchange stirred the remaining tent tenants.

“What’s going on?” Manfred asked.

“The tent’s leaking,” Herbert answered.

“What are we going to do about it?” Manfred asked.

“I’m going to double up my blanket and take it out and spread it over the leak area,” Detlev announced.

“You’ll freeze your ass with just one blanket,” Manfred warned.

“I’ll substitute my overcoat for the blanket.”

“I don’t think it’s a good idea, Detlev,” Herbert said.

“Why not?”

“The blanket will saturate and the leak will resume,” Herbert answered.

“Well, we’ll just have to go out and wring out the blanket every so often,” Detlev commented with some annoyance. “At least it is a partial solution.”

“I still don’t think it is a good idea,” Herbert said.

“Do you guys have a better idea?” Detlev asked.

When he received no answer, he grinned and said, “Since we will be utilizing my blanket, you three guys can take turns wringing it.”

Detlev’s brother broke into the discussion by yelling, “Hey, I’m trying to get a little more shuteye! Do whatever you like, but let me get a little more sleep!”

“Easy for him to say,” Manfred said. “He’s probably got the only dry spot in here.”

Detlev’s idea worked somewhat.

After the boys spent a week in the tents, the Luftwaffe rolled up two more caravans alongside the gun emplacements. By draw, gun crews number one and number two won the privilege to move in. The caravans each had four two-tiered bunk beds, which were located in the four corners of the vehicle. Each caravan also had a table, several chairs, and a potbellied stove.

After gun crew number one had evacuated their tent and moved into their assigned caravan, Manfred Romke said, "All we have to do now is to get some firewood for the stove."

"Where are you going to find firewood? Have you looked around? You can look in all directions, and as far as the eye can see, there are no trees. All you see are heath shrubs," Detlev responded.

"Well, maybe the Luftwaffe will supply us something with which to fuel the stove," Manfred said and added, "At least we are out of the rain."

On the following morning, after roll call, Oberwachtmeister Besler said, "I have bad news. Hamburg was hit by a heavy daylight raid on October 25. The flak position we vacated was hit hard. Three Luftwaffe Auxiliaries and an Unteroffizier were killed. Several boys were hurt, and one boy's foxhole was filled in by debris of a nearby bomb blast. The good news is that his buddies were able to get him out alive."

The boys had listened in silence.

Before he dismissed them, the Oberwachtmeister said, "I know that you feel for those who were killed and those who are hurting, but don't be developing a guilt complex if you also feel that we were fortunate to get out of there when we did."

One night, several days after moving into the caravan, Herbert had the 12:00 to 2:00 A.M. watch.

Shortly before the end of his watch, he roused Rolf Ganther, who was to relieve him and who now was quartered in the caravan that had been assigned to gun crew number two.

"How are you doing?" Rolf asked as he stepped outside.

"I'm cold, and I haven't worn a pair of dry socks ever since we've been here."

"Yeah, I know what you mean. Those caravans do keep us out of the rain, and you can hang stuff up, but without fuel for the stove, nothing dries," Ganther said. Looking at Herbert, he added, "Well, I suppose you're ready for some shut-eye."

"Yeah," Herbert mumbled. As he was about to leave, Ganther said, "I know where we can find some long poles that we could saw for firewood."

"Where would you find long poles around here?" Herbert asked.

"The Luftwaffe erected several camouflaged areas to park aircraft along the southern end of the field. They put up poles about half the length of telephone poles and draped camouflage netting over them to hide the aircraft from above. Several poles were left over and are just lying around."

"Are any aircraft parked there now?" Herbert asked.

"No. If there were, we wouldn't be able to go after the leftover poles; the parked aircraft would be guarded."

"Maybe they haven't finished the job, and they will be back to erect additional parking areas," Herbert suggested.

"Nah, there isn't any netting left. I'm sure they are done."

"What are you going to use for tools?"

"I've been scouting around. There is a crosscut saw, which we could borrow, in the engineers' tool shed. The saw takes two guys to operate it. Later on we can also borrow an axe to chop the blocks."

"You don't think we'll get into trouble?" Herbert asked.

"Nah, all we'll be doing is cleaning up the leftovers!"

Herbert thought for a while and finally said, "All right, count me in. When do you want to do this?"

"I'll wake you just before I go off guard duty. Meet me just after 4:00 A.M. at the fence that runs along the southern perimeter of the airfield."

"All right, I'll see you later."

As Herbert walked toward the perimeter fence, the sparse light of a crescent moon enabled him to see that Rolf, with the crosscut saw tucked under his arm, was already waiting for him. They walked in silence eastward along the perimeter fence. After they had walked about halfway along the southern perimeter, Herbert could just barely make out the camouflaged areas just ahead that Rolf had mentioned to him.

Tugging Herbert's sleeve, Rolf, keeping his voice low, said, "The leftovers are lying along the fence this side of the camouflaged areas."

After they reached the half dozen or so poles, Rolf pointed toward an area strewn with sawdust and whispered, "We'll have to move the poles to where the construction crew evidently did their sawing. Sawing the poles in place would be a dead giveaway."

Herbert said, "I can understand why we are whispering," and then added, "but how are you going to convince the saw to keep the noise down?"

"I brought a can of grease with me. We'll grease the blade now and then to dampen the noise. C'mon, help me roll one of those suckers into that area."

The boys started sawing. Although the grease did dampen the noise of the sawing process, to Herbert, in his apprehensive state, the noise sounded like a clarion piercing the still of the night. When they stopped occasionally to grease the blade, they would listen in an attempt to ensure that they had not attracted someone's attention.

After they were about half done sawing the first pole and were about to resume their labor, Herbert got Rolf's attention by letting go of his saw handle and uttering, "Shh!"

"What's the matter?" Rolf asked.

"I thought I heard some rustling coming from the heath shrubs behind the fence."

Both boys listened intently for about a minute.

"I think you're imagining things. I didn't hear anything.

"C'mon, this is taking a lot longer than I thought. Let's finish up this first pole—hide the blocks somewhere and then hightail it out of here."

They hid the blocks in shrubs they had passed on the way to the camouflaged area.

As they were walking back toward the battery emplacement, Rolf said, "We don't want the guy doing guard duty to see us as we return."

"Why not?"

"It doesn't behoove us to advertise what we are doing."

"We'll be advertising the minute we light up the potbellied stoves with that wood!"

"We'll just tell everyone who wants to know where the wood came from, that a local farmer took pity on us after we told him how we are freezing our asses out here," Rolf countered.

Herbert broke out in a smile and said, "Hey, good thinking."

After Herbert slipped back into his caravan, he took off his boots and his wet socks, and he lay down in his bunk fully clothed and wrapped himself in his blankets. He couldn't fall asleep right away. He worried that he indeed had heard someone rustling in the brush, that someone had been spying on them.

Chapter 45

Shortly before roll call that very morning, Unteroffizier Knabe confided to the battery commander that two boys had been seen cutting up poles that were intended for some construction on the south side of the airfield.

"Two of our boys?" the Oberwachtmeister asked.

"Yes."

"Who saw them?"

"One of the local farmers—"

"And he told you?"

"Yes."

"When did he see them?"

"About 4:30 this morning."

"How do you know they were our boys?"

"The farmer recognized them as Luftwaffe Auxiliaries."

Seated at the caravan table, the Oberwachtmeister scrutinized Unteroffizier Knabe intently. With furrowed brow, he pondered the sequence of events just made known to him. He wondered why a local farmer would be strolling around the perimeter of the field in the early morning hours and why Knabe would be out there to talk to him through the wire-mesh fence, since the airfield was off limits to civilians. Also, the boys always wore their fatigues—in the darkness they would be indistinguishable from regular Luftwaffe personnel!

"Do you have any evidence?"

The Unteroffizier reached toward his bunk and produced one of the blocks that the boys had cut off earlier.

"Well, then we'll have to question the boys, won't we?"

"Yes, sir!"

Immediately after roll call Oberwachtmeister Besler announced, "I have been told that two Luftwaffe Auxiliaries, seeking firewood, availed themselves of government property. They were seen dissecting poles that were intended to be used to support the camouflage netting that is being set up on the south end of the airfield. Unteroffizier Knabe, show us the evidence."

Unteroffizier Knabe pulled the block, which he had shown the battery commander, out of a small canvas bag he was holding. As he held the block up he said, "Destruction of government property is a court martial offense!"

The words *court martial* spread through the formation like wildfire.

Oberwachtmeister Besler motioned with his hand for Unteroffizier Knabe to back off, and shouted, "Attention!" to quell the disturbance in the ranks.

After ordering at ease, the Oberwachtmeister said, "Since you are the only auxiliaries around here, the two boys involved must be part of this contingent. I want those two to step forward. Now!"

Rolf and Herbert broke rank and positioned themselves in front of the formation. The battery commander sensed that the two boys had been rattled by Unteroffizier Knabe's remark. Both were blinking a lot to keep the tears from shedding.

"I want you to report to me in the command trailer at 10:00 A.M. sharp," he brusquely told them and added, "I also want all the Unteroffiziere to be present."

He scanned the formation and then said, "Unteroffizier Junger, you can dismiss them."

When the two boys entered the command trailer to report to the battery commander, he and the Unteroffiziere were already present. The Oberwachtmeister was sitting at the table, and the Unteroffiziere were seated on the lower tiers of the two nearest bunk beds.

"Come and sit with me at the table," the Oberwachtmeister said to the boys.

After they sat down, he looked at Rolf and asked, "So, tell me, Ganther, why you guys went out there and started to cut up those poles."

"We were cold, sir. We've been in those caravans for a week now, and we are still staring at a useless stove because we don't have any fuel."

"That doesn't give you the right to just go out and start demolishing government property."

"The poles that are out there are leftovers."

"How do you know that?" the Oberwachtmeister asked.

"For one thing, there wasn't any netting left to construct another camouflaged area."

"Perhaps additional netting was on its way," the Oberwachtmeister suggested."

"No. I observed the Luftwaffe guys while they were working out there for several days. They always left their tools at the worksite—they would cover them up, but they left them at the site overnight. Once the tools were gone, I figured that the job was done."

"I see," the Oberwachtmeister said. He turned to Herbert and asked, "Klug, why did you take part in this mishap?"

"I too was cold. I was cold, and all my clothing has been damp since the second day after we got here."

"I've been here for as long as you have, but my clothing isn't damp," the Oberwachtmeister remarked.

"With all due respect, sir, you didn't have to sleep in a leaking tent for the first week we were here."

The battery commmander shook his head and said, "I didn't realize that you guys were in such dire straits. I wish you would have come to talk to me about it instead of going ahead with plans of your own."

"It wouldn't have done any good," Herbert commented.

The Oberwachtmeister frowned and asked, "What do you mean?"

Herbert pointed at the potbellied stove and said, "You, too, don't have any fuel."

The Oberwachtmeister nodded and said, "The Luftwaffe was supposed to supply us with heating fuel as soon as they rolled up the first caravan. Unfortunately, that has not happened, in spite of my many complaints."

Glancing at the Unteroffiziere, he said, "I think we have to take into account some very extenuating circumstances for what the boys did."

"Extenuating circumstances or not, destruction of government property remains a court martial offense," Unteroffizier Knabe responded.

The boys cringed. The battery commander turned in his chair toward Knabe and shouted, "Stop your court martial prattling. We are going to handle this as an internal affair. The boys have committed a misdemeanor, nothing more."

Having regained his composure, the Oberwachtmeister asked his liaison Unteroffizier, "Junger, what are the appropriate punitive measures for this type of misdemeanor?"

The Unteroffizier thought for a moment before he said, "Latrine duty always tops the list, and KP runs a close second." The two boys exchanged anxious glances.

"We don't have latrines or kitchen facilities," the battery commander observed.

"No, but the Luftwaffe compound has both," Unteroffizier Junger said. He added, "Consecutive guard duty shifts are also effective."

"Thank you, Junger," the battery commander said. He stroked his chin for a moment and then directed his attention to the two boys. "As punishment for your misdeed, and hopefully as a future reminder of what awaits you should you decide to do things on your own that you are not supposed to be doing, you will alternately do four hours of guard duty here or four hours of kitchen police at the Luftwaffe facilities every day for the next three weeks, starting tomorrow. You can decide among yourselves who does guard duty and who reports for KP tomorrow. After that, you will switch roles each day until the three weeks are up. Did I make myself clear?" the Oberwachtmeister asked.

In unison, the boys muttered, "Yes, sir."

"I can't hear you!"

"YES, SIR!"

"That's more like it."

The Oberwachtmeister looked at Unteroffizier Junger and said, "Junger, you will please revise your sentry roster and make the necessary arrangements with the Luftwaffe kitchen personnel." Returning his attention to the boys, he said, "You two can go now."

After the boys had left, the battery commander said, "I'd like to talk to Unteroffizier Knabe, alone. Junger, why don't you go and make the arrangements with the Luftwaffe personnel.

Kimmel and Latner, you can run your gun crews through some exercises."

✦ ✦ ✦

Once the three Unteroffiziere had left the caravan, the battery commander invited Unteroffizier Knabe to take a seat at the table.

"Knabe, I'm curious about the farmer that reported this incident to you. Do you know the guy?"

"No."

If you don't know him, how do you know he is a farmer? Maybe he is a blacksmith or some such thing."

"What difference does it make? This is farm country, and I just assumed that he is a farmer."

"You don't know where he lives? I'd like to have a few words with him."

"I never saw him before last night."

"I see."

The Unteroffizier avoided the battery commander's stare by fixing his eyes on the table top.

"Did you talk to him through the fence?"

"No."

"Of course, you didn't. You would have had to be out there at the same time the farmer was, and you certainly wouldn't have had a reason to be traipsing around out there in the early morning hours."

"Of course not."

The battery commander paused for a moment and then asked, "I take it that the farmer was on the airfield, when you talked to him."

"That is correct."

"Hmm, that is interesting. I'm going to have to check with the main gate personnel whether a farmer for whatever reason was allowed access to the airfield. Their logbook entries would give us the answer. If there is no such entry, then we would have to assume that he climbed the fence. This would open up another can of worms."

Unteroffizier Knabe appeared somewhat nervous as he asked, "What are you getting at?"

"Well that would be a security breach. There would have to be an inquiry, and you would be called upon to testify, since you were the only one who talked to him."

As the battery commander reached for the phone, Unteroffizier Knabe, visibly agitated, put up his hand and said, "You don't have to make that call. There was no farmer!"

"There was no farmer?" the battery commander asked, feigning surprise.

"No. I got up early in the morning because I had to take a leak. Once outside, I saw Klug and Ganther walking along the fence. One of them had a large saw under his arm. I decided to follow them to see what they were up to, but on the outside of the fence. You already know the rest of the story."

The battery commander sighed and said, "Yes, I know the rest of the story, but I didn't know that you were watching them before they even made the first cut. Why didn't you stop them?"

"That Klug kid sticks in my craw. He was born in New York, and he didn't come to Germany until shortly before the war started. Did you know that?"

"Yes. The teacher told me about his history."

"Well, he seems to be lukewarm about whose side he should be on. Some time ago I was talking to him and the subject of the U.S.A.'s entry into the war came up. Do you know what he said to me? He said, 'It was your Fuehrer that declared war.'"

"If I recall correctly, that is exactly what happened," the battery commander replied.

"Yes, but don't you see, he said *your* Fuehrer; he did not say *our* Fuehrer!"

"Well, what did you expect? One day he is an American citizen; then, overnight, he is told that he is German. Just because he didn't come to you to teach him how to goosestep is hardly a reason to want to try him by court martial."

When Knabe didn't respond, the battery commander asked, "What about the other kid?"

Unteroffizier Knabe shrugged and said, "Collateral damage."

"Collateral damage!" the battery commander gasped. He looked at the Unteroffizier in barely controllable anger and said, "Knabe, you are a bastard! I suppose that if this incident had gone your way, you would have gone bragging to your former cronies at the Gestapo that you managed to put two guys up for court martial."

Oberwachtmeister Besler took a moment to quell his rage. He then said, "If you ever mention just one word about this to your cronies, I'll come down hard on you. I'll suddenly remember certain things that I chose to forget during the inquiry that was directed at you some time ago. I'll have that inquiry reopened even though my forgetfulness may be hard to explain. Do you get my drift?" The Unteroffizier mumbled, "Yes, sir."

"Good, now get out of here. At the moment, I can't stand the sight of you!"

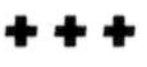

Unteroffizier Junger returned to the caravan shortly thereafter. "I have modified the sentry schedule, and I have advised the Luftwaffe people that we are offering them some kitchen help," he reported to Besler.

"Good. You didn't give them any particulars, did you?"

"No, sir."

"Good. Listen, Junger, why don't you have one of your Hiwis retrieve the wood that the boys have hidden in the bushes. When the Luftwaffe gets around to it, they will be giving us dried peat moss and some kindling to fire up the stoves. That peat moss doesn't ignite easily, and I'm afraid the boys will need more kindling than the Luftwaffe allocates until they get the hang of firing up peat moss. The Hiwis can chop the blocks to provide that extra kindling."

"Don't you think you might become an accessory in the destruction of government property if you have them do that?"

"Nah, it's already destroyed. The Luftwaffe doesn't know about it, and, if they find out, I have their commitment in writing that they were to supply us with fuel from day one. They are as much to blame for this incident as anyone else, and they're not going to put their own ass in a sling."

Chapter 46

Herbert and Rolf started their assigned penalties on the following morning. After about two weeks their fingers acquired a brownish tinge from peeling seemingly never ending quantities of potatoes in the Luftwaffe kitchen facility. Thorough scrubbing notwithstanding, with what in those days passed for soap, the stains would not readily disappear. The KP duty did have a redeeming element: Whoever was part of the KP detail was fed in the Luftwaffe mess hall.

The four-hour sentry duties also were a drudgery; however, at times they would partially coincide with alerts, when all crew members had to be in their gun emplacements. In those instances, time spent in the gun emplacement was credited as sentry time.

Both boys were relieved when they completed their sentences at the end of November.

Shortly thereafter, the barrack for gun crew number three was completed. It had been given priority over the remaining housing, including the command barrack, in order to move crew number three out of their tents as soon as possible. Completion of the remaining barracks occurred in approximately one-week intervals.

Once the final barrack, the one that would serve as a classroom and the teacher's quarters, was finished, Mr. Vogt returned to the battery, and the boys were able to continue their schooling.

After the barracks were up, the Luftwaffe finally supplied fuel with which to heat them. True to Oberwachtmeister Besler's prediction, they supplied dried peat moss.

+++

On an early December morning, loud explosive charges followed by popping noises caused some of the boys to leave the barracks to find out what was going on. They saw that several miles to the north V-1s were being launched from their ramps. The loud noise was due to the charge that fires the missile off the ramp. The succeeding put-put sound came from the pulse-jet engine that powers the missile to its target.

"I didn't think that the V-1 has the range to reach England from here," Herbert said to Detlev Wolfert.

"It probably doesn't, but, as you can see, those are being aimed to the southwest. To targets in England, they'd have to be aimed considerably more westward. They are probably headed for Antwerp."

"Antwerp? Sounds to me like we're going back in time. Antwerp was taken by German forces over four years ago!" Herbert responded.

Detlev shrugged and said, "In some instances we may be going backward; on the other hand, those missiles up there have been active for not more than six months, and they are already being superseded by the V-2."

As they watched several more launches, one of the missiles, after it attained altitude, apparently had a faulty directional system. It suddenly veered off course and proceeded to fly in a circle. Since the V-1 installation was bounded by the North Sea to the west and by open country in all other directions, no attempt was made to shoot it down. Consequently, the missile kept on circling until the pulse jets shut off, thereby causing it to drop and to explode in a field.

Herbert had counted the number of missiles launched. He thought four out of five—a 20 percent failure rate!

+++

Several days later, during an alert, Herbert watched the bombers coming out of the west in a clear blue sky. Since the formations were still at about 15,000 feet, on their way to the usual over-target altitude of some 20,000 feet, Herbert could identify the aircraft with the help of binoculars. Those in his field of vision were B-17 four-engine bombers.

Since the aircraft were readily visible to the naked eye, Herbert put the binoculars aside and started to count: 1, 2, 3—after he reached a count of 700 about an hour later, he tired of counting and stopped—but there were still more bombers coming.

When he told Unteroffizier Kimmel of his count, the Unteroffizier said, "You shouldn't be looking just to the west; there is also a threat from the east. That is where the cripples come from, aircraft that have had a malfunction that has forced them to leave the formation. Those guys are always looking for targets of opportunity, and we are one of the targets."

+++

In mid-December, Unteroffizier Kimmel's prescience was fulfilled.

Six of the boys, with provision containers strapped on their back, were on their way to return the empty containers to the Luftwaffe kitchen facilities. Herbert was among them.

The boys had decided to make a beeline for the Luftwaffe compound, instead of using the paths along the field's perimeter, as they were supposed to do. Herbert was dawdling behind the group by some twenty yards.

"Aircraft—two o'clock!" someone hollered, just before they reached the intersection of the two runways. When Herbert looked in that direction, he saw the four-engine bomber approaching from the east on a path that would cause it to pass directly overhead. The aircraft had lost altitude but was still well out of the range of the guns.

"Hit the deck!" one of them yelled.

Everyone lay down in a prone position. As Herbert hit the turf, he felt a dank wetness around the back of his neck. Oh, shit! he thought, the lid of my provision container is not properly sealed, and now the dregs of the potato soup that we had for dinner are running around my neck. He tried to remove the mess with his hands while his eyes remained focused on the approaching aircraft.

When he saw the bombs tumbling out of the aircraft, he cringed. Herbert stuck his nose into the turf and clasped his sticky hands behind the back of his head.

As the first bomb impacted, he found himself crawling to catch up with the boys that lay ahead of him. He checked himself and thought, why are you doing this? Strength in numbers? Nah, you're just plain scared out of your wits!

The bombs had impacted about 150 yards to the northwest of the intersection. Some of them found the runways.

When all was quiet, a trembling voice said, "Let's hightail it out of here." The boys resumed their trek toward the kitchen facilities in double time.

✦ ✦ ✦

For the Christmas holiday of 1944, three crew members of gun number one had acquired passes; therefore, only five boys and Unterofffizier Kimmel were in the barrack on Christmas Day. Four of the boys had received Christmas parcels from home; Herbert had received none. He knew that his mother would have sent something, and he figured that his package had been either held up in the ever weakening postal system or destroyed during an air raid while in transit; however, the four boys shared their cookies and other goodies with one another and with Herbert. Even Unteroffizier Kimmel shared a cake with them.

✚✚✚

In early January, Herbert was told to report to Unteroffizier Junger in his office in the new command barrack.

"You're going to Lueneburg!" Junger announced.

"Lueneburg? What's in Lueneburg?"

"You are going there to receive noncom training."

Herbert thought baby-flak being trained as noncoms? Germany must really be scraping the bottom of the barrel!

"Who else is going?"

"Gerhard Zeitler from gun crew number three."

"Why us?"

"I don't know. Maybe the Oberwachtmeister wants to get the two of you out of his hair for a while."

Herbert glanced at the Unteroffizier with a grimace.

Junger returned the grimace and said, "You'll be leaving tomorrow morning."

Herbert asked, "At what time do we leave in the morning?"

"Report to me at 7:00 A.M. I'll have your travel orders ready."

"Yes, sir."

✚✚✚

The noncom training center was situated in a brick building at one end of a fully operational fighter airfield on the outskirts of Lueneburg. The air-raid trenches that had been dug on two sides of the building portended that the boys would be spending some time in them.

The training center essentially was self-contained; the living quarters and the classrooms for the trainees were all located in the brick building.

The training course consisted of classroom instructions and hands-on training in the use of light and heavy machine guns. The enrollees were regular Wehrmacht and Luftwaffe personnel and two Luftwaffe Auxiliaries.

The classroom instructions were intended to teach the trainees the rudiments of leading an infantry squad. Emphasis was placed on reconnaissance and assault squads.

Herbert wondered, with the Soviets deep inside Poland and with the German attempt to split the U.S. and British forces in the west seemingly stalled, are the Germans planning to send Luftwaffe Auxiliaries into the front lines?

During the fourteen-day course, the trainees spent many hours in the air-raid trenches—during the night, when British bombers were overhead and during the day, when P-47 Thunderbolt fighter bombers were nearby.

On the final day, the trainees were given a pass-fail test. Herbert passed—the other boy did not.

Late that evening, Gerhard and Herbert were on their way to retrace their route back to Nordholz. They would again change trains in Hamburg and also in Cuxhaven for the remaining short ride to the airfield.

After the boys had transferred in Hamburg, the train, just ten minutes after leaving the Hamburg main station, made an unscheduled stop at a suburban station because an air-raid alert was in effect. Everybody was ordered off the train.

Under heavy flak, the boys walked about a city block before an air-raid warden waved them into the basement of an apartment building.

They sat among strangers. When the air-raid warden came inside and closed the heavy basement door behind him, everyone knew that it was no longer safe to stand outside.

Immediately thereafter, somber glances were exchanged, and the crying of the younger children was heard when nearby bomb impacts caused the building to tremble.

After the all clear sounded, the boys headed back to the station. During the short walk, they saw that several houses on both sides of the street were burning.

Upon his return to the battery emplacement, Herbert found out that his Christmas package had arrived.

"When did this get here?" he asked Klaus Wolfert.

"Yesterday," Klaus replied.

While Herbert was unwrapping the package at the barrack table, seven guys impatiently crowded around the table to see what was inside. When he took the large cookie container out of the box, he remembered how his friends had shared with him on Christmas Day. Herbert took a handful of cookies out of the container and then shoved the container to the center of the table.

"Help yourself," he said, before adding, "Save a few for Unteroffizier Kimmel."

He read the note his mother had enclosed in the package. She was worrying that she and the girls soon would have to leave Altburgund.

That evening, when the OKW announced that the Soviets were advancing on Warsaw, Herbert worried, too.

Chapter 47

At 6:00 A.M. on the morning of 19 January, 1945, Hertha was awaked by a blaring loudspeaker. The announcement said: All those wishing to move westward are to assemble at the town square this morning no later than 8:00 A.M. Wagon transport will be available to take you to a train depot for evacuation. Bring only what you can carry. Timeliness is of the utmost importance. The wagon convoy will not wait for stragglers!

Hertha rose and looked out the window. She saw the truck bearing the loudspeaker slowly moving down the icy, snow-covered street, repeating the message over and over.

She cried out, "Romi, Hannelore, get up! We're moving out!"

+++

Having doubled up on some of the clothing articles they were wearing to protect them against the extreme cold outside and having thrown as much additional clothing as they deemed they could carry into a small duffel-bag, they arrived at the town square an hour and a half later.

Horse-drawn farm wagons, lined with straw, were aligned in the square and along the roads leading into it. Hertha and the girls were assigned a wagon along with an elderly couple and a woman with two small children. At 8:00 A.M. sharp, among rumbling of gunfire in the distance, the wagon column started to move.

"Why couldn't they just have us board a train at the Altburgund station?" Hertha asked the elderly gentleman. "My guess is that the Gauleiter has not lifted his evacuation ban, and this is happening without his knowledge. Apparently the local authorities have taken things into their own hands and have assembled a train wherever they could."

"Oh."

After the column had been underway for about half an hour, Hertha suddenly cried out, "Oh, my God!"

Taken aback, Romi asked, "What's the matter?"

"The satchel, the little satchel! I left it on the kitchen table!"

Romi shrugged and asked, "Is it that important?"

Hertha looked at Romi wide-eyed with anxiety, and said, "It may contain the key to your future—your, your brother's, and Hannelore's American birth certificates are in it. Your father always made it a point that they not be lost! It also contains all the money I have squirreled away for this kind of occasion. I have to go back and retrieve the satchel!"

"I'll go with you." Romi said.

Hertha looked at the young woman with the two children and asked, "Would you look after my youngest for a while? We forgot something and must go back." She acknowledged the woman's nod with a nod of her own and said, "We'll meet you at the depot.

"Let's go," Hertha said. She saw the wagon that was trying to pass theirs, but Romi did not.

"Look out!" Hertha yelled, but not soon enough.

Romi had jumped off the wagon just before the passing horse was almost alongside her. She spooked the horse, and it reared. Romi barely escaped its menacing hooves.

After her daughter had caught her breath, Hertha admonished, "Romi, please be careful. We don't need any more problems."

✚✚✚

Hertha and Romi drew some inquisitive looks as they walked in the opposite direction the wagons were moving. They were just back inside the town limits when a German staff car pulled up alongside them. "Where are you going?" the officer in the passenger seat asked.

"We're part of the wagon column that just left town a while ago. We forgot something, and we came back to pick it up," Hertha told him.

"Haven't you noticed that the sound of the guns is getting louder by the minute? What can be so important to you to want you to still be lollygagging around here?"

"We forgot some personal papers," Hertha answered.

"I see. Where do you live?"

"On the other side of town," Romi answered.

"Hop in the back," the officer said. "We'll take you there. If you hurry up, we'll drive you back to the depot."

When they reached the Klug apartment, Hertha quickly got out of the car and went inside. She picked up the satchel and was about to leave when she happened to glance at the Fuehrer picture, still facing the wall in the living room. She took a few steps, took down the picture and threw it into the wastebasket. She hesitated for a moment; then, with an impish grin, she put her foot into the wastebasket and pressed down until the glass shattered.

"Hurry, ma'am! We must go now," the officer called out as he was approaching the door to the apartment.

Before Hertha could answer, he stuck his head through the doorway. Seeing Hertha, with her foot in the wastebasket, he asked, "What on earth are you doing?"

"I...I just...I just squashed a cockroach," Hertha said with a smile.

"Lady, this is no time to be going after cockroaches."

"It is for me," Hertha replied. "I've been wanting to get that particular one for a long time."

As promised, the officer told his driver to head back to the depot. When Hertha and Romi got out of the car, the officer said, "Don't be going back another time. The Russian tanks are advancing in a pincers movement around this whole area. Just keep moving westward as fast as you can; the Russians do not take kindly to German civilians. Good luck to you."

Hertha thanked him for his efforts and said, "Good luck to you, too."

After the officer left, Hertha looked at the train cars standing on the rail siding. They were freight cars. The sliding doors were open, and she could see that the car floors were covered with straw. Each car had a stove, and in one corner of each car stood a pail. Those would be the toilet facilities, Hertha thought. Her glance shifted to the mob of people who were waiting to board the train.

"C'mon, we have to find Hannelore," she said to Romi.

"Do you think we should split up?" Romi asked.

"No, no. We are already split up enough!"

They finally found Hannelore and their acquaintances huddled on the floor of one of the depot sheds. Hannelore was quietly holding her doll. Hertha looked at Hannelore with a smile and said, "We're back!"

Hannelore looked up to her mother. With tears welling in her eyes, she said, "Please don't ever leave me like that again."

"Oh, honey, we had to walk fast when we had to go back for

the papers. I thought it would be easier on you if you stayed with the wagon."

Lowering her head, Hannelore supplicated, "Don't leave me again."

Hertha reached down and hugged her youngest. She said, "I'm sorry. I wasn't thinking. I should have left Romi with you. I promise that we won't leave you again."

Railway employees divided the crowd into groups of approximately twenty and assigned each group to one of the freight cars. Immediately after everyone boarded, the train left the depot. Initially, the train moved along at great speed. It was moving so fast that the sideways lurching of the freight cars made Hertha question the engineer's sanity, but she remembered what the German officer had said; therefore, she realized that the engineer was racing to avoid the Russian encirclement attempt. She kept that information to herself.

After about half an hour, the train slowed down to a crawl. At times the train was shunted to a spur track and came to a complete stop.

Hertha heard someone ask, "Why are they doing this?"

"Because eastbound traffic gets priority," someone else answered, adding, "Presently, almost all the traffic is eastbound."

The stop and go mode of the train, moving along at a slow rate and being shunted to a spur track, continued for the remainder of the day and the next day. At some of the spur stops soup kitchens had been set up. One could get some food by standing in line, but only if one's turn in line occurred before the food ran out.

By the end of the second day, the stove had run out of fuel. Hertha and the girls tried to stay warm in the now icy freight car by huddling close together and covering themselves with straw. They tried to sleep but could only doze. On the morning of the third day, Hertha noted that their clothing was covered with hoarfrost.

Romi said, "Ow! My legs and my feet hurt."

"You're not the only one who's hurting," her mother replied.

"What are these grayish-white patches on my legs?" Romi asked.

Hertha avoided the question by saying, "Just rub them a little to improve the circulation." She did not want to alarm her daughter, but she knew the cause: frostbite!

Luckily, the third day was not as cold as the preceding ones, and a little warmth was supplied when some ingenious person in the car decided, "Since we don't have wood, let's burn the straw!"

On that afternoon the train arrived in Kuestrin, a city located along the river Oder. The occupants were told to disembark.

A trip that normally took two hours by passenger train had taken almost three days!

The train platforms of the Kuestrin train station were occupied by a mass of teeming humanity. People from all points east were trying to evade the Russians. Fear and anxiety were etched on many faces. The mood of the crowd was approaching an "everyone for himself" attitude.

Hertha and the girls squirmed and pushed their way to the station waiting room where several soup kitchens had been set up. After standing in line for over an hour, they were able to get some soup and a slice of bread for each. After their respite, Hertha asked a station official when the next train for Berlin would be available.

"Lady, our normal scheduling procedure has been temporarily superseded by chaos. We don't know when trains will be available or where they will be going," the official advised. He added, "All you can do at the moment is to listen to the public address system and hope that it announces a train heading for Berlin."

Hertha sighed. She turned to the girls and said, "Let's see if we can find a place to sit down."

Three hours later there was an announcement that a train to Berlin would be pulling in on platform number four. The announcement added a caveat: This train is for *"Mutter und Kind"* only!*

"That's us!" Hertha exclaimed.

As she and the girls neared the designated platform, they saw that the train had already pulled in. Barriers had been put up along the platform to keep the crowd at bay. Hertha noticed that there was only one conductor for every three train cars to monitor the boarding.

Hertha and the girls got in line to get on the train. When it was their turn, the conductor pointed at Romi and said, "She can't get on."

"What do you mean, 'she can't get on,' she is my child."

"Is she sixteen or younger?"

"No. She is celebrating her eighteenth birthday today if you can call this celebrating. Can't you make a small concession and allow her on the train?"

"Not if she is over sixteen."

Hertha rolled her eyes and said, "Oh, for heaven's sake."

She pulled Romi aside, out of earshot of the conductor, and whispered, "You must get on the train. Do you see those cars that presently are not being monitored?"

Romi nodded.

"Walk along the barriers until you get to the first one, but stay on this side of the barriers. As soon as you get a chance,

* See footnote number 4 on page 152.

make a run for it and get into that car." Hertha grabbed Romi's hand and said, "Remember, your only concern is to get on that train."

As the conductor watched Romi walk away, Hertha asked him, "Are you satisfied?"

Just as she and Hannelore were boarding, Hertha heard a commotion coming from the barriers. Looking back, she saw that the crowd, ignoring the "Mutter und Kind" caveat had overturned the barriers and was swarming toward the train. She took another look, but she no longer could see Romi!

✚✚✚

Hertha and Hannelore seated themselves in one of the train compartments. Hertha was almost beside herself worrying about whether Romi was able to get on the train. Hannelore said to her mother, "Don't worry, Mama, Romi is just like you. She can be tough, when she has to be."

The train aisle rapidly filled with people. Social amenities quickly disappeared in the atmosphere filled with fear. With more people pushing and shoving to get on the train, some of the folks in the aisles soon spilled into the compartments as standees. After the shoving and pushing seemed to quiet down, Hertha turned toward a man standing near the compartment door and said, "I'm trying to find out whether my older daughter was able to get on the train.

"Please pass a question toward the rear of the train. I need to know whether a Rosemarie Klug is on board."

The man nodded. Hertha heard, "Is there a Rosemarie Klug on board?" three or four times. With each repetition, the message became less audible to her as it was passed along.

Little Hannelore glanced at her mother. She noticed that her mother was shivering.

The car jerked, signaling that the train was getting underway. Hertha sighed.

About ten minutes later, Hertha heard a return message, "Yes, there is a Rosemarie Klug on board."

She thanked the man near the door, gave Hannelore a hug and said, "Thank God!"

Shortly thereafter, Romi had been able to wiggle her way forward through the aisles such that she could see and wave at her mother and sister in their compartment.

Like the freight train that had brought them to Kuestrin, the passenger train also moved along at a slow pace. It also was shunted onto spur tracks an innumerable number of times, where it might have to wait for half an hour before starting up again.

Soup kitchens were again set up at some of the spur tracks, but no one dared to leave the train, for fear that one might not get back on again. Instead, folks would open a compartment or aisle window to accept sandwiches through the window and pass them on inside the car. Not everyone would receive a sandwich. Most would share with the unfortunates; a few would not.

Unlike the freight train, the interior of the passenger train grew tepidly warm, because of the mass of humanity confined in the relatively small space. A downside was the mixture of body odors emanated by that mass of humanity.

A call of nature could not be relieved until about half an hour later; it took about fifteen minutes to get to the toilet and another fifteen minutes to await one's turn.

Thirst became a problem. When the train wound up on a dual spur, it stopped such that Romi's aisle window was directly opposite the cab of a locomotive that was stopped on the other spur. Seeing the icicles hanging from the roof of the engineer's cab, she opened the window and asked him to hand her several icicles. The engineer obliged, and Romi passed some of them on to her mother's compartment.

When Hertha waved at her in acknowledgement, Romi called out to her mother, in English, "I'd much rather have a Popsicle!"

✚✚✚

Sixteen hours after leaving Kuestrin, the train finally arrived in Berlin. Once in the station concourse, Hertha walked to the nearest operational phone booth to let Walther know that they had arrived.

After the hugs and kisses upon Walther's arrival at the station, he took a closer look at his wife and the girls and said, "You all look like you've been put through the wringer."

Hertha told him about their four-day nightmare. She also told him about the incident when the German officer surprised her while she had her foot in the waste basket. "You're taking some unnecessary risks, Hertha. What if the officer had looked into the waste basket?"

Hertha shrugged and said, "He didn't strike me as the Nazi type." After a pause, she added, "And I had no way of knowing that he would follow me into the house."

"Well, it's water over the dam," Walther replied. He picked up their duffel bag and said, "Let's go. I'll introduce you to Mrs. Kampert."

"Who is Mrs. Kampert?" Hertha asked.

"She is the lady with whom you will be staying for a few days."

"Oh, now I remember," Hertha remarked, after she recalled their discussion that had taken place months earlier.

"You will be able to get some rest for several days, but within a week, we will have to make the necessary arrangements for your trip to your cousin in Treuen," Walther told Hertha.

"Why so fast?" she asked.

"There are several reasons," Walther replied. "You will be very cramped in Mrs. Kampert's two-room apartment. Also, I don't want you to stay in Berlin any longer than absolutely necessary. Berlin is being subjected to air raids almost on a daily basis."

"Are there any other reasons?" Hertha asked.

"Yes, there is one more," Walther replied. After a pause he said, "Within ten days, I'll be shipped to France."

"Oh! No!" Hertha cried out.

Chapter 48

After Herbert completed the 8:00 to 10:00 P.M. watch on a February evening, Unteroffizier Junger asked him to deliver the battery's provisioning requirements, based on the headcount for the remainder of the month, to the Luftwaffe administration building. At about 11:00 P.M., he left the building to return to the battery.

Once he stepped outside, the cold night air stung his face. His eyes took a while to accommodate to the mandated total blackout, which meant that, but for the intervals when the cloud cover briefly parted to allow a crescent moon to cast a dim light on his surroundings, he would remain practically sightless. Even during such intervals, patches of ground fog tended to negate the dim light of the moon.

Herbert ventured through the darkness on what he thought would be a direct path to the intersection of the runways. After he had reached the runway pavement, he heard the sound of aircraft engines overhead. He thought, since there is no alert in effect, that must be a German aircraft.

He hoped that the runway lights would turn on so that he could reorient himself; the lack of visual references might have caused him to stray from his intended straight line course toward the battery emplacement.

Herbert knew that the lights would be turned on in an emergency only and that they would stay on for only a second or two, because prolonged illumination would present a target to undetected enemy aircraft in the vicinity.

The aircraft had circled and apparently was making another pass. He heard the aircraft engines being throttled back.

The runway lights did come on several times; however, because of the scattering effect of the ground fog, their blue light merely enveloped Herbert in a blue haze, which was useless for him to establish his bearings.

As the sound of the throttled-back engines drew nearer, he panicked and started to run in the direction he thought would get him off the runway. Suddenly, the aircraft landing light briefly came on—the beam of light hit Herbert head-on. He raised his hands to his eyes and instinctively turned his back toward the beam. Seconds later, Herbert was again surrounded by complete darkness, but the multicolored spots that were dancing in front of him indicated that his eyes had not taken kindly to the blinding shaft of light. He was too bewildered to remember from which direction the light had come.

Holy crap, he thought, I am trying to get off the runway, but I am finding myself on a collision course with an airplane! In the dark, I must have wandered off my intended beeline by nearly.... The squealing tires contacting the tarmac and the increasing rumble of the approaching aircraft interrupted his thought. He envisioned two scenarios: If the pilot saw me, he might rev the engines and initiate a go around, and by running, I risk walking into a prop. If the pilot didn't see me, he will continue his landing roll, and I merely risk getting run over. The choice was obvious, so Herbert hit the deck. He lay there, as the aircraft approached. He attributed his trembling to the cold air, rather than to the fear that had gripped him.

As the aircraft was almost upon him, the props dispersed

the ground fog and a break in the black clouds revealed the crescent of the moon. Split seconds later, Herbert saw the silhouette of an Me-110 wing glide over him.

The landing direction of the aircraft allowed Herbert, albeit much more dramatically than he had bargained for, to ascertain the runway orientation, and he was able to reorient himself. He was out of there like a shot. He thought being caught in the wrong place at the wrong time would only feed Unteroffizier Knabe's affinity to babble about court martials.

✚✚✚

Several days later, Rolf Ganther relieved Herbert of guard duty.

"Do you remember the camouflaged areas the Luftwaffe built on the south side of the airfield a while back?" Rolf asked.

Herbert grimaced and replied, "How could I forget?"

"Well, they now have two aircraft parked there. They are much smaller than a normal single-engine fighter."

"What kind are they?" Herbert asked.

"A Luftwaffe guy told me they are Me-163As. He said that they are rocket propelled!"

"Rocket propelled?" Herbert asked incredulously. "That guy must be putting you on."

Rolf answered with a shrug.

✚✚✚

While engaged in gun maintenance a week later, the boys of gun number one were surprised by a roaring sound. When they looked toward the runways, they saw a small aircraft taking off at an incredible speed. Flames were emitting from the rear of the aircraft as it raced along the runway during takeoff. Just after leaving the ground, its landing gear fell off and the little craft proceeded to climb at an incredible rate at an angle of about seventy degrees.

"Hey, how's that guy going to land?" Klaus Wolfert shouted. "He lost his landing gear!"

The aircraft climbed to about 12,000 feet. It seemed to glide at that altitude for several minutes. Then, with another rocket burst, it flew several wide circles at an incredible speed. Finally it glided in circles back down and landed, on skids protruding from its undercarriage, in a grassy area of the airfield.

"Wow, would you look at that!" Klaus exclaimed. "He shed the landing gear on purpose, probably to reduce the air resistance; then, he came back in on the skids."

Someone said, "That must be one of the new weapons that the Fuehrer has been promising us."

All of the crew, including Herbert, was impressed by the speed of the little craft. They had never seen any aircraft move so fast. While impressed, Herbert thought, you'll need a lot more than two of those, if you want to stop the bombers from flying over the Reich.

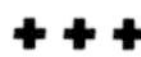

In the first week of March, Herbert was ordered to report to Oberwachtmeister Besler in the command barrack. When he got there, both Oberwachtmeister Besler and Unteroffizier Junger were present.

"Have a seat, Klug," the battery commander said from behind his desk. After Herbert complied, Besler said, "Because of Unteroffizier Kimmel's expertise in range finding, he is being transferred, and I also have to give up another Unteroffizier. I won't be getting any replacements. Unteroffiziere Kimmel and Knabe will leave tomorrow morning. Unteroffizier Junger will take over for Knabe, but I don't have anyone to take Kimmel's place." Besler paused and asked, "Are you with me, so far?"

Herbert nodded.

"I'm thinking of having you replace Kimmel," Besler said.

Herbert couldn't hide his surprise, when he asked, "Me? Why me? Why not someone else?"

"You are the only one that has the required qualification. The rule book says that a gun commander must have successfully passed a noncom training course, and you are the only one of the Auxiliaries who has done that," Besler answered. He looked at Herbert and asked, "Do you think you can handle the job?"

"I can handle the job," Herbert said, although without great conviction.

"You'll still be doing your normal routines, such as sentry duty. Your added duties will consist of making sure everyone in your crew is in the gun position during alerts, overseeing gun maintenance, and...and telling them to shoot, when there is something to shoot at. It's a simple assignment, and I don't think you'll have any problems."

"Will I get to wear an Unteroffiziers's insignia?"

The Oberwachtmeister laughed and said, "No, no. There are no such rank distinctions in the Luftwaffe Auxiliary."

"Well, will I be moving into Unteroffizier Kimmel's former quarters?"

Besler laughed again. Turning to Unteroffizier Junger, he quipped, "Listen to this guy. I offer him a piece of cake, and he wants the whole bakery!" He thought, I have to start remembering that I'm overseeing a bunch of sixteen-year-old kids. Then, in a more serious vein, he said, "Keep what I'm about to tell you under your hat, until after I make the announcement following roll call tomorrow morning: Unteroffizier Kimmel's former quarters are being modified and outfitted with a separate entrance for a visitor who will be staying with us for a while."

"A visitor?" Herbert asked.

"A visitor," Besler answered, adding, "Beyond that, neither you nor anyone of the other boys has a need to know."

When Herbert did not respond, the Oberwachtmeister asked, "So, do we have a deal? Will you accept the new assignment?"

"Yes, sir."

"Good, I will make the announcement tomorrow morning, along with the visitor thing."

✚✚✚

On the following morning, when Oberwachtmeister Besler announced the forthcoming arrival and stay of a visitor at the battery emplacement, he was very emphatic when he told the boys, "I don't want you to converse with him, unless he initiates the conversation. If he does, you will address him with 'Sir.' Under no circumstances are you to question him about his stay with us. Your best behavior is to pretend he is not here, insofar as that is possible."

When the boys of gun number one had returned to their barrack after the roll call, Herbert's crew members congratulated him on his "promotion."

Then the teasing started. Detlev asked, "Of whom does he remind you?" When no one responded, Detlev said, "He has the same stature as Napoleon."

Detlev's brother Klaus said, "Nah, he's a little taller than Napoleon but not by much." Turning to Herbert, he said, "Tuck your right hand partially into your tunic like Nappy did when he was modeling to have his picture painted. I want to see if there is a resemblance."

"Careful, guys," Manfred chimed in, "we may be looking at our next kaiser."

His whole crew laughed.

Herbert squelched the needling when he said, "Napoleon had an army to back him up; all I have is a bunch of wise-asses."

This time, they all laughed.

The talk soon switched to Oberwachtmeister Besler's announcement of the anticipated visitor. Detlev asked Herbert, "Did Papa Besler tell you anything, besides what he told us?"

"Nope."

"Maybe we are getting another teacher to help Mr. Vogt out," Hans Scherer, the loader for gun number one, suggested.

"Nah. Why should we be restricted from conversing with another teacher?" Detlev countered.

Several days later the visitor arrived. When Herbert first cast his eyes on him, he saw a white-haired man, approximately in his late fifties, who wore the uniform of a Luftwaffe private. Something about the uniform intrigued Herbert. It did not look like it had been taken off a rack; it was immaculate and seemed to have been tailored for the man. The man, himself, had the unmistakable bearing of a German officer!

At mealtimes, the visitor did not share in the provisions the boys were allotted; he was catered to by two Luftwaffe types. Herbert noticed that the two were always the same men. Who is this guy? Herbert wondered.

About a week after the visitor's arrival, Herbert walked past the open door of the visitor's quarters. As he glanced inside, he saw an olive-drab cap of the Afrika Korps that lay on a chair near the door. Herbert kept on walking. Whoa! Herbert thought, this guy probably was an officer with the Afrika Korps under Field Marshal Rommel. If I recall correctly, Rommel later became involved in a complicity to overthrow Hitler, although he had no direct part in the assassination attempt of the previous July. Had the visitor been part of that complicity or the attempt to assassinate the Fuehrer? Is he running from the Gestapo? A shrug of the shoulders. Maybe the cap belonged to someone else. But why is he holed up here without any function other than to be catered to by two Luftwaffe types? Why did Papa Besler transfer Knabe rather than Unteroffizier Latner? Was it because Knabe had some prior links with the Gestapo, and Besler did not want him snooping around? Why did Besler tell us to stay clear of the visitor? Why should we be addressing a Luftwaffe private with "sir"?

If he is on the run, who is concealing him? To what extent is Besler involved? Are they trying to save this man from the hangman's noose? Am I making a mountain out of a molehill? Hell, I don't know! In any case, the whole affair is no skin off my back.

Starting about this time, the Oberwachtmeister's morning roll calls were followed by announcements of the names and ranks of those who had been found wanting in their duties to Fuehrer and Fatherland. Mobile court martial units hunted them down, and convictions drew the death sentence. The ranks of those executed ranged from lieutenant colonel to private.

Chapter 49

"*Jabos*[12] at three o'clock!" the lookout, crouched on the fender of the lead truck, yelled. The empty trucks of the supply column, on their way back to the rear area supply depot, quickly stopped. Most of those on board the trucks made it to the ditch adjacent to the road; some did not. They became victims of the P-47s that quickly turned their trucks into funeral pyres.

After Walther and other survivors had assisted medics to get the wounded into ambulances and to lay the dead alongside the roadway, they waited in a grove of trees to hitch a ride with the next returning supply column.

"Has this been an unnecessary trip, or what?" Joseph Reiner, who had been ordered to France with Walther from their unit in Berlin, asked. "We just crossed the border back into Germany a while ago. When we arrived in France about seven weeks ago, they told us that there had been a screw up. We were supposed to have arrived about a month earlier, in time for the start of the German counteroffensive in the Ardennes, because our people were expecting to need help to interrogate large numbers of prisoners. When that didn't materialize, they

12 German contraction for *Jagdbomber:* fighter bombers.

had us guarding bridges against resistance fighters, who also never showed up."

Walther nodded and with a chuckle continued Reiner's train of thought, "Once the bridges no longer needed guarding, because they were already in Allied hands, we were handed a rifle and told that we now were part of the rear guard. And three days ago, we were ordered back to Berlin. Our commanding officer told us that he didn't have any transport available to take us to the nearest functional railhead. He didn't even know where such railhead might be located."

Reiner shook his head and said, "Then he suggested that we hitch a ride on a supply column heading back from the front."

"His parting words to us were anything but reassuring," Walther recalled. "Do you remember what he said?"

"How could I forget?" Reiner replied. "He said, 'At this moment in time, I wouldn't wish my worst enemy a transfer back to Berlin.'" With a sardonic smile, Reiner added, "I expect Hitler knows that the doomsday clock for Germany is in its final hour, but he will tell his constituents that, by unveiling a decisive secret weapon in the last minute, he will beat the clock."

Walther laughed and derisively commented, "Yeah, but what happens to us in the meantime? We've already had to hightail it out of two trucks in as many days just before they were incinerated by the Jabos!"

On a clear early April night, Herbert had the 2:00 to 4:00 A.M. watch. At about 3:30, he heard aircraft engines. As he looked upward, he was startled momentarily: he could make out the silhouette of a Mosquito bomber apparently circling at about seven thousand feet.

Being close to gun number one, he ran into the gun emplacement, picked up the phone of the one-way line that connected to the loudspeaker in the barrack, and yelled, "Get your asses out here, on the double! Mosquito bomber overhead!"

He thought, it's a good thing that we always turn the loudspeaker to full volume before we turn in for the night. They'll wake up with a jolt, but they will wake up!

Herbert quickly started to remove the tarpaulin off the gun. His crew came running out of the barrack before he was done. He had to snicker, when he saw them. They were in their long johns. Some of them were barefoot, while others were tripping over their untied shoelaces.

"There is a Mosquito bomber circling overhead! I think he's going to make another pass!" Herbert yelled.

The engine noises grew louder, and when the aircraft was almost directly above them, they could see its silhouette against the background of the star studded sky.

"Fire at will!" Herbert shouted.

Boom! Boom! Boom!

The K1 took his foot off the pedal and was adjusting the azimuth angle.

"Decrease your lead angle a little bit!" Herbert shouted. "The tracer showed your aim to be somewhat ahead of the target."

"'Decrease your lead angle.' I can hardly see the aircraft," the K1 mumbled. He again depressed the firing pedal, and the gun responded: Boom! Boom! Boom!

The ensuing silence, after the last shot emptied the magazine, was quickly interrupted by the loudspeaker of the transceiver system, which tied the gun positions via phone lines not only to the battery command barrack, but also to the Luftwaffe airfield administration.

"STOP FIRING IMMEDIATELY!" a strange voice blared out of the loudspeaker.

Herbert picked up the transceiver mike and reported, "We are shooting at a Mosquito bomber!"

"I DON'T CARE WHAT YOU'RE SHOOTING AT. YOU ARE TO CEASE FIRING IMMEDIATELY!" the loudspeaker blared again.

All eyes of his crew were directed at Herbert.

"Are you sure that we were shooting at a Mosquito bomber?" Detlev asked him.

"I had no doubts whatever," he responded. "Couldn't you guys identify it?" he asked.

Klaus Wolfert answered, "Hey, we came out here after we had been aroused from sleep. Just about the time we took our positions, you were already shouting, 'Fire at will!'"

Herbert wondered whether he might have been mistaken. He said, "Go inside and put some more clothes on; then, come back out. We have to clean the gun barrel."

✚✚✚

Some of the boys from the other guns had been roused by the firing of the gun. They stopped by to inquire about what was going on. While the gun crew was cleaning the gun barrel, Papa Besler also made an appearance. He said, "It has been a bad night so far. First, you guys wake me up. Then, I receive a phone call from the airfield commander. He chews my ass for not distributing his advisory to you guys that a captured British aircraft was being flown in here for retrofitting. When I told him that even I had not been put in the loop, he left the mike open and I heard the dressing-down he was giving to someone on the other end of the line. Somebody on that end forgot to tell us what was going on."

Herbert felt as though a heavy load had been lifted from his shoulders.

"You guys did the right thing," the Oberwachtmeister said, and, "I understand that the pilot was very annoyed. He radioed in that your last tracer convinced him to change course to his alternate airport." As the Oberwachtmeister turned to go back to the command barrack, he added, "You guys did well I guess—in this case almost too well."

After the crew of gun number one had returned to their barrack, one of the boys asked, "What would they be doing with a captured British aircraft?"

Detlev said, "I've heard that after they change the markings, they send the aircraft aloft to fly alongside daylight incursions of bomber formations to report the position and the altitude of the formations to the German Air Defense Command. Being Allied aircraft, they do not rouse suspicion."

Chapter 50

After Hedwig, Grandfather Werner's niece, found out that Hertha and the girls were seeking refuge, she accepted them with open arms in early February. Cousin Hedwig now lived alone in the upper floor of the big two-storied house. The bakery store, which took up the ground floor, had been closed because her husband and her two sons all were in the service.

The little town of Treuen, having been spared the ravages of war, became an idyllic refuge for Hertha and the girls; however, as with the rest of the country, the food situation became ever tighter as the war progressed. Vegetables, consisting mostly of turnips and a few potatoes, plus a few slices of bread, became the order of the day.

In the first week of April, cousin Hedwig's son, Heinz, came home on convalescent furlough. His left arm, which he supported with a sling, had sustained several shrapnel injuries. Anticipating that the Americans would soon occupy Treuen and hoping to avoid detention in a POW camp, Heinz soon switched to civilian clothing,

He knew his way around the area, and he would go out to forage for food. Most of the time he came home empty-handed; however, one day he was able to barter something or other in return for a bagful of canned meat.

Toward the middle of April, the Americans were closing in. The burgomaster of the town ordered the inhabitants to display white flags to save his town from destruction.

Two days later, the Americans arrived. The tanks came in first, followed by infantry, followed by two-and-a-half ton trucks carrying more infantry, followed in turn by swarms of jeeps!

Hertha and the girls hid their enthusiasm from the German populace, but they were thrilled to see the Americans moving into town. The Americans started going from house to house, looking for German soldiers and weapons.

Looking out the window, Romi saw two Americans approaching cousin Hedwig's house. When they pounded on the door, she opened it and asked, "What took you guys so long?"

Both soldiers were taken aback, not by the impertinence of the question, but by the presence of a young lady who spoke perfect English albeit with a Brooklyn accent.

The taller of the two stammered, "Are there any German soldiers or weapons in this house?"

"No soldiers and no weapons…" Romi responded, adding, "If you like, you can come in and look for yourself."

"That won't be necessary," the soldier said. After a pause, he asked, "Where did you learn to speak English like that?"

"In New York."

"In New York?" the soldier interrupted incredulously. "What are you doing here?"

Romi briefly told him her tale of woe.

"Wow!" he exclaimed, after the brief rendition of her story. Then he said, "Maybe we'll be able to talk some more, at another time."

As the soldiers turned to leave, Romi heard him tell his buddy, "The guys won't believe me when I tell them that a young lady from Brooklyn lives in that house."

The Americans requisitioned the house next to cousin Hedwig's home. Apparently, the soldier who had talked to Romi spread the word as promised. The guys next door anxiously waited for Romi to come out into the back yard, to hang up wash or to tend to the flower beds, in order to have a chance to talk to an American female.

At first, cousin Hedwig worried that there might be repercussions for fraternizing with the enemy if the German army were to retake the area; however, her worries seemed to dwindle, when Romi's new acquaintances brought assortments of canned food and real soap when they came to chat.

Several days after the GIs arrived, Romi told her mother that her whole mouth hurt and she could barely swallow. When Hertha took a look, she saw that Romi's mouth was full of grayish ulcerations. The tissue surrounding the ulcerations was severely inflamed. Hertha immediately left to find a doctor.

She returned an hour later, not with a doctor, but with a GI. Romi recognized him as one of those with whom she had been conversing. She remembered that his name was Allen.

"I couldn't find a German doctor, so I asked for help next door," Hertha said.

After Allen looked at her mouth, he said, "Rosemarie, be ready to go to the dispensary at eight o'clock tomorrow morning. I will take you there. Make sure that you bring your American birth certificate with you. I'm sure the doctor can prescribe the necessary medication."

The following morning, Allen pulled up in a jeep and took Romi to the dispensary. He led the way as they entered the dispensary. Rosemarie blushed when he prankishly hollered at the guys who were lined up to see the doctor, "Pull up your pants! A young lady is coming through!"

The guys in line stared at Romi in wonder, and their gaze remained fixed on her as Allen led her to the reception desk. The medic at the desk did not even ask to see her birth certificate, when he noticed the Brooklyn accent as she talked to him.

When a GI came out of the doctor's office, Allen motioned her to go in.

"Won't I be bucking the line?" Romi asked.

"Yeah, but they won't mind," Allen responded.

✚✚✚

"You must be the young lady for whom Allen made an appointment," the doctor said.

Romi nodded.

"Well, let's take a look."

While he examined her mouth, the doctor inquired how she had been caught up in war-torn Germany. Romi reiterated her story that she had told so many times in the last few days.

After the doctor concluded the examination, he said, "I believe you have trench mouth. What kind of meat have you been eating recently?"

"We don't get to eat a lot of meat, but I did have a little canned meat a while ago."

"Aha! Canned meat could be the cause if its shelf life has been exceeded, or if it was not processed properly in the first place. I don't have the proper medication for you, but I can send you to a dentist who does. Come back tomorrow morning. You will have to go to another town down the road. We're taking a bunch of GIs there tomorrow, and you can ride along in the ambulance."

✚✚✚

When Romi climbed into the ambulance the following morning, she again drew a lot of stares. The GIs had many questions for her: What was it like to live under Hitler? How did the population put up with the ravages of war? When was she returning to the United States? The dentist confirmed that she had trench mouth, and he gave her the required medication. After several return trips the ulcerations disappeared.

Chapter 51

By the time Walther and his buddy, Joseph Reiner, returned to Berlin in mid-March, the British and American POWs had been evacuated westward. When Walther inquired why he and Reiner had been ordered back to Berlin, the commanding officer told him that they originally were to rejoin their old unit; however, those plans had been superseded by an order of the Berlin garrison that all able-bodied Wehrmacht personnel now in Berlin were to be assigned to combat units.

Two days later, Walther and his friend, Joseph Reiner reported to a unit that was deployed in the elevated terrain known as the Seelow Heights, just west of the city of Kuestrin. The Russians already had taken the city and had established a bridgehead on the west bank of the Oder River. A mere thirty-five miles now separated them from the Berlin city limits.

There was a lull in the fighting, while the Russians busied themselves amassing troops, artillery, and tanks in the bridgehead for the assault on the Seelow Heights that constituted the last natural barrier that lay between the Russians and Berlin.

When the assault started about mid-April, thousands of guns pounded the German line. This initial attack failed, because the German commander, sensing a disaster, had moved his troops back to a second line of defense. Just days later, utilizing strong air support, the Russians resumed their attack. They soon breached the second line of defense. Walther's comrade, Joseph Reiner, was killed by a machine gun burst during that action. When yet a third line was overrun, constant retreat became the only option for the remaining German forces. After a few days, the German lines had been pushed back to the eastern suburbs of Berlin.

✦✦✦

Walther peered out of the basement window of an apartment complex in one of those suburbs. He and two of his comrades had taken up positions in the complex while they waited for the next Russian attack. They were shell shocked from the slaughter at the Seelow Heights and dead tired for lack of sleep.

Germany has been fighting a losing war for some time now, Walther thought, but the fighting goes on unabated. Everyone here knows that the end is near, but the fighting continues, if only to allow as many refugees as possible to flee westward ahead of the Russian hordes. Like the heralding of a deadly plague, the reports of atrocities committed by the Russians in East Prussia have spread and instilled intense fear among the population.

He wondered, what are my options in this endgame? If I survive and become a POW, I still may be shot dead on the spot, or at best, I will have to join the multitudes that are being transported to gulags somewhere in the bowels of Mother Russia. If I run now, I risk being caught by a mobile court martial and hung from a lamp post with a sign around my neck that reads: I was a coward.

He sighed as he concluded that he was just another pawn in this game. There were no viable options available either from friend or from foe.

Soon artillery fire, mortar bursts, and machine gun chatter signaled the next Russian attack. No activity was evident from the view out of the basement window.

"I think they are bypassing the apartment complex," one of Walther's buddies shouted.

The gunfire continued. Suddenly, a loud explosion tore a big hole in the brick wall that separated the basement from the adjoining one. A large chunk of debris hit Walther squarely on one side of his helmet. Just before he blacked out, Walther, squinting through a cloud of mortar dust, saw two Russians standing on the other side of the hole. They had their PPSh-41 submachine guns trained on him and his comrades.

✚✚✚

The insistent prodding of a rifle barrel compelled Walther to come to. When he looked up, he saw that four Russian soldiers were now in the basement. After he got up, a Russian with shouldered rifle motioned Walther to clasp his hands over his head. Walther complied and the Russian frisked him. With more rifle prodding, Walther and his two buddies were led out of the apartment complex.

Once outside, the first thing the Russians did was to deprive the prisoners of their rings. When one of the Russians shouted, *"Uhr! Uhr!"* the captives knew that they were about to lose their watches. Finally, the three Germans had to empty their pockets. After Walther pulled a handkerchief out of his pocket, one of the Russian soldiers, a Mongol, pointed at it and questioned its utility by giving Walther a quizzical look. Walther put the handkerchief to his face and mimicked blowing his nose.

The Russian broke out laughing, and after shaking his head several times, he demonstrated an easier way. He closed one of his nostrils with one finger, while he cleared the other one by forcefully exhaling through it. Still laughing, he snatched the handkerchief away from Walther and threw it on the ground to indicate that he had no use for such decadence.

When the Russians had concluded their search and seize operation, two of them escorted the captives to a POW assembly area.

+ + +

After the morning roll call, sometime in the third week of April 1945, Papa Besler announced that an engineering unit would be dismounting the thirty-seven millimeter guns and replacing them with heavy machine guns mounted on tripods. When someone asked the reason for the change, the battery commander tersely replied that the thirty-seven millimeters were required in the front lines.

"Unteroffiziere Junger and Latner will train the crews of gun numbers two and three," Papa Besler announced and then asked, "Klug, do you remember what they taught you about the heavy machine gun in Lueneburg?"

When Herbert hunched his shoulders, Besler said, "I'll assist you with your crew training."

Several days later, Herbert, responding to a call of nature, took the long walk to the navy compound. While sitting in one of the stalls, he heard low-flying aircraft and gunfire. Suddenly, the remnants of the commode of the adjacent stall were ricocheting around his feet. Pulling up his trousers, he was out of there in no time. Holding his pants up, he ran outside and toward his gun position. Looking to his right, he saw a P-47, closely followed by an Me-109, coming directly toward him. The aircraft appeared to be no more than fifty feet off the ground. Armor-piercing rounds burrowing into the ground directly ahead of him caused him to hit the deck. After the planes passed overhead, he got up, but promptly tripped over a pant leg. He continued toward his gun emplacement holding his pants up with both hands. Gasping for breath when he arrived, he shouted, "Why aren't you shooting?"

Manfred Romke answered, "Papa Besler was on the intercom; he told us not to fire." Looking at Herbert he said, "He probably was afraid that we might shoot down the wrong one."

Still looking at Herbert, he added, "Unless you're going back to the john, you probably ought to button and zip up your pants."

✚✚✚

As the end of April neared, Oberwachtmeister Besler made another announcement: The battery no longer was to shoot at airborne targets. Ammunition was to be reserved for the expected ground fighting.

Herbert thought, Bremen, only about forty miles from here, already is in British hands. Are we going to be engaged in ground combat before this war is over?

On 30 April, Herbert had the 8:00 to 10:00 A.M. watch. Toward the halfway point of his watch, he saw an Me-110 taking off. To his surprise, the Me-110 was towing a small aircraft. It was an Me-163A, the aircraft type that he and his buddies had watched as it performed a short, rocket-powered test flight sometime earlier. As he wondered whether the small aircraft was being evacuated to a safer haven, he heard additional engine noises.

Looking into the sun, he saw three P-47s diving in formation directly at the Me-110, which now had attained an altitude of about one hundred feet. A short burst from the lead

P-47 vaporized the Me-110 in a huge ball of flame. The pilot of the small aircraft was able to unhook the tow line and, after circling sharply, to land in a pasture.

"Apparently the American fighters did not see the towed aircraft, or they paid it no mind, because they mistook it for a glider not worthy of their attention," Herbert reasoned.

On 1 May, the radio broadcast the news of Hitler's death. On 2 May, the Germans blew up the runways at the Nordholz airfield with preset charges. On 4 May, German forces in northwest Germany surrendered unconditionally to Field Marshal Montgomery. All heavy weapons were dismounted and thrown on a pile along with all hand held guns. On 5 May, the British tanks rolled in.

As the tanks arrived, Herbert made an attempt to converse with the incoming troops. However, he soon gave it up; their Scotch brogue did not jell well with his Brooklyn accent.

During the first two weeks the disarmed Germans stayed in their assigned quarters. Herbert thought that the cursed sentry duties finally had come to an end, but he soon was disappointed.

Across the road that ran along the outside of the western fence of the airfield stood a food warehouse. Some genius had decided to post an armed sentry outside of the warehouse after nightfall. One morning, Herbert was tasked with the 4:00 to 6:00 watch. He was issued an unloaded rifle.

Toward the end of his watch, he heard the slow gait of a horse. Looking toward the road, he saw that the approaching horse was hitched to a buggy. On the buggy seat were two British soldiers. Both had a sub-machinegun on their lap.

Herbert took one of them to be an officer. He assumed that the enlisted man seated next to the officer probably was his orderly. The enlisted man was the first to see Herbert. He shouted, "Lieutenant, there's a Kraut with a rifle!"

Keeping the buggy between themselves and Herbert, both men immediately jumped off the buggy and trained their guns on him.

The officer yelled, "Put your hands up!"

The enlisted man yelled, "Drop the rifle!"

Herbert put his hands up and thought, how do I drop my rifle with my hands raised?

Keeping his arms extended, he ever so slowly turned his upper body to the right until the rifle strap slipped off his shoulder, and the weapon fell to the ground.

As the Brits came closer, the enlisted man said, "The bloody sod is just a kid. What's he doing with a rifle?"

Herbert thought, these guys are not Scotch. I can understand them. He didn't know what "bloody sod" meant, but he thought it had a nice ring to it; therefore, he said, "From one bloody sod to another: I was doing sentry duty with an unloaded rifle."

His remark caused four raised eyebrows. Herbert reached for his rifle to show them that it was not loaded.

"Stay away from the rifle!" the enlisted man shouted.

The commotion had attracted the attention of several German POWs. "Offizier! Offizier!" the lieutenant hollered at them, indicating that he wanted to talk to a German officer.

When a German major arrived, the British officer asked whether he spoke English. After the major nodded, the lieutenant told him that there had been a flagrant violation of the surrender terms.

"I'm just trying to keep thieves away from the warehouse. I issued an unloaded rifle to the sentries to let the riffraff know that we mean business," the major said in his defense.

"I understand your problem, but your solution is not viable. Your sentry knows the weapon is not loaded, but my people do not. You are putting your guys at risk, because some hothead might open fire without ever challenging your sentry," the British officer said. The German major did not respond.

"I have to advise my superiors of this incident, and I request that you accompany us on our way back to our battalion headquarters," the lieutenant said. The major nodded. The Brits got back on the buggy and turned it around to go back whence they had come.

Herbert watched them leave. The sight of the German major, trudging beside the buggy bearing the two Brits, underscored the recent events. Herbert thought, Germany has lost the sequel to the war that had been hoped to be the war to end all war. He also thought, with some disappointment, the Brits never commented on my good grasp of the King's English.

The British collected the Germans captured on the airfield and the surrounding area and transported them to makeshift POW camps, which they established on farms approximately eight miles south of the airfield.

Soon after the move, Herbert ran into Oberwachtmeister Besler. "Whatever happened to the visitor?" Herbert asked.

"I don't know. Maybe he took off for home," Besler said.

"Were you hiding him from the Gestapo?" Herbert asked.

Besler laughed and said, "No, the Gestapo were the ones who sent him to us. His stay with us was somewhat of a house arrest."

"What brought that on?"

"The Gestapo intercepted a letter that he had written to his wife wherein he implied that the war was lost. The Gestapo charged him with defeatism and sidelined him here."

"Coming from the Gestapo, wasn't that a light sentence?"

"Not if you consider that he had been demoted from lieutenant colonel to private before they sent him here."

At the end of May, the British moved out, and the Americans moved in. According to the Allied plan to partition Germany at the end of the war, the country had been divided into four zones. Enclosed within the British zone, an enclave was provided that was to be under United States jurisdiction to provide harbor facilities for the American occupation forces. In a northerly direction, the enclave extended just past the airfield at Nordholz.

Two days after the Americans moved in, a convoy of two-and-a-half ton trucks pulled up at the makeshift POW camp. The POWs were ordered onto the vehicles. Half an hour later, the trucks arrived at the Nordholz airfield.

An American sergeant, speaking broken German, lined the POWs up and told them that their job would be to break up and haul away the wrecked concrete of the erstwhile runways, because the Americans were anxious to repave them.

As the sergeant started to form the POWs into groups of about twenty for subsequent work area assignments, an American soldier, with shouldered rifle, approached the sergeant.

Herbert was within earshot when the soldier said, "Hey, Joe, the mess sergeant says he needs some help. How about letting him have one of these guys?"

Because he was in the middle of a count, the sergeant waved him off. After he had established another group, he said, "Yeah,

yeah, go ahead and select one." After a pause, he added, "Don't pick one of the stronger guys; pick one of the runts."

The soldier with the shouldered rifle scanned the lineup. He pointed at Herbert and beckoned him to step forward. He then pointed at Herbert, then at himself, and then toward the administration buildings at the other end of the field. With a wave, he indicated that the boy was to follow him.

As Herbert trolled behind the soldier, he gave the soldier a once-over. He was a young fellow, maybe nineteen, and very tall. Herbert estimated about six foot, five inches. He was wearing khaki fatigues. A shock of red hair stuck out from under his fatigue cap. Herbert thought, he'll be the first American I'll talk to since I left the U.S. six years ago.

Herbert quickened his gait. When he was almost abreast of the soldier, he tapped him on the shoulder and asked, "Hey, Red, how are the Dodgers doing?" Red kept on walking without responding. Herbert surmised that the guy had not heard him. He tapped him a little harder and repeated, "Hey Red, how are the Brooklyn Dodgers doing?"

The soldier stopped, whirled around, looked down at Herbert, and responded, "Jesus Christ! Where did you learn to speak English like that?"

"In Brooklyn."

"In Brooklyn! What are you doing here? How come you're wearing that uniform?"

Herbert told Red about his recent past.

"Well, I'll be damned," Red said. Then he asked, "How did you know my nickname?"

"With that hair, it had to be either Curly or Red. I just took a wild guess."

"Smartass!" Red said with a grin. "C'mon, I'll introduce you to my buddies."

Herbert walked beside the soldier as they continued on their way to the administration buildings.

✦ ✦ ✦

Breakfast was being served when he and the soldier arrived at the mess hall. Once inside, the soldier called out, "Hey you guys, see this kid next to me? This kid's from Brooklyn!"

"Aw, you're full of shit, Red! Is this another one of your goofy jokes?" one guy cried out.

"What's a kid from Brooklyn doing in that uniform?" another one hollered. "Nah, he ain't from Brooklyn!"

Red did not reply; instead, he picked Herbert up by the waist and stood him up on one of the tables and said, "Tell them, kid tell them what you told me!"

Herbert recited his story to a mess hall filled with GIs. While he was talking, he noticed that one GI had taken up position in the doorway that apparently led to the kitchen area. When Herbert concluded his resume, the GI, who had been standing in the doorway, approached the table onto which Herbert had been deposited and said, "Hi, I'm Manuel. I'm the mess sergeant. You will be working for me, OK?"

Herbert nodded.

"Are you hungry?" Manuel asked.

Herbert nodded again.

"Follow me," Manuel said, as he started back toward the kitchen area.

✦ ✦ ✦

The mess sergeant told him to take a seat at one of the kitchen tables and asked one of the kitchen help to whip up a couple of sandwiches for the boy. When the sandwiches were served, Manuel asked Herbert what he would like to drink.

"Do you have a Coca-Cola?"

"Yeah, we got Coke."

"Oh boy, I'll have a Coke."

He wolfed down the sandwich, but he sipped the Coke—he wanted it to last as long as possible.

After he had eaten, Manuel said, "C'mon, I'll show you where you'll be working. You can take the bottle with you."

Once outside, he took Herbert to where the GIs were cleaning their mess kits. He said, "I can't have all these guys traipsing through the kitchen. As you can see, they do their dishwashing out here, after they throw any leftovers into a garbage can inside the building." He pointed to the metal trash cans that were set up in pairs with a gasoline burner under each can. "Each pair of cans forms a dishwashing unit. One can, with soapy water, is for washing, the other is for rinsing. We have two pairs of cans set up to keep the traffic moving. Are you with me, so far?"

Herbert nodded.

"Your job is to fill the cans, to heat the water, and to change the water occasionally. There's a small handcart around here somewhere that you can slide the cans onto when the water needs to be changed. You'll have to dump the water somewhere outside of the traffic area." Manuel looked at Herbert and asked, "Do you think you can handle that?"

"I can do that," Herbert answered.

"OK, I'll leave you out here so that you can get acquainted with the job and perhaps with some of the guys. I understand that from now on your group will be arriving here an hour earlier than you did today. That will give you plenty of time to prepare for the breakfast crowd."

Herbert did get to talk to many of the GIs. While most of them asked him personal questions, some just wanted to know whether he knew of anyone who wanted to sell a Luger or a camera.

When the trucks arrived at the airfield on the following morning, a different sergeant was there to group the POWs for their work area assignments. Herbert did not hang around. He broke rank immediately to head for the mess hall. When the sergeant challenged him in broken German, Herbert, in his best English, said, "I have orders to report directly to the mess sergeant." He kept on walking. Looking back without breaking his stride, he had to chuckle when he saw the sergeant's open-mouthed stare.

The daily truck convoys to the airfield and back to the POW camp were accompanied by a small detachment of guards, perhaps one guard for every three trucks. The guards always rode shotgun in the truck cab. Since the majority of trucks had only the driver occupying the cab, Herbert thought, rather than being smothered in the mass of humanity in the back of the truck, I might as well ask one of those guys whether I can ride up front.

At first, he got some astonished looks whenever he climbed on a truck fender and asked the driver whether he could ride up front with him. After a few days, he didn't have to ask anymore he would hear one of the drivers holler, "Hey, Brooklyn, you can ride in the cab with me!"

Two weeks into the job, Herbert went to see the mess sergeant in his office and told him, "If you can give me two more garbage cans and the burners to go with them, I can streamline that operation out there."

"How will two more cans streamline the operation?" Manuel asked.

"With only two lines to the dishwashers, traffic gets backed up quite a bit at times. Adding another line would help to eliminate that problem."

"I'll see what I can do," Manuel told him.

Two days later, Herbert had two more cans and two additional burners. He set up the new cans some distance from the existing ones and posted a sign that read: One week's worth of laundry = two packs of cigarettes or two chocolate bars. He soon was doing a thriving business.

The first time Manuel saw the sign, he said, "You conned me, you little shit!" But he was laughing as he walked away.

✚✚✚

On an afternoon in late June, Herbert, not being busy, was sitting in the mess hall listening to the gramophone Manuel had set up. Some of the available recordings, he had heard before, such as "Once in a While," some were new to him, among them, Glenn Miller's "In the Mood." Those two became his favorites, and he played them over and over again.

While listening, he was leafing through the U.S. Armed Forces magazine *Stars and Stripes* and came across an article that drew his attention. According to the article, the four Allied occupation zones of Germany had been finalized. Looking at the map that accompanied the article, his heart sank. Both the British and the Americans were yielding substantial areas to Russian occupation. The area ceded by the Americans included the Vogtland, where his mother and sisters had intended to seek refuge when the Russians reached Warsaw.

Herbert did not know whether they had been able get out of Poland in time, but even if they did, they now would be back at square one. This time, another flight westward would be difficult, because the Russians barred inter-zonal traffic.

They couldn't go to the Lienhofs in the Sudetenland; the Czechs were already kicking all the Germans out!

Herbert went to Manuel to ask him why this was happening.

The mess sergeant said, "The zoning was established long before the war ended, and it was confirmed recently when the Allies conferred at Yalta." He looked at the boy and asked, "Why does this bother you?"

"Our home in Hamburg was destroyed during an air raid in 1943. My father, who is in the army, was stationed in an area of Poland that was annexed to Germany after the Polish campaign, and my mother and sisters went to live there to be near him. Besides, they had no place else to go.

"When my father was transferred to Berlin, he told my mother to get out of that annexed area no later than when the Russians took Warsaw. I don't even know whether they got out in time, and if they did, this map tells me that the Russians now are taking over the area where they were going to seek refuge."

"Don't you people ever write one another to convey your latest whereabouts?" the mess sergeant asked.

"People wrote, but there was no guarantee that the mail would reach its destination. I suspect a lot of mail was destroyed en route, and now the German postal system is in complete disarray. Germany is kaput, Manuel," Herbert replied.

"Why are you so concerned about the Russians?" the mess sergeant asked.

Herbert looked at him and said, "Sarge, after you guys have taken a German town, fraternization is one of the first things that comes to mind. When the Russians enter, they rape and pillage!"

"How do you know that?"

"Just ask the thousands of eye witnesses who were able to escape."

The mess sergeant thought a while and said, "How much longer are you going to be a POW? Who has jurisdiction over you?"

"In the camp, I'm still under German jurisdiction. I understand that the British have jurisdiction to demobilize the POWs in this area. Even though you guys are here, as far as the POWs are concerned, this area is still considered to be part of the British occupation zone."

"What will you do, once they let you go?"

"I'll start to look for my family," Herbert answered.

"How are you going to do that?" the mess sergeant asked.

"My family established a rendezvous point in the event that we were separated at war's end," Herbert responded.

"Listen," Manuel said, "if you can't find your family, you come back here. In about four months my unit will have enough points to be shipped back stateside, and we'll take you with us."

"How are you going to do that?" Herbert asked.

"I don't know yet," Manual replied. Looking at the boy, he said, "You're small enough to squeeze into a duffel bag. Could you hold still long enough for someone to tote you across a gangplank to board a ship?"

Herbert laughed and said, "I don't know."

"Well, that would be one way of doing it, maybe not the best way, but my GIs will think of something. Those guys can come up with some amazing ideas. Whenever I give them a seemingly impossible task, they take it as a personal challenge to find a way to get it done. Just remember, if you can't find your family, come back here!"

"You're kidding me, aren't you?" Herbert asked.

"About what?"

"About stuffing me in a duffel bag and all that."

"No, I'm not!"

Herbert was overwhelmed by the mess sergeant's offer. In a choking voice, Herbert muttered, "Thanks…thanks for wanting to help me," and, "I'd…better get back to work."

He left quickly; he didn't want Manuel to notice that he was close to tears.

Chapter 52

One night in early July, Romi was awaked several times by heavy truck traffic. She did not dwell on the commotion, thinking that the Americans might be assembling for a big parade somewhere. In the morning, she asked her mother whether she too had heard the noise. Hertha shook her head and said, "I didn't hear anything."

Shortly thereafter, cousin Hedwig knocked on their bedroom door; she cracked it and said, "You may want to come in here and listen to the radio announcement that is being repeated every ten minutes." Hertha went into the living room.

The announcement advised that according to previous negotiations among the Allies, the Americans were yielding the provinces of Thuringia and Saxony to the Russians.

Citizens were to remain in their homes during the imminent arrival of the Russian occupation troops. All travel between occupation zones remained prohibited.

Cousin Hedwig pulled the window curtain aside to peek outside. "The imminent arrival has already taken place," she said to Hertha. "Take a look." Hertha was shocked when she saw the many Russian soldiers in their brown uniforms. Some were on foot, some were in horse drawn wagons, and many were on horseback. Some of the horsemen were raising lingering clouds of dust, while showing off their riding skills by galloping up and down the dirt road that led past cousin Hedwig's house. Occasionally, she saw a jeep with a red star emblazoned on its hood.

"Why weren't we given some advance notice?" she asked cousin Hedwig.

"Any advance notice probably would have set off a stampede toward the west," Hedwig answered.

"Well, we're going to have to leave. If I had known this was to happen, we'd have left a lot earlier," Hertha said as she rushed back to the bedroom.

"Romi, Hannelore, we're leaving tomorrow," she told her daughters. "Romi, you'll have to help me to get our laundry done and to pack."

"What's the big rush?" Romi asked.

"Take a look outside!"

Hertha hurried back into the living room to talk to cousin Hedwig. When she returned with an armful of clothing, Hannelore was crying. Hertha turned to her youngest and said, "Don't be afraid. We've escaped from those guys once before; now we're going to do it one more time!"

Romi pointed to the clothes her mother was holding and asked, "What's that stuff for?"

"These are Heinz's castoffs. You will be wearing them tomorrow when we leave."

Romi contracted her brows and asked, "Mama, you're not going to make me look like a boy, are you?"

"That is exactly what I'm going to do."

"It won't work, Mama. My long hair will give me away."

"You'll pin your hair up and cover it with Heinz's old hat. If you don't want to do that, I'll have to cut your hair before we leave."

Romi sighed. She didn't want to masquerade as a boy, but she knew that her mother would insist. "My voice will give me away," Romi said as she tried once more to change her mother's mind.

"Then don't talk," Hertha replied.

The following afternoon, a middle-aged woman, a ten-year-old girl, and a fair-complexioned young man left cousin Hedwig's house. The woman and the young man carried a backpack between them. The child, carrying a satchel, followed close behind.

Heinz accompanied them to the railroad station. He tried to talk Hertha into staying, but she was adamant.

"Where will you be going?" Heinz asked.

"To Hamburg, eventually," Hertha answered.

"Why Hamburg? Your former home is now a pile of rubble."

"When Walther left for France, he reminded me that in the event we lost touch with one another at war's end, we would reunite in Hamburg. A former colleague of his promised to take us in, if the need arose."

"You could just as well reunite here," Heinz suggested.

"As it turns out, it would be in the Russian zone of occupation. Walther always told us to stay one step ahead of the Russians, so now we have some catching up to do."

As they boarded the train, Heinz asked, "How far will this train take you?"

"To Erfurt," Hertha replied.

"And then?"

"We'll find out when we get there."

After the train arrived in Erfurt, Hertha inquired about rail connections to the north or west. She was told that there weren't any, that the only serviceable line was the one they came in on.

"What do we do now?" Romi asked.

"Now we start hoofing it!" Hertha replied. Both Romi and Hannelore groaned.

They did not have to ask for immediate directions when they left the station; they merely had to join the trek of refugees that was intent on getting out of the Russian occupation zone. There were refugees from the eastern provinces and folks who had lost their homes to the bombs, all wanting to start over in the west. Some of the refugees had horse and wagon, some had little handcarts; most had only what they could carry. None of them knew how they would manage to cross the zonal border.

Because some folks moved faster than others, the trek soon thinned out. Hertha listened intently while she and the girls walked with another small group. She found out that the best way to arrange overnight lodging when reaching a village was to seek out the burgomaster. The burgomaster usually would direct the refugees to farms, and the lodging almost always would be a spot in the barn or in the hayloft. Hertha's apprehension quickened, when someone cautioned to be off the road before dark.

On the first night, after Hertha and the girls had been assigned a farm, they were invited into the house for some soup; then, they were shown a spot in the barn to spend the night.

Hertha roused the girls at daybreak. She wanted to get back on the road as soon as possible, and she wanted to use the rising sun to orient herself. She knew that if they kept the sunrise at their back, they would be moving in a westerly direction. She told herself to avoid the main roads and to try to keep on moving in a northwesterly direction.

The trek had thoroughly dispersed, and Hertha and her daughters now walked alone most of the time. Occasionally, they were able to hitch a ride on a farm wagon going from one village to another. On one such ride they sat among several pickle barrels. The barrel tops were uncovered, and with every pothole, pickle brine squirted in all directions. At the end of the ride, they, themselves, smelled pickled.

In the afternoon of the second day, they came to a small roadside inn. Hertha said, "Let's stop here for some fruit juice." After she and the girls were seated, two Russian soldiers entered. Hertha took them to be officers. The two Russians gave the threesome more than occasional glances. Hertha became uneasy and said, "Drink up, and let's get out of here." When they were back on the road, Romi, glancing over her shoulder, noticed that the Russians also had left the inn; they were still staring at them, but then they walked away.

That evening, Hertha thanked the lady of the farmstead, to which they had been assigned, for the sandwiches she prepared for them. After the woman had shown them to the barn, Hertha told the girls, "Let's save some of the sandwiches for tomorrow. With some luck, they'll only have to last us until tomorrow night."

On the third day, opportunities to hitch rides on farm wagons grew more scarce than heretofore. Hertha and the girls continued to plod along isolated dirt roads. Little Hannelore complained and cried a lot. Hertha thought, no wonder, she probably has to take three steps for our every two.

Toward evening they approached another village. It was like all the other villages they had passed, except that it seemed to be enveloped in deadly silence. Not a soul or farm animal was to be seen. When they found the burgomaster's residence, Hertha asked him, "What's going on? This place seems like a ghost town!"

The burgomaster replied, "We had some problems here last evening. Three of our young women were raped by drunken Russian soldiers." He saw the dread etched on Romi's and Hertha's faces and said, "You'd best get off the road as soon as possible. I know a nearby farm family who surely will take you in. You may have to pound on the door a while, but don't become disheartened."

The burgomaster's warning to be insistent proved to be prescient. No one responded after Hertha had knocked on the door of the farm house several times. After her next attempt, a window curtain was pulled aside, and soon someone cracked the door.

"What do you want?" a male voice asked.

"We're seeking refuge for the night," Hertha said.

The window curtain was pulled aside once more, and a woman's voice said, "Let them in."

Once the threesome was inside, the lady of the house said, "I'm Maria, and this is my husband Jakob." Hertha reciprocated by introducing herself and her daughters.

Maria said, "I'm sorry to have kept you waiting so long. We are all a little fidgety right now. Yesterday evening Russian soldiers intercepted three girls coming home from the fields and had their way with them."

Hertha nodded and said, "The burgomaster told us what happened."

Romi took off her hat, removed several pins, and dropped her bunched up hair down to her shoulders.

"Ah, the young man really is a young woman!" Maria exclaimed as she watched the long hair unfurl. To Romi she said, "I suspected as much, but only because your mother introduced you as Rosemarie. Looking at Hertha, she said, "It was wise of you to put her in man's clothing I'm assuming that it was you who prompted her to don the disguise."

Hertha nodded.

"The mere perception of having a young man in the group should be helpful," Maria said.

Romi countered with, "Let's hope the perception is not put to the test!"

Maria gave her a sympathetic look and nodded. Then she asked, "When did you eat last?"

"We had one or two leftover sandwiches this morning," Hertha replied.

"Well, you must be starved," Maria said. "I have a casserole on the stove. Why don't you join us?"

After the meal, Jakob told Hertha that she and her daughters could safely spend the night in the hayloft. Once they were in the loft, he would take the ladder down and hide it overnight. In the morning, he would bring the ladder back.

Hertha did not sleep well that night. At daybreak, she heard a scraping sound coming from the loft entrance. She cautiously investigated and saw that Jakob had replaced the ladder. "Good morning," Hertha called out.

"Good morning," Jakob responded. "I hope I didn't wake you."

"No, no. It's time for us to get ready to leave."

"Before you leave, come inside. Maria will have breakfast ready."

"She needn't go out of her way for us."

"No problem," Jakob said.

After Maria fed them, Hertha, Romi, and little Hannelore were back on the road. Hertha and Romi, carrying the backpack between them, led the way; Hannelore, occasionally shifting the satchel from one hand to the other, followed close behind.

"Did you ask Maria for directions to the new zone demarcation line?" Romi asked.

"I asked, but she doesn't know. All she could tell me was to keep moving westward. I already knew that."

As they moved along the road, the pasture land on either side gave way to grain fields. The wheat and rye fields were shoulder high, thereby obscuring any reference points except for what could be seen when following the path of the road. After having walked for several hours, they had yet to meet another soul.

"Mama, I have to go to the bathroom!"

Hertha and Romi stopped. "Well, go into the field a little ways," Hertha said.

"I need some toilet paper."

Hertha groped through the backpack until she found the remnants of a roll. "Don't use more than you have to. That is all we have left."

"I won't."

While waiting out Hannelore's excursion into the grain field, Romi said, "We now have everything in common with those other people."

"What other people?" her mother asked.

"I'm thinking about the refugees I occasionally helped off the freight trains back in Altburgund. They were hungry; now we are as hungry as they were. They had nothing but the clothes on their back; now we have but a little more. They pooped in the streets; now we poop in the fields. They were dirty and smelled bad; now we are like them," Romi said while brushing away her tears.

"Honey, we have joined their ranks. We, too, are refugees. Yes, we are unkempt, but be thankful that we have been sheltered and given food these past few nights. We can't expect the farmers to run full service hotels for us."

Hertha gave her daughter a hug and said, "Things will get better, once we can cross over to one of the western zones."

"You really mean 'if' we can cross…don't you?" Romi countered. Her mother sighed and did not answer.

They continued to trudge along the desolate road in the scorching heat of the July sun. Varying air densities of the hot summer day caused mirages of puddles along the road. By mid-afternoon, the threesome was exhausted.

"I think we're going to have to find a place to rest for a few days," Hertha said. "My feet are starting to swell from all this walking."

After the grain fields on their right gave way to woodland, they soon spied a small inn tucked in the woods. Hertha and her daughters were relieved when the innkeeper told them that he had a room available.

✚✚✚

Three days later, Hertha and the girls were on the road again. The rest period at the inn had buoyed their spirits.

A short way from the inn, the road was again bracketed by grain fields on either side. Hertha noticed that the road had taken a turn toward the north.

Toward noon, a commotion coming from the grain stalks just ahead and to the left side of the road caused Hertha and her daughters to stop dead in their tracks.

"Quick, hide in the grain," Hertha whispered.

As they watched, a man stuck his head out of the wheat field and scanned the road on both sides. He motioned to someone behind him that the coast was clear. Out of the grain field stepped three German soldiers.

Hertha breathed a sigh of relief and said, "C'mon, let's ask them for directions."

This time, it was the soldiers who were astonished to see a woman, a young fellow, and a child appear out of nowhere.

"Where are you headed?" one of the soldiers asked.

"We're trying to cross into one of the western zones," Hertha answered.

"How long have you been on the road?" the soldier asked.

"We left Erfurt seven days ago, but we stopped to rest the last three days."

"Erfurt? Erfurt must be close to fifty miles from here!"

Hertha shrugged and asked, "Where are you heading?" "We just crossed the demarcation line yesterday. We're headed to our homes further east."

"Are we going in the right direction if we keep following this road?" Hertha asked.

"No, you should head west right now," he said, as he pointed into the wheat field. "If you go any further north and then turn west, you are likely to run into a Russian bivouac in a wooded area. Just turn west here. Eventually you will come to the woods; by staying low in the underbrush while you pass through, the Russians won't be able to see you."

"What comes after the woods?" Hertha asked.

"More grain fields. You won't want to stay on any roads. You'll be entering a no-man's land. The roads will be patrolled; the Russians will try to intercept you. If you run, they will shoot to kill!"

Hertha showed her distress by covering her face with her hands.

The soldier tried to reassure her, "You'll be all right. Just take your time and always look before you leap." He gave Romi what she interpreted as a knowing smile and patted Hannelore on the cheek; then, he signaled his companions that it was time to leave. The soldiers disappeared into the grain field on the opposite side of the road.

Hertha said, "We won't be able to walk two abreast with the backpack between us. I'll strap the pack on my back. Romi, you take the satchel and follow me. Hannelore, you stay close behind Romi. Let's go!"

After an hour, they came to the woods. Peering out of the field, Hertha could see that the Russians had erected tents in the woods an appreciable distance to the right from where she stood. Two Russian tanks were parked at the edge of the woods near the tents. Hertha studied the underbrush and whispered to the girls, "If we keep our heads down, they won't be able to see us." She admonished, "No talking until we're through the woods."

They moved forward, slowly. Every time one of them snapped a twig, they instinctively stopped. Soon they were able to see the grain fields, to which the German soldier had alluded.

After they were once again concealed in the fields, they plodded onward. At intervals the fields were crisscrossed by dirt roads. Each time they came upon such a road, a scan in both directions preceded their scurrying across into the field on the other side. In late afternoon, the threesome reached another crossing point. This time the intersection was not another dirt road, it was a river embankment!

Hertha's spirits sank when she saw the river. They sank even more when she saw the bridge a short way downstream: The inner piers of the bridge had been blown away, causing most of the roadway to drop into the river. The superstructure, lacking the support of the inner piers, had dropped toward the water, such that its center now was only about a foot above the river; the main beams that had horizontally spanned the river, now formed an inverted arch between the remaining bridge piers.

Hertha studied the bridge. She noted that the main beams, although deformed, had not been broken. She also noted that a pedestrian handrail, its balusters anchored to the nearer main beam, had followed the deformation of the main beam, and it appeared to be unbroken.

"What do we do now?" Romi asked.

"We'll stay hidden until after dark, then we will cross the bridge."

"There is no roadway in the center portion of the bridge!" Romi exclaimed.

"We'll walk across, by stepping sideways along that main beam and holding onto the handrail."

"What about her?" Romi asked as she nodded toward Hannelore. "Won't she be too frightened to go across?"

"Hannelore is little. I'll keep her directly in front of me as we maneuver across to the other side. I'll carry the backpack. There is a length of rope in the backpack. You can use the rope to tie the satchel to your shoulder. That way, you'll have both hands free to hold onto the handrail."

"When do you want to do this?" Romi asked.

"We'll have to wait until after dark," Hertha said, "but first, we'll rummage through the backpack for the darkest clothes we can wear."

While they hid in the wheat field and waited for nightfall, Hertha told Hannelore how they were going to cross the bridge.

Hannelore's tears glistened as she wailed, "What will I do if you fall?"

"Shh!" Hertha admonished. "Get that out of your head. I am not going to fall!" she whispered.

They approached the bridge under a starlit sky. Hertha thought, thank God that there is no moon.

She showed Hannelore how to place her feet on the main beam and to hold onto the handrail. She then straddled the little girl from behind and said, "We are going to cross the bridge by taking little steps sideways. Hertha placed her right foot on the outside of Hannelore's right foot; then she moved her left foot toward the river, all the while holding onto the handrail. She told Hannelore, "Now you shift your feet close together until your left foot is next to, but not on, my left foot." Hannelore giggled nervously. "Then, you reposition your hands, one at a time. After you have done that, I will again put my right foot next to, but not on, your right foot." Hannelore giggled again. "And then we keep doing that over and over again until we have crossed the bridge. OK?"

Hannelore nodded.

"Romi, you follow us," she whispered. "Don't look down at the water!" She did not remind the girls that neither she nor they could swim.

✚✚✚

An hour and a half later, they reached the other bank.

"What now?" Romi asked.

"Now, we scurry up to the wheat field we saw from the other side."

"And then?" Romi asked.

"Then we get some well-earned rest," her mother replied.

After they lay down in the field, Hannelore said, "The croaking of the frogs is keeping me awake."

"Pretend that they are singing a lullaby for you," her mother suggested.

Chapter 53

A week after the mess sergeant offered to help him to return to the U.S., Herbert's cushy job at the mess hall abruptly came to an end. One evening, after the POWs had been transported from the airfield back to the camp, he was told to report to the ranking German officer of the camp.

The officer turned out to be the major who had been involved in the controversy that had evolved while Herbert was on guard duty at the warehouse.

"Klug, I understand that you are fluent in English."

Herbert stood at attention and replied, "Yes, sir!"

"Where did you learn the language?"

"I was born in New York, and I lived there for eleven years."

"I see. I am going to send you to a former German division staff in Cuxhaven. The British are developing a program to clear the German harbor entrances of mines. To do this, they are looking for German volunteers to man the minesweepers."

"Are you asking me to volunteer?" Herbert asked.

"No, no. All the paperwork is in English; therefore, a German division staff has been tasked to translate it into German. Do you think you can be of any help?"

"I suppose so, sir."

"Good, be here at seven o'clock in the morning, and bring all your stuff with you since you may not be coming back here."

+++

A British sergeant rolled up in a jeep on the following morning to drive Herbert to Cuxhaven. Herbert sat up front with the sergeant. On the way, they engaged in small talk and exchanged cigarette brands. Herbert offered the sergeant a Chesterfield, while he tried one of the sergeant's Players.

When they arrived at a school, the sergeant said, "Your people are set up in the school gymnasium."

Herbert acknowledged with a nod and said, "Thanks for the ride."

As he entered the gym, he noticed that it had been converted into a workroom. Many desks had been brought in, and both German and British personnel busied themselves at their respective workstations.

Herbert had barely set down his duffel bag, when a German captain turned toward him and said, "Hey, orderly, how about getting me a cup of coffee?"

Herbert stood at attention and said, "I'm not an orderly, sir."

With furrowed brow, the captain asked, "If you're not an orderly, what are you doing here?"

"I'm here to help you translate the British documents."

Herbert's response elicited a chuckle, "You're going to help us with the translations?" and then laughter. The officer turned serious and fired three questions in quick succession at Herbert in English. Herbert's answers came just as quickly also in English.

"Well, well," the captain said with a smile, "perhaps you can be of some help. Wait here, while I find someone to brief you on an assignment."

After the captain left, Herbert looked around the gym. He noticed that the next lowest German rank after his lowly grade of Luftwaffe Auxiliary was that of first lieutenant!

+++

Having spent the night outdoors, Hertha and the girls resumed their trek through the grain fields at daybreak.

Toward mid-morning, they came upon a paved road that crossed the field. "Let's follow this road to the north for a while," Hertha suggested.

"The soldier said that we should stay off the roads," Romi reminded her mother."

"There's no one here. If we see or hear someone, we'll mosey back among the grain stalks."

They continued on the blacktop until they came to a fork in the road: one branch turned toward the northeast, the other to the northwest.

They stopped. "What now?" Romi asked.

"Honey, I have no idea where we are, but we certainly want to stay away from any path that leads us farther east," her mother replied.

They selected the left fork and trudged onward. When the road took another turn to the left, they saw the barrier, similar to that of a customs gate, blocking the road. Two tanks were parked just beyond the barrier, one on each side of the road.

"They're not Russian, Mama!" Romi cried out.

"How do you know?" Hertha asked.

"The stars on the gun turrets. They're not red, they're white! Those are American tanks, Mama!"

Romi was beside herself with joy. She handed the man's hat she was wearing to her mother and started to run toward the barrier. While running, she removed the hairpins and let her freed tresses fall to her shoulders. Hertha and Hannelore also started to run.

As the three females approached the barrier, a bewildered GI held up his hand and told them in broken German that he was not allowed to let anyone pass.

"But we're Americans!" Romi cried out.

Taken aback, the GI asked, "You're what?!"

"We're Americans! We got stuck in Germany soon after the war started, and now we're trying to go back home."

"Holy sh…" the GI caught himself. He glanced backward over his shoulder and shouted, "Hey Mac, come here, but watch your language. I'm talking to a young lady from the U.S. of A."

Mac sauntered to the barrier and said, "Larry, I think you've been away from home too long. What are you hallucinating about?" he asked.

"These ladies and the little girl are Americans. They're trying to get out of the Russian zone. Turning to Romi, Larry said, "Tell him what you told me."

After Romi obliged, Mac said, "Well, I'll be…"

By this time, a seemingly whole platoon of GIs had gathered at the barrier.

"Why can't you let us pass?" Hertha asked Mac.

"We can't let anyone pass without the captain's permission," Mac answered. "I'll try to reach him on the phone. Just be patient and hang around."

"We won't be going anywhere," Hertha called out after him, as he strode toward one of the tanks.

Hertha and Romi told the GIs of their recent experiences. Even little Hannelore, whose dormant English came back to life, was talking to some of the soldiers. She soon was clutching a fistful of chocolate bars.

Everyone looked up when a jeep came tearing down the road

toward the barrier on the soldiers' side. After hitting the brakes, a young officer got out of the jeep.

Pointing at the threesome, Mac said, "Sir, these are the folks I called you about."

Romi and Hertha, who had seated themselves in the roadside grass, got up and approached the barrier.

The captain rested his hands on the barrier and asked, "Who wants to be the spokesperson?"

Romi, her heart pounding wildly because their immediate fate now was up to this man, lifted her hand. She thought, I hope he is as compassionate as he is handsome.

Then she told him her story. When she finished, she added, "My sister's and my U.S. birth certificate are in that satchel my mother is holding."

The captain smiled and said, "Your accent has already convinced me that you could not have been born anywhere else but in Brooklyn. But I'll gladly take a look at your birth certificates."

While Hertha put the certificates back into the satchel, the officer asked her for her ID. As Hertha handed him her papers, she noticed that he was wearing a ring embossed with the Star of David.

The captain studied her ID and repeatedly shifted his glance from the ID to her. Hertha thought, is he trying to match my countenance to the picture, or is he wondering whether the swastika on the validation stamp of my ID singles me out as a Nazi?

The captain returned the ID to Hertha and said, "Boys, let the two girls pass..." He took another look at Hertha and added, "and the mother too."

Romi yelled, "Hurray, I could kiss all of you!" Her comment elicited several responses, such as: "Me first!" "Why not?" and "Anytime, honey."

As the captain climbed back into the jeep, he motioned to Mac and said, "Take them to our canteen and get them some sandwiches and something to drink."

"Yes, sir."

When the captain's jeep pulled away, both Romi and Hertha had tears in their eyes. Hannelore continued to munch a chocolate bar.

✚ ✚ ✚

When the threesome was on the road again, they felt reborn. No longer did they have to hide in the fields; no longer did Romi have to masquerade as a boy.

"Where are we going now?" Romi asked.

"We're heading for the major highway up ahead which will take us to Kassel. In Kassel, we'll look up your father's parents. Perhaps we can stay with them for a few days and get some rest."

"How do you know there is a highway up ahead and that it will take us to Kassel?"

"I told Larry that we had no idea where we were. When he told me that we were about twenty miles east of Kassel, I asked him for directions," Hertha replied.

✚ ✚ ✚

After Hertha and the girls had walked along the highway shoulder for a short time, a jeep, occupied by a single GI, pulled up alongside of them. "Hey, Brooklyn, do you need a lift?" the driver asked Romi.

"How do you know…?"

The GI responded with a grin and said, "The grapevine is working overtime."

Romi took the seat next to the driver; Hertha and Hannelore climbed in the back.

"Where are you headed?" the soldier asked Romi.

"Right now, we're trying to go to Kassel."

"Well, I can save you about seven miles of walking," he said.

During the short ride, Romi answered his many questions about her being in Germany and having to roam the German countryside with her family members.

When the driver had to turn off the highway, the threesome continued their walk along the shoulder. At times, one of the ubiquitous two-and-a-half ton U.S. Army trucks would pass by. Romi decided to hitch a ride. The next time one of the trucks came along, she thumbed the driver and yelled at the top of her lungs, "Hey, we need a ride!" As the truck passed, Romi dropped her arm in disappointment.

Suddenly, new hope: the truck brakes squealed, and the truck began to back up. When the cab was alongside Romi, the driver leaned toward the highway shoulder and asked, "Did I just hear what I thought I heard? Did you say you need a ride?"

"That's what I said!"

"Are you CIA or something?"

"Nah, I'm a displaced person from Brooklyn."

"What are you doing way over here?"

"I'll tell you all about it, if you can take me and my mother and sister to Kassel."

"I can take you to the southern suburbs of the city. From there you can follow the river all the way into the city center."

"OK."

"Help your mom and little sister to hop in the back; then, you can ride up front and tell me all about it."

After Hertha and Hannelore were settled in the back and the truck took off again, Hannelore asked her mother, "How come Romi gets to sit up front all the time?"

"She gets to sit up front because she is a young lady, and these young soldiers haven't been able to talk to a young lady in a long time," her mother said. After a pause, she added, "I'm glad you're still a little girl."

"Why?"

"Well, if you weren't, I'd be sitting back here all by myself."

Hannelore gave her mother a hug and said, "No, you wouldn't."

Hertha thanked the driver when he dropped them off at the river. They could see the skyline of Kassel, more specifically, the remnants of the skyline that had not been turned into rubble.

"This place looks as bad as Erfurt," Romi said to her mom.

"I expect all the cities through which we'll be passing will look the same way," Hertha replied as she remembered the destruction she had seen in Erfurt and in Hamburg after the raids of the summer of '43.

They started walking north on the path that wound its way along the river bank. Soon, Hertha and the girls came upon a boat landing. A small river boat was docked at the landing, and four GIs were on board. The GIs waved at the threesome. Romi waved back and yelled, "Hey, are you guys planning on cruising downstream?"

As if on command, all eyes aboard focused on Romi.

"What did you say?" one of the soldiers asked.

"I'm wondering whether you can give us a lift to the city center."

Instead of answering the question, one of the GIs asked,"Where did you learn to speak English like that?"

"We took a wrong turn in Brooklyn some time ago, and wound up in this mess," Romi responded.

Romi noted the animated discussion that took place among the soldiers. When she saw them all nodding in unison, she knew that she, her mother, and her sister were about to be invited to take a river cruise.

+++

The threesome took to the rubble-strewn streets after the soldiers dropped them off in downtown Kassel. They found Grandfather Klug's apartment to be unscathed; however, the lady, who answered the door and now occupied the apartment, told them that the elderly couple had been evacuated. After some searching, she was able to give Hertha the address of Walther's oldest sister, Ella, who lived on the outskirts of the city.

Ella did not recognize Hertha and the girls immediately. It had been five years since she had last seen them, and now they stood on her doorstep, disheveled from being on the road for days on end.

"I'm Hertha and these are my daughters, Rosemarie and Hannelore."

Ella puzzled retrospectively for a moment and then said, "Yes, of course." She pointed at Hannelore and said, "That one was only about five years old when I last saw her. C'mon in." Once they were inside, she asked, "What brings you here?"

"Well, we had to run from the Russians when they advanced into the Warthegau back in January; a little over a week ago, we ran again when the Russians claimed their occupation zone. We had sought refuge in the Vogtland, but when the Russians marched in, we moved out."

"The Russians let you out?" Ella asked.

"Are you kidding? We stumbled upon an American checkpoint along the zonal border. When we showed the girls' American birth certificates to the soldiers, they let us enter the American zone." Hertha replied.

"You were lucky to get out. Where are your menfolk?"

Sighing, Hertha said, "We haven't heard from either one since early March. Walther was transferred to France in late January."

Ella's eyes clouded with tears. "Walther...we named our only child after him," she said. "Our son's class was evacuated from Kassel. He would still be alive, if he had stayed with us. He died in the evacuation camp shortly after contracting pneumonia."

"Yes, I remember your letter."

"Your son, Herbert, where is he?"

"He's been with an antiaircraft unit since late '43!"

"So you don't know where they are or whether they survived the war," Ella said.

"That's about it," Hertha replied

"What are your plans?" Ella asked.

"Well, we have to go back to Hamburg. We decided long ago to meet there in the event we lost contact with one another at war's end. A former colleague of Walther's, Hans Kurscharper, suggested his home as a rendezvous point as a matter of fact, he offered to take us in if we had no place to go. We stopped here hoping that we could rest for a day or two before we continue our journey."

"That won't be a problem. Why don't the three of you go clean up a bit while I fix us some supper," Ella said.

When they sat down at the supper table, Hertha asked,

"Where is Fritz?"

"My husband is temporarily out of work. As you know, he's been with the postal service for years, but with most of the infrastructure being in shambles, they are unable to move stuff at the present time, so he went to help out on his brother's farm not far from here. I expect him to be back home in another week."

During supper, Romi told Ella of their flight through the Russian zone.

"You were lucky that you didn't run into a Russian patrol," Ella said after Romi had recounted their experiences. "Now you only have to cross into the British zone at some point to get back to Hamburg."

"Do you know of a good spot to sneak across?" Hertha asked.

"You won't have to sneak across," Ella replied. "The British and the Americans have opened their zones to folks who have been displaced and are now traveling to return to their original dwelling place. All you have to do is to verify your hometown by showing your ID at the border checkpoint, and they will let you cross."

"That's a relief," Hertha said. "Are the railroads back in operation?"

"Well, you won't find any long distance service from here to Hamburg. Many roadbeds have been cobbled back together as single track only; therefore, at the present time, the railroad people are limited to performing a shuttle service between the larger cities. You will have to make your way back in stages."

"If that's the way it has to be, so be it. Having to transfer from train to train certainly beats having to walk," Hertha said.

Two days later, in early morning, Hertha and the girls joined the crowd at the Kassel main station. While waiting for the announcement of a northbound train, the threesome stood close to three German soldiers who had placed their duffel bags on the platform and were sitting on them. Two of them were older men; the third man was a youngster. Hannelore watched the younger man as he retrieved a small container from his duffel bag. After sitting down again and opening the container, he proceeded to spread margarine on a slice of bread. When he was finished, he noticed the little girl's stare. Without a word, the young soldier broke the slice in halves and offered one to Hannelore. Hannelore looked at her mother. When Hertha nodded, the little girl accepted the tidbit.

After Hertha thanked the soldier, he asked, "Do you mind if my buddies and I travel with you?" Pointing to the other two, he added, "They are headed for Berlin, and I'm bound for Hamburg." He introduced himself as Artie.

"We're also traveling to Hamburg," Hertha replied, and "We won't mind your company a bit." After waiting for hours, a train heading for Hanover was announced.

"That's for us!" Romi said.

The three soldiers formed a phalanx for the three females and elbowed their way onto the train. Being first on, they were able to acquire seats for Hertha and the girls.

During the train ride to Hanover, Hertha complained about an abscess on her neck. Artie mentioned that he also had one, but on his upper arm.

"It throbs all the time," he said.

Hertha nodded and said, "Same here."

"Once we're in Hanover, I'm going to ask the Red Cross people to direct me to a doctor to have it lanced. Maybe you want to come along and have yours done, too," Artie said.

"I might take you up on that," Hertha replied.

It was after dark when the train pulled into Hanover. When a railroad official told them that no trains would be available until morning, the three soldiers and Hertha and her daughters sought overnight refuge.

The train station and the immediate vicinity had been heavily bombed. They traipsed through rubble until they came upon several barracks that had been abandoned by the Wehrmacht. Although other refugees had already made themselves at home there, they were able to find two vacant rooms that were adjacent to one another. The soldiers occupied one room, and Hertha and the girls settled in the other one. The rooms were completely unfurnished, which meant that they would be sleeping on the floor. On the far end of the hall, one room had the word *Toilet* scribbled on the door. The scribbling was superfluous because the stench emanating from the room left no doubt as to what was on the other side of the door.

The room was as bare as the others, except that a walkway had been erected along its perimeter. A continuous low railing, affixed to the inside of the walkway served as the bench that one would normally find in an outhouse. Beyond the walkway, the floor of the room was covered with sand.

Several rakes leaned against the walls of the room. Essentially, the "toilet" was a litter box for humans. It had one redeeming element: an inside door lock.

"Who would even think of putting up such a room?" Romi asked her mother.

"Probably someone who knew that this part of the city has lost its water supply." Hertha answered.

On the following morning, the two older soldiers left the group, since they would now be heading in a different direction. Artie asked whether it would be alright if he could continue to travel with Hertha and the girls. Hertha told him that that would be fine and that she and the girls would feel a lot safer having a man accompany them.

The foursome stood in line at a Red Cross soup kitchen, where they were given soup and a cup of coffee. After they had received a little nourishment, Artie inquired whether a doctor was available. He was directed to a Red Cross tent adjacent to the soup kitchen.

"Mrs. Klug, I found a doctor. Let's go and see whether we can get our boils lanced," Artie said.

Hertha looked at him apprehensively but said, "Anything is better than having to put up with this pain."

She and Artie walked to the tent while Romi and Hannelore sat down on a nearby bench.

When they returned an hour later, Hertha said, "The good news is that the doctor took care of our needs. The bad news is that the doctor strongly advised us to come back in two days so he can verify that the infections have been cleared."

"We won't have to go back to those barracks. The doctor gave me the address of a school where we might find shelter."

Hertha and the girls, with Artie in tow, wandered through more debris until they found the school which had survived the bombing raids unscathed. It was teeming with refugees, and, at best, it would be a shelter from the elements. They soon found out that in order to bed down, one had three choices: requisition a bench, arrange three chairs, or accept the floor.

They spent two monotonous days in the school building.

Exacerbating the monotony was the fare offered by the Red Cross soup kitchen, which they visited three times a day: In the morning, the menu consisted of a slice of bread with ersatz coffee for adults or skimmed milk for children; at noon and in the evening, the soup kitchen offered a bowl of either potato or turnip soup, depending on which of the two had been declared the soup du jour.

After the doctor determined that both Hertha and Artie were clear of infection, the foursome trudged back to the Hanover station where they boarded a train that took them to Celle, a town some forty-five miles to the northwest. Not knowing anyone in town and not wanting to miss the possibility of a train heading northward, they decided to spend the night in the station waiting room.

Artie went out to find a soup kitchen and returned with a little sustenance.

In the morning, the station PA system announced a train that would terminate in a southern suburb of Hamburg.

"Hurray!" Hertha cried out. "This will be a big step forward!"

Once again, with Artie in the lead, they jostled their way onto a train. Six hours later, the train arrived in the Hamburg suburb of Harburg.

Upon inquiring about train service into the city, Artie was told that all service was limited to freight; there was no passenger service.

"What do we do now?" Romi asked.

"Since there is no passenger service, let's meander over to the marshalling yards," Artie suggested.

After they arrived at the yard, they could see from their vantage point that two freight trains were being assembled on the second and third tracks nearest to them. Several freight cars, empty and decoupled, stood on the first track.

"You and your daughters best hide in one of those decoupled cars while I do a little reconnaissance. We want to stay out of sight of the railroad security guards," Artie said to Hertha. He helped them into one of the cars before he left.

Dusk was setting in by the time Artie returned.

"The train that is being assembled on the third track is headed for Hamburg," he said.

"How do you know that?" Hertha asked.

"A railroad official told the train engineer what his assignment would be after he completed the Hamburg run."

While the foursome looked longingly through the fading light at the train on the third track, they saw a woman walking stealthily along the side of the train. Suddenly, she stopped and rolled open a car door. She climbed inside and the door of the car rolled shut.

"That's for us," Artie said. "Remember which car that was. When it gets a little darker, we will join that lady."

When Artie rolled open the door of the freight car, he could barely discern the group of about ten people that were huddled on the floor at one end of the car.

He was greeted with antagonistic whispers, "Shh!" "Stay out!" "Close the door!"

Artie whispered back, "There's enough room for four more!" He helped Hertha and the girls aboard; then, he hoisted himself into the car.

But for a shaft of waning light entering through a screened window near the top of the car, total darkness would have reigned after Artie rolled the door shut as quietly as he could. Many scowling eyes gazed at the newcomers.

"Hey, don't be getting all bent out of shape," Artie said, keeping his voice low. "We have as much right to be here as you have."

"Just let's keep it quiet," someone whispered.

They sat in silence. Now and then the car would receive a jolt, indicating that another car or string of cars had been added to the train.

Suddenly, an old man fell victim to a coughing spell.

"Keep him quiet!" someone murmured.

"How?" someone else asked.

"Put a hand over his mouth," Artie suggested.

The coughing stopped, but the ensuing silence was broken by a voice from outside that said, "They're in here!"

With that, the door was rolled open, and one of two railroad security guards scanned his flashlight over the huddled group.

"Everybody out! You should know by now that regulations forbid your hitching a ride!" he shouted.

Amidst sullen complaints, the car was evacuated.

"I want you to leave the marshalling yards immediately!" the guard with the flashlight demanded.

The group dispersed. "What now?" Romi asked.

As Hertha shrugged, the train started to move. Thoroughly disheartened, the threesome watched the train slowly pick up speed.

"Where is Artie?" Romi asked.

"I don't know," her mother replied.

Crestfallen, the threesome continued to watch the freight cars roll by. As the caboose passed by, they could just make out the waving figure sitting on the top step—it was Artie!

"Mama, he's leaving us!" Romi cried out.

"It would appear that way," Hertha said. She looked at Romi and said, "Don't begrudge his going on his own. He's close to home and we do tend to hold him up."

They watched as the taillights of the caboose seemed to fade; then Hertha said, "C'mon girls, let's go back to the Harburg station and try to get some rest because tomorrow we'll have to start hoofing it again."

✚✚✚

Hertha and the girls wandered two more days through the annexed suburbs of Harburg and Wilhelmsburg on their way to Hamburg proper. During that interim, they spent a night, along with many others, in the waiting room of the Wilhelmsburg train station.

In areas that had been devastated by the bombings, the threesome walked along streets barely cleared of debris that now seemed to lead nowhere. They saw folks scavenging the rubble for reusable bricks and building timber. After chipping the mortar off the bricks, they were using them and the beams to refurbish the basements of bombed out houses into temporary living quarters. Those folks were driven by the singular purpose of getting a roof over their head, and they paid little mind to the refugees walking the streets.

When the threesome reached the former city limits of Hamburg, they headed for the nearest subway station. They were overjoyed when they found out that connections were available to Blankenese, the western suburb of Hamburg where the Kurscharpers resided. Hertha now faced a new worry: had the Kurscharper home survived the bombings? She did not mention her concern to her daughters.

After the subway reached the terminal station of Blankenese, Hertha noted that the suburb had remained relatively untouched by the raids. As they rounded the curve in the road that would bring the Kurscharper home into view, Hertha sighed with relief—the house was intact!

Ilse Kurscharper answered the doorbell.

"Well, look who's here!" she exclaimed.

Hertha's trepidations prevented her from abiding by the usual greeting courtesies. In a voice trembling with anxiety, she asked, "Have you had any word from Walther or my son, Herbert?"

"I'm afraid not," Mrs. Kurscharper answered.

Now near tears, Hertha said, "Ilse, we have no place to go. Is your offer still good?"

"Of course it is. Please come in."

Chapter 54

Herbert had little trouble translating the assignments given him at the former division staff, although he frequently did have to reach for one of the technical English-German dictionaries.

After he had been with the staff for about a week, he still was intimidated being in the midst of the much higher German ranks; after all, his grade of auxiliary was not even acknowledged as a rank in the German military. Whenever one of the German officers addressed him at his workstation, Herbert would raise himself out of his chair and stand at attention.

One morning, a British officer stopped by at Herbert's desk and said, "I've been observing your reaction whenever one of your people comes to your desk—you don't have to do that anymore."

"I don't have to do what anymore?" Herbert asked.

"You don't have to stand at attention when they address you," the Brit replied.

"I do it, because they are still my superiors," Herbert said.

"No they're not! Your army is defunct. That means it doesn't exist anymore. There are no more privates, captains, or majors. You guys are all alike now!"

Herbert responded by hunching his shoulders, but later, he did follow the Brit's suggestion. He no longer stood at attention when addressed by the German officers, and the officers did not fuss; however, it took a while for him not to stand up and keep his middle fingers on his pant seams when they talked to him.

✦✦✦

Shortly after the translation of the British documents had been completed in late July, Herbert became part of a truckload of other POWs who were being sent to a demobilization center near the city of Flensburg just south of the Danish border.

The center was nothing more than a collection of farmsteads. Thousands of POWs sought shelter in barns, while awaiting the individual exit interview conducted by the British and the subsequent delousing procedure, before being allowed to go home.

Heavy rains had fallen, and the excessive traffic of the many detainees soon turned the farm yards into quagmires.

To stay out of the mud, the POWs had to either remain confined in the barns, or, weather permitting, while away the time in the surrounding pastures.

One morning, while walking in one of the grassy fields and chatting with some of his fellow POWs, Herbert heard a voice behind him cry out, "Herbert?" He didn't react immediately, thinking that he probably wasn't the only one with that name in the mass of humanity surrounding him. The voice persisted with another, "Herbert?" This time he turned around and found himself facing Oscar Diebohl, the ship steward who had befriended his parents back in the States.

He had not seen the steward since he occasionally stopped by to visit briefly with the Klugs aboard ship on their way to Germany.

Noting Diebohl's coast guard uniform, Herbert said, "Uncle Oscar, it looks like they transferred you to another ship."

"That they did," was Diebohl's reply.

"How did you wind up in this dump?" Herbert asked.

"The Brits fished me out of the North Sea."

"They fished you out of the sea?"

"Yeah, after first sinking my ship."

"Oh."

"What kind of outfit did you get dragged into?" Diebohl asked.

"I was with the flak. I was stationed in Hamburg for most of '44. In October of '44, my battery was transferred to an airfield located at Nordholz which is just south of Cuxhaven."

"Where is your family?" Diebohl asked.

"I don't know!" Herbert reiterated to Diebohl what he had told the American mess sergeant.

"Well, did they get out of the Vogtland in time?" Diebold asked.

"I don't know! I don't even know whether they got out of Altburgund in time! The last communication I had from my mother was a Christmas package which arrived about four weeks late. I haven't heard from my father since I saw him in Berlin on my way back from a furlough in Altburgund. If he remained in Berlin and survived, he most likely wound up as a Russian POW."

"What are you going to do, once you get out of here?"

"My parents established a rendezvous point in Hamburg where we would meet if we were split up at the end of the war."

"What will you do if you don't find them there?"

Herbert shrugged and said, "Hang around, I guess, until I can find out something definitive."

Diebold looked at the boy a moment, and then he said, "I'm scheduled to go for my exit interview tomorrow morning, so I'll be leaving here before you do. I'm going to give you my address in Lokstedt, which is a suburb of Hamburg. If you can't make contact with your parents, come and see me. Maybe my wife and I will be able to help you find your parents." With that, he scribbled his address in a notebook, tore out the page, and handed it to Herbert.

"Thank you, Uncle Oscar."

"Don't lose it," Diebohl said. After a pause, he said, "I'd best get back to the barn and try to get some of this muck off my boots, so I won't look like a complete slob at the interview tomorrow." After he had started to leave he turned around and said, "Good luck to you, and take care of yourself."

Herbert nodded.

Herbert had to spend another week on the farmstead before he became part of a contingent that was scheduled for the exit interview. The selected POWs were trucked to a nearby school and lined up outside of the school gymnasium.

The British had again turned a school gymnasium into a work area. They had distributed many desks throughout the gym, and the desks were manned by British junior officers to conduct the individual exit interviews. When Herbert was beckoned into the gym, a young lieutenant called him to his desk. After inviting Herbert to sit down, the officer asked him, in broken German, "How old are you?"

In English, Herbert responded, "I just turned seventeen a few months ago."

The lieutenant did a double take, and after reverting to his mother tongue, said, "You sound like a Yank. Where did you learn to speak English?"

"In New York."

"In New York, eh? How did you wind up in that uniform?"

"The German authorities did not recognize my American birthright. Since my father was a German national and I was a minor, I was considered German according to German law."

"I see. How long have you been in the service, and what kind of service did you perform?"

"I've been in the Luftwaffe Auxiliary since 1943. I was with an antiaircraft outfit," Herbert said.

"Were you drafted?"

"Because of the bombings, my high-school class was evacuated from Hamburg to Hungary in the spring of '43. Upon our return seven months later, we were given one of two choices: commit to either attending a Hitler Youth leadership school or joining the Luftwaffe Auxiliary. Most of my classmates chose the latter."

"That is interesting," the lieutenant commented. "Why would most of your classmates choose the Luftwaffe Auxiliary?"

"Have you been to Hamburg?" Herbert asked.

"Yes, I have," the lieutenant responded.

"Have you seen the devastated areas?"

The lieutenant nodded.

"Well, when we returned from Hungary, the sight of those areas became the determining factor for joining the Luftwaffe Auxiliary," Herbert said.

"I see," the lieutenant replied. He then busied himself with one of the demobilization forms that each of the POWs received upon completion of the exit interview. After entering Herbert's personal data on the form, he handed it to him and said, "There is one more thing I have to do. Please roll up your left sleeve."

Herbert complied and asked, "What are you looking for?"

The officer smiled and said, "An SS tattoo. I presume that you were not in the SS, but I'm obliged to check each interviewee's left arm."

After the lieutenant completed his inspection, he asked, "Are you planning on returning to the United States?"

"Yeah, if they will allow a former enemy combatant to reenter," Herbert said.

"Well, I wish you the best of luck. Go and get yourself deloused. After that, you can be on your way."

"Yes, sir."

✦ ✦ ✦

Herbert joined a truckload of POWs that was headed for Hamburg. After the driver dropped them off at the Hamburg main railroad station, Herbert, with considerable trepidation, boarded a subway for the trip to Blankenese. He thought what if the Kurscharpers have not had any word from Mama or Papa—what will I do—how will I go about trying to find them?"

✦ ✦ ✦

His apprehensions peaked when he stood in front of the Kurscharper residence. With trembling hand, he pushed the doorbell. When Ilse Kurscharper came to the door, he said, "I… I'm Herbert. Have…have you…do you have any news of the whereabouts of my parents?"

Instead of answering, Mrs. Kurscharper turned around and shouted into the house, "Hertha, come and see who is here!"

Herbert sighed with relief. There were hugs and kisses; there were more hugs and kisses when Romi and Hannelore came to the door. Even Mrs. Kurscharper, whom he had last seen four years earlier, gave him a hug.

After he had entered the house, Herbert asked his mother, "How long have you been here?"

She said, "Let's see…we're in mid August, and we arrived in late July, so we've been here for about three weeks…isn't that right, Ilse?"

Mrs. Kurscharper nodded.

"Then you left the Vogtland, when the Russians marched in," Herbert said.

"We left, when the Russians were already there," Hertha replied.

"I didn't even know whether you got out of the Warthegau in time," Herbert told his mother.

"I wrote to you several times while we were with cousin Hedwig. You didn't receive any of my letters?" Hertha asked.

Herbert shook his head. "The last mail I received from you was your Christmas package."

"I'm sorry that the lost letters caused you needless worry," his mother said. "Where have you been since war's end?"

"I was captured by the British. After their tanks rolled in, I tried to talk to the tank crews, but they were Scots and I hardly could make out a word they said. They couldn't understand me either and probably thought I was some smart-ass kid trying to impress them with my sophomore English.

"Shortly after the British arrived, the airfield where I had been stationed became part of an enclave which the Americans took over. The German POWs in the vicinity of the airfield were trucked to the airfield every day to help repair the runways, which had been blown up by the Germans just days before the war ended. I lucked out and was assigned to work for an American sergeant who ran the mess hall. The first thing he did, after he found out that I was born in Brooklyn, was to feed me steak sandwiches, and guess what? I had my first Coca-Cola in six years!"

"Lucky you!" Romi commented.

"After about a month, I was again put under British jurisdiction. I was sent to a former German division staff, in Cuxhaven, where I helped translate some British documents into German."

"A German division staff?" Romi asked. Did you have to work with a bunch of German officers?"

"Yeah," Herbert answered. He laughed and said, "At first they thought that I was someone's orderly. After that job was done, I was trucked to a demobilization camp in Flensburg."

"Why all the way to Flensburg?" Hertha asked.

Herbert hunched his shoulders. He said, "I guess the British wanted to process all their POWs through one large demobilization center. I had to go through an exit interview, and after a delousing procedure, they let me go."

"What did they ask you during the interview?" Romi asked.

"They wanted to know what kind of outfit I was in, and they checked my left arm for an SS tattoo."

"Why would they check a kid like you for an SS tattoo?" Romi asked.

"I don't know. Maybe they thought I might be some Nazi big shot in disguise."

Romi rolled her eyes and said, "Yeah, right."

Herbert turned toward his mother and asked, "Where is Papa? When did he come back?" The ensuing mood change told him that his questions had quickly turned the joyous atmosphere of the reunion to foreboding.

"We haven't had word from your father since the end of January," his mother said.

"He didn't write to you from Berlin after you arrived in the Vogtland?" Herbert asked.

"He had orders to go to France just a few days after we left Berlin on our way to cousin Hedwig," Hertha said.

"To France?" Herbert cried out.

His mother nodded. Herbert thought if Papa was in France, his chance to survive would have been far greater than if he had to take part in the endgame in Berlin.

In an effort to reassure his mother, he said, "He's probably an American POW, and after the Americans found out that he speaks the language, they put him to work to help them out, like the Brits did to me. He'll be home soon."

"Do you really think so?" Hertha asked.

Suppressing some serious doubts, he answered, "Yes, Mama."

Several days after his arrival at the Kurscharpers, Herbert decided to try to contact Karl Rothman, his former classmate who had not passed the physical requirements for the Luftwaffe Auxiliary. He knew that Karl's home, which was located not far from the former Klug residence, had survived the raids of 1943, but he did not know what happened thereafter. He got on the subway to downtown Hamburg to find out.

Before seeking out Karl's house, Herbert decided to take a look at the remains of the apartment building where his family had lived. As he walked along the ruins of the Iffland Strasse, he noticed the many small placards pasted on surviving walls or street lamps. The placards conveyed to family and friends the whereabouts of those who had been made homeless.

Herbert had expected to see a burned out shell at the site of the former family residence, but what he found was a rubble-strewn lot. The apartment house had been completely demolished. While he looked at the ruins, an old man came shuffling toward him from the end of the block where several houses had survived the bombings. As the old-timer was about to pass Herbert, he stopped and said, "You won't be finding a forwarding address from anyone who was in that house when it was hit; there were no survivors."

"How do you know that?" Herbert asked.

"I was here when it happened. That house took a direct hit!"

"Five-hundred pounder?" Herbert asked.

"At least," the old man answered as he shuffled on his way.

Herbert sighed. He thought, Papa may well have saved three

lives, when he urged Mama and the girls to spend the summer of '43 in Schildberg.

He took another look; then he walked toward the street where he hoped to find the Rothman house intact.

He gave a sigh of relief when he saw that the house had survived.

Mrs. Rothman, Karl's mother, answered the doorbell. Before he could introduce himself, she said, "I know you. You're one of Karl's former classmates. You're Herbert, right?"

When Herbert nodded, she said, "C'mon in."

Mrs. Rothman ushered Herbert to her son's room. Karl responded to the knock on the door and exclaimed, "Hey, look who's here! How are you doing, Herbert?"

"I'm OK. I was just released from a British POW camp."

"How come they kept you so long?"

"When the war ended, I was asked to help translate some documents for the Brits. After that, I just had to hang around until it was my turn to be released."

"Where did you get the black uniform?" Karl asked.

"I'm still wearing my grey uniform because I have nothing else to wear; it has been dyed black in accordance with the edict issued by the British occupation forces. The decree states that continued wearing of uniforms is permitted only if all medals and rank insignias are removed and the uniforms are dyed black."

Herbert laughed and said, "I didn't have to worry about the first two requirements."

"Why the edict?" Karl asked.

"I suppose the Brits don't want the populace to be reminded of Third Reich images, such as Luftwaffe grey and Wehrmacht green."

"Yeah, but why black?"

"I don't know; maybe the Brits forgot that the panzer crews wore black. But can you imagine what would have happened if the edict had called for orange or pink?"

"Yeah, nobody would have paid any attention to it," Karl said.

"Exactly!" They both chuckled. "What have you been up to?" Herbert asked.

"After the Brits dismantled our school in the summer of '43, I had to switch to another school. I just got my high school diploma this past spring, and I will start an apprenticeship in another two weeks. Were you guys, who were with the flak, able to finish up the high school curriculum?"

"Yeah, we got our diplomas last April."

"Did Mr. Vogt stay with you all that time?" Karl asked.

"Yep. He stayed on base Monday through Friday and conducted classes as the situation allowed. He normally spent the weekends at home, but there were times when he stayed over on Friday to conduct a class on Saturday. On several occasions, when we were falling behind schedule, he even returned on a Sunday to help the class make up for lost time."

"He's a pretty good Joe, isn't he?" Karl said.

"Yes, he is."

Herbert broke the ensuing silence, "So, what do you want to do? Want to go to a movie?"

"All the neighborhood theatres are burnt out. We'll have to take a trolley."

"That's OK. Let's go."

When the feature film ended, the theater PA system blared an announcement: The occupation forces have requested that the audience remain seated until the following newsreel has been shown.

Herbert and Karl looked at each other and sat down again.

The newsreel chronicled the arrival of the Allies at the concentration camps of Belsen, Buchenwald, and Auschwitz. When the theater lights came on, a silent audience made its way toward the exits.

Once the boys had left the movie theater and were back on the trolley, Karl asked, "Can you believe what we just saw? The commentator said that most of the victims were Jews and that the perpetrators did not differentiate between man, woman, or child."

Herbert replied, "What we saw today makes us eyewitnesses, after the fact, of what the Allies uncovered upon their arrival. If someone had told me about this, I wouldn't have believed it. Why? Because it is just too gruesome to accept by word of mouth. Such hearsay can only lead to a supposition that something might be true, but I never even heard such hearsay, did you?"

"No. You don't think the films could be a hoax?" Karl asked.

"No. The piles of bodies...the emaciated survivors...even Hollywood would be hard pressed to come up with such diabolic scenes. "Whoever was in charge of the camp operations must have kept a tight lid on them," Herbert replied.

"These seem to have been big operations," Karl said. "How would you keep them secret with the overall administration, all the transportation requirements, and the camp personnel involved?"

"I don't know. Conceivably, the administration and transportation aspects could have been camouflaged to give the appearance, to most of those involved in the operation, that it was part of the resettlement program," Herbert said.

"What about the SS guys who were recruited for assignments in the camps?" Karl asked.

"They probably were given a choice: either the camp, or the eastern front. If they chose the camp assignment, they probably were not told what it entailed."

"What if they objected, once they found out?" Karl asked.

"They probably could still go to the eastern front, but they would go as members of a penal battalion." Noting Karl's quizzical look, Herbert added, "Hey, you know damn well that those camp honchos had to be a bunch of low-lifes!"

When Herbert had to get off the trolley to transfer to the subway, he said, "I'll see you around, and...and I'm sorry I suggested going to the movie."

Karl mumbled, "Me too."

One morning in the second week of September, while Mrs. Kurscharper was out shopping and her husband was at work, the doorbell rang. When Hertha opened the door, she uttered a scream and started to cry. Her children came running to find out what was happening.

In the doorway stood Walther.

"What have they done to you?" Hertha sobbed, as she led him inside.

His filthy uniform hung on an emaciated body that appeared to be in limbo between life and death. The yellow tinge of his hollow-eyed features and his shaved head aged him way beyond his years.

Still sobbing, Hertha asked, "Where have you been?"

Easing himself into a chair, Walther said, "I was captured by the Russians in Berlin."

"In Berlin?" Hertha asked. "But you were transferred to France in January."

"Yes, I was transferred to France, and I also was transferred back to Berlin in March. Didn't you get any of my letters?"

Hertha shook her head.

"I was one of the lucky ones," Walther said. "They made me work until I could work no longer; then they let me go. Most of the younger guys were hauled off to God knows where, probably a one-way trip to Mother Russia."

Hertha started to cry again. She cried and she cried.

✦ ✦ ✦

The following weeks were devoted to nursing Walther back to health. With food still severely rationed, this was difficult to do; however, a little self-denial by the other family members at mealtime soon showed some promise.

The Kurscharper apartment now was really crowded. Hertha and Walther slept in a small attic room. Mr. Kurscharper had moved out of the bedroom and slept on the living room couch so that the girls could share the bedroom with Mrs. Kurscharper. Herbert slept on the living room floor.

Not wanting to impose on the Kurscharpers any longer than necessary, Hertha and Walther soon visited the housing authority to acquire accommodations. With the housing situation a shambles, the authority was compelling renters of large apartments to share space with the needy. As a result, the Klugs were able to sublease one large room not far from the Kurscharpers' apartment. Privacy did not extend beyond that one room because kitchen and toilet facilities had to be shared with the original renters.

✦ ✦ ✦

The fall of 1945 was quickly ceding to winter. Hertha's anxieties about the lack of winter clothing her family was facing were lessened with the arrival of a letter from Walther's sister Elfriede.

In her letter, postmarked two months earlier, Elfriede assumed that her brother's family might be in need of additional winter clothing. She went on to say that she had been able to collect some women's clothing, a few men's items, and several blankets from friends. She stated that she was hesitant to send a package via the postal system for fear that winter might be over by the time the package arrived if it arrived at all. She suggested that the men folk pay her a visit to pick up the clothing items.

✚✚✚

Two days later, Walther and Herbert were at the Altona railroad station waiting for the express train to Cologne to pull into the terminal station.

Since rail travel, specifically passenger rail travel, was still very sporadic, they had arrived at the station early enough to give them a good chance to get on what most likely would be an overcrowded train.

As the train slowly made its way into the terminal station, Herbert watched from near the platform edge as the train car doors slowly moved by. They moved by in pairs since the rail cars were joined by trucks of four wheels that coupled the rear of one car to the front of the next car, and the rail cars had but one door on each end to provide access from the boarding platform.

Walther turned toward his son and said, "We're lucky we got here early. Take a look at the crowd behind us."

Herbert did not have to look. He could feel the push of the crowd behind them intensifying whenever the car doors moved past where they stood. When the cars were just inching past, Herbert was hoping that the train would stop when the next pair of doors, now a little more than half a car length away, would be adjacent to where he and his father stood on the platform.

His wishful thinking was interrupted by a high-pitched scream. Looking in the direction from where the sound emanated, Herbert saw that a woman had fallen into the open space between the oncoming cars to the roadbed below.

"Look, Papa!" Herbert yelled, as one of the woman's legs came in contact with the car's undercarriage, causing her to perform a backward somersault beside the rails.

By the time Walther saw what was happening, two men had jumped into the void between the two cars and coaxed the woman to lie still until the train came to a full stop.

All eyes watched as the two men ministered to the woman.

She was unhurt.

As quickly as the woman's distress cry had directed the crowd's attention toward her, the squealing of the brakes redirected that attention back toward the train. There was a frantic surge of the crowd to get on the train. Walther and his son, located close to the platform's edge and aligned with a car door, were engulfed by that surge and transported onto the train with hardly any conscious effort on their part.

After the train arrived in Cologne, Herbert asked his father, "How much farther is it from here to the town where your sister lives?"

"Siegen is about forty-five miles east of Cologne."

Walther soon found out that passenger rail service between Cologne and Siegen had not yet been reinstated.

"What do we do now?" Herbert asked.

"We'll hunt up the freight terminal and sneak a ride in one of the freight cars."

"How will we know which train to pick?"

"Any train with the locomotive facing east most likely will pass through Siegen unless it turns toward the north about ten miles this side of Siegen, in which case we may have to hitch-hike the rest of the way," Walther answered.

"How do you know all that?"

"I checked the area map when I found out that passenger rail service had not yet been resumed between here and Siegen."

✚✚✚

On the following morning, Elfriede Klug greeted her brother with teary eyes and open arms.

Herbert was surprised at how youthful his aunt looked. He was aware that she was his father's junior by eleven years; which would make her thirty-four; however, he thought that she could easily pass to be in her late twenties.

"Let me look at you," she said to Walther. "You've spent some time in a Russian POW camp, haven't you?" she asked.

"How can you tell?" Walther asked.

"The few that they let go…you all look alike…malnourished to where you are a mere shadow of your former selves." She folded her arms and shivered, as though she were cold.

Turning to Herbert, she asked, "And who might this young fellow be?"

"Don't you recognize him?" Walther asked. When she shook her head, he said, "That is my boy, that is Herbert. He is a little taller now than when you last saw him when we visited Kassel in 1939."

"Ah, yes…I remember now. The other two take after the mother. Both have the dark hair and the dark eyes."

✚✚✚

Over lunch, Walther told Elfriede about his capture and subsequent confinement by the Russians and how Hertha and the girls had eluded the Russians on two different occasions. After Herbert told his aunt about his encounter with the Americans, she exclaimed, "Well, your war certainly ended on a happy note."

Herbert nodded.

"Are you still the assistant director of the girl's high school here in Siegen?" Walther asked.

"I'm still employed by the high school, but the current assistant director now reports to me," Elfriede answered.

"Congratulations. That sounds like a well deserved promotion," Walther replied.

"Thank you!"

Two days later, after nightfall, Walther and Herbert were heading back to the marshalling yards, in hopes of catching a ride back to Cologne. The two duffel bags, empty upon their arrival, now contained miscellaneous winter clothing.

After arriving at the dimly lit marshalling yards, they saw two freight trains on the tracks. Both were coal trains—coal cars loaded with briquettes of coal dust compressed into approximately 2x3x8in. forms. The nearer train appeared ready to go, while the cars of the other one were still being coupled together.

"The locomotive of the nearer train is heading in the right direction, so we should be able to get out of here fairly soon. We'll just stay out of sight between two of the cars until the train starts moving; then, we will climb the ladder to the top of one of the cars."

"Why not just stay on the ladder?" Herbert asked.

"Stay on the ladder—on a mid-November night—with hoarfrost covering everything you touch and a duffel bag on your back? I don't think so! We'll be a lot safer riding on top of a coal pile." Walther replied.

Soon a rippling effect ran through the train as the slack in the car couplings gave way to the demands of the locomotive. As the car started to move, Herbert climbed the ladder with his father close behind.

When Herbert neared the top of the car, Walther tugged on the boy's pant leg and said, "They load these cars from the top until the briquettes start falling off the car sides; therefore, from your vantage point, the car will look like it has a shallow gabled roof made up of briquettes. You want to make sure you walk, or crawl, so that you distribute your weight between both sides of the ridge line."

"Why?"

"Well, the briquettes are just dumped into the car; therefore, they do not stack in an orderly manner. They fall on one another as melting ice floes do when they run aground in early spring: sort of helter-skelter. The briquettes don't afford the best footing when they are loaded like that. Your best bet to maintain your balance is to not lose your footing under both feet simultaneously, and the best way to do that is to straddle the ridge line."

"Oh!"

After Walther reached the top of the car in the waning light of the marshalling yards, he followed his son for several steps and then said, "We can stop here."

In turning toward his father, Herbert promptly forgot what Walther had just told him and planted both feet on the same side of the ridge line. The briquettes under both feet gave way, and he fell and started to slide down the pile. Walther instinctively reached out and grabbed his son's duffel bag. "See what I mean?" he asked as he pulled him back up to the top of the pile. Walther sighed and said, "I'm beginning to wonder whether getting on this coal train was a smart thing to do. We're going to have to figure out a way to keep from slipping off this coal pile during the next two hours or so. If we don't, we'll slip to the car's edge and over, since there won't be anything to hold onto."

Walther thought for a while and then said, "Your duffle bag is only about half full. Take it off and let me have it."

After Herbert complied, Walther said, "I'm going to redistribute the contents of the bag evenly and then lay the bag down at right angles to the ridge, sort of like a mattress." After he had placed the bag, he said to his son, "Now, you are going to sit down on the bag on one side of the ridge, facing the nearer car side, while I will sit down on the other side of the ridge, facing the other side of the car. We will be sitting back to back. Before I sit down I will take off my duffel bag and expand the shoulder straps as far as they will go—"

"Whoa, whoa!" Herbert cried out. "What do you want me to do, after you lay my bag down?"

Walther reiterated what he had said. He stopped, and then asked, "OK so far?"

Herbert nodded and sat down.

"Now I will take off my duffel bag, expand the shoulder straps, and have you place the bag in front of you—just put your arms under the straps and hug the duffle bag."

"Why do you want me to do that?" Herbert asked.

"You'll see in a minute. I will now sit down behind you, and we will be sitting back to back. Then, I will place my arms through the shoulder straps of the bag you are holding. Now, can you get up?"

"No! I can't get up! You've practically strapped yourself to my back!" Herbert cried out.

"That is absolutely correct. And I can't move freely because I have strapped you to my back. Neither one of us can move freely; therefore, neither one of us will slide off this coal pile. You can even fall asleep, and you will still be safe," Walther said.

"I won't fall asleep," Herbert replied with some disdain.

After fifteen minutes of silence, Walther asked, "Are you staying awake?" He waited about five minutes before he repeated the question. Still not hearing a response, Walther smiled and thought, "So much for 'I won't fall asleep.'"

Two and a half hours after leaving the marshalling yards in Siegen, the coal train decelerated to a crawl when it entered another marshalling yard at the outskirts of Cologne. "Let's get ready to disembark," Walther said."Just strap your duffle bag loosely on one shoulder and throw the bag overboard before you jump."

"Where do we go from here?" Herbert asked.

"We'll hop a trolley to the main railroad station and make arrangements for the trip back to Hamburg."

Herbert with his mother during his furlough in the fall of '44

Воинская часть
полевая почта
№ 61964

СПРАВКА

Бывший военнопленный
(фамилия, имя, отчество)

1945 г.

освобожден из лагеря для военнопленных и следует по месту своего постоянного жительства в г.

место
для
печати

полевая почта № 61964

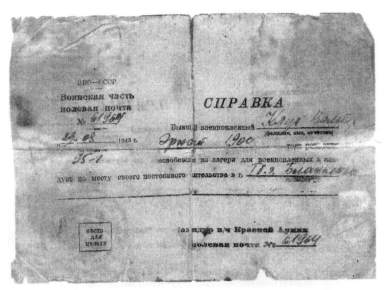

Walther's POW release certificate issued by the Red Army.

Chapter 55

After their return to Hamburg, Walther, although not yet fully recovered, soon became restless. He found a job as an interpreter in the maintenance department of an RAF command center in Blankenese. The job did not pay much, but he was fed twice during each shift. The two meals, normally just a side benefit, became the main attraction of the job since he was still seriously malnourished.

Herbert also found a job. He went to work as an apprentice in a small machine shop which, although located within the firestorm area of the 1943 raids, had somehow survived.

To reach the shop from the subway stop, Herbert had to walk a considerable distance through the ruins of what had been five-storied residential blocks. They were completely burnt out, with only the outside walls left standing. Herbert's trek through the ruins was far enough to take him out of hearing range of any background noise. Midway between the subway stop and the shop, all he could hear were his steps striking the path that had been stamped by others into this manmade wilderness. When he stopped, he was surrounded by a graveyard silence.

One morning, while surrounded by this crypt-like muteness, he looked around and thought some, who perished here, were never found; for them, this is their final resting place; the walls that tower over them have become their tombstones.

With shortages abounding, a considerable part of the German economy was being relegated to the black market. Twenty cigarettes now were worth more than twenty German marks. Many goods, including food items, became part of a barter system. As a result, even food ration stamps at times became worthless. Storekeepers, faced with a shortage of some items, had to tell customers that their food stamps could not be honored once those items had run out.

Walther quickly found a way to alleviate that situation. He found a job for Romi at the RAF command center. She was assigned to work in the noncom officers' mess as a waitress, and, most important, she would be fed at least once a day. She was hired with the understanding that she could double up as an interpreter for the British occupation forces when dealing with the German help.

One evening Herbert was washing his hands at the washstand that the Klugs had set up in their one-room apartment in order to not spend an inordinate amount of time in the bathroom being shared with the original apartment renters.

While Herbert was busy at the washstand, his mother noticed his discomfort.

"What is the problem?" his mother asked.

"I'm having trouble getting my hands clean; I don't dare scrub over these blisters."

"What blisters? Let me see," she said.

As she inspected his hands, she asked, "What kind of work are they having you do to cause such blisters?"

"Every morning I have to break up chunks of calcium carbide and mix them with water to generate acetylene, which, in combination with oxygen, is used for welding. The carbide is very corrosive, and that is why I have the blisters."

"Don't they give you any gloves?" his mother asked.

"Yes, I have gloves, but they are old and worn out."

"Can't the company get you new ones?" she asked.

"Mama, just like so many other things nowadays, new gloves are not available!" Herbert responded.

"Well, you can't continue on like this. Here, let me see," his mother said, as she turned his hands over to look at his palms. Shaking her head, she said, "If you were to continue as you have been, you would literally work your fingers to the bone. This is no good. Does your father know about this?"

"No," he said as he shook his head.

"Well, let's let him in on this. He will know what to do."

✚ ✚ ✚

Herbert had just finished drying his hands, when Romi walked into the Klugs' rental lodging.

"Hi, Mama. Hi, Herb. Where is the rest of the gang?"

"Hannelore is visiting a neighbor's kid, and your father is not home from work yet," Hertha responded. She then asked, "How did it go?"

"It didn't."

"What didn't go?" Herbert asked.

"I took the afternoon off from work and went downtown to our old neighborhood, in the hope that I might re-establish contact with Werner," Romi said. "You remember Werner, don't you?"

"Werner…Werner…you mean the guy you were sweet on back in 1942…the guy who wanted to become engaged to you back then, but didn't, because you had the good sense to tell him that you were both too young and that you thought it best to wait until the war was over…you mean that Werner?"

Romi looked at him and nodded.

"Wow! When was the last time you saw him?"

"Just before we left Hamburg in June of '43 to spend the summer in Altburgund."

"So, what do you do? Do you go downtown and ring his doorbell, but no one is ever home?" Herbert asked.

"No, silly! His family's residence was destroyed during the summer raids of '43. I don't know where the family moved to or even whether they survived."

"So, you just walk the streets in the hope that you will run into him?" Herbert asked.

"No!" Romi replied. With a beseeching look, she said to her mother, "Tell your son to not be so obtuse!"

Hertha honored the request with "Herbert, don't be obtuse."

Romi shook her head and mumbled, "Oh, you guys…no, I don't roam the streets expecting to run into him by chance. I have two girlfriends who still live in the neighborhood whose homes were spared. I've gone to see them and asked them to let me know if they should hear of his whereabouts."

The tears in Romi's eyes prompted Herbert to ask, "You're pretty serious about this guy, aren't you?"

As she nodded, he said, "Well, I hope you find him."

On the following Saturday, Walther announced that he had some errands to run, and he asked Herbert to go with him.

After they left the house, Walther asked, "How is the job coming along? Your mother told me about the calcium carbide burns to your hands."

"My hands are a lot better than they were. I now alternate with another apprentice on that particular assignment, so I only have to do it every other day."

"I've been thinking: perhaps your mother and I were a little hasty in giving our blessings to your acceptance of that apprenticeship," Walther said.

"Why do you say that?" Herbert asked.

"Well, aside from the hand blisters, I think the job is taking too much out of you. It is manual labor, and you are not getting enough nutritional input for the output that the job demands. It will take you four years to complete the apprenticeship, and you won't learn the good stuff until the last two years. The first two generally are gofer years. Do you really want to stay in this disaster area for another four years?"

"Do I have any choice?" Herbert asked.

"I have written a letter to your Uncle Emil in New York. I have eaten crow and have asked him whether he and your Aunt Ida would consider sponsoring Rosemarie's and your return to the United States. Once an American consulate is reestablished and your uncle has agreed to sponsor the two of you, you should be free to leave. Your mother and I, on the other hand, will most likely have to get on a quota list before we can return with Hannelore if they let us return at all!

"I haven't been able to contact your uncle yet, because the capabilities of the German postal service are still very limited. I'm looking for a go-between that will enable me to get in touch with him."

"Do you have any idea when a U.S. consulate will return to Hamburg?" Herbert asked.

"One of the British officers at the RAF command center indicated to me that a U.S. consulate would be operational here sometime in April of next year."

"That's about four months away. If I quit my job, what do I do in the meantime?" Herbert asked.

"Just give your boss two weeks' notice. I'm pretty sure that I can find you a job at the RAF command center."

Herbert did not doubt his father's ability to find him a job at the command center, but he did feel that his father might be overly confident to assume that, by flashing his birth certificate, his re-entry into the United States would be guaranteed; after all, he had been an enemy combatant!

Chapter 56

By the end of November, 1945, Herbert also was working for the RAF command center. As was the case with Walther and Romi, the offer of a meal a day was the governing factor in accepting the job. Herbert soon received tutorage, both from his father and his sister, as to which one of the guards, at the various command center exits set up for the hired help, was the least attentive. As a result, Hertha's and Hannelore's diet supplements received another boost, and by Christmas the Klug pantry was in better shape than it had been in a long time.

+ + +

In early January, Romi made another trip downtown in search of her boyfriend. This time Hertha did not have to ask about the results. Romi was in tears as soon as she entered the room. "Another futile trip?" Hertha asked.

Romi shook her head.

"Then why are you crying?"

"I ran into him, completely by chance."

"Well, that's wonderful—isn't it?"

"No, Mama. It is not. He is marrying someone else!"

"Marrying someone else…" Hertha absentmindedly repeated. "But he can still change his mind, can't he?"

"No, Mama. He can't. She is carrying his child!" Romi replied amidst another flood of tears.

+ + +

One evening in late February, Romi asked her father, "Do you know Ernest Budd?"

"Mr. Budd, the medical sergeant at the RAF command center? Yes, I know him. Why do you ask? Is he your new boyfriend?"

"I'm not ready for a new boyfriend, Papa. Besides, he is married. Whenever I talk to him, he is always telling me how he is looking forward to being discharged so he can return home to his wife—"

"How did you get to know him?" Walther interrupted.

"I helped him decorate the NCO's canteen for a party some time ago. I've talked to him several times since then, and I told him that you were trying to establish contact with Uncle Emil in New York."

"And?" Walther asked.

"And he said that he could help you out," Romi replied.

"I can't just walk up to the man and tell him that you told me that he could help me to communicate with my brother-in-law in the United States."

"You don't have to do that. He has offered several times to walk me home—he's just trying to get away from the military environment once in a while. I'll take him up on his offer one of these days and then ask him in. If he is serious about wanting to help you out, he then can tell you himself what he has in mind."

"All right, we can try that," Walther said.

+ + +

All of the Klug family, except Hannelore, was present when Mr. Budd, Mr. Ernest Budd, made his first appearance at the

Klug household. He made a good impression in his dress uniform and boots that were polished to a high luster, and he assured that the introductory formalities were kept short-lived by pulling a small container of teabags out of his tunic pocket and saying to Hertha, "I've got the tea, if you can provide the hot water."

While Hertha served cookies, Mr. Budd said to Walther, "I understand that you are trying to contact your brother-in-law in New York."

"Yes, I have written a letter to Hertha's brother in New York, primarily to let him and his family know that we have survived the war. I have also asked him whether he could assist us in our endeavor to return to the United States.

"Now that I have written the letter, I don't know what to do with it—the German postal system is still hard pressed to deliver mail just blocks away, and handling international mail will be a pipe dream for the foreseeable future."

"Well, all you need is a go-between. All you have to do is to advise your brother-in-law that I will be the intermediary to facilitate the correspondence between you and him and to give him my address in Canterbury.

"I will send your letters, sealed in an envelope addressed to your brother-in-law, to my wife. She, in turn, will apply the necessary airmail postage to your envelope and send it on its way. Conversely, my wife will send any mail from your brother-in-law to me, and I will be most happy to personally deliver his letters to you!"

"I appreciate your offer, Mr. Budd," Walther said, "but I'm not sure that I can accept it."

"Why not?" Mr. Budd asked.

"I feel it would be placing an imposition not only upon you, but also upon your wife. And I won't be able to compensate you for the postage. I would assume the airmail postage between London and New York is rather steep and our currency at the moment is almost worthless," Walther replied.

"Well, it looks to me like I have already been imposing upon you and your daughter. There have been many times when I have kept either you or Rosemarie past your normal quitting times to translate for me while I was dealing with the German help—"

"That is part of the job description!" Walther injected.

"But not after hours!" Mr. Budd declared.

Walther sighed, and looking at Mr. Budd said, "The letter is very important to me. Unless I can find someone in the United States to sponsor Rosemarie and Herbert's return, they won't be going anywhere soon. My wife and I won't be allowed to return at this time and Hannelore is too young to be separated from her mother, so I'm hoping that Hertha's brother, Emil will vouch for the two older kids.

"I'll accept your help while at the same time hoping that I can make it up to you sometime in the future," Walther conceded.

"Good," Mr. Budd said. "I'll be able to route your letter to my wife tomorrow."

✚ ✚ ✚

In the following weeks, Mr. Budd became a frequent visitor at the Klug household, and as the visitor became a friend, the original formality yielded to vocalizing on a first name basis, except for Herbert and Romi, who continued to address Ernest as Mr. Beetle. He was so called by his British contemporaries, probably because part of his responsibilities as a medical sergeant was to periodically disinfest the command center kitchen and dining areas of bugs.

✚ ✚ ✚

Four weeks later, Ernest dropped in at the Klugs completely unannounced.

"I have a response to your letter from an Emil Werner in New York!" he proclaimed.

All five Klugs reacted with a cheer that probably had the landlord wondering whether the sub-renters had won some kind of lottery. Ernest handed the letter to Walther, who opened it with shaking hands and started to read, with Hertha looking over his shoulder. Looking up, Walther used Emil's nickname when he said, "Ene and Ida are relieved that we have made it through the war OK, and they want to know when we will be able to return. Ene says he and Ida will sponsor all of us. In the event that not all can return at the same time, he says, 'Send the kids—we will assume guardianship.'"

Walther handed the letter to Ernest. There was silence while Ernest read the letter, and Hertha and Walther fought back the tears.

When Ernest laid the letter on the table, Walther turned to him and said, "You have done us a huge favor in establishing this link with Emil. This letter will be of tremendous help to us once the American Consulate returns to Hamburg and we can petition for the two older kids' return to the U.S. One of the main concerns of the consulate is that entering displaced persons or returning citizens be properly sponsored to ensure that they do not become wards of the state—in this case the federal government.

"Emil's letter gives us a head start in that he has anticipated the need for sponsorship and has gone beyond that by accepting guardianship.

"Hertha and I thank you, Ernest, for going out of your way to help us in this matter."

Ernest smiled and said, "There will be follow-up letters to Uncle Emil. Don't hesitate to let me know when you are ready to send them."

Chapter 57

On a morning in mid May of 1946, Walther, Romi, and Herbert were sitting in the waiting room of the newly opened American consulate in downtown Hamburg. Walther was leafing through a tattered copy of the *New York Times,* and Romi and Herbert were scanning several dog-eared editions of the *Saturday Evening Post* while waiting their turn to see one of the vice consuls.

About one half hour after their arrival, the receptionist told Walther and his progeny that a vice consul was now available to see them and that she would guide them to his office. Walther picked up the folder he had brought with him and stayed close to the receptionist as she led them down a long hallway, while Romi and Herbert followed at a much slower pace.

"Aren't you a little scared?" Romi whispered.

"About what?" Herbert asked.

"About going back to the States by ourselves," she said.

"I'm only scared that they may not allow me to go back," Herbert remarked.

"Why wouldn't they?"

"Because…because of the Luftwaffe Auxiliary thing."

"But you didn't have any choice."

"I didn't have much choice, but I still wound up as an enemy combatant."

"I don't think that they will hold that against you."

"I hope you're right."

"But you won't be scared if you can go?"

"Nope."

"I think I would be too scared to go by myself. The only time I have been away, from whatever was home in these past seven years, was the time I spent in the Sudetenland and the time I was away because of the stupid farm service requirement."

"I've been away from home for almost half the time since we arrived in Germany, so I'm used to it," Herbert countered.

"Well, I sure hope they let you go, because I don't think I could bring myself to go alone."

When the receptionist stopped at a door toward the end of the hall, Walther looked back toward his kids. Surprised that they were still only halfway from the reception room, he induced them to hurry by motioning with outstretched hands, and while waving his hands toward himself, saying,

"C'mon, let's go! This is all about you!"

Speaking German, the vice consul bade them to sit down and said, "I am vice consul Bob Langston. How can I help you?"

After Walther introduced himself and his offspring, also in German, he added in English, "I am here to request the repatriation of my two older offspring to the U.S.A."

"How many more children do you have besides these two?" the vice consul asked.

"I have another daughter. Hannelore is only eleven and at this time is too young to be separated from her parents."

Mr. Langston acknowledged with a nod and said, "Your English is good." Pointing toward Herbert and Romi he asked, "Do they also speak the language?"

Instead of answering the vice consul, Walther, still speaking English, said, "Herbert, tell Mr. Langston what you asked the first American soldier you talked to at war's end."

"I asked him, 'How are the Brooklyn Dodgers doing?'"

Mr. Langston laughed and asked, "Well, did he know?"

"Nah. He was from Tennessee, and he didn't have a clue."

"If you're still wondering, I don't think they did very well last year," the vice consul said and then asked, "How did you get to talk to an American soldier, when Hamburg had fallen to the British?"

"At war's end my unit was captured by the British on an airfield just south of Cuxhaven, where we had been stationed.

"Since the Americans needed access to the harbor facilities of Bremerhaven, they negotiated with the British for an enclave in the British zone. The airfield became part of that enclave, and the German POW's located there temporarily were placed under U.S. jurisdiction," Herbert explained.

The vice consul was frowning when he asked, "Were you in some kind of Hitler Youth outfit that was supposed to make a last minute stand at the end of the war?"

Herbert shook his head and said, "No! We were members of the Luftwaffe Auxiliary."

"Whoa! Whoa!" Mr. Langston interjected. "What's this Luftwaffe Auxiliary? It sounds very much like a military organization!"

"It was a military organization," Walther responded. "By 1943, many of the ground-based antiaircraft personnel were transferred to the front lines and had to be replaced."

Mr. Langston was scowling as he pointed to Herbert and asked, "How old are you right now?"

"I just turned eighteen," Herbert answered.

Still scowling, and holding his clenched right fist palm side up, the vice consul started a backward count. Beginning at the count at forty-six, he straightened his thumb. At forty-five, he straightened his index finger. He continued the count, until at a count of forty-three he had straightened his ring finger, re-clenched his fist, and again started a backward count, this time starting the count at eighteen and continuing until he again straightened the ring finger at fifteen.

"You were just fifteen years old in 1943! What did you do? Did you volunteer to join that outfit?" Mr. Langston asked.

Walther intervened by saying, "As high school sophomores, the boys were given a choice of either joining the Luftwaffe Auxiliary or enrolling in a Hitler Youth leadership school. The leadership school offer was a ruse.

"It was given as an alternative so that the populace could not say that fifteen-year-olds were being drafted to become antiaircraft gunners. In fact, it turned out to be an unnecessary alternative. A great majority of Hamburg's fifteen-year-old high school students, who either had witnessed the raids of July 1943 or subsequently saw what had been done to Hamburg, elected to join the Luftwaffe auxiliary!"

Mr. Langston shook his head and mumbled, "Fifteen-year-old AA gunners…"

Turning his attention back to Walther, Mr. Langston asked, "Were all the children born in the United States?"

When Walther nodded affirmatively, the vice consul asked, "But you are not requesting repatriation of the whole family?"

"No." Walther replied, "My wife and I are German nationals; therefore, we are not eligible for repatriation. I realize that in order for my wife and me to return, we will again have to go through the immigration procedures, but we don't want to apply at this time because my wife's brother, instead of sponsoring only the two eldest children, would have to sponsor all five of us. I'm unwilling to burden him to that extent."

The vice consul looked at Walther and said, "The subject of your return is somewhat moot at this time. At present we are not accepting immigration applications from German nationals. We have our hands full tending to the repatriates and assisting the large numbers of displaced persons, who are looking for a place to call home. Once we start accepting applications from German nationals again, the applicants will have two additional requirements to contend with: 1. The applicant must be able to prove that he/she was not a Nazi and 2. Male applicants, who served in the German military must show they did not do so voluntarily, and must provide character references from at least half a dozen non-German sources.

"How long were you in the U.S.?" the vice consul asked.

"We were there from 1925 until 1939," Walther answered.

"Did you acquire United States citizenship?"

"Yes, I was a U.S. citizen from about 1936 until 1941."

"What happened in 1941?" Mr. Langston asked.

"I renounced my American citizenship."

"Why did you do that?"

"By midsummer of 1941, Lend-lease was in full swing, and the United States' entry into the war seemed a foregone conclusion. Once that happened, I knew I would be interned, and my family would be without a breadwinner," Walther explained.

"But up until then, your family could have left the country, right?" Mr. Langston supposed.

"Wrong!" Walther countered. "The children and I perhaps could have left if we were willing to board a neutral vessel and brave the mined waters; however, that was not an option. Why? My wife was a German citizen when she emigrated to the U.S., and she returned a German citizen.

"After Hitler closed the borders, soon after the war started, she could not leave the country. She was trapped, and since we could not leave her, we all were trapped!"

Walther's recollections strained his composure. He sighed before he continued, "That renunciation had all kinds of repercussions. I was drafted into the Wehrmacht about four weeks later. The renunciation turned the children into Germans overnight, since German law assigns citizenship of minors to that of the father.

"Overnight, Rosemarie was required to have to perform one year of farm service, as were all German girls.

"Overnight, Herbert was required to join the Jungvolk, a division of the Hitler Youth, as mandated for all German boys in the age group of ten through fourteen years. In the spring of 1943, his school class was evacuated from Hamburg to Hungary because of the increased intensity of the air raids, and upon their return in late '43, the members of the class were given the choice of either the Hitler Youth leadership school or the Luftwaffe Auxiliary."

Shaking his head, the vice consul asked, "When was it that you returned to Germany?"

"We came back in June of 1939," Walther replied.

"Well, I think you would have been better off if you had missed that boat. You traded a Depression in the U.S. for a war over here—not a good move," the vice consul said.

"I agree with you completely, but you will have to concede that hindsight is never available until after the fact," Walther countered.

"Yeah, I suppose you are right," Mr. Langston said. He then asked, "Have you been able to contact your brother-in-law about sponsoring these two youngsters?"

"Yes, I sent him a letter and received a reply recently," Walther answered as he drew the letter out of his coat pocket and handed it to the vice consul.

"How did you manage to establish contact?" Mr. Langston asked.

"A British sergeant, whom the family befriended, sent the letter to his wife in Canterbury, England, and she in turn applied the required airmail postage and forwarded the letter to New York. Return mail is handled in like manner.

"It is sent to Canterbury and then forwarded by our British friend's wife to Hamburg," Walther replied.

"I assume you have Rosemarie's and her brother's birth certificate with you?" the vice consul inquired.

Walther pulled several papers out of his folder. "I brought all three with me," Walther said.

"I only need the two for the older offspring I just want my secretary to make copies for me—then you can have them back. You want to make sure you don't lose the certificate for your youngest daughter—it will be a plus when you file your immigration request, sometime in the future."

After the secretary had returned with the copies, Mr. Langston said, "I have also copied your brother-in-law's address. I will advise him of what will be expected of him as a sponsor of the two youngsters. Once that is squared away, we will apply for the necessary passports for them."

"Are you reasonably confident that the requested passports will be granted?" Walther asked.

"Yes, I am," the vice consul replied. "Your daughter is a shoo-in. As for Herbert, yes, he was an enemy combatant, but he also was a victim of circumstances, and well…" Mr. Langston raised his hands and added, "Our judicial system just doesn't provide for legal proceedings against combatant minors!"

Both Herbert and Romi broke out in smiles: he because a heavy load had been lifted off his shoulders, and she because she would not have to cross an ocean by herself!

"So, where do we go from here?" Walther asked.

"I would suggest that you take Herbert and Rosemarie to have passport pictures made and to drop them off at this office. We will advise you when the passports can be picked up. Thereafter, it will be a matter of waiting for instructions from the U.S. Army Civil Censorship Division and the shipping company as to how the repatriation will proceed."

"OK," Walther said. "I want to thank you for your help, Mr. Langston, and I hope I can count on your assistance, once you again will be accepting immigration petitions from German nationals."

"I'll see what I can do," the vice consul replied.

"Kids, say thank you to Mr. Langston, and let's go and look for someone who can supply you with a passport picture," Walther said as he motioned them to follow him.

✚✚✚

One evening in early June, Walther came home from work two hours later than usual. "Where have you been?" Hertha asked. "We waited for you for about an hour, but then, we decided to go ahead with supper."

"I had a call from the vice consul. He said that the kids' passports could be picked up at any time, so I did."

"I'm surprised that the consulate is open that late," Hertha said.

"It isn't," Walther replied. "Mr. Langston made arrangements with the security desk so that I could pick up the passports after hours."

"So, where are the passports?" Romi inquired.

"Give your father a chance to have some supper," Hertha interjected.

"It's not a problem; I have them right here," Walther said, as he reached into his coat pocket and pulled out the documents.

"Here is yours," he declared, as he handed Romi one of them, and, "Here is yours," as he offered the remaining one to Herbert.

"Where is mine?" little Hannelore wanted to know.

"You will get yours about two years from now when you and your mother and I will be returning to the United States," her father told her. Looking at the older two, he said, "Don't forget to sign them. They are invalid without your signature."

As Herbert leafed through his passport, he suddenly exclaimed, "Uh, oh! I've got a problem!"

"What is the problem?" his father asked.

"The consulate gurus have interchanged my first and middle names. According to this passport I am now Horst Klug, not Herbert Klug!" With an anguished look, he cried out, "How could they make such a dumb mistake?"

"Well, let's check what it says on the birth certificate," Walther suggested.

"You won't have to do that," Hertha injected. "I remember clearly that the birth certificate reads Horst Herbert—"

"Then why has everybody been calling me Herbert for the past eighteen years?"

Hertha couldn't suppress a smile when she said, "We only called you Herbert for seventeen and a half years. When you were six months old and it was time for you to be baptized, we realized that Horst was a little too close to the English word horse and that unless we changed your first name, we would leave you open to derision by your playmates and eventual classmates."

"What Mama is saying is that she was afraid that the other kids would nag you a lot with a name like Horst," Romi said as she dwelled on "nag" to emphasize the double meaning.

"I understand," Herbert responded. "What I don't understand is why my birth certificate wasn't changed."

"At the time, we had every intention of doing that, but somehow we never got around to it," Hertha said.

"Aw, gee whiz!" Herbert interjected. Turning to his father, he asked, "What am I going to do?"

"Just sign your name as the consulate has written it!"

"But it isn't my real name!" Herbert crabbed.

"What difference does it make?" Walther asked him. "When you introduce yourself to someone, you don't grope in your coat pocket and pull out your passport and open it to the page that lists your name and point to it and tell your new acquaintance that this is who you are—or do you?"

"No, of course not," Herbert replied. "I just thought that perhaps we could ask Mr. Langston to have it corrected."

"We don't want to do that," his father declared.

"Why not?" Herbert asked.

"You heard the vice consul tell me how busy he was with repatriation requests and displaced person applications. If we were to go back to him now to tell him that the order of your forenames on your passport is incorrect, your application for repatriation might go back to the bottom of the pile, and you just might miss the boat."

"Let me see your passport," Romi requested.

"What for?" Herbert asked.

Romi shrugged and said, "I just want to see if the photographer did as good a job with your picture as he did with mine." After he handed her his passport, Romi said, "Your picture turned out real nice." She turned to her mother and asked, "How do you like his picture?"

"I think it's fine. He looks very debonair in his suit jacket," Hertha replied. She studied the picture a moment longer and said to her daughter, "That suit is made of the same type of synthetic fiber that you once characterized as being itchy when you wear it and fussy about how you clean it. After you and he leave, make sure that he does not add the suit to the laundry pile; when it needs cleaning it has to be dry-cleaned!"

"Did you hear what Mama said, Horst?" Romi asked with an impish smile.

Herbert, who had been engrossed in a newspaper, looked up and said, "Yeah, yeah, I heard: dry-cleaning only."

+++

One week later, at the supper table, Hertha announced that she had paid a visit to her friend Ihde Johte and that Ihde had told her that her daughter Annalisa was scheduled to return to the United States on a liberty ship named *Marine Flasher* leaving Bremerhaven on July 5.

During the third week of June, Walther received a letter from the consulate advising him that Romi and Herbert were to report to the U.S. Army in Bremen on 29 June for processing to board the *Marine Flasher* scheduled to leave Bremerhaven on 5 July for New York.

"Well, at least one of the passengers will recognize you," Hertha said. "Annalisa will be happy to know that she will have two friends aboard."

Upon arrival in Bremen, the repatriates and displaced persons were separated from their entourage family and/or friends to be deloused and to be assigned to youth hostel dorms after being separated once more according to sex.

On the following morning the U.S. Army Censorship Group interrogated the prior day's arrival of repatriates and displaced persons who had been granted passage on the *Marine Flasher.* The censorship folks were primarily interested in written, or printed, material that the returnees and the emigrants had on their person or in their luggage. Herbert guessed that the U.S. Army was not keen on having copies of *Mein Kampf* shipped into the United States.

When the soldier who was inspecting Romi and Herbert's only piece of luggage—a duffle bag which they shared—he came upon the British chocolate bars and Player cigarettes that the RAF personnel had given them when they left their jobs at the command center. He also found the pack of Chesterfields that was a leftover of Herbert's stint with the Americans. The soldier asked Romi, in German, "Where did you guys get this stuff? Were you dealing in the black market?"

He did a double take when Romi replied in English, "No, we were not involved in the black market. We worked for the RAF and—"

"You both worked for the RAF?" the soldier asked.

Romi and Herbert both nodded.

In a more conciliatory tone, the soldier said, "In that case, please forgive my presumptuous attitude." He paused for a moment and then asked, "Will you be going back to Brooklyn?"

Romi asked, "How do you know that we're from Brooklyn?"

"Your accent is a dead give-away," the soldier replied.

"Oh...no, we're not heading back to Brooklyn; we'll be staying with an aunt and uncle who live in Manhattan."

"I see," the soldier remarked. He hesitated for a moment and then said, "Well, we've looked through your duffle bag. Let's now look through the rest of your stuff," as he expectantly peered over the counter for additional luggage that they might have set down.

Romi and Herbert looked at one another; Herbert merely shrugged, and Romi said, "There is no 'rest of your stuff'. Except for the clothes on our back, what you saw in the duffle bag are all of our worldly possessions."

"You mean, what's in the duffle bag, that's it?" the soldier asked in a tone now noticeably bereft of the cockiness he had previously used when insinuating their black market ties.

"That's it!" Romi said.

The soldier seemed somewhat at a loss for words when he said, "I guess some folks like to travel light."

"Some do, because they have no choice," Romi said and added, "Are we all done?"

"We're all done. You guys have a good trip going home."

✦ ✦ ✦

During the next four days, Herbert and Romi were free to spend time with their family. On 3 July, Annalisa arrived with her mom and dad, and the elders and kids of the two families got a chance to become reacquainted.

On the morning of 5 July, the repatriates and displaced persons were loaded onto two-and-a-half ton trucks for the trip to Bremerhaven, where they would transfer to a train that would take them to where the *Marine Flasher* was berthed. Prior to loading, the soon to be ship's passengers were issued a travel ticket, issued by the shipping line, an embarkation card to board the *Marine Flasher* stating the sailing date and the name and shipboard accommodation of the bearer, and a notice issued by the Travel Censorship Division verifying that the bearer had submitted all written and printed material in his/her possession.

They had been advised to say their goodbyes on the preceding evening, since they would be subjected to a final delousing session early in the morning of 5 July and a quarantine from family and friends thereafter. When it was time to board the trucks, any last minute goodbyes therefore were done from afar—a wave here, a blown kiss there. Impersonal as the final goodbyes were, they did not prevent a tear or two from being shed.

Once the trucks entered the dock areas of Bremerhaven, repatriates and refugees were transferred to rail freight cars that would take them to where the *Marine Flasher* was berthed.

"This reminds me of the freight cars that we had to board when we were running from the Russians," Romi said.

"Well, this will be just a very short ride," Herbert responded.

"How do you know?" his sister asked.

"If we still had a considerable distance to go, they wouldn't have taken us off the trucks. I would guess that the shipping quays probably border directly on one side of this marshalling yard, and there is no truck access to the ship."

Herbert's supposition was soon validated when the train made a sharp right-hand turn around several dock-side warehouses that had hidden the ship from view. It was painted grey. When the embossed lettering on the port side of the bow became distinguishable as *Marine Flasher*, loud cheers erupted from the oncoming boxcars.

"It isn't very big," Romi observed when she saw the ship.

"I would guess that it is about half the size as the liner we were on when we came here," Herbert volunteered.

"If it's only half the size, I'll probably be twice as seasick going back," Romi lamented.

After the train came to a stop, a shipboard loudspeaker advised the new arrivals to have their passenger ticket, their embarkation card, and their U.S. Army censorship clearance ready for embarkation. They were then advised to line up in twos at one of two available gangplanks located at the bow and the stern of the ship respectively.

Romi and Herbert selected the bow gangplank. Once aboard, a ship's officer directed the female passengers to above main-deck cabins and the males to the forward hold.

"While you check out where you will be bunking for the next ten days, I am going to find out where they put me. My embarkation card lists my accommodation as BII-103. I'll see you back on deck in about fifteen minutes," Herbert suggested.

Romi nodded and said, "OK."

Herbert followed a group of fellow male passengers down a flight of stairs into the forward hold of the ship. Bright sun-light quickly was replaced by incandescent lighting that barely managed to illuminate the forward hold. He noticed that the better part of the area, normally used to carry cargo, contained rows of three-tiered bunk beds. Each row had ten beds that were aligned in head to foot-end fashion across the width of the ship, and the ten beds of each row were separated by small cabinets that housed three footlockers, one for each bed tier.

The rows of beds were separated from one another by walk-through aisles, and there were nine such aisles, thereby providing bedding for three hundred individuals.

The bow area of the forward hold contained shower and toilet facilities. Considering the number of beds and available shower stalls, Herbert concluded that the lines at each shower stall would be ten deep, if all three hundred forward-hold dwellers woke up and decided to shower at the same time.

Herbert took his embarkation card out of his coat pocket, and after some searching, he found out that the top tier of bed number ten in section BII would be his pad for the duration of the trip.

When he got back on deck, Romi was already waiting for him.

"Did you find your cabin?" he asked.

"Yeah."

"How many do you have to share it with?"

"There are four girls in the cabin. How many guys do you have to share your accommodations with?" Romi asked.

"When all the beds are taken, two hundred and ninety-nine."

"Two hundred and ninety-nine?" Romi gasped.

"It's just a big open area with a bunch of three-tiered beds," Herbert replied.

"Yeah, but three hundred people in one area—"

"So?" Herbert interrupted.

"So, I hope you have good ventilation down there."

"Hey, I'm saving about sixty-six bucks on my fare for sleeping down there. Your cabin accommodation costs you two hundred dollars."

"You mean, it cost uncle Ene and Ida two hundred two hundred dollars."

"Well yeah, but eventually you're going to have to pay it back," Herbert commented. "They live in a walk-up as we did, except that theirs is in Manhattan, while ours was in Brooklyn. I would guess that the almost three hundred and forty dollars, which they had to cough up for our tickets, put a crimp in their savings account."

"I know." Romi replied. How long do you think it will take me to repay the two hundred dollars?"

Herbert shrugged and said, "Let's assume that you can find a job paying a dollar an hour. I think that's an unrealistically high assumption, but let's go with it. So, you'll gross forty bucks a week. Taxes probably will cut your take home to thirty-two dollars. It seems reasonable to me that each of us contribute fifteen dollars per week for groceries and upkeep. That would leave you with seventeen dollars. Assuming that you can get by with seven dollars per week for expenses—"

"I only get to keep seven dollars out of every forty that I earn?" Romi lamented.

"Let me finish," Herbert said. "Assuming you can get by on seven dollars per week, you'll have ten dollars left; therefore, you might be able to pay the two hundred bucks back in twenty weeks."

"I'll be a pauper for the first twenty weeks," Romi said.

"You'll be much less a pauper than you are right now," Herbert said. "Besides, I just pulled some numbers out of…out of…I just guessed at some numbers. Perhaps you will be able to find a job that pays two dollars an hour. Then you could reimburse them in four weeks." He thought for a moment and added, "It doesn't really matter how quickly we reimburse them, as long as we come up with a doable weekly amount and stick with it."

"Oh, I agree that we should repay them as soon as we can even though we may be monetarily challenged for a while," Romi said.

The ship's PA system, announcing that lunch was being served in the dining room, curtailed the discussion.

+++

As Romi and Herbert neared the dining room entrance, they ran into Annalisa Johte. "Where have you been? We were wondering why we had not yet run into you," Herbert asked.

"I was in one of the cars in the rear of the train. Since the transfer from train to the ship was done incrementally by starting with the first car and gradually working back to the rear of the train, I did not get to board until about twenty minutes ago."

"Are you all settled in as far as your accommodations are concerned?" Romi asked.

"Yep, I'm in one of the cabins on the starboard side of the B deck," Annalisa said.

"Wow, you sound like an old hand at this sort of thing!" Romi exclaimed.

Annalisa smiled and said, "When in Rome, do as the Romans do!"

As Romi and Herbert nodded in agreement, Annalisa backed off and said, "As I boarded and showed the purser my embarkation card, he said, 'You're over on the starboard side.' I, myself, wouldn't know the difference between a starboard deck and a poop deck!"

Herbert thought, I noticed the change when she arrived in Bremen with her parents several days ago. She has changed from the somewhat taciturn fourteen-year-old I met when her mother altered my ill-fitting uniforms back in 1943 and has become an attractive young lady. "We're headed for the dining room," he said, "Why don't you join us?"

"OK."

Folks, waiting for the dining room to open, already had formed a line that wound its way from the amidships located entrance all the way beyond the superstructure and well into the forward part of the main deck.

After they joined the line, Annalisa asked Herbert, "How many passengers would you guess that this ship can accommodate?"

He hunched his shoulders and said, "Perhaps five hundred—why do you ask?"

"Well, the only Americans I ever ran into, while in Germany, were you and Romi. Now, quite suddenly, I am surrounded by repatriates, and it seems that Germany must have been overrun by folks born in the U.S."

Herbert chuckled and said, "You used the correct wording when you said 'it seems.' In a country of eighty million with an influx of one thousand foreigners, the native born will outnumber the foreigners by a factor of eighty thousand to one. Even an influx of three or four thousand, while it changes that ratio, the change has no significance."

"Do you think all the people lined up here are repatriates?" Annalisa asked.

Romi joined the conversation by saying, "I haven't been eavesdropping, but in passing, I couldn't help overhearing parts of the conversations of other passengers. I've heard folks talking German, others talking Polish, and still others conversing in what sounded like French to me. I believe that many of these folks are displaced persons."

"I wonder how they will manage, once they are in the United States," Annalisa said.

"When they realize that in order to be understood they have to pick up the language, they will make it a priority to do so," Herbert responded.

"I thought your vocabulary was very good when you talked

to the ship's officer right after we joined the food line," Annalisa commented."

"Well, I took English classes in high school, mainly to give me more time for my German studies. As a result, I stayed somewhat current in English. Additionally, my close association with the Americans and the British while a POW enabled me to broaden my vocabulary significantly. If my English now is better than it was when I arrived here in 1939, it is so because I occasionally happened to be at the right place at the right time since then," Herbert explained.

When the line had advanced sufficiently to where he could look through the windows into the dining room, Herbert was somewhat disappointed. He had expected a dining room layout similar to the one he remembered of the liner that had brought his family to Germany: linen tablecloths and upholstered chairs, with a battery of stewards catering to the passengers. Instead, he saw metal tables with plastic-covered tops and eight metal stools per table all bolted to the deck. The battery of stewards had become superfluous since the modus operandi was cafeteria style and therefore self-service.

"It looks like there won't be any table service," Herbert advised the two girls.

Annalisa merely shrugged, while Romi asked, "Since we are now aboard an American ship, we are considered to be on American soil, isn't that right?"

"I guess that is true," Herbert replied.

"Well, since I haven't had any American cuisine in seven years, I'm really looking forward to an American lunch, and I don't care whether it is served by several stewards or whether I have to go and get it myself!"

Once they had served themselves at the food counters and had seated themselves at one of the tables, Romi commented, "When I mentioned American cuisine earlier, I was thinking hot dogs and corn on the cob, but I'll accept the alternative the ship's chef has come up with: bratwurst and sauerkraut!"

Annalisa and Herbert both laughed, and Annalisa said, "I would assume that it also has been a while since you had bratwurst."

"You're right," Romi responded, and added, "Anything on the menu would have seemed like a delicacy to me."

After lunch, the threesome went on deck to reconnoiter their new surroundings. Another train bearing additional passengers had arrived, and Herbert and the girls watched as the newcomers ascended the two gangplanks. Shortly after the last passengers of the second train had boarded, the ship's PA system announced that the *Marine Flasher* would be getting underway at 5:00 P.M. that afternoon.

Herbert pulled three of the many available deckchairs side by side and invited Annalisa and his sister to sit down.

"There won't be enough deck chairs available, once all the passengers are settled in," Annalisa commented.

"They won't need one for every passenger," Herbert replied. "Look at how some are making themselves at home on the cargo-hold covers. They have noticed that the huge steel covers are in turn covered with a tarpaulin, and they have discovered that the tarpaulins substitute very nicely as beach blankets. Hopefully, they won't discover that lying there too long will result in a nasty sunburn."

✦✦✦

After spending about an hour in the sun, Herbert said, "I think I've had enough exposure for one day." Both Romi and Annalisa nodded agreement.

"Romi, you can show me your cabin, and I also want to take some of my stuff out of the duffel bag and take it down to the hold with me," Herbert told his sister.

When they reached the B deck level, Annalisa said, "Well, I'd better scoot over to my cabin on the other side of the ship. I'll see you later."

"Just remember that your cabin is located on one of the starboard decks; it's not located on the poop deck," Herbert said, tongue in cheek.

"Yeah, yeah," Annalisa replied

"Will you be coming back down to the main deck when it is time for the ship to cast off?" Herbert asked.

Annalisa, who was already walking toward her cabin, turned her head toward him and said, "I'm planning on it."

Chapter 58

The main deck was already crowded with fellow passengers when Romi and Herbert returned there minutes before the ship was to leave. They found a spot on the port side deck railing, and they were soon joined by Annalisa.

The gangplanks had been pulled in, and at precisely 5:00 P.M. the bow and stern lines were untied. On the starboard side, a tug maneuvered the ship away from the quay and pointed it toward the breakwater. Once the tug disengaged, *Marine Flasher's* captain eased his ship toward the harbor entrance. The mood of all the passengers assembled on the main deck was buoyant as *Marine Flasher* passed the breakwaters and attained full speed; however, shortly thereafter both Romi and Annalisa started fussing about their now windblown hair.

"C'mon, I'll show you my cabin," Annalisa announced. Romi nodded acquiescence, but Herbert decided to remain on deck a while longer.

After the girls left, he made his way to the stern of the ship. He was somewhat overwhelmed as he leaned onto the deck railing and watched the German shoreline slowly recede.

He thought, I've been looking forward to this day for a long time. I did so when I was in the annexed part of Czechoslovakia; I did so after I was evacuated to Hungary without knowing one word of the hunky language; I did so when I was with the Luftwaffe Auxiliary, albeit to a lesser extent, because then, at times, I had serious doubts that I would live long enough to celebrate my twentieth birthday. I did so when I was an American POW and with heightened confidence because of Manuel's offer to have his guys stow me away if I were unable to link up with my family.

Herbert's gaze turned from the ship's wake to the receding shoreline, without registering what he saw.

He thought, Manuel's offer knocked me for a loop at the time, and it still does. He once again recalled Manuel's words: "You're small enough to squeeze into a duffel bag." As always, the memory of that scene had an emotional impact that brought him close to tears.

He wished he hadn't lost the notebook that contained the names and addresses of some of the GIs whom he had met while working in the mess hall.

Herbert continued to gauge *Marine Flasher's* progress by watching Bremerhaven becoming more distant. Soon *Marine Flasher* was far enough from shore such that a few burnt out high-rise buildings were all that remained visible of the shoreline. As the ship distanced itself further, Herbert's visible horizon continued to change, and the high rise shells appeared to gradually sink into the ocean. He thought, too bad that all the destruction that has befallen this continent in the past few years can't be made to disappear as were the remnants of that skyline a few minutes ago. After gazing for a minute or so at the now unobstructed horizon of sky meeting water, he added, I hope the destination continent of this trip never experiences the agonies that have befallen the one I have just left.

✚✚✚

"Where have you been?" Romi cried out after Herbert returned to the main deck. "Annalisa and I have been looking all over for you for the past half hour."

"I was back on the fantail."

"What's a fantail?" she asked.

"It's the back end of a ship."

"What were you doing there for the last two hours or so?" she asked.

"I was reminiscing about how often I had dreamt about this day during the last six years."

"Two hours wouldn't be sufficient for me to recount all the times I yearned for this day," Romi said.

"Well, I didn't count each time I dreamt about it, just when I was moved about, like: Germany to the Sudetenland, Sudetenland back to Germany, Germany to Hungary, Hungary to Poland, and so on. I didn't bother with individual scenes, but counted only the feature presentations, so to speak," Herbert clarified.

"Well, in about ten days it will be a dream come true—what will you be dreaming then?" Romi asked.

"With this dream coming true, all the others will fall into place," Herbert ventured.

"If all the others include this evening's supper, it's not going to happen," his sister said.

"Why not?"

"Because it is 8:30 P.M. and the dining room closed at 8:00," she declared. We looked for you at 7:00, but when you couldn't be found, Annalisa and I decided to go and eat."

"It's not a problem. I'm not hungry. As a matter of fact, it's been a long day, and I'm ready to turn in. Where is Annalisa?"

"She was tired, too. She went back to her cabin just before you came back to the main deck."

"Well, I'm going to head downstairs. You probably should

turn in too," he said.

"Yeah, I think I will. Sleep well."

"You, too."

✚✚✚

After Herbert returned to his assigned bed, he checked out the clothing items that he had brought down from Romi's cabin. There were several sets of underwear, several polo shirts, and his suit pants. He put the underwear and the shirts in his assigned locker, and then he gave the suit pants a once-over. They were severely wrinkled from the extended stay in the duffel bag.

Herbert remembered how he had kept his Luftwaffe trousers reasonably pressed. He checked the mattress support. Seeing closely placed slats of wood, he lifted the mattress and placed his suit pants on the slats, such that the wrinkles would be lessened and the pant creases enhanced when placed between the slats and the mattress.

Once satisfied with his housekeeping chores, Herbert stripped to his underwear and climbed into his third-tier resting place for a good night's sleep. As he lay down, he noticed the close proximity of the approximately 9.5-inch diameter, cast-iron pipe, barely visible in the sparse light of the hold, that ran lengthwise above his bed. Once he was stretched out, he realized that there was less than a foot of clearance between him and the intrusive pipe. He lay down with considerable trepidation but eventually closed his eyes and fell asleep.

✚✚✚

The rocking motion awoke Herbert. Drowsy and barely aware of his surroundings, he raised his upper body, which immediately placed his head on a collision course with the overhead pipe.

Impact was unavoidable. "Damn it!" Herbert cried out as his forehead bounced off the accursed pipe.

He lay back down until the pain and the stars dancing before his eyes subsided. The wall clock in the sparsely illuminated hold told him that it was 5:30. Herbert thought, that would be A.M., as he climbed down from his "third floor" perch.

He told himself, there isn't a soul in the shower area. I might as well get cleaned up now…before the herd shows itself.

As he walked well into the bow area, he noticed that the bobbing sensation increased as he walked further into the front of the ship and thought, that is to be expected. After all, walking toward the extreme bow area of a ship is equivalent to being on a seesaw plank. According to that analogy, the up and down motion would be zero at midships, and maximum at the bow and stern.

He wondered what caused the increased turbulence of the sea, since no storms had been forecast.

While showering he recalled being on the much bigger ship when his family was on its way to Germany in 1939. Even the big liner had experienced the choppiness on the last two days of the voyage. He remembered that Oscar Diebold, the ship's steward, had told his father that the choppiness was a well-known phenomenon of the English Channel.

✦✦✦

"How did you get that bump on your forehead?" Romi wanted to know as he met her and Annalisa in the cafeteria for breakfast.

"I had a collision with a cast-iron pipe," Herbert responded.

"How did you manage to do that?" Romi asked. "Don't tell me…you were probably daydreaming and just happened to walk into it, right?"

"Wrong, and I didn't walk into it. I was awakened by the roughness of the water. While still half asleep, I rose and hit my head on the pipe that runs just above my third-tier bed. You, being located sort of midships, perhaps didn't even notice; however, since I have to use the showers that are located in the most forward section of the bow area, the bobbing sensation there was severe enough to almost make me seasick.

"I wonder why the water got so choppy," Romi said.

"Probably, because we entered the English Channel," Herbert replied.

"You've been to the Channel only one time. What makes you say that?" his sister asked.

"I just remember Oscar Diebohl telling Papa that the Channel is known for its short, broken waves."

"How long will we stay in the English Channel?" Romi asked.

"Till we get out of it," he replied.

Romi sighed and addressing Annalisa asked, "Do you see why I sometimes have to address him as smarty-pants?"

Annalisa answered with a noncommittal smile, while Herbert tried to make amends by saying, "I'd have to know how fast we're going and how long the channel is, and I know neither."

When they finished breakfast, Herbert offered that, if they wanted to take advantage of the sunny weather, he would requisition three deck chairs on the main deck. The girls were agreeable and indicated that they would look for him about half an hour later.

While setting up the chairs, Herbert heard the ship's PA system announce the following message: *Marine Flasher* will make a stop at Le Havre to take on several additional passengers. Arrival time at Le Havre is estimated to be 2:00 P.M.

✚✚✚

Herbert was back at the starboard-side deck railing by 1:30 P.M. Close by, and leaning against the railing stood a member of *Marine Flasher's* crew. Herbert noted that the crew member appeared to be not much older than he himself was. Just as he was about to engage the sailor in conversation, another crew member approached and called out, "Hey, Ray, are you enjoying your first transatlantic voyage?"

"Yeah, George, I like it real well," the youngster standing next to Herbert replied.

Herbert took George to be in his late twenties. "Pretty soon you will get your first look at the French coast," George said after he positioned himself next to Ray.

"Will we be tying up at a pier in Le Havre?" Ray asked.

"I understand we are stopping to take on several more passengers, but they will board via motor launch. I don't know why they are going that route," George said.

"How do the additional passengers come aboard?" Ray asked.

"They use an accommodation ladder," George replied.

"What's that?"

"It is a portable stairway that will be fastened to the side of *Marine Flasher* to allow the new passengers to board the ship from the launch. Unlike a gangway, which usually is oriented at right angles to the ship, the accommodation ladder is oriented parallel to the ship's side. We'll be able to watch the guys mount the ladder in a little while. Right now it is stored on one of the midship decks."

Fifteen minutes later, the French coastline came into view and half an hour later, the breakwaters and the harbor of Le Havre.

"That's why we are taking on the additional passengers by launch…" George noted when he saw that the harbor facilities had been heavily damaged and several vessels had been sent to the bottom. Only the upper sections of their superstructures remained visible to attest to their fate.

Pointing toward the wrecks, Ray asked his shipmate, "Do you think they were ours?"

George shook his head and said, "No. Those are German ships."

"How do you know?" Ray asked.

"I was in this area a little over two years ago. I was working aboard a troop transport that was depositing the boys into LSTs just off the Normandy beaches. All that happened about sixty miles southwest of here. At the time Le Havre was in German hands and was not a target in the invasion attempt," George replied. He thought a moment and then said, "Besides, we never would have approached an enemy-held port with an invasion contingent and expected to offload the troops on one of its piers."

Ray responded with a deferential, "Wow!"

✚ ✚ ✚

Soon *Marine Flasher* had slowed down sufficiently for the captain to drop anchor on the seaward side of the breakwater.

The accommodation ladder was put into place, and shortly thereafter a motor launch pulled up alongside *Marine Flasher.* All eyes on the starboard-side main deck watched as about two dozen additional passengers were added to the ship's manifest.

As the launch left the scene, the rattling of the anchor chain indicated that *Flasher* was ready to continue her voyage. During the first three days out of Bremerhaven, pleasant summer weather enticed many passengers to spend time on deck. Early on day four, the weather turned stormy, and it stayed that way during days five and six. The girls did not leave their cabins, and Herbert sought refuge midships, having already been made aware that being closer to the ship's center of gravity would produce less nausea. He visited the ship's recreation center and occasionally would briefly go onto the main deck to heave, while hanging over the deck railing, all the while hoping that the severity of the storm did not increase to where the deck would be declared off limits.

Although feeling wretched at dinner time on day four, Herbert made his way to Romi's cabin to ask whether she would be going to the dining room. He encountered four crabby women who unanimously told him that at the moment they just could not stand the sight of any kind of food. After he asked Romi how Annalisa was holding up, she told him not to bother Annalisa, since Annalisa had already told her that she wouldn't be going to dinner.

"Well, I've been puking my brains out, but I'm going to try to keep some food down. I'll see you when the weather changes," Herbert said, as he left for the dining room.

Herbert selected a bowl of pea soup and did manage to empty the bowl. Unfortunately, the soup never reached its intended destination—an extra large trough between wave crests caused the bowl to skid off of his tray thereby depositing the contents on the floor, but not before bouncing off his pant leg—the right pant leg of his suit pants!

He was relieved that there were only a few witnesses to his mishap. He now attempted to retrieve the errant bowl, but the pea soup-splattered cafeteria floor only fleetingly horizontal because of the storm—caused him to almost lose his balance and set his efforts at naught.

A crew member, brandishing a mop, pushed him aside and cleaned up the mess.

Too embarrassed to return to the food counters, Herbert decided to go back to his bunk bed. While walking toward the forward hold, he thought, the dark green of the pea soup is not going to blend too well with the light tan of my pants. Mama told me to have them dry-cleaned, but how can I do that on a haphazardly converted former troop transport? I'm just going to have to take a chance and wash them. The only other pants I have are my old uniform pants, and the seat of those pants is so worn that its reflectivity could put a mirror to shame! I wouldn't want to walk ashore in those pants!

When he was back at his bunk bed, he retrieved his uniform pants out of his assigned foot locker. He told himself, "Once I switch pants, I'll take my suit pants to the shower area and wash them. Maybe the need for dry-cleaning is just an old wives' tale; maybe the pants won't mind a little water!"

He felt like he was riding an elevator as he walked toward the shower area nestled in the bow of the ship. With every step the alternating up and down excursions, both in extent and acceleration, became greater and appeared to be initiated with greater force the closer he got to the bow.

He anticipated that his laundry chore would be interrupted by several trips to one of the toilet stalls to heave up more bile, which seemingly was all his stomach had left to offer.

Having situated himself at one of the sinks, he contemplated his task. He thought, I have a sink with hot and cold running water. Each sink has a cake of the ubiquitous GI soap, with which I became familiar while working for Manuel in the mess hall. My effort will be restricted to that part of the right pant leg that was stained by the pea soup. When I'm done washing and rinsing, I will not wring the water out, but will squeeze it out by wrapping the pant leg in a towel and applying pressure.

Perhaps I'll be able to fool the pant leg into thinking that it was dry-cleaned!

When he was done, he returned to his bunk bed and carefully arranged his suit pants under his mattress for an overnight press.

Exhausted from having fasted for most of the day—some of it voluntary, some of it not—and from having to deal with this calamity, Herbert stretched out in his bunk and soon fell asleep.

✚✚✚

The wall clock in the hold indicated 5:00 A.M. when Herbert awoke. He gingerly avoided the overhead steel pipe as he got out of bed. His very first task was to retrieve his suit pants from under the mattress. Since the night lighting would not be switched to daytime illumination of the front hold until 7:30, he could not tell how well he had eradicated the pea soup stain from his right pant leg. He could tell that the pant leg had dried overnight.

He carefully slipped out of his bunk onto the hold floor and put on the pants. Cool air around his right ankle indicated that the pant leg did not reach as low as the left one did. Herbert thought, the right pant leg probably is wrinkled and therefore is not reaching my ankle. He gave the pant leg a downward tug. When the tug was instantaneously felt at his waist, he knew that his wrinkling theory had been a figment of his imagination, contrived to avoid the thought that the pant leg might have shrunk. But it had shrunk! It had shrunk, not only in length, but also in girth.

The pant cuff now almost hugged his leg about three inches above his ankle.

"Shit!" Herbert cried out, aloud.

"What's the problem?" a voice from the second-tier bunk inquired.

"I washed my good pants, Brian, and they shrunk," Herbert responded.

"So your pants are a little shorter than anyone else's. That won't make you the worst dressed person aboard this vessel," Brian opined.

"You don't understand. Only one pant leg has shrunk," Herbert replied.

"How did you manage to do that?"

"I only spilled soup on one pant leg; therefore, I only washed that pant leg!"

"Well, then the solution to your problem is simple. You just have to treat the other leg the same way," Brian offered.

"All I'll be doing is to shorten both pant legs. Wearing the pants like that will still make me look like a dork."

"No, it won't. People who do notice will think that you are wearing knickers and that you just did not gather the pant legs at the knee. No big deal!"

"You really think so, Brian?"

"Absolutely!"

That evening, Herbert made his way back to the shower area to wash the left pant leg in exactly the same way he had washed the right one.

The storm did not let up until six days after *Marine Flasher* had left Bremerhaven. Early in the morning of the seventh day the seas had turned calm amidst bright sunlight.

At 7:30, Herbert was knocking on Romi's cabin door.

"Are you ready for some breakfast?" he asked as she opened the door.

"Yeah, I'm ready…C'mon in," she said. As he entered, her first words were, "What in the world did you do to your pants?"

"I spilled some pea soup on them several days ago."

"You spilled soup on them, and then you washed them, didn't you?"

Herbert nodded sheepishly.

"Mama warned you that they required dry-cleaning."

"Yeah, but she didn't tell me what to do if I spilled pea soup on them during a storm in the middle of an ocean while aboard a ship that didn't have the simple amenity of a dry-cleaning facility."

Romi rolled her eyes and said, "You're lucky my cabin mates aren't here. They would have had a good laugh…at your expense."

"Where are they?" he asked.

"They left for the cafeteria about half an hour ago."

"C'mon, let's go and see if they left us any breakfast," she said as she opened the door for them to leave.

"One of my buddies down in the hold said folks would think I'm wearing knickers when they see me in these pants. What do you think?"

"Uh-uh!"

"Why not?"

"Knickers don't have cuffs!" she exclaimed as she burst out laughing and took him by the arm to lead him to the cafeteria.

✚ ✚ ✚

The passing of the storm left both passengers and the ship's stewards in an elevated mood—the passengers because they no longer were seasick, and the stewards because they no longer had to put up with the whining of their seasick charges.

In the following days, Herbert, Romi, and Annalisa spent much time sunbathing on the main deck. On one of those days, Herbert, who was standing at the main deck railing, called out to his sister and their friend Annalisa, "Hey, come take a look. You'll get to see flying fish!"

Annalisa, who, like Romi was lounging in one of the deck chairs, commented, "He's pulling our leg, isn't he? Whoever heard of flying fish?" Turning toward Romi, she asked, "There is no such thing—or is there?"

Looking up from the book she was reading, Romi said, "I remember seeing them while we were aboard ship on our way to Germany. Go and take a look. It's not an everyday occurrence, even aboard ship, to be able to watch them."

"I'll come and take a look, but if you guys are pulling my leg, I won't…" she was groping for an appropriate retaliation and laughingly said, "I won't talk to you guys for one whole hour!"

After she joined Herbert at the railing and after scanning the waters close to the horizon, she asked, "Well, where are they?"

"They glide just above the waves," Herbert said. "You have to look close to the ship—almost straight down—if you want to see them."

"Oh yeah, I see them," Annalisa cried out, "and it looks like they are trying to race the ship. Romi, you have to come over here and see this! You yourself said that it is not an everyday occurrence to be able to watch them."

After she had coaxed Romi to the railing, she asked, "But how can they fly? They aren't birds!"

"I read somewhere that they have exceptionally large fins for their size and that the large fins allow them to glide above the waves after they thrust themselves out of the water," Romi responded.

"They seem to be able to almost keep up with the ship, while they are gliding," Annalisa exclaimed while watching the flying fish.

After a while, she looked up and said, "Thanks guys, for sharing this with me. It is something I had not yet seen."

Sunny weather and calm seas continued unabated. In the

afternoon of day ten, *Marine Flasher's* PA system announced that the ship would be docking at a Hudson River pier at approximately 2:00 P.M. on the following day. The PA system further announced that landfall would occur at around noon.

Romi and her brother made sure to have an early breakfast in order to be on deck in time to witness the anticipated landfall. They reserved several deck chairs for Annalisa and for a few acquaintances they had made since coming aboard.

While waiting for the others to join them, Herbert lit a cigarette.

"I thought you were all out of cigarettes," Romi commented.

"I was, but I bought another pack," he responded.

"But I bought another pack," she mimicked. "What did you do? Did you ask one of the crew members to sell you a pack, and where did you get the money?"

"I bought it at a PX that is located one deck below the cafeteria."

"What's a PX?"

"PX is an abbreviation for post exchange. It is a store normally located at an army base where soldiers can buy stuff not supplied to them, such as shaving and grooming utensils, as well as tobacco and cigarettes beyond their normal allotment. I'm familiar with the term because the Americans had a PX right next to the mess hall where I worked for them while a POW. As a former troop transport, *Marine Flasher* would have had a PX, and evidently the PX was retained after the ship's mission changed," Herbert explained.

"Oh," Romi replied before asking, "So where did you get the money?"

"Mama had a few American coins squirreled away. She gave me a twenty-five cent piece shortly before we left."

"So you bought a pack of cigarettes with your quarter?"

"Yep! The pack cost me one U.S. dime, so I have fifteen cents left. They have chocolate bars down there. You can have the fifteen cents and buy one or two of those, if you like."

"Nah, I'd just as soon have you keep the money. I wouldn't want you to arrive in the United States penniless."

"Hey, I'll be assumed penniless by anyone who sees me in my suit pants."

Romi laughed and asked, "Now whose fault is that?" After a while Annalisa and several of the new acquaintances joined the Klug kids on the sunny deck.

In anticipation of being scattered to the winds once *Marine Flasher* had been tied up to a New York pier later that afternoon, the newly found friends exchanged addresses with one another, so that they could retain contact after they went their separate ways.

Shortly before noon someone toward the bow of the ship bellowed, "Land ho!"

All eyes looked in the direction the ship was headed. Through the hazy atmosphere, what seemed to be white cliffs, seen from afar, had appeared at the horizon.

"I don't recall any cliffs being in the New York harbor area," Annalisa opined to the members of her group.

"Once we get closer and the haze disperses, what right now might remind us of the cliffs of Dover will turn out to be part of the New York skyline. The skyscrapers in the bay area of New York come right up to the water's edge," someone else in the group responded.

A little while later, the prediction of the someone else was validated. What seemingly had appeared as a sighting of cliffs on the far horizon turned into a view of the still far away New York waterfront, whose hazy appearance was slowly transformed into the world renowned marvel of the New York skyline as *Marine Flasher* approached closer. Many "Ohs!" and

"Ahs!" were voiced by those who were seeing this marvel for the first time as well as by those who remembered it from another day.

When *Marine Flasher* glided past the Statue of Liberty, the "Ohs!" and "Ahs!" of the skyline sighting turned into shouts of "Hurrah!" and "God bless America!" Many of the cheers were voiced in the various accents of the displaced persons.

Marine Flasher slowed down as she eased into the Hudson River. She soon was intercepted by two tugs that gingerly guided her to a pier crowded with people who had awaited the arrival of the ship.

After their group had dispersed, Romi, Herbert, and Annalisa managed to position themselves at the railing adjacent to the pier. Looking down at the crowded pier, some thirty feet below the main deck of *Marine Flasher,* brought to mind the images of newsreel pictures taken of Times Square just before midnight on a New Year's Eve. Amidst a background of joyful cheers, many of the ship's passengers soon were able to recognize family and or friends on the pier and to engage in shouted discourse with them.

"I think I see my aunt and my uncle toward the back of the pier. I'm going to move to where I'll be closer to them, maybe I'll be able to draw their attention to me," Annalisa said.

"OK," Romi responded. "If we don't see you later on, remember to stay in touch." Turning to her brother, she asked, "Have you recognized anyone yet?"

"No, but I just now saw a little kid holding up a sign with your name on it."

"Where…?"

"Over there," Herbert replied as he pointed toward the right side of the pier. "I don't know why we didn't notice him earlier. Perhaps he was holding the sign such that we couldn't make out what it said."

"That's Nicky!!" Romi cried out, "And Uncle Ene and Ida are standing right behind him."

"Yeah, I see them now. Boy, except for Nicky, they don't look any older than when we left," Herbert commented.

"Nicky was just a baby then. Uncle Ene was thirty-four and Ida was twenty-eight. Ida always looked much younger than her age. I can remember us likening her to a teenager at times; maybe that's why we never addressed her as Aunt Ida," Romi conjectured, as she waved to the crowd on the pier.

"It won't do any good," Herbert commented.

"What won't do any good?"

"Your waving. We were eleven and twelve years old when we last saw them. There haven't been any photo exchanges since then, and we have matured from little kids to big kids. We have changed sufficiently to where they would have difficulty in recognizing us," Herbert said.

"I realize that," she said, as she continued to wave. "Just let me live this long anticipated moment."

Herbert understood, but he said, "Let's transfer our waves to where the forward gangplank will be located, so that we won't be the last ones to go ashore."

✚ ✚ ✚

Coming off the gangplank, Romi and Herbert had to work their way through the crowd to where they had last seen their aunt and uncle. Herbert, closely behind Romi, kept nudging his sister toward the right to where he had last seen their kinfolk. When Romi spied her uncle, she held up her hand and yelled at the top of her lungs, "Uncle Ene, I'm Rosemarie!!"

Her clarion-like outburst got the attention of her relatives, plus that of many others who were assembled on the pier to greet new arrivals.

Herbert's and Romi's reunion with their Uncle Ene and his family was a joyous one. Little Nicky was the only one who did not shed any tears. He just gave the newcomers a wide-eyed look in apparent wonder as to what all the fuss was about.

After the hugs and kisses, Ida asked, "So where do we have to go to claim your luggage?"

"What luggage?" Romi inquired.

"Your suitcases or trunk or whatever contains all your clothing and stuff," Ida answered.

"All our stuff is in here," Romi said as she pointed to the duffel bag slung over her shoulder.

"All of your possessions are in that bag?" Ida asked.

Romi and Herbert both nodded.

Ida's eyes again flooded with tears as she gave the newcomers a once-over, and said, "Well, it looks like we'll be busy doing some big time shopping during the next few days; but right now, let's go home!"

BREMEN TRAVEL CENSORSHIP SUB-SECTION
GROUP "B" CIVIL CENSORSHIP DIVISION
APO 751 US ARMY

The below named person has submitted for approval all written and printed matter in his/her possession.

NAME: H. Klug

DATE: 29 JUN 1946

TC CCD

EMBARKATION CARD
Einschiffungskarte

S/S MARINE FLASHER

Sailing-Date: 5. Juli 1946

Accommodation
Schiffsplatz B II - 103

Mr. ~~Mrs. Miss~~ KLUG, HORST HERBERT

F 0989 A 7626

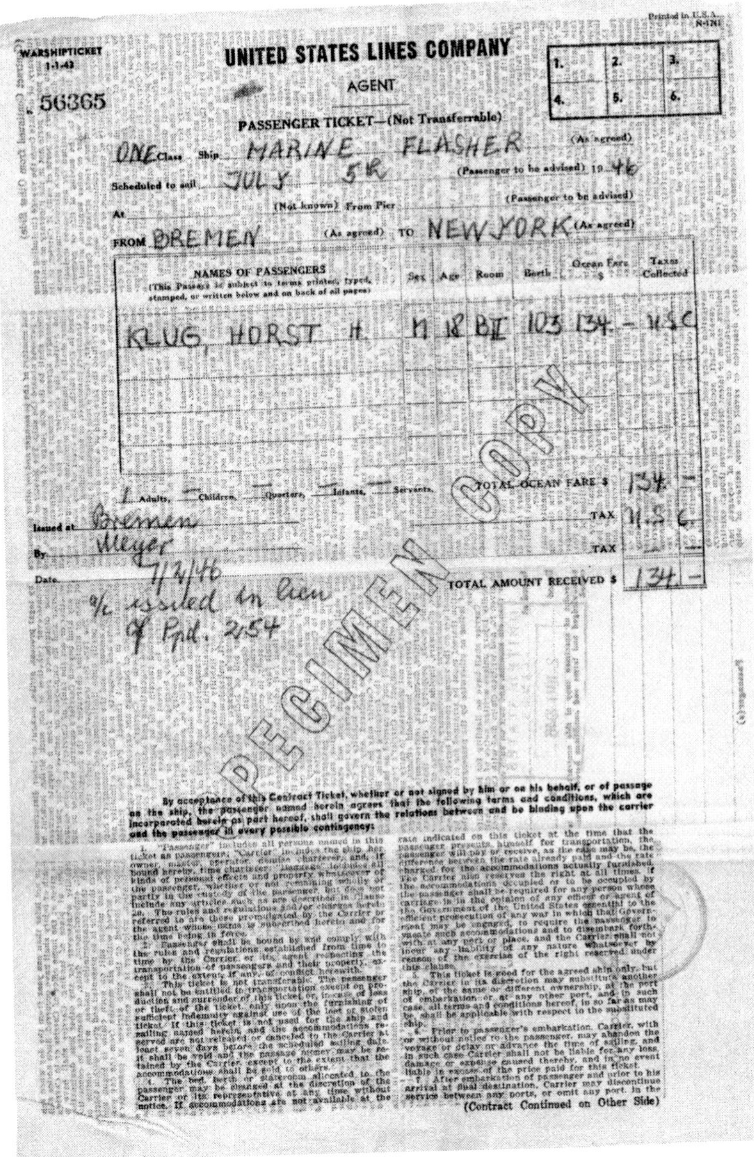

Printed in U.S.A.
N-1781

WARSHIPTICKET
1-1-43

No 56365

UNITED STATES LINES COMPANY

AGENT

PASSENGER TICKET—(Not Transferrable)

1.	2.	3.
4.	5.	6.

ONE Class Ship MARINE FLASHER (As agreed)

Scheduled to sail JULY 5th (Passenger to be advised) 1946

At (Not known) From Pier (Passenger to be advised)

FROM BREMEN (As agreed) TO NEW YORK (As agreed)

NAMES OF PASSENGERS (This Passage is subject to terms printed, typed, stamped, or written below and on back of all pages)	Sex	Age	Room	Berth	Ocean Fare $	Taxes Collected
KLUG, HORST H.	M	18	B II	103	134.–	USC

1 Adults, – Children, – Quarters, – Infants, – Servants. TOTAL OCEAN FARE $ 134.–

Issued at Bremen TAX U.S.C.

By Meyer TAX –

Date 7/4/46 TOTAL AMOUNT RECEIVED $ 134.–

o/c issued in lieu of Ppd. 254

SPECIMEN COPY

By acceptance of this Contract Ticket, whether or not signed by him or on his behalf, or of passage on the ship, the passenger named herein agrees that the following terms and conditions, which are incorporated herein as part hereof, shall govern the relations between and be binding upon the carrier and the passenger in every possible contingency:

1. "Passenger" includes all persons named in this ticket as passengers; "Carrier" includes the ship, her owner, master, operator, demise charterer, and, if bound hereby, time charterer; "Baggage" includes all kinds of personal effects and property whatsoever of the passenger, whether or not remaining wholly or partly in the custody of the passenger, but does not include any articles such as are described in Clause ... The rules and regulations and/or charges herein referred to are those promulgated by the Carrier or the agent whose name is subscribed hereto and for the time being in force.

2. Passenger shall be bound by and comply with the rules and regulations established from time to time by the Carrier or its agent respecting the transportation of passengers and their property, except to the extent, if any, of conflict herewith.

3. This ticket is not transferable. The passenger shall not be entitled to transportation except on production and surrender of this ticket or, in case of loss or theft of the ticket, only upon the furnishing of sufficient indemnity against use of the lost or stolen ticket. If this ticket is not used for the ship and sailing named herein, and the accommodations reserved are not released or canceled to the Carrier at least seven days before the scheduled sailing date, it shall be void and the passage money may be retained by the Carrier, except to the extent that the accommodations shall be sold to others.

4. The bed, berth or stateroom allocated to the passenger may be changed at the discretion of the Carrier or its representative at any time without notice. If accommodations are not available at the rate indicated on this ticket at the time that the passenger presents himself for transportation, the passenger will pay or receive, as the case may be, the difference between the rate already paid and the rate charged for the accommodations actually furnished. The Carrier also reserves the right at all times, if the accommodations occupied or to be occupied by the passenger shall be required for any person whose carriage is in the opinion of any officer or agent of the Government of the United States essential to the efficient prosecution of any war in which that Government may be engaged, to require the passenger to vacate such accommodations and to disembark forthwith at any port or place, and the Carrier shall not incur any liability of any nature whatsoever by reason of the exercise of the right reserved under this clause.

5. This ticket is good for the agreed ship only, but the Carrier in its discretion may substitute another ship, of the same or different ownership, at the port of embarkation or at any other port, and in such case, all terms and conditions hereof, in so far as may be, shall be applicable with respect to the substituted ship.

6. Prior to passenger's embarkation, Carrier, with or without notice to the passenger, may abandon the voyage or delay or advance the time of sailing, and in such case Carrier shall not be liable for any loss, damage or expense caused thereby, and in no event liable in excess of the price paid for this ticket.

7. After embarkation of passenger and prior to his arrival at final destination, Carrier may discontinue service between any ports, or omit any port, in the

(Contract Continued on Other Side)

Associated Reading

Altner, Helmut. *Berlin Dance of Death.* Havertown PA.: Casemate, 2002

Beck, Earl R. *Under the Bombs.* Lexington KY: The University Press of Kentucky, 1986

Biedermann, Gottlob Herbert. *In Deadly Combat.* Lawrence KS: University Press of Kansas, 2000

Black, Jeremy. *World War Two: A Military History.* London: Routledge, 2003

Cooper, Alan. *Target Dresden.* Bromley, Great Britain: Independent Books, 1995

Davidson, Edward, and Manning, Dale. *Chronology of World War II.* London: Cassell & Company, 1999

Hastings, Max. *Armageddon.* New York: Alfred A. Knopf, 2004

Johnson, Eric A. *Nazi Terror.* New York: Basic Books, 1999

Kane, Robert B. *Disobedience and Conspiracy in the German Army 1918–1945.* Jefferson NC: McFarland & Company, 2002

Middlebrook, Martin. *The Battle of Hamburg.* London: Cassell & Company, 1980

Mitcham, Samuel W. *Why Hitler?* Westport CT: Praeger Publishers, 1996

Ponting, Clive. *Armageddon.* London: Reed Consumer Books, Ltd., 1995

Sorge, Martin K. *The Other Price of Hitler's War.* Westport CT: Greenwood Press, Inc., 1986

Zijlstra, Gerrit. *Diary of an Air War.* Austin TX: Eakin Press, 1991